OUT WITH GARIBALDI

FRANK ENGAGED IN A TOUGH FIGHT WITH THE OFFICER
WHO HELD THE FLAG. (PAGE 136.)

OUT WITH GARIBALDI

A STORY OF
THE LIBERATION OF ITALY

BY

G. A. HENTY

Author of "The Lion of St. Mark" "No Surrender" "St. George for England"
"Under Wellington's Command" &c.

WITH EIGHT ILLUSTRATIONS BY W. RAINEY, R.I.

ISBN 1-59087-096-4

ROBINSON BOOKS
2002

Copyright 2002 by

Althouse Press &
Oregon Institute of Science and Medicine

PREFACE

The invasion of the Kingdom of the Two Sicilies by Garibaldi with a force of but a thousand irregular troops is one of the most romantic episodes ever recorded in military history. In many respects it rivals the conquest of Mexico by Cortez. The latter won, not by the greater bravery of his troops, but by their immense superiority in weapons and defensive armour. Upon the contrary, Garibaldi's force were ill-armed and practically without artillery, and were opposed by an army of a hundred and twenty thousand men carrying the best weapons of the time, and possessing numerous and powerful artillery. In both cases the invaders were supported by a portion of the population that had been reduced to a state of servitude, and who joined them against their oppressors. There is another point of resemblance between these remarkable expeditions, inasmuch as the leaders of both were treated with the grossest ingratitude by the monarchs for whom they had gained such large acquisitions of territory. For the leading incidents in the campaign I have relied chiefly upon Garibaldi's Autobiography and the personal narrative of the campaign by Captain Forbes, R.N.

G. A. HENTY.

CONTENTS

CHAP.	Page
I. Awaiting the attack	1
II. A desperate defence	21
III. Troubles	40
IV. A sudden summons	56
V. On the way	76
VI. The Villa Spinola	95
VII. The expedition sails	116
VIII. Palermo	134
IX. Hard fighting	149
X. With Bixio	170
XI. A hazardous expedition	189
XII. An ambuscade	208
XIII Across the straits	225
XIV. A discovery	244
XV. The advance from Reggio	264
XVI. Naples	284
XVII. The Battle of the Volturno	303
XVIII. Capua	323

ILLUSTRATIONS

	Page
"FRANK ENGAGED IN A TOUGH FIGHT WITH THE OFFICER WHO HELD THE FLAG" . . . . *Frontis.*	136
"WALKING UP AND DOWN THE ROOM LIKE A CAGED LION"	24
"HIS ASSAILANT FELL BACK AND DISAPPEARED"	82
"THE HINGES OF THE DOOR WERE BROKEN OFF"	152
"IN HER EXCITEMENT SHE FELL ON HER KNEES"	196
"'SILENCE, SIGNORS!' HE SAID IN A LOUD VOICE"	236
"IT WAS NOT UNTIL NULLO ORDERED FOUR MEN TO LOAD . . . THAT HE WOULD ANSWER"	300
MAP SHOWING POSITION OF THE OPPOSING FORCES AROUND CAPUA	305
PLAN OF THE BATTLE OF THE VOLTURNO	311
"HE WENT UP TO PERCIVAL AND PUT HIS HAND ON HIS SHOULDER"	330

OUT WITH GARIBALDI

CHAPTER I

AWAITING THE ATTACK

ON April 29th, 1849, two men were seated in a room whose open windows commanded a view down the Tiber. A sound of confused uproar rose from the city.

"I am afraid, Leonard," the elder of the two men said, "that the crisis is at hand. The news that the French are landing to-day at Civita Vecchia is ominous indeed. It is true that Oudïnot has sent a message saying that the flag he has hoisted is that of peace and order. The people will not believe that he comes as an enemy; but, for my part, I have no doubt of it."

"Nor have I," the other replied. "It was bad enough that we had Austria against us, Sardinia powerless, and all the princelings of Italy hostile; but that France, having proclaimed herself a republic, should now interfere to crush us and to put the Pope back upon his throne is nothing short of monstrous. I feared that it would be so, but Mazzini had so much faith in his influence with members of the French Assembly that he has buoyed up the hopes of the populace, and even now the people generally believe that the French come as friends."

"It is doubtless the influence of their new president, Napoleon, that has turned the scale against us," the other said gloomily. "I do not suppose that he cares about the Pope one way or the other, but it is his interest to pose as his champion. By so doing he will gain the good opinion of Austria, of Naples, and the ducal rulers of the Italian states. Even Prussia, protestant as she is, would view with satisfaction the suppression of a rising like ours, for her throne well-nigh tottered in last year's explosion. Russia, too, which perhaps more than any other power has reason to fear a popular rising, would feel grateful to Napoleon for undertaking to crush free thought in Rome. It is evident that the French President's move is a politic one. Do you think that we shall fight, Leonard?"

"I fancy so. I have no belief in Mazzini's courage, president though he may be. Garibaldi is the popular hero, and I know him well enough to be sure that if he has but a handful of men to back him he will fight till the end. We had the odds as heavily against us when we were comrades-in-arms at Rio, with but the *Susie* and a merchantman with three or four guns against the whole Brazilian navy, or when, with the Italian volunteers, two hundred strong, we several times withstood the assault of five times our number. You will see we shall fight; but there can be no question what the end must be. We may repulse Oudinot's attack; but France could send any amount of reinforcements to him, while we have no friends to go to. It is well that your wife, Muriel, and the boy were sent off a month since to Leghorn, where, if we escape from what must happen here, we can join them and take ship for England."

"I am sorry that you should be involved in this affair, Leonard."

"I am not sorry," the other said. "In the first place, after being here more than ten years, I have come to hate the tyranny and oppression, I don't say of the Pope himself, but of his underlings, as much as you do. In the second place, I would fight by the side of Garibaldi in almost any quarrel. I do not agree with him in his love for republics, but he has infected me with his hatred of tyrants and his burning patriotism. He is a glorious man; and after having been his comrade, I may almost say his brother, in adventures, hardships, and battles for two years, it would be strange indeed if I hesitated to join him in his crusade to rid Italy of her tyrants. I am a soldier, and I own a fondness for fighting when convinced that the cause is a just one. I know your opinions on the subject; but I suppose you do not propose to fight yourself?"

"I do indeed, Leonard. I do not say that I should be a match for a strong and active man in a bout with swords, though of course I learned the use of the rapier when a student, but at fifty I can at least use a musket as well as a younger man, and if Rome fights I fight with her. Ah, here comes Garibaldi!"

The door opened, and a man entered, whose appearance, even if he had not been dressed in a red shirt, blue trousers of rough cloth, and a soft, broad-brimmed wideawake, would have been remarked wherever he went. Of middle height, he was exceptionally wide across the shoulders and deep in the chest; he wore his hair and beard long—both were of a golden yellow, giving a remarkably leonine look to his face; his eyes were blue, and the general expression of his face, when not angered, was pleasant and good-tempered, although marked also by resolution and firmness. At that time his name was comparatively little known in Europe, although the extraordinary bravery and enterprise that he had shown at Rio and Monte Video had marked him as a leader of guerilla warfare, possessing many characteristics that recalled the exploits of Lord Cochrane. It was only when, after his services had been declined by Carlo Alberto, King of Sardinia, he was, with a few hundred followers, making his way to aid in the defence of Venice against the Austrians, that, on hearing that Rome had risen, he hurried to aid the movement, and on his arrival there was greeted with enthusiasm by the populace, who had been informed by Mazzini of his exploits.

"You have heard the news?" he said as he entered.

"Yes; we were just talking it over," Leonard Percival said, "and conclude, as I suppose you do, that the French come as enemies."

"There can be no doubt about it, my friend," Garibaldi said. "If they had said that they came as enemies I might have doubted them; but after the evasive answer their general gave to the deputation Mazzini sent them this morning, I have no question whatever that they will attack us to-morrow."

"And you will fight?"

"Of course. We shall beat them, I think; in the end Rome must fall, but our resistance will not have been in vain. The stand we shall make against tyranny will touch every heart throughout Italy. It will show that, ground down as the people have been for centuries, the old fire of the Romans is not extinct. This will be but the beginning. When it is seen that the despots cannot maintain their authority save by the aid of foreign powers, there will be revolt after revolt until Italy is free. There were some grand lines you once told me as we sat round a camp fire, Percival, that exactly express my thoughts."

"I know what you mean," the Englishman said. "They were Byron's:

> For freedom's battle once begun,
> Bequeath'd by bleeding sire to son,
> Though baffled oft, is ever won."

"They are splendid and true," Garibaldi said enthusiastically. "So shall it be with us. This is our first battle— we cannot hope to win it; but our guns will tell Italy and Europe that we have awoke at last, that, after being slaves so long that we had come to be looked upon as a people content to be ruled by despots, we are still men, and that, having once begun the fight for freedom, we will maintain it until freedom is won."

"And now, what are your plans for to-morrow?"

"As soon as the French are seen approaching the city the church bells will ring and the alarm be beaten in the streets. The word has been passed round that all are to assemble instantly. The troops that have been organized will first pour out; the rest will follow with such arms as they have. We shall simply rush upon the French. In such a fight there is no need for manœuvring; and it is well that it is so, for there the French would be our superiors. We shall simply attack and drive them back. We may take it for granted that, being boastful creatures and believing that they have but to show themselves and we shall lay down our arms and implore their mercy, they will be wholly taken by surprise and disconcerted by our onslaught. Can you recommend anything better, my friend?"

"No. With such a force as yours, newly raised and wholly unused to discipline, it is probable that at the first engagement, and with the advantage of surprise, they will, as you say, drive back the French; but you will have to adopt different tactics afterwards: to stand on the defensive and prevent their entering the city as long as possible, and to defend every street and lane, as the Spaniards did at Saragossa. They may take the city at last, but at so terrible a cost of blood that we may be sure that when you rise again the French people will not allow another expedition to be undertaken for a cause in which they have no concern, and which would entail such heavy sacrifices."

"Will you have a separate command, Percival? You have but to choose one, and it is yours."

"I will fight by your side," the Englishman said briefly. "I know that I shall get my full share of the work then."

"And you, professor?"

"I shall go out with the rest. The students have elected me their captain, and I shall, of course, lead them. It is a simple matter. I see the enemy in front, and I go at them. Even I, a man of peace all my life, understand that. I shall have with me at least a dozen of my colleagues, and if I am shot they can direct our boys as well as I can."

"Good!" Garibaldi said. "If I thought that you could keep the students in hand, and then dash into the thick of it if you see our men wavering anywhere, I should say do so; but I know that it would be impossible. They will long to be in the front rank and to set an example to others, and I shall feel confident that, wherever they may be, there will be no faltering. Your chief difficulty will be in restraining their ardour. Well, my friends, I have many things to arrange, so must be going. You will find me in my quarters at nine o'clock this evening, Percival. The officers and the heads of the various quarters of the town are to meet me there at that hour, to arrange where the assembling-places are to be when the alarm is given, and the streets through which they must move when we see at which point the French are going to attack us."

"I will come down with him," the professor said. "I will send word to my colleagues where to meet me an hour later, so that I can inform them of the arangements."

And with a nod Garibaldi, who had been unanimously elected general of the Roman forces, strolled away.

Leonard Percival had been a captain in the British army, but having become tired of garrison life during the long peace, had sold out in 1837, and sailed for South America, where there were always opportunities for a man of action to distinguish himself. He took part in the struggle of Rio Grande for separation from Brazil. Here he first made the acquaintance of Garibaldi, and shared with him in the many perilous adventures and desperate fights of that war. Becoming disgusted with the factions and intrigues that were rampant at Rio, he left the service of the little republic and returned to England.

He was the second son of a wealthy English gentleman, who had viewed with much disapproval his leaving the army and undertaking the life of a soldier of fortune when there was no occasion for his doing so, as he had an allowance amply sufficient for him to live upon. His father was not much surprised when, after staying for a month at home, Leonard told him that, having a taste for art, he had made up his mind to adopt it as a profession, and should go out to

Rome to study. This seemed to him better than wandering about the world fighting in quarrels in which he had no concern, and he had no valid reply to his son when the latter said,—

"You see, father, you cannot expect me to spend my life in absolute laziness. I must be doing something. The life of a club lounger is the last I should choose. I have no liking for a country life—if I had I would go out to Australia or Canada and settle; but I know that in a few months I should be home again, for I could not stand a life of solitude. If you can suggest anything better I shall be ready, as far as possible, to be guided by your wishes."

"You may as well have your own way, Leonard. I suppose it will come to that in the end, and therefore you may as well do it first as last; and at any rate, a few months in Rome will be a change for you, and I shall not be expecting by every post a communication saying that you have been killed."

So Captain Percival went to Rome, without any idea of staying there more than a year. His plans, however, were changed when he met and fell in love with Muriel, the only child of Professor Forli, a man of almost European reputation for his learning and attainments. His wooing had been an uneventful one. His income was amply sufficient, in the professor's eyes, to keep his daughter in comfort, and, moreover, the master under whom Leonard was studying gave an excellent account of his ability and industry, and in 1842 the marriage took place. Previous to this Leonard had obtained his father's consent to his intended marriage, although not his approval.

"I consider that it is one more piece of folly," he wrote.

"There was no reason in the world why you should not have settled at home and made a good marriage. I had specially hoped that this would have been the case, as Tom still remains a bachelor. However, there are some redeeming points in the matter. I have, through a friend, who is a member of the Athenæum, learned that Professor Forli's name is well known, and that he is considered one of the most learned men in Italy. In the next place, the young lady's mother is, as you have told me, an Englishwoman of good family, and her daughter is therefore only half an Italian. From your description of her, allowing for the usual exaggeration in such cases, she takes after her mother, and might pass anywhere as of unmixed English blood, so I may hope that I shall not have black-haired, swarthy little grandchildren running about. I shall add a couple of hundred a year to your allowance, as I always intended to do when you married."

A year later Captain Percival brought his wife home to England, and stayed there for some time; and here a son was born, who was christened Frank, after his grandfather. Whatever objections the latter might at first have felt to his son's marriage, they were altogether removed by this visit; neither in appearance nor in speech did his wife betray her foreign origin, for her mother had always conversed with her in English, and she spoke it without the slightest accent. She was now twenty, was strikingly handsome, and very graceful in her movements. He would gladly have kept her and his son with him; but when they had consented to her marriage, her parents had bargained that she should, at any rate, spend a large portion of her time with them, as they had no other children. Moreover, her husband was now devoted to art, and although he had only been working for two years, his pictures were already beginning to attract attention.

Mr. Percival was, therefore, obliged to content himself with the promise that they would come over every year for at least four months. The arrangement, however, was not carried out, for, a few months after their return to Italy, Mr. Percival died suddenly. His death made no difference pecuniarily to his son, as he had settled upon him a sum sufficient to produce an income equal to that which he had before been allowed. His elder brother came out a year later, and stayed for a few weeks with him.

"You must send this little chap over to England to be educated, Leonard," he had said, "if you will persist in sticking in this rotten old city. I don't suppose I shall ever marry; and if not, of course some day he will come in for the property."

"But why on earth shouldn't you marry, Tom? You know what a trouble it was to our father that you did not do so—it was a real grievance to him."

"Well, I should really have been glad to oblige him; but somehow or other I never saw any girl whom I earnestly desired to make my wife, or, as I suppose you would call it, fell in love with. I very much prefer knocking about in my yacht, or travelling, to settling down. Of course I always spent a month or two, twice a year, at my father's, and was in town three months in the season—that is to say, when I did not get sick of it. Then I either went up the Mediterranean or to the West Indies, or knocked about round England for three or four months, and finished the year with a run up the Nile, or out to India or China. Now I feel even less inclined to marry than I did before, for if I did, it would simply mean eight months in the year down in the country, and four in London. Of course, if I ever do fall in love—and at forty it is hardly likely—I shall marry; I don't bind myself in any way to remain single. Anyhow, I am glad that you are married, and that, when I go, there will be another Frank Percival, who we must hope will be of a more settled disposition than either of us, to reign in the old place."

So things had gone on quietly until, in 1848, the revolution in Paris was followed by an upheaval all over Europe. The ascent of Pius IX. to the papal chair was hailed by the liberal party in Italy as the commencement of a new era. He was accredited, and not unjustly, with liberal views, and it was believed that he would introduce reforms into the Papal States, and act as a centre round which patriots could rally. Unfortunately, the party of reform in Italy was divided into two classes; of one of these the Marquis d'Azeglio was the leading spirit; he was a moderate reformer, and looked to a union of Italy under a constitutional monarch. Carlo Alberto, the King of Sardinia, seemed to him the only man who could assume that position, and for years d'Azeglio had worked quietly to this end.

A more violent spirit was however working with as much zeal and energy in another direction. Mazzini was an extreme republican of the narrowest kind; he was in communication with men of the same type in France, and had formed secret societies all over Italy. He and those with him were anxious to obtain the countenance and prestige which a Pope of advanced liberal opinions would give to their party, and Pius IX, was received with enthusiastic acclamations by the republican party of Rome. But, liberally inclined as he was, he shrank from committing himself wholly to the reformers. He was a weak man; and although his vanity was gratified by his reception, and although he had sincerely desired to introduce broad reforms, he hesitated when called upon to carry those reforms into action. The King of Sardinia had been pushed forward by the Mazzinians, until he compromised himself, and made advances to the Pope, when in 1847 Austria violated the Papal territories at Ferrara. But the Pope hesitated. His army was already near the frontier; but he declared that he had no intention of making war, and desired only to protect his territory.

The news of the movement had reached Monte Video; and Garibaldi, believing that the Pope would stand forth as the champion for the freedom of Italy, wrote, offering his services and those of his followers, the greater part of whom were Italians who had been exiled for their political opinions. No answer was received from him; and Garibaldi took the matter into his own hands and with eighty-five Italians sailed for Europe. On arriving at Alicante he learned that a revolution had broken out in Paris, that Carlo Alberto had given his people a constitution, that Lombardy and Venice had risen, that the Milanese had driven the Austrians out of the city, that there were insurrections in Vienna and Berlin, that Tuscany and Rome were sending thousands of volunteers to fight in the national cause, and that even Ferdinand of Naples had promised his people a constitution. Garibaldi was unavoidably detained for some time at Nice, his native town, and before he was able to move a change had set in.

The Lombards and Venetians had both quarrelled among themselves. Mazzini's party were struggling against those who would have made Carlo Alberto King of Italy. The Piedmontese, after brilliant successes at first, were obliged to retreat. The Roman volunteers had been forced to capitulate. Garibaldi went to see the king, and offer to act with his volunteers in his service; but his application was slighted, and this threw him into the hands of the revolutionary party. It was a grievous mistake on the part of the king; but the latter could not forget that Garibaldi had been a rebel against him, nor could Garibaldi forget that it was the king who had sentenced him to death and had sent him into exile. He therefore hurried to Milan, where he was received with enthusiasm. The king moved to the aid of Milan, against which the Austrians were advancing; but in that city the party of Mazzini was predominant, and they refused to open the gates to him; and early in August the king came to terms with the Austrians, and Milan surrendered.

For a time Garibaldi's following alone maintained the war. Carrying on a guerilla warfare, he, with fifteen hundred men, was surrounded by five thousand Austrians, but he effected a marvellous retreat, and retired into Switzerland. Here he was taken ill, and was forced to rest for some months. He then went to Genoa. The extraordinary skill and bravery which he had shown during the campaign induced the king of Sardinia to offer him the rank of general in his army, that being the grade that he had held in Monte Video. But Garibaldi refused, and with two hundred and fifty volunteers started for Venice, which was besieged by the Austrians. On hearing, however, of the rising in Rome and the flight of the Pope—who had now abandoned his liberal professions, and had thrown himself into the hands of Austria—Garibaldi changed his course, and his ranks being swollen as he marched along, he arrived at Rome at the head of fifteen hundred men. Here he met his comrade in the struggle at Rio and Monte Video.

During his six years' residence in Rome Captain Percival had imbibed that hatred of the Austrians and detestation of the despotisms under which the Italian States groaned, that was felt by all with whom he came in contact, his father-in-law, Professor Forli, being one of the leaders of the liberal party in Rome. His wife, too, was an enthusiast in the cause; and although he felt no sympathy whatever with Mazzini and the revolutionary party, he was, even before the arrival of Garibaldi, resolved to take up arms should Rome be attacked. The presence of Garibaldi still further confirmed this resolution; but as soon as he heard that a French expedition had set sail, he had insisted that his wife and child should leave the city, for he by no means shared the general belief that the French were coming as allies. Her mother accompanied her to Leghorn, for the professor was as anxious as Percival that his wife and daughter should be in a place of safety.

They were most reluctant to go, and only yielded when Signor Forli and Captain Percival declared that their presence in Rome would hamper their movements and render it impossible for them to make their escape if the city should be taken, which both foresaw would be the case. They promised that when they found all was lost they would leave the city and join them at Leghorn. Madame Forli was to take her maiden name again; and as two English ladies staying at an hotel at Leghorn they would be safe from annoyance even if a French or Austrian army marched through the town. The professor spoke English well, and once out of the city he and Leonard would be able to pass as two English tourists travelling from Naples to Florence.

Had the Pope sought refuge in Capua or Malta, events might have taken a very different turn; but he threw himself into the hands of the King of Naples, and went the length of pronouncing him to be a model monarch, a pattern to the rest of Europe, and this at a time when the disclosures that had been made respecting the horrible dungeons into which all Neapolitans suspected of entertaining liberal views were thrown, were filling Europe with horror.

This change of front extinguished the hopes of those who had imagined that the Pope would become the centre of liberal thought in Italy, rendered the people of the papal dominions desperate, and vastly increased the party of Mazzini and the extreme republicans. On February 9th a constituent assembly was held in Rome, and the republic was proclaimed. Garibaldi was appointed to defend the frontier. Volunteers poured in from all parts of Italy, and as the King of Sardinia had again taken up arms, a force was moving forward to support him, when the news came of his defeat at Novara, followed by his abdication and the succession of Victor Emmanuel to the throne. Austria, Naples, and Spain were now eager to crush the revolution in Rome; but the resolution of the Romans was unshaken, and they still hoped to be able to maintain themselves with, as they expected, the aid of France.

The terrible blow that had been inflicted on finding that the French were coming as enemies, instead of as friends, did not shake their determination, although it was now with a courage of despair rather than of hope that they prepared for the conflict. Rome must fall; but at least it would prove itself worthy of its best traditions, and set an example that would not be lost upon the peoples of Italy. Anything, they felt, would be better than the reign of a pope in close alliance with the tyrant of Naples; and the evening after the French landing saw Rome tranquil and grimly determined. Doubtless many of those who were resolved to fight till the last were buoyed up with the hope that in any case they would be able to make their escape when the action was over. Rome covered a great extent of ground, and the French army was not of sufficient strength to form a cordon round it.

Captain Percival had, a fortnight before, sent his finished and unfinished canvases and all his most valuable belongings down to Civita Vecchia, and had shipped them for England. He knew the reckless destruction carried out by an army after a successful assault, and that possibly, if it came to street to street fighting, a considerable portion of the city might be burnt. The professor had similarly sent away his very valuable collection of coins, books, and manuscripts. At nine o'clock they went down to the mansion that Garibaldi occupied. A long discussion took place and routes were decided upon for the various contingents to follow when the alarm was given. News had been brought in from time to time during the day as to the movements of the French, and the point at which they would probably assault was therefore now known. It would be either at the Porta Cavalleggieri or at the Porta San Pancrazio.

Captain Percival and the professor returned to the former's house, where the professor had taken up his residence since his wife had gone to Leghorn, and sat talking until a late hour. They were roused early the next morning by the ringing of the great bells of the cathedral, which were joined almost immediately by those of all the other churches in the city. Captain Percival had lain down fully dressed, and springing to his feet, he buckled on a sword, placed a brace of pistols in his belt, and then ran down to the Porta San Pancrazio, where, as he knew, Garibaldi would take up his post. The general, indeed, had not slept at all, but, fearful that the French might attempt an assault under cover of darkness, kept watch round the western wall, along which he had posted the men he could most depend upon. Even before the Englishman joined Garibaldi the roar of the guns on the wall told that the French were already advancing.

"It is like old times, comrade," Garibaldi said, with a strong grip of his hand, "only it is on a larger scale than we were accustomed to in South America. Oudinot is beginning with a blunder, for he is making for the Porta Cavalleggieri, which is flanked by the walls of the Vatican. He is over-confident, and I do not imagine that he expects anything like a serious resistance. I think we shall certainly beat him back there, and that then he will attack us here. Will you go to the other gate? All my old comrades know you, and, indeed, all the volunteers, as you have assisted to drill them."

Oudinot, indeed, had believed that the force of regular troops he had with him would easily brush aside the resistance of a half-armed mob.

Captain Percival hurried away. The volunteers were already gathered on the walls, and in every street the townspeople were hurrying out, armed with weapons of all kinds. On the roofs and at the windows of the houses women were clustered thickly, waving their handkerchiefs and scarves, and shouting words of encouragement and applause to the men. To the roar of cannon was now added the rattle of musketry. When he reached the gate he found a heavy column of volunteers drawn up there, while behind them was a dense crowd of excited citizens. From the wall he saw the French advancing; the leading regiment was but a few hundred yards away. They were moving steadily forward, apparently heedless of the cannon that thundered on their flank and face. The musketry they could afford to despise, for they were beyond the distance at which any accurate shooting was possible; and, indeed, the firing was of the wildest description, as comparatively few of the men had ever handled a gun until a few weeks previously. Captain Percival went up to the officer who was in command, and with whom he was well acquainted. Although the massive walls still stood, the gates had long since disappeared, their places being occupied simply by barriers, where the duty on provisions and goods coming into the city was collected.

"The men are clamouring to be let out," he said. "What do you think, Captain Percival?"

"I should let them go soon. They are full of dash and enthusiasm at present, and would fight far better on the offensive than they would if they are kept stationary. I should keep them in hand till the French are within seventy or eighty yards of the gate. By that time they will be answering the fire from the walls, and even those in the front lines, whose muskets are still loaded, will only have time for one shot before our men are upon them. I should place three or four hundred of your steadiest men on the wall here, so that if the sortie is repulsed, they can cover the retreat by their fire."

"I think that is good advice," the other said. "Will you come down with me, and tell them that they shall go, but that they must not move till I give the order, and that no man is to fire until he is within ten yards of the enemy's line."

It was difficult to make their voices heard above the crack of musketry and the shouts of the excited crowd; however, their words were passed from man to man, and so back among the people behind. Now that they knew that they were to have their way, and that the critical movement was at hand, the shouting abated, and a stern look of determination settled on their faces. Leonard Percival joined a group of officers who were at the head of the volunteers, and the officer in command resumed his place on the wall, as it was all-important that, if the sortie were repulsed, he should lead his men down and oppose the entrance of the enemy until the retiring force had rallied.

It was not long before a roll of musketry broke out, showing that the assailants were now returning the fire of the Garibaldians on the wall. It grew louder and louder; and then, when the head of the French column was some eighty yards away, the officer on the wall gave the order, and the volunteers followed by the citizens poured out with a mighty shout. The French halted for a moment in surprise, not having dreamt that the defenders of the town would venture upon sallying out to attack them. Then there was a scattered fire of musketry; but most of the barrels were already empty, and few of the balls took effect. Without replying, the volunteers rushed forward, opening out as they ran to something like order. When within ten yards of the French bayonets every man delivered his fire, and then hurled himself upon the broken ranks. The struggle was a short one. The weight and impetuosity of the attack, supported as it was by a surging crowd of excited citizens, was irresistible, and the regiment broke and fled hastily to the shelter of the troops following it, leaving the ground strewn with dead and wounded. Then the bugles at the gate rang out the order to the exulting crowd to retire. The officers threw themselves in front of the men, and with great difficulty checked the pursuit, and caused them to withdraw to their original position behind the wall.

CHAPTER II.

A DESPERATE DEFENCE

AFTER a short halt the French, having re-formed, changed their course and marched along parallel to the fortifications. Captain Percival had, on his returning from the sortie, joined the officer on the wall, and watched alternately the movements of the French and the scene in the city. This was one of wild excitement—the men cheering and shouting, shaking each other by the hand, placing their hats on their bayonets, and waving them in answer to the wild applause of the women on the housetops. Some, however, were not content at being called back, instead of being allowed to complete what they considered their partial victory; forgetting that they would have been met in a very different manner by the troops in support, who would have been prepared for the attack and would have reserved their fire until the last moment. As soon as it became evident that the French intended to make their next move against the gate of San Pancrazio, the greater portion of the volunteers marched in that direction, Captain Percival accompanying them.

"You have done well so far," Garibaldi said, as he joined them. "Now it will be our turn, and we shall have tougher work than you had, for they will be prepared. I suppose your loss was not heavy?"

"Very trifling indeed; there were but three dead brought in, and there were some ten or twelve wounded."

"It was just the sort of action to raise the spirits of the men, and they are all in the humour for fighting. I shall therefore lead them out here. But we cannot hope to succeed with a rush as you did—they will be prepared for us this time; the best men would be killed before we reached them, and the mass behind, but few of whom have guns, would be simply massacred."

The volunteers, who had undergone a rough sort of drill, were assembled before the French had concluded their preparations for an assault. Garibaldi appointed Captain Percival to take charge of the gate, having with him two hundred of the volunteers, behind whom were the armed citizens. These clamoured to go out as before; but Garibaldi raised his hand for silence, and then told them that he would not lead them to a useless massacre against an army of well-armed soldiers.

"Your duty," he said, "is to remain here. If we have to fall back, you will open to let us pass. We shall be ready to do our share when necessary; but the defence of the gate will be for a while entrusted to you. If the enemy force an entrance, fall upon them as you would upon wild beasts; their discipline and their arms would be of no great advantage in a hand-to-hand fight. Each man must fight as he would were he protecting his family from a band of wolves—hatchet and pike must meet musket and bayonet, those who have knives must dive among the throng and use them fearlessly. It is a great charge that we entrust to you: we go out to fight; you will guard the city and all you hold dear."

A loud cheer showed that he had struck the right chord, and the mob drew back as he led out some five thousand

A DESPERATE DEFENCE

volunteers. These advanced to within musket-shot of the enemy, and then scattering, took shelter behind houses and cottages, walls and ruins. The French cannon opened fire as the movement was going on. These were answered by the guns on the walls, and as the French advanced a murderous fire was opened by their hidden foes. The battle raged for several hours. Sometimes the French advanced close up to the position held by the Garibaldians, but as soon as they did so, they were exposed also to the fire from the men on the walls; and in spite of Captain Percival's efforts, groups of men made their way down the road and joined the firing line, lying down until the moment should come when they could spring like wild cats upon the French.

Once or twice, when the assailants pressed back the Garibaldians in spite of their efforts, they found themselves presently opposed by a crowd that seemed to leap from the ground, and who, with wild shouts, rushed upon them so furiously that they recoiled almost panic-struck before so unaccustomed an enemy. Men were pulled down, and as Garibaldi had given strict orders that no French soldier should be killed except when fighting, these were carried back triumphantly into the city. At last General Oudinot, seeing that his troops were making no progress, and that even if they could force their way into the city, they would suffer terribly in street-fighting with such assailants, gave the order for his men to retire. This they did sullenly, while a roar of triumphant shouting rose from the volunteers, the men on the walls, and the crowd that covered every house and vantage-ground, from which a view of what was passing outside could be obtained.

The Italian loss was only about a hundred men killed

and wounded, whereas the French lost three hundred killed and wounded and five hundred prisoners. So unprepared was the French general for such a resistance, that he had to undergo the humiliation of sending in to Garibaldi to ask him to supply him with surgeons to dress the wounds of the French soldiers. During the fighting the French artillery had done far more injury to works of art in Rome than they had inflicted upon the defenders, as the artillery played principally upon the dome of St. Peter's and the Vatican, both of which buildings were much damaged.

The joy caused in Rome by this victory was prodigious. Fires blazed that night on all the hills, every house was illuminated, the people thronged the streets, shouting and cheering. They had, indeed, much to be proud of: five thousand almost undrilled volunteers had defeated seven thousand of the best troops of France.

The French retired at once to Palo on the road to Civita Vecchia. Garibaldi gave his troops a few hours' rest and then moved out to attack the French, and took up a most advantageous position. His troops were flushed with victory, while the French were cowed and dispirited; and he was on the point of attacking, when General Oudinot sent a messenger to treat for an armistice, and as a proof of his sincerity offered to give up Ugo Bassi, a priest who had remained by the side of a wounded man when the Garibaldians had for a moment retired. Garibaldi would peremptorily have refused the request, for he was confident that he should defeat and capture the whole of the French. Mazzini, however, with his two associates in the triumvirate, still clung to the hope that the French would aid them, and determined to accept the armistice, fearing that were the whole

WALKING UP AND DOWN THE ROOM LIKE A CAGED LION.

French army destroyed, the national feeling would be so embittered that there would no longer be any hope whatever of an alliance. Garibaldi protested, declaring that the armistice would but enable the French reinforcements to arrive. Mazzini, however, persisted in the decision, and actually released the five hundred prisoners in exchange for the priest.

The folly of this violent democrat sealed the fate of Rome. Had Garibaldi been permitted to carry out his plans, the French army would have been destroyed or made prisoners to a man, and the enthusiasm that such a glorious victory would have excited throughout all Italy would have aroused the whole population to burst their bonds. Furious at this act of folly, Garibaldi and his troops re-entered Rome. He was greeted with enthusiasm by the people, but disliking such ovations, he slipped away with Captain Percival to the latter's house. Professor Forli had taken no part in the fighting outside the walls, but stationing himself with the troops that manned them, had kept up a vigorous fire whenever the enemy were within gunshot. After the repulse of the second attack he had returned home.

"The stupidity of these people is incredible," Garibaldi, who had scarcely spoken a word since he had turned back towards Rome, burst out, waving aside the chair that the professor offered him, and walking up and down the room like a caged lion. "We held the French in the palms of our hands, and they have allowed them to escape. A fortnight, and we shall have three times their number to face, and you know what the result will be. I regard the cause as lost, thrown away by Mazzini—a man who has never taken part in a battle, who kept himself shut up in the capital when the fighting was going on, a man of the tongue and not of action. It is too disgusting. I am a republican; but if a republic is to be in the hands of men like these, they will drive me to become a monarchist again. Carlo Alberto was weak, but he was at least a man; he staked his throne for the cause, and when it was lost, retired. Mazzini stakes nothing, for he has a safe-conduct; if he loses, he will set to to intrigue again, careless who may fall or what may come to Italy, if his own wild ideas cannot prevail; he desires a republic, but it is a republic that he himself shall manipulate. Well, if it must be, it must. I am no statesman, but simply a fighting man. I shall fight till the last; and the failure must rest upon the head of him who has brought it about."

"It is a bad business," Captain Percival said quietly. "I thoroughly agree with you, Garibaldi, in all you say; but as you know of old, I am not much given to words. I began this thing, and shall go through with it. I think as you do, the cause is lost; but every blow we strike will find an echo in Italy, and a harvest will grow from the seeds some day. As to Mazzini and his two companions, I am not surprised. When you stir up muddy water, the scum will at first rise to the top. So it was in the first throes of the French Revolution, so it is here; the mob orators, the schemers, come to power, and there they remain until overthrown by men of heart and action. After Robespierre and Marat came Napoleon, a great man whom I acknowledge I admire, heartily, enemy though he was to England; after Mazzini Italy may find her great men. I know you do not like Cavour; I admire him immensely. He is obliged to be prudent and cautious now; but when the time comes he will be regarded as the champion of free Italy; and from what I have heard of him, the young King Victor Emmanuel will be a sovereign worthy of him."

"I hope it may prove so," Garibaldi said shortly; "at present the prospect does not seem to me a fair one. And you, professor?"

"I shall carry out my plans, and when Rome falls, as fall it doubtless will, I shall, if I escape, join my wife at Leghorn, and go and establish myself in England. I have friends and correspondents there, and I have my son-in-law, who has promised me a home. Here I could not stay—I am a marked man; and the day that the Pope enters in triumph I should be consigned to a dungeon under St. Angelo."

"There should be no difficulty in escaping," Garibaldi said. "With fifteen miles of wall it would need fifty thousand men to surround them; and the French will want all their strength at the point where they attack us."

It was evident that some time must elapse before there would be any change in the situation at Rome. Mazzini was sending despatches to Ledru Rollin and the French Assembly, imploring them to abstain from interference that would lead to the destruction of the Roman Republic; and until these could be acted upon, or, on the other hand, fresh troops arrived from France, matters would be at a standstill. In the meantime, danger threatened from another quarter; for the King of Naples was preparing to move with ten thousand men to reinstate the Pope. This force, with twenty pieces of cannon, had advanced as far as Albano. Three days after the battle, Garibaldi told Captain Percival that he was about to start that evening with four thousand men to meet the Neapolitan army, and asked him to accompany him.

"The troops will not be warned till an hour before we set out. It is important that no whisper shall reach the enemy as to our intentions or strength."

"I shall be glad to go with you," the Englishman said. "After the way your men fought against the French, I have no doubt that they will make short work of the Neapolitans, however great the odds against them. Bomba is hated by his own subjects; and it is hardly likely that they will fight with any zeal in his cause. They are very different foes from the French."

Accordingly, at eight o'clock on the evening of May 4th, Captain Percival mounted and joined Garibaldi and his staff, and they rode to Tivoli, halting among the ruins of Adrian's Villa.

The next morning scouts were sent off towards Albano, and returned in the evening with the news that the Neapolitans were still there, and showed no signs of any intention to advance, the news of the defeat of the French having, no doubt, greatly quenched King Ferdinand's ardour.

On the 8th the Garibaldians moved to Palestrina, and the general despatched a body of men to drive back the scattered parties of Neapolitans who were raiding the country. This was done with little loss, the Neapolitans in all cases retiring hastily when approached. Garibaldi had information that evening that orders had been given for the main body of the enemy to advance and attack him on the following day. The information proved correct; and before noon the Neapolitan force was seen approaching, seven thousand strong. Garibaldi had no cannon with him, having set out in the lightest marching order. He distributed a portion of his force as skirmishers, keeping the rest in hand for the decisive moment. The Neapolitan artillery opened fire, and the main body advanced in good order; but as soon as a heavy fire was opened by the skirmishers, much confusion was observed in their ranks. Two other parties were at once sent out; and these, taking every advantage of cover, soon joined in the fray, opening a galling fire upon each flank.

Several times the Neapolitans attempted to advance, urged on by their officers; but the skirmishing line in their front was strengthened from the reserves whenever they did so, until the whole of the Garibaldians, with the exception of a thousand of the steadiest troops, were engaged, and an incessant fire was maintained against the heavy ranks of the enemy, whose artillery produced but little effect against their almost unseen foes. For three hours the conflict continued; then, as the Garibaldian reserve advanced, the confusion among the enemy reached a point at which it could no longer be controlled, and Ferdinand's army fled like a flock of sheep. Garibaldi and his staff had exposed themselves recklessly during the fight, riding about among their troops, encouraging them, and warning them not to be carried away by their impetuosity into making an attack, until the enemy was thoroughly shaken and the orders issued for a general charge.

A heavy fire was maintained upon the staff by the Neapolitans; and it seemed to them that Garibaldi had a charmed life, for although several of the staff fell, he continued to ride up and down as if altogether oblivious of the rain of bullets. He did not, however, escape unscathed, being wounded both in the hand and foot. The fugitives did not halt until they had crossed the frontier into Neapolitan territory. The Garibaldians remained for two or three days at Palestrina; and seeing that the Neapolitans showed no signs of an intention to advance again, returned by a rapid march to Rome.

Mazzini's efforts had been to some extent successful. The French Assembly declared that for France to aid in suppressing a people determined to obtain their freedom was altogether in contradiction with the condition on which the republic had been instituted, and sent M. de Lesseps as an envoy to Rome. Napoleon, however, was of opinion that the reverse to the French must be wiped out, and on his own authority despatched large reinforcements to Oudinot.

To the indignation of Garibaldi's friends and of the greater part of the population of Rome, it was found, on the return of the force to the capital, that, in spite of the brilliant successes that had been gained, Mazzini and the demagogues had superseded him in his command, and had appointed Colonel Roselli over his head. This step was the result of their jealousy of the popularity that Garibaldi had gained. His friends advised him not to submit to so extraordinary a slight; but the general simply replied that a question of this kind had never troubled him, and that he was ready to serve, even as a common soldier, under any one who would give him a chance of fighting the enemy of his country. On the 14th the Neapolitan army again advanced and occupied Palestrina; and the Roman army, now ten thousand strong, marched out on the 16th. Garibaldi, with two thousand men, moved in advance. Although Roselli was nominally in command of the army, he was conscious of Garibaldi's greater abilities, and deferred, on all points, to the opinion of the man who was regarded by all as being still their Commander-in-chief.

When within two miles of Velletri Garibaldi met a strong column of Neapolitans; these, however, after but a slight resistance, took to flight, and shut themselves up in the town. Garibaldi sent back for reinforcements, but none arrived until too late in the day for the attack to be made; and in the morning it was found that the enemy had evacuated the place, the soldiers being so cowed by their superstitious fear of Garibaldi that the officers in vain attempted to rally them, and they fled in a disorderly mob. The panic reached the other portion of the army, and before morning the whole had again crossed the frontier. Garibaldi, at the head of his division, followed them up; and receiving authority to carry the war into the enemy's country, was marching upon Naples, when he was recalled in all haste to aid in the defence of Rome, Oudinot having given notice, in spite of a treaty agreed upon between M. de Lesseps, on the part of the French Assembly, and Mazzini, that he would attack Rome on Monday, June 4th.

Oudinot was, however, guilty of an act of gross treachery, for, relying upon his intimation, the city was lulled into a sense of security that no attack would be made until the day named, whereas before daybreak on the 3rd his troops stole up and took possession of the buildings just outside the gate of San Pancrazio, and, before the Roman troops could assemble, captured the Porta Molle, after a desperate resistance by a few men who had gathered together on the alarm being given. The firing was the first intimation that Rome received of the treacherous manœuvre of Oudinot. Again the church bells pealed out, and the populace rushed to defend their walls. Garibaldi felt that the occupation by the enemy of two great villas, a short distance from the wall, would enable them to place their batteries in such close proximity to the San Pancrazio gate that it was necessary at all hazards to recapture them; and, with his brave Lombard volunteers, he sallied out and attacked the French desperately.

All day long the fight continued, both parties being strongly reinforced from time to time; but in fighting of this kind the discipline of the French soldiers, and the military knowledge of their officers, gave them a great advantage over the Italians, who fought with desperate bravery, but without that order and community of effort essential in such a struggle. In vain did Garibaldi and Colonel Medici, the best of his officers, expose themselves recklessly in their endeavours to get their men to attack in military order and to concentrate their efforts at the given point; in vain did the soldiers show a contempt for death beyond all praise. When night fell the French still held possession of the outposts they had gained, and the Italians fell back within the walls.

That night Garibaldi held a council of war, at which Captain Percival was present. The latter and Colonel Medici were strongly of opinion that a renewal of the fighting of that day would be disastrous. The loss had already been very great, and it had been proved that, however valiantly they fought, the volunteers were unable to wrest the strong positions held by a superior force of well-disciplined men; for the French army now numbered forty thousand, while that of the defenders was but twelve thousand, and of these more than half had joined within the last three weeks. A series of such failures as those they had encountered would very quickly break the spirit of the young troops, and would but precipitate the end. These opinions prevailed, and it was decided that for the present they should remain on the defensive, maintaining a heavy cannonade from the walls, and making occasional sorties to harass the besiegers. In the meantime, the bridge across the Tiber should be destroyed, and, if possible, mines should be driven to blow up the batteries that would be erected by the French under cover of the positions they held.

These tactics were followed out. The French engaged upon the erection of the batteries were harassed by continuous cannonade. Sorties were frequently made, but these were ere long abandoned; the loss suffered on each occasion being so heavy that the troops no longer fought with the courage and enthusiasm that had so animated them during the first day's fighting. The attempt to blow up the bridge across the river by means of a barge loaded with explosives failed, and none of the defenders possessed the knowledge that would have enabled them to blow in the centres of the arches. The mines were equally unsuccessful, as the French countermined, and by letting in the water formed a streamlet that ran into the Tiber, filled the Italian works, and compelled the defenders to desist from their labours. Nevertheless, the progress of the siege was hindered, and although it was certain that the city, if unaided, must fall ere long, Mazzini still clung to the hope that the treaty made by Lesseps and carried by him to Paris would be recognized. This last hope was crushed by the arrival of a French envoy with the declaration that the French Government disavowed any participants in the Convention signed by M. de Lesseps.

Even Garibaldi now admitted that further resistance would only bring disaster upon the city and cause an absolutely useless loss of life. Mazzini and his two colleagues persisted in their resolution to defend the town to the last, even if the French laid it in ashes, and they even reproached Garibaldi with cowardice. On the night of the 21st the French gained possession of the San Pancrazio gate, having driven a passage up to it unnoticed by the defenders. They at once seized the wall and captured two bastions, after a desperate defence by Garibaldi. They then planted cannon upon these and began to bombard the city. Twelve guns were also planted in a breach that had been effected in the wall, and terrible havoc was made among the villas and palaces in the western part of the city.

Roselli proposed that the whole defending force should join in an attack on the French batteries; but to that Garibaldi would not consent, on the grounds that these could not be carried without immense loss, and that, even if captured, they could not be held against the force the French would bring up to retake them. Gradually the assailants pushed their way forward, encountering a determined resistance at the capture of the Villa Savorelli. On the evening of the 27th no fewer than four hundred of its defenders fell by bayonet wounds, showing how desperately they had contested every foot of the advance. On the morning of the 30th three heavy columns of French advanced simultaneously, and carried the barricades the Romans had erected. Garibaldi, with the most determined of his men, flung himself upon the enemy; and for a time the desperation with which they fought arrested the advance. But it was a last effort, and Garibaldi sent to Mazzini to say that further resistance was impossible.

He was summoned before the triumvirate, and there stated

A DESPERATE DEFENCE

that unless they were resolved to make Rome a second Saragossa, there was no possible course but to surrender. In the end the triumvirate resigned, issuing a proclamation that the republic gave up a defence which had become impossible. The assembly then appointed Garibaldi as dictator, and he opened negotiations with the French. So enthusiastic were the citizens that, in spite of the disasters that had befallen them, many were still in favour of erecting barricades in every street and defending every house. The majority, however, acquiesced in Garibaldi's decision that further resistance would be a crime, since it would only entail immense loss of life and the destruction of the city. For three days negotiations were carried on, and then Garibaldi, with four thousand men, left the city and marched for Tuscany, while the French occupied Rome. But in Tuscany the patriots met with but a poor reception, for the people, though favourable, dared not receive them. The French had followed in hot pursuit; the Austrians in Tuscany were on the look-out for them; and at last, exhausted and starving, they took refuge in the little republic of San Marino. Here they were kindly received; but an Austrian army was advancing, and the authorities of the republic were constrained to petition that the Garibaldians, now reduced to but fifteen hundred men, should be allowed to capitulate, and that they themselves should not be punished for having given them refuge.

These terms were granted, but the Archduke insisted upon Garibaldi himself surrendering. The general, however, effected his escape with his wife and twelve followers, embarking on board a fishing-boat, and they reached the mouth of the Po; the rest of the band were permitted by the Austrians to return to their homes. Garibaldi, alone, with his dying wife, was able to conceal himself among some bushes near the river; his companions were all taken by the Austrians and shot. Nine other boats, laden with his followers, could not get off before the pursuing Austrians arrived; and a heavy fire being directed upon them, they were forced to surrender. Garibaldi's faithful wife, who had been his companion throughout all his trials, died a few days later. The Austrian pursuit was so hot that he was forced to leave her body; and after many dangers he reached Genoa. He was not allowed to remain in Sardinia; and from thence took ship to Liverpool, and there embarked for New York.

Fortunately for Captain Percival, he and Professor Forli had, when on June 27th Garibaldi himself recognised that all further resistance was useless, determined to leave the city. When he stated his decision to Garibaldi, the latter warmly approved.

"You have done all that could be done, comrade," he said; "it would be worse than folly for you to remain here, and throw away your life. Would that all my countrymen had fought as nobly for freedom as you have done for a cause that is not yours!"

"I have a right to consider it so, having made Rome my home for years, and being married to the daughter of a Roman. However, we may again fight side by side, for assuredly this will not be the last time that an attempt will be made to drive out the despots; and I feel sure that Italy will yet be free. I trust that you do not mean to stay here until it is too late to retire. You must remember that your life is of the greatest value to the cause, and that it is your duty, above all things, to preserve it for your country."

"I mean to do so," Garibaldi said. "As soon as all see that further resistance is useless, I shall leave Rome. If I find that any spark of life yet remains in the movement, I shall try to fan it into flame; if not, I shall again cross the Atlantic until my country calls for me."

That evening Captain Percival and the professor left the town. There was no difficulty in doing so, as the whole French force was concentrated at the point of attack. The professor had exchanged his ordinary clothes for some of his companion's, and their appearance was that of two English tourists, when in the morning they entered Ostia, at the mouth of the Tiber, by the road leading from Albano. As many fugitives from Rome, had, during the past month, embarked from the little port, and it was no unusual thing for English tourists to find their way down there, they had no difficulty in chartering a fishing-craft to take them to Leghorn, it being agreed that they should be landed a mile or two from the town, so that they could walk into it without attracting any attention, as they would assuredly be asked for passports were they to land at the port.

The voyage was altogether unattended by incident; and on landing they made a detour and entered the town from the west, sauntering quietly along, as if they had merely been taking a walk in the country. Ten minutes later they entered the lodging that Madame Forli had taken, after staying for a few days at an hotel. Great indeed was the joy which their arrival excited. The two ladies had been suffering terrible anxiety since the fighting began at Rome, and especially since it was known that the French had obtained possession of one of the gates, and that a fierce struggle was going on. They were sure their husbands would keep their promise to leave the city when the situation became desperate; but it was too likely that Captain Percival might have fallen, for it was certain that he would be in the thick of the fighting by the side of Garibaldi. It was, then, with rapturous delight that they were greeted, and it was found that both were unharmed.

It was at once decided to start by a steamer that would leave the next day. Both the ladies possessed passports: Muriel that which had been made out for her husband and herself on their return home from their visit to England; while her mother had one which the professor had obtained for both of them when the troubles first began, and he foresaw that it was probable he might have to leave the country. Therefore no difficulty was experienced on this score; and when the party went on board the next day the documents were stamped without any questions being asked. Not the least delighted among them to quit Leghorn was Frank, who was now four years old. He had found it dull indeed in their quiet lodging at Leghorn, and missed his father greatly, and his grandfather also, for the professor was almost as fond of the child as its parents.

There were but few passengers besides themselves, for in the disturbed state of Italy, and, indeed of all Europe, there were very few English tourists in 1848; and even those who permanently resided in Italy had for the most part left. The passengers, therefore, were, with the exception of the two ladies and Captain Percival, all Italians, who were, like Signor Forli, leaving because they feared that the liberal opinions they had ventured to express—when it seemed that with the accession of a liberal pontiff to the papal chair better times were dawning for Italy—would bring them into trouble now it was but too evident that the reign of despotism was more firmly established than ever.

The steamer touched at Genoa, and here the greater portion of her passengers left, among them Professor Forli's party. They took train to Milan, where they stopped for a few days, crossed the Alps by the St. Gothard's Pass, spent a fortnight in Switzerland, and then journeyed through Bâle, down the Rhine to Cologne, and thence to England. They were in no hurry, for time was no object to any of them, as they were well supplied with money; and after the excitement and trouble of the last few months, the quiet and absence of all cause for uneasiness was very pleasant to them. On their arrival at Tom Percival's town residence in Cadogan Place sad news awaited them. Only a fortnight before, his yacht had been run down at sea, and he and the greater part of the crew had perished.

CHAPTER III

TROUBLES

THE death of Tom Percival naturally made a great difference to his brother's position. He was now a large land-owner, with a fine place in the country and a house in town. The next nine years of his life were unmarked by any particular incident. Signor Forli and his wife were permanently established in Cadogan Place. The professor had never been accustomed to a country life, and in London he was able to indulge in all his former pursuits. He had always laid by a certain amount of his income, and could have lived in some comfort in London, as until the troubles began he had received, in addition to his modest salary as a professor, the rents of a property he possessed near Naples, of which place he was a native. But neither Captain Percival nor his wife would hear of his setting up an establishment of his own.

"We shall not be up in town above three months of the year at the outside," the former said; "and of course Muriel will always want to have you with us for that time, for I know very well that you will seldom tear yourself from your work and come down and stay with us in the country. It will be far better for us that the house shall be always used, instead of being left for nine months in the year to caretakers. You can fit up the library with cases for your coins and manuscripts. You have already made the acquaintance of many of the scientific and learned men you formerly corresponded with, and will soon get a very pleasant society of your own. It will be better in all respects. You can shut up the rooms you don't use, while the servants whom I keep to look after the house must in any case be told to consider you as their master; and you can, if you choose, get a couple of Italian servants as your own special domestics." And so, after much argument, it was settled, and for some years things went on to the satisfaction of all.

When ten years old Frank was sent to a preparatory school for Harrow, and three years later to the great school itself. Just at this time the professor determined to pay a visit to Italy. Since the fall of Rome everything had gone on quietly there; and although persons suspected of liberal ideas had been seized and thrown into prison without any public inquiry, he considered that now that he had been settled in England for years, and had become a naturalised British subject, he could without any risk go over to make an effort to obtain a reversal of the confiscation of his property in the Neapolitan territory. Before starting he had called upon the official representative of the Neapolitan government, and had been assured by him that his passport as a British subject would be respected, and that if he refrained from taking any part in politics he could travel in King Ferdinand's territories without any fear of his movements being in any way interfered with.

Up to this time Captain Percival and his wife had been strongly against the proposed visit, but after the professor had received this official assurance they believed with him that he could in perfect safety undertake the journey. He wrote on his arrival at Naples, stating that he had, as soon as he landed, called upon one of the ministers, and reported to him the assurance that the envoy in London had given him, and had been told that, while expressing no opinion upon the probability of his obtaining a reversal of the confiscation of his estate, there could be no objection whatever to his endeavouring to do so, but that he did not think the government would authorise his establishing himself permanently in the kingdom, as his well-known political opinions would naturally render him obnoxious. He had given his assurance that he had no intention whatever of remaining beyond the time necessary for the purpose for which he had come; that he had now permanently settled in England, and had only come over for the purpose that he had specified; and that on no account would he hold any political discussions with such personal friends as he had in Italy, or give any expression whatever of his own views. He wrote that, as he had said before starting, he did not intend to call upon any of his former acquaintances, as, if he did so, it might bring them into discredit with the government.

No other letter was received from him. After waiting for three weeks, Captain Percival wrote to the proprietor of the hotel from which the previous letter was dated, asking if he was still there, and if not, if he was aware of his present address. The answer was received in due time, saying that Professor Forli had gone out one morning, a week after his arrival, with the intention, he believed, of visiting his former estate, but that he had not returned. Two days later a person had arrived bearing a letter from him, saying that he had changed his plans and should not return to Naples, and requesting that his luggage and all personal effects should be handed over to the bearer, who would discharge the amount owing for his bill. He had complied with the request, and had since received no communication from Professor Forli. Captain Percival went at once to call upon the minister for foreign affairs, stated the whole circumstances to him, and the assurance that the professor had received from the Neapolitan envoy before starting, and said that he felt sure that, in spite of his assurance and the protection of his passport as a British subject, his father-in-law had been seized and thrown into prison.

"If that is the case, a serious wrong has been committed," the minister said. "But we cannot assume that without some proof. He may have been seized by some brigands, who by a ruse have obtained possession of his effects; possibly the person now in possession of the estate, fearing that he might be ousted from it, has taken these means for suppressing a claimant who might be dangerous. However, what you have told me is sufficient for me to commence action, by making a complaint to the Neapolitan government that a British subject, duly furnished with a passport, is missing, and requesting that measures shall at once be taken to ascertain what has become of him."

Correspondence went on for three or four months, the Neapolitan government protesting that they had made inquiries in every direction, but had obtained no clue whatever as to Professor Forli's movements from the time when he left his hotel, and disclaiming any knowledge whatever of him. It was now January, 1858, and Lord Palmerston, who was then prime minister, took the case up warmly, and Captain Percival had several interviews with him.

"I quite agree with you, sir," the minister said, "that he is probably in a Neapolitan dungeon; but at present we have no absolute proof of it; if we had I should summon Ferdinand to release him under a threat of war."

"I am quite ready to go out, sir, to make personal inquiries; and if you could obtain for me an order to visit the various jails and fortresses in the Neapolitan territories, I may succeed in finding him."

"I will obtain for you such an order," Lord Palmerston said decidedly. "If they refuse my request, I shall be forced to the conclusion that they are afraid of your finding him there—not that I think it is likely you will do so. Indeed I regard it as certain that he would be removed from any prison before you arrived there, or if still there, that his dungeon would not be shown to you. At the same time, you would be doing good work. Already there have been some terrible disclosures as to the state of the Neapolitan prisons. These, however, have chiefly been made by men who have been confined there, and have been denounced as calumnies by the Neapolitan government; but coming from you, armed with the authority of our foreign office, they could not but make a profound impression. They might force the authorities to ameliorate the present state of things, and would certainly enlist the sympathy of the British public with the cause with which Professor Forli was associated, and for which I am aware you yourself fought."

A fortnight later Captain Percival was again sent for by the foreign minister.

"Here," the latter said, "is a royal order from the King of Naples for you to view any or all the prisons in his dominions without let or hindrance, in order to assure yourself that Professor Forli is not an inmate of any of them."

Two days later Captain Percival started. On arriving at

Naples, he first called upon the Neapolitan minister, who expressed himself with some indignation on the fact that the assurance of the government that they knew nothing of Professor Forli's disappearance had been doubted; but stated that they were ready to offer him any facility in his search. Before commencing this, Captain Percival went out to the professor's estate, near Capua, and saw the proprietor, who assured him that he had neither seen nor heard anything of its late owner; and although his assertions would have weighed but little if unsupported, Captain Percival's investigation in the town and of several persons upon the estate all tended to show that the professor had not been seen there. His appearance was familiar to many, and he could hardly have visited the place without being recognised. Captain Percival went to see several of Signor Forli's old friends, upon whom he would almost certainly have called before going to the estate, and from whom, indeed, he would have received far more information as to its condition than he would have obtained by direct application to a man who could not but have regarded him with hostility; none of them, however, had heard of his return to Italy.

After stopping two or three days there, he returned to Naples and began his inspection of the prisons. The Royal order being presented, he was everywhere received courteously, allowed to inspect them from the lowest dungeons to the attics under the roofs, and also to hold conversations with the prisoners. He had no idea that he would actually find the professor; his great hope was that he should learn from prisoners that he had been confined there, as this would enable the British government to demand his instant release. Terrible as had been the descriptions he had heard of the treatment of the prisoners and the state of the jails, they fell far short of the reality; and he not only sent detailed reports to the government, but also to *The Times,* which published them in full. They were copied into every paper in the kingdom, and created a general feeling of indignation and disgust.

Failing to obtain the smallest information as to the professor at Naples, Captain Percival then went down to Salerno, and left there with the intention of visiting the prisons in Calabria and at Reggio, and afterwards of crossing into Sicily and trying the gaols there. Four days after he left Salerno, the servant he had engaged in Naples returned to the town with the news that the carriage had been attacked by brigands, and that his master, who always carried a brace of pistols, had offered a desperate resistance, but had been killed. The horses had been taken out of the carriage, and they and Captain Percival's luggage had been carried off to the hills. He himself had been allowed to return. The Governor of Salerno at once sent the man to Naples; the news was officially communicated to the British envoy, who telegraphed at once to London. A message was returned, saying that an official communication would be addressed to the government, and in the meantime he was to send down one of the officers of the embassy to inquire into the whole matter. He was to request the Neapolitan government to furnish an escort from Salerno, and was also to demand that steps should be taken to pursue and bring the brigands to justice.

The secretary of the legation had no difficulty in obtaining the order for an escort; and taking with him the servant who had brought the news, proceeded to the place where the affair had occurred. The carriage was found overthrown by the roadside. There were two or three bullet-holes in it; there was a dark patch evidently caused by blood in the road close by; and a few yards away was a bloodstained cap, which the servant recognised as being that of Captain Percival. Following up a track which led off the main road from here, they came upon some fragments of letters, among them one on which were the words, "Your loving wife, Muriel." For two or three days the hills on each side of the track were searched, but no sign whatever was found of Captain Percival's body. In the meantime, a strong force of carabinieri searched the mountains, and three weeks after the return to Naples of the search party from the legation, came the news that they had surprised and killed a notorious brigand leader with three of his followers, and had taken prisoner a fourth. This man was sent to Naples, and there questioned by a judicial official in the presence of the secretary of the legation.

He acknowledged that he had been one of the party, consisting of their leader and seven followers, who had attacked the Englishman's carriage. They had not intended to kill him, but to carry him off for ransom; he, however, resisted so desperately that he was shot. Although very seriously wounded, they had carried him up to the mountains, believing that he would recover, and that they might still make money out of him. The man himself had been sent down to Salerno to ascertain whether the authorities were taking any steps to hunt down his capturers. As soon as he learned that a strong force of carabinieri had been ordered out in pursuit, he had returned to the hut occupied by his chief. He found that during his absence the prisoner had died. He had never asked where he had been buried, for it was a matter that did not concern him. The contents of the portmanteau had been divided among the party; he was himself now wearing the boots and one of the shirts of the dead man. That was all he knew.

The captain of the carabinieri testified that he had found an English portmanteau and many articles, some of which bore the initials "L. P." upon them; there was a brace of handsome pistols of English make, which were used by the chief of the brigands in the fight; and in a cupboard among other things was the royal order for Captain Percival to visit his majesty's prisons. A diligent search had been made in the neighbourhood of the hut, but the grave of the English gentleman had not been discovered. In due time the brigand was placed on trial, and was sentenced to imprisonment for life; and so the matter ended, save for the two widowed women and Frank.

It had been a heavy blow indeed for the lad, who was passionately attached to his father, and had also loved the professor, who had always been extremely fond of him. He was at home for Easter when the terrible news arrived. Neither his mother nor grandmother expressed a doubt that his father had been murdered; and when the news of the confession of one of the band and the discovery of Captain Percival's belongings in the hut of the brigands arrived, they gave up all hope of ever seeing him again.

Madame Forli, however, while not doubting that Captain Percival had been killed, believed that the Neapolitan government were at the bottom of the matter. "I know what the methods of the Neapolitans are," she said; "and the sensation caused by Leonard's letters to the papers here may have decided them to put an end by any methods to further revelations, and they may very well have employed these brigands to carry out their purpose. Every one knows that in many cases these men are in alliance with the officers of the police; and the latter are well paid to wink at their doings, and even to furnish them with information of the persons worth robbing, and to put them on their guard when, as occasionally happens, a raid is made by the carabinieri in the mountains. A capture is hardly ever effected; and while there is little chance of a political prisoner shut up in their dungeons making his escape, notorious brigands frequently succeed in doing so. Nobody dares to speak of their suspicions; but there can be little doubt that the prison officials are bribed to connive at their escape, knowing well enough that the government will not trouble over the matter, while on the other hand the escape of a political prisoner brings disgrace and punishment upon all the prison officials."

"I cannot think—I will not think so, mother," Muriel exclaimed; "for were it so, the same treatment might be given to him that has, we have no doubt, befallen my father. A thousand times better that Leonard should have been killed, than that he should drag out his existence in such utter misery as that which he has described as being the lot of prisoners in the dungeons of Bomba. The brigands may have been set on by their government. That is possible—I can believe that iniquitous government to be guilty of anything—but whether Leonard was attacked merely for plunder, or for ransom, or by the connivance of the government, I cannot and will not doubt that he is dead; the story of one of the band can leave no doubt of this, and it is confirmed by his servant, who saw him fall. Never try to shake my confidence in that, mother. It was almost more than I could bear to think of my father as confined in one of those dungeons; if I thought for a moment that Leonard could be there too, I believe that I should lose my reason."

Frank returned to school after the short holidays. His mother thought that it would be better so, as the routine of work and play would give him little time for moping over his loss. He worked harder than he had ever done at school before; but obtained leave off cricket, and spent his time out of school in long walks with one or other of his chums. After the summer holiday he was himself again. He was quieter than he had been, and held aloof from fun and mischief, but joined in the sports vigorously, and regained the ground he had lost, and came to be regarded as likely some day to be one of the representatives of the school.

When it seemed that the search for the body of Captain Percival had failed, Mrs. Percival wrote to the secretary of the legation in Naples, saying that she would be glad if her husband's courier would come over to see her.

"I naturally wish to know," she said, "as much as I can of the last movements of my husband from the only person who was with him; and I would willingly bear the expenses of his journey both ways, and pay him fifty pounds. I did not receive any letter from my husband during the fortnight preceding his death, and want to learn as much as possible about him."

The secretary, on receiving the letter, sent the note to the chief of the police, in whose charge the man had been while the investigations were proceeding; an answer was returned saying that the man Beppo Paracini was not now in his charge, but that perhaps he could find him in the course of a few hours, and would, on doing so, send him to the legation at once.

Instead of seeing the man himself, however, the officer went to the director of the secret police. "As this affair has been in your department rather than in mine, signor, I thought it best to bring you this note I have just received from the British legation before taking any steps in the matter."

The official read the note through. "You have done quite right," he said. "The affair has been a very troublesome one, and now that it has practically come to an end, it would not do to take any false step in the matter. You shall hear from me in the course of the day."

He sat thinking deeply for some minutes after the other had left him, then he touched a bell.

"Luigi," he said, when a man entered, "go and fetch Beppo Paracini; if he is not in, find where he has gone and follow him."

Half an hour later the courier entered. When before the court he had been dressed in the fashion affected by his class; now he was in dark, quiet clothes, and might have been taken for an advocate or a notary.

"Beppo," he said, "I thought that we had finished with that troublesome affair of the Englishman; but there is again occasion for your services in the same direction. Here is a letter from the secretary of the British legation saying that he wishes to see you, for that the Signora Percival has written to him to say that she is anxious to learn more of the last days of her husband, and is willing to pay your expenses to England and to give you fifty pounds for your services, if you would be willing to go to her for a few days.

I regard this as a fortunate circumstance. The woman's husband and her father have been constant enemies of the kingdom. Percival was a bosom friend of Garibaldi; her father was also his friend, though not to the same degree. Ever since they established themselves in England his family, who are unfortunately rich, have befriended Italian exiles.

"Forli was acquainted with all his compatriots in London, who, like himself, were men of education and position, and had escaped from justice. In that house any plot that was on foot, especially if Garibaldi was a leading spirit in it, would certainly be known. No doubt the loss of her husband will make this woman more inveterate against us than ever. I have often wished that I could establish an agent in her house, to keep me informed of what was going on there, who visited it, whether any meetings and consultations were held there, from whom they received letters, and the purport of them, but I have never before seen my way to it. The woman Forli is herself English, and consequently since her husband's death no Italian servants have been kept in the house. This letter gives me the opportunity I have desired. I wish you to go to the British legation, and to express your willingness to accept the offer that is made, and if possible to obtain a situation in the house.

"You could represent that you were anxious to obtain a place of any kind in England, for that, owing to the part that you have taken in the search for Percival's body—a search which brought about the death of the brigand Rapini and the breaking up of his band—your life was no longer safe there from the vengeance of his associates. You can say that before you became a courier you were in the service of several noble families—of course you will be provided with excellent testimonials—and as it was your zeal in her late husband's behalf that had brought you into this strait, it is quite possible that she may offer you a post in the household. You can declare that you do not desire high wages, but simply a shelter. You will, of course, report yourself on arriving in London to the head of our secret agents there, and will act generally under his directions. I need not say that you will be well paid."

"I will gladly accept the mission, signor, for, to say the truth, I am not without some apprehensions such as you suggest. I have changed my appearance a good deal; still, I cannot flatter myself that I could not be detected by any one on the search for me, and I do think that some of Rapini's band, knowing that I was with the carabinieri, may have vowed vengeance on me; and, as you know, signor, a man so threatened cannot calculate on a very long life."

"That is so, Beppo. Then we may consider the matter settled. If you cannot succeed in obtaining a position in the house of this family, I shall instruct my agent in London to utilise your services there, at any rate for the next six months. After that time you may return without much risk, for when it is found that you have disappeared from all your former haunts, the search for you is not likely to last long. At any rate, you might as well mention to those who have known you as a courier, that you intend to establish yourself either in Paris or Berlin. For as you speak both French and German as well as English, that would in any case be the course that a prudent man would adopt, after being mixed up in an affair that ended badly for the brigands. Well, in the first place, you had better go at once to the legation and accept the terms. Come here at eleven o'clock tomorrow, and I will give you further instructions."

Thus it happened when Frank came home next time from school, he was surprised at having the door opened to him by a grave-looking servant in plain clothes, who said in English, with a very slight foreign accent: "The Signora Percival is in the drawing-room, sir. I will see to your baggage and settle with the cabman."

"Whom have you got hold of now, mother?" he said, after the first greeting—"an Italian? Isn't he a fearfully respectable-looking man? Looks like a clergyman got up as a valet."

"He was your dear father's courier, Frank. I sent for him to come over here, as I wished to learn all about your father's last days. The poor fellow was in fear of his life, owing to the evidence that he had given against the brigands. William had given me notice that he was going to leave only the day before; and as Beppo had served in several noble families, who had given him splendid testimonials, and was afraid to return to Italy, I was very glad to take him in William's place, especially as he only asked the same wages I paid before. I congratulate myself on the change, for he is quite the beau-ideal of a servant—very quiet in the house, ready to do anything, gets on well with the other servants, and is able to talk in their own language to any of his countrymen who come here, either as visitors or as exiles in need of assistance. He has, indeed, saved me more than once from impostors; he has listened to their stories, and having been a courier, and knowing every town in Italy, on questioning them he found out that their whole story was a lie."

"That is all right, mother; if you like him, that is everything. I own that I liked William; I am sorry that he has gone. I shall be some time getting accustomed to this chap, for he certainly is fearfully grave and respectable."

CHAPTER IV.

A SUDDEN SUMMONS

ONE Saturday early in March, 1860, Frank, now sixteen years of age, on starting for the football ground, was told that the house-master wished to see him, and he at once went into his study.

"Percival, I have received a note from your mother, asking me to let you out till Monday morning. She says that she particularly wants to see you, and will be glad if you will start at once. Of course I will do so; you had better catch the next train, if you can."

"What in the world can the mater want to see me in such a hurry for?" Frank said to himself in a rather discontented tone as he left the master's study. "It is a frightful nuisance missing the match this afternoon! I don't know what Hawtrey will say when I tell him that I cannot play. Ah! here he is."

"What is up, Percival?"

"I am awfully sorry to say that I have just received a message from my mater calling me up to town at once. I have no idea what it is about; but it must be something particular, for I told her when I wrote to her last that this was going to be the toughest match of the season; still, of course I must go."

"I see that, Percival. It is a terrible nuisance; you are certainly the third best in the house, and now I shall have to put Fincham in, I suppose, and I am afraid that will mean the loss of the match."

"He is as strong as I am, Hawtrey."

"Yes; he is strong enough and heavy enough, but he is desperately slow. However, I must make the best of him."

Frank hurried upstairs, and in ten minutes came down again, dressed. He ran the greater part of the way to the station, and just caught the up train. The disappointment over the football match was forgotten now. Thinking it over, he had come to the conclusion that either his mother or grandmother must have been taken seriously ill. It could hardly be his mother, for it was she who had written; still she might have managed to do that, even if she had met with some sort of accident, if it was not too serious. If not she, it must be the signora, as he generally called her, and as he was very fond of her, he felt that her loss would be a heavy one indeed. His anxiety increased as he neared London; and as soon as the train stopped at Euston he jumped out, seized the first hansom, and told the cabman to drive fast to Cadogan Place. He leaped out, handed his fare to the cabman, ran up the steps, and knocked at the door.

"Is every one well, Beppo?" he asked breathlessly, as the servant opened it.

"Yes, sir," the footman replied, in his usual calm and even voice.

"Thank God for that!" he exclaimed. "Where is my mother?"

"In the dining-room, sir, with the signora."

Frank ran upstairs. "Mother, you have given me quite a fright," he said. "From your message I thought that some one must have been suddenly taken ill, or you would never have sent for me when you knew that we played in the final ties for the house championship to-day. I have been worrying horribly all the way up to town."

"I forgot all about your match, Frank," his mother said. "I have had a letter that put it out of my head entirely."

"A letter, mother?"

"Yes, Frank; from your hero, Garibaldi."

"What is it about, mother?" Frank exclaimed excitedly, for he had heard so much of the Italian patriot from his father, and of their doings together in South America and the siege of Rome, that his admiration for him was unbounded.

"Sit down, Frank, and I will tell you all about it. The letter was addressed to your dear father. Garibaldi, being in Caprera, probably has but little news of what is passing at Naples. He had heard of my father's disappearance, but was apparently in ignorance of what has happened since."

She took out the letter and read:

"'MY DEAR COMRADE AND FRIEND,—

"'When I last wrote to you it was to condole with you on the disappearance of that true patriot and my good friend, Professor Forli. I hope that long ere this he has been restored to you; but if, as I fear, he has fallen into the clutches of the rascally government of Naples, I am afraid you will never hear of him again. Several times, when you have written to me, you have told me that you were prepared to join me when I again raised the flag of Italian independence, though you held aloof when France joined us against Austria. You did rightly, for we were betrayed by the French as we were at Rome, and my birthplace, Nice, has been handed over to them. You also said that you would help us with money; and, as you know, money is one of our chief requisites. The time has come. I am convinced that the population of the Neapolitan territories are now reduced to such a state of despair by the tyranny of their government that they will be ready to hail us as deliverers.

"'My plan is this: I am sure a thousand or so of the men who fought with me in the Alps will flock to my standard, and with these I intend to effect a landing in Sicily. If I capture Palermo and Messina I think I can rely upon being joined by no small number of men there, and by volunteers from all parts of Italy; five thousand men in all will be sufficient, I think—at any rate, that number collected, I shall cross to the mainland and march upon Naples. You may think that the adventure is a desperate one, but that is by no means my opinion; you know how easily we defeated the Neapolitan troops in 1848. I believe that we shall do so still more easily now, for certainly very many of them must share in the general hatred of the tyrant. Come, dear friend, and join us; the meeting-place is called the Villa Spinola, which is a few miles from Genoa.

"'I do not anticipate any great interference from Cavour; he will run with the hare and hunt with the hounds, as your proverb has it. He dare not stop us; for I am convinced that such is the state of public opinion in Italy, that it might cost his master his crown were he to do so. On the other hand, he would be obliged to assume an attitude of hostility, or he would incur the anger of Austria, of the Papacy, and possibly of France; therefore I think that he will remain neutral, although professing to do all in his power to prevent our moving. I am promised some assistance in money, but I am sure that this will fall short of the needs. We must buy arms not only for ourselves, but to arm those who join us; we must charter or buy steamers to carry us to Sicily. Once there, I regard the rest as certain. Come to me with empty hands, and you will receive the heartiest welcome as my dear friend and comrade; but if you can aid us also with money, not only I, but all Italy, will be grateful to you. I know that you need no inducement, for your heart is wholly with us, and all the more so from this disappearance of madame's father, doubtless the work of the tyrants. Need I say that our first step in every town and fortress we capture will be to release all political prisoners confined there?—and it may be that among these we will find Professor Forli. Turr will be with me, Baron Stocco of Calabria, Bixio, and Tuckory; and Madame Carroli has written to tell me that she places her three sons at my disposal in the place of their brave brother, and will, moreover, supply me with money to the utmost of her power. Come, then, dear friend, aid me with your arm and counsel, and let us again fight side by side in the cause of liberty.'"

Frank leapt to his feet. "You will let me go in my father's place, mother, will you not? Many of those who will follow Garibaldi will be no older than myself, and probably not half so strong; none can hate the tyranny of Naples more than I do. It is the cause for which my father and grandfather fought; and we now have greater wrongs than they had to avenge."

"That is what I thought you would say, Frank," his mother said sadly. "'Tis hard indeed to part with a son after having lost father and husband; but my father was an

Italian patriot, my husband fought for Italy; in giving you up I give up my all; yet I will not say you nay. So fierce is the indignation in England at the horrors of the tyrants' prisons that I doubt not many English will, when they hear of Garibaldi's landing in Sicily, go out to join him; and if they are ready in the cause only of humanity to risk their lives, surely we cannot grudge you in the cause not only of humanity, but of the land of our birth."

"I feel sure that father would have taken me, had he been here," Frank said earnestly.

"I believe he would, Frank. I know that he shared to the full my father's hatred of the despots who grind Italy under their heel; and besides the feeling that animated him, one cannot but cherish the hope that my father may still be found alive in one of those ghastly prisons. Of course my mother and I have talked the matter over. We both lament that your studies should be interrupted; but it can be for a few months only, and probably you will be able to return to Harrow when the school meets again after the long holiday—so that, in fact, you will only lose three months or so."

"That makes no odds one way or another, mother. In any case, I am not likely to be a shining light in the way of learning."

"No—I suppose not, Frank; and with a fine estate awaiting you, there is no occasion that you should be, though of course you will go through Oxford or Cambridge. However, we need not think of that now."

"And will you be sending him any money, mother?"

"Certainly. Your father put by a certain sum every year in order that he might assist Garibaldi when the latter again raised the flag of freedom in Italy—a cause which was sacred in his eyes. At the time he left England, this fund amounted to £10,000; and as he never knew when the summons from Garibaldi might arrive, he transferred it to my name, so that he need not come back to England, should a rising occur before his return. So you will not go empty-handed."

"That will be a splendid gift, mother. I suppose I shall not go back to school before I start?"

"No, Frank. Since you are to go on this expedition, the sooner you start the better. I shall write to your headmaster and tell him that I am most reluctantly obliged to take you away from school for a few months; but that it is a matter of the greatest importance, and that I hope he will retain your name on the books and permit you to return when you come back to England."

"If he won't, mother, it will not matter very much. Of course I should like to go back again; but if they won't let me, I shall only have to go to a coach for a year or two."

"That is of little consequence," his mother agreed; "and perhaps, after going through such an exciting time, you will not yourself care about returning to school again. You must not look upon this matter as a mere adventure, Frank; it is a very, very perilous enterprise, in which your life will be risked daily. Were we differently situated, I should not have dreamt of allowing you to go out; but we have identified ourselves with the cause of freedom in Italy. Your grandfather lost everything—his home, his country, and maybe his life; and your father, living as he did in Rome, and married to the daughter of an Italian, felt as burning a hatred for the oppression he saw everywhere round him as did the Italians themselves; perhaps more so, for being accustomed to the freedom Englishmen enjoy, these things appeared to him a good deal more monstrous than they did to those who had been used to them all their lives. He risked death a score of times in the defence of Rome; and he finally lost his life while endeavouring to discover whether my father was a prisoner in one of the tyrants' dungeons. Thus, although in all other respects an English boy—or Italian only through your grandfather—you have been constantly hearing of Italy and its wrongs, and on that point feel as keenly and strongly as the son of an Italian patriot would do. I consider that it is a holy war in which you are about to take part—a war that, if successful, will open the doors of dungeons in which thousands, among whom may be my father, are lingering out their lives for no other cause than that they dared to think, and will free a noble people who have for centuries been under the yoke of foreigners. Therefore, as, if this country were in danger, I should not baulk your desire to enter the army, so now I say to you, join Garibaldi; and even should you be taken from me, I shall at least have the consolation of feeling that it was in a noble cause you fell, and that I sent you, knowing that my happiness as well as your life hung upon the issue. I want you to view the matter then, my boy, not in the light of an exciting adventure, but in the spirit in which the Crusaders went out to free the Holy Sepulchre, in which the Huguenots of France fought and died for their religion."

"I will try to do so, mother," Frank said gravely; "at any rate, if the cause was good enough for my father and grandfather to risk their lives for, it is good enough for me. But you know, mother," he went on, in a changed voice, "you can't put an old head on to young shoulders; and though I shall try to regard it as you say, I am afraid that I shan't be able to help enjoying it as a splendid adventure."

His mother smiled faintly. "I suppose that is boy nature. At any rate, I am sure that you will do your duty, and there is certainly no occasion for your doing it with a sad face; and bear in mind always, Frank, that you are going out not so much to fight, as to search every prison and fortress that may be captured, to question every prisoner whether he has heard or known any one answering the description of your grandfather, or—or——" and her lip quivered, and her voice broke.

"Or, mother?"—and he stood surprised as Mrs. Percival burst suddenly into tears, and the signora, rising from her seat, went hastily to her, and put her arm round her neck. It was a minute of two before Mrs. Percival took her hands from her face and went on,—

"I was going to say, Frank, or of your father."

Frank started, as if he had been suddenly struck. "My father," he repeated, in a low tone. "Do you think, mother —do you think it possible? I thought there was no doubt as to how he was killed."

"I have never let myself doubt," Mrs. Percival went on. "Whenever the thought has come into my mind during the past two years I have resolutely put it aside. It would have been an agony more than I could bear to think it possible that he could be alive and lingering in a dungeon beyond human aid. Never have I spoken on the subject except to my mother, when she first suggested the possibility; but now that there is a chance of the prison doors being opened, I may let myself not hope—it can hardly be that—but pray that in God's mercy I may yet see him again." And as she again broke down altogether, Frank, with a sudden cry, threw himself on his knees beside her, and buried his face in his arms on her lap, his whole figure shaken by deep sobs.

Mrs. Percival was the first to recover her composure, and gently stroked his hair, saying: "You must not permit yourself to hope, my boy; you must shut that out from your mind as I have done, thinking of it only as a vague, a very vague and distant possibility."

"But how, mother, could it be?" he asked presently, raising his head. "Did we not hear all about his being killed, how Beppo saw him shot, and how one of the band testified that he was dead and buried?"

"So it seemed to me, Frank, when my mother first pointed out to me that all this might be false, and that just as the government of Naples declared they were absolutely ignorant as to your grandfather's disappearance when it appeared to us a certainty that it was due to their own act, so they would not hesitate a moment to get rid of your father, whose letters as to the state of their prisons were exciting an intense feeling against them in every free country. She said it would be easy for them to bribe or threaten his servant into telling any tale they thought fit; he or some other agent might have informed the banditti that a rich Englishman would be passing along the road at a certain time, and that the government would be ready to pay for his capture and delivery to them. The prisoner taken may have been promised a large sum to repeat the story of the Englishman having died and been buried. It was all possible, and though I was determined not to think of him as a prisoner, my mother, who knew more of these things than I did, and how matters like this were managed in Italy, thought that it was so. Still to my mind there were, and still are, reasons against hope, for surely the Neapolitan government would have preferred that the brigands should kill him, rather than that they themselves should have the trouble of keeping him in prison."

"Possibly they would have preferred that," Signora Forli said, speaking for the first time. "They knew that he was an Englishman, and doubtless learned that he carried loaded pistols, and may have reckoned confidently upon his resisting and being killed, and may have been disappointed because the brigands, hoping for a large ransom, carried him off wounded."

"But even then," Mrs. Percival said, "they could have sent up their agents to the brigands and paid them to finish their work."

"Yes, possibly that is what they did do; but though I have never spoken to you on the subject since you told me not to, I have thought it over many and many times, and it seems to me that they would scarcely do so, for they might thus put themselves into the power of these bandits. Any one of the band might make his way to Naples, go to the British legation, and under the promise of a large sum of money and protection denounce the whole plot. It seems to me more likely that they would send an agent to the chief brigand, and pay him a sum of money to deliver the captive up to the men who would meet him at a certain place. It is probable that the chief would, on some excuse or other, get rid of all his band but two or three, hand over the prisoner, and share the money only with those with him, and when the others returned, tell them that the prisoner had died and that they had buried him. Then the carabinieri would use every effort to kill those who were in the secret, and being in earnest for once, they probably did kill the chief and those with him. Probably the man who gave his evidence was not one of the party at all, but some prisoner charged with a minor offence, who was promised his liberty as the price of telling the story that he was taught. If Leonard had been killed and buried, as they stated, his grave must surely have been found—the earth must still have been fresh; and, indeed, nothing is more unlikely than that the brigands should have taken any extraordinary trouble to hide the body, as they could not have anticipated that any vigorous search would be made for it. For these reasons I have all along believed that Leonard did not come to his end as was supposed. He may have been killed afterwards by those into whose hands he was delivered; but even this does not seem likely, for one of them might betray the secret for a large reward. He may have died in a dungeon, as so many thousands have done; but I believe firmly that he did not, as reported, die in the brigands' hut. I have never since spoken on the subject to your mother, Frank, for I agreed with what she said, that it would be better to think of him as dead than in a dungeon, from which, as was shown in the case of your grandfather, there was no chance of releasing him. Now, however, if Garibaldi is successful, as every prison will be searched, and every political prisoner freed, there is a prospect that, if he is still alive, he may be restored to us."

Frank, with the natural hope of youth, at once adopted the signora's view; but his mother, although she admitted that it might possibly be true, still insisted that she would not permit herself to hope.

"It may be that God in His mercy will send him back to me; but, though I shall pray night and day that He will do so, it will be almost without hope that my prayer will be granted, —were I to hope, it would be like losing him again if he were not found. Now let us talk of other matters. The sooner you start the better, Frank; you will not have many preparations to make. The Garibaldian outfit is a simple one—a red shirt, trousers of any colour, but generally blue, a pair of gaiters and one of thick, serviceable boots, a wideawake, or, in fact, any sort of cap with perhaps a red feather, a wellmade blanket wound up and strapped over one shoulder like a scarf, a red sash for the waist, a cloak or great-coat strapped up and worn like a knapsack, and a spare shirt and a pair of trousers are all the outfit that you require. You had better take a good rifle with you, and of course a pair of pistols. All the clothes you can buy out there, and also a sword, for no doubt Garibaldi will put you on his staff."

"In that case I shall not want the rifle, mother."

"No; and if you do you can buy one there. In a town like Genoa there are sure to be shops where English rifles can be bought, and you might have difficulty in passing one through the customs—luggage is rigorously examined on the frontier and at the ports. A brace of pistols, however, would be natural enough, as any English traveller might take them for protection against brigands if he intended to go at all out of beaten tracks. As to the money, I shall go to the bank on Monday, and request them to give me bills on some firm in Genoa or Turin. Garibaldi will find no difficulty in getting them cashed. I should say that your best course will be to go through Paris and as far as the railway is made, then on by diligence over Mont Cenis to Turin, and after that by railway to Genoa. In that way you will get there in three or four days, whereas it would take you a fortnight by sea."

"Then it seems to me, mother, that there is nothing at all for me to get before I start, except a brace of pistols; but of course I must have my clothes up from Harrow."

"I will write for them at once, Frank. It would be better that you should not go down—you would find it difficult to answer questions put to you as to why you are leaving; and of course this enterprise of Garibaldi must be kept a profound secret. One cannot be too prudent in a case like this, for if a whisper got abroad the Italian government would be compelled to stop him."

"You will not see Beppo here when you come back," Mrs. Percival said to Frank on Monday evening. "I gave him notice this afternoon,"

"What for, mother? Anyhow, I am not sorry, for I have never liked him."

"I know that you have not, Frank, and I begin to think that you were right. My maid said to me this morning that, though she did not like to speak against a fellow-servant, she thought it right to tell me that when I am out of the house and before I get up of a morning he is often in the drawing-room and dining-room, in neither of which he has any business; and that when she went up yesterday evening—you know that she is a very quiet walker—she came upon him standing outside the drawing-room door when we were chatting together, and she thought, though of this she was not quite sure, that he had his ear at the keyhole. He knocked and came in the instant he saw her, as if he had only that moment arrived there; but she had caught sight of him before he saw her, and was certain that he was listening.

"Of course, she might have been mistaken; but thinking it over, it seems to me that she was probably right, for once or twice since he has been here, it has struck me that the papers in my cabinet were not in precisely the same order as I had left them. You know that I am very methodical about such matters; still, I might each time, when I took them out, have omitted to return them in exactly the same order as before, though I do not think it likely that I could have done so. However, I thought nothing of it at the time; but now that I hear that he has been spying about the rooms and listening at the door, I cannot but connect the two things together, and it may be that the man has been acting as an agent for the Neapolitan government. You know, when we were talking the matter over on Saturday, my mother suggested that it was possible that the courier had been in league with the brigands. Possibly he may also be an agent of the government; and there was so great a stir made at that time that I cannot regard it as impossible, knowing how she and I are heart and soul with the Italian patriots, that he was sent over to watch us."

"I think it not only possible but probable," Signora Forli put in. "I know that in Italy the police have spies in every household where they suspect the owner of holding liberal opinions; and knowing that our house was frequented by so many exiles, they may have very well placed this man here. I regret now that at the time this man came over at your mother's request, we listened to his plausible tale and took him into our service, but I had not at that time any strong suspicions that the attack on your father was a preconcerted one, and I should hardly have mentioned the idea to your mother had it occurred to me. However, it is of no use thinking over that now; the great point is to consider how it will affect your plan."

"In what way, signora?" Frank asked in surprise; and Mrs. Percival added, "I don't see what you mean, mother."

"I mean this, dear: if this man is a spy, you may be quite sure that he has had false keys made, by which he can open your cabinet, your drawers, and your writing-desk. It is quite probable that he knows Garibaldi's handwriting, for, knowing that the general was a great friend of your father, he would almost certainly be furnished with a specimen of it; and, if that was the case, we may take it for granted that wherever you put any letter from Garibaldi, he would get at it and read it. That in itself can do comparatively little harm, for rumours of the general's proposed expedition are already current. But he will know that, immediately on receipt of that letter, you sent for Frank. Doubtless there are other Neapolitan spies over here, and every movement you have made since will, in that case, have been watched, and you will have been seen to go to the bank to-day. It is not likely that they would know how much we have drawn out, for your conversation was with the manager in his private room; but knowing your devotion to Garibaldi's cause, they might well suppose that the amount would be a considerable one. We have made no secret of the fact that Frank will start the day after to-morrow to travel in Italy for a time; and he will guess that Frank is the bearer of this money to Garibaldi—possibly, as it seems that he listened at the doors, he may even had heard you tell Frank how much you were going to send. Yesterday evening we were talking over how the bills had best be concealed, and he may have heard that also; if he did, you may be pretty sure that they will never reach Garibaldi, unless our plans for their concealment are changed."

"You frighten me, mother."

"I don't know that there is anything to be frightened about," the signora said. "I do not for a moment suppose that he contemplates any actual attack upon Frank; though he will,. I am convinced, try to get the money—partly, no doubt, for its own sake, partly because its loss would be a serious blow to Garibaldi. After the disappearance of his grandfather, and the commotion there was over the death or disappearance of his father, an attack upon Frank would appear to be a sequel of these affairs, and would cause such general indignation that the ministry would take the matter up in earnest, and the result would be far more disastrous for the government of Naples than could be caused by any amount of money reaching Garibaldi, whom they must regard as an adventurer who could give them some trouble, but who could not hope for success. Therefore, I do not think that there is any danger whatever of personal injury to Frank; but I do think there is grave fear that the money will be stolen on the way. If our suspicions are well founded as to Beppo, no doubt two or three of these agents will travel with him. If he stops to sleep at an hotel, his room would be entered and his coat carried off; he may be chloroformed when in a train and searched from head to foot; his baggage may be stolen on the way, but that would only be the case if they do not find the bills on his person or where we agreed last night to hide them."

"I dare not let him go," Mrs. Percival said, in a trembling voice.

"Why, mother," Frank said almost indignantly, "you don't suppose, now that I am warned, I shall be fool enough to let these fellows get the best of me? I will carry a loaded pistol in each pocket; I will not sleep in an hotel from the time I start till I have handed the bills to Garibaldi, and will take care always to get into a carriage with several other passengers. If I hadn't had fair warning, I dare say I should have been robbed; but I have no fear whatever on the subject now that we have a suspicion of what may occur. But if you think it would be safer, I do not see why you could not send the bills by post to an hotel at Genoa."

Signora Forli shook her head. "That would not do," she said. "You do not know what these Neapolitan spies are capable of. If they find that you have not the money with you, they would follow you to your hotel at Genoa, bribe the concierge there to hand over any letter that came addressed to you, or steal it from the rack where it would be placed, while his attention was turned elsewhere. However, I have an old friend at Genoa, the Countess of Mongolfiere; we exchange letters two or three times a year. She is, of course, a patriot. I will, if your mother agrees with me, enclose the bills in an envelope addressed to you, put that in another with a letter saying that you will call at her house when you arrive at Genoa, and request her to hand the letter to you. I will say that it vitally concerns the cause, and beg her to place it under lock and key in some safe receptacle until you arrive."

"That is an excellent idea, mother," Mrs. Percival said, "and would seem to meet the difficulty."

Frank rose from his seat quietly, stepped noiselessly to the door, and suddenly threw it open. To his surprise his mother's maid was sitting in a chair against it, knitting.

"It is all right, Hannah," he said, as she started to her feet. "I did not know you were there. I thought that fellow might be listening again," and he closed the door.

"I asked her to sit there this evening, Frank," Mrs. Percival said. "I knew that we should be talking this matter over, and thought it better to take the precaution to ensure our not being overheard."

"Quite right, mother; I am glad you did so. Then you think that that plan will answer?"

"Yes, I think so; but you must be sure and take care of yourself, just as if you had the money about you."

"That I will, mother; you can rely upon that."

"And above all," Signora Forli said, "you must beware, when you go to the Countess for the money, that you take every possible precaution. Call in the daytime, go in a carriage and drive straight from her place to the Villa Spinola; better still, go first to Garibaldi, tell him where the money is, and ask him to send three of his officers to your hotel on the following morning. Then take a carriage, drive to the Countess's, and take it to the general with four of you in the carriage. They would not dare to attack you in broad daylight."

"That is an excellent plan," Mrs. Percival said, in a tone of great relief. "Certainly, if they do manage to search him on the way, and find that he has not got the bills upon him, they will watch him closely at Genoa, where, no doubt, they will get the assistance of some of Francisco's agents. There are sure to be plenty of them in Genoa at present; but however many of them there may be, they would not venture to attack in daylight four men driving along what is no doubt a frequented road, more especially as they would know that three of them were Garibaldi's men, which is as much as to say desperate fellows, and who would, no doubt, like yourself, be armed with pistols."

"We had better take one more precaution," Signora Forli said. "It is believed that you are going to start on Thursday morning. Your packing can be done in five minutes; and I think that it would be a good plan for you to have everything ready to-night, and send Mary out for a hansom tomorrow morning, so that you could, when it comes up to the door, go straight down, get into it, and drive to the station. I don't say that they might not be prepared for any sudden change of our plans; but at least it would give you a chance of getting a start of them that they can never recover—at any rate, not until you get to Paris."

"How could they catch me there?" Frank said.

"Francisco's agents here might telegraph to his agents in Paris, and they might be on the look-out for you when you arrived, and take the matter up. You were going *viâ* Calais. Let me look at the Bradshaw."

"Yes," she said, after examining its pages; "the train for the tidal boat leaves at the same time as the Dover train. If, when you get into the cab, you say out loud, 'Victoria,' so that Beppo may hear it, you can then, when once on your way, tell the cabman to take you to Charing Cross. In that way, if there is any one on the look-out when the Calais train comes in, they will be thrown altogether off the scent."

"It seems ridiculous, all these precautions," Frank said, with a laugh.

"My dear, no precautions are ridiculous when you have Francisco's agents to deal with. Now, I will write my letter to the Countess at once, so that she may get it before your arrival there. You will, of course, go out and post it yourself."

CHAPTER V

ON THE WAY

AFTER posting the letter, Frank made several small purchases, and was more than an hour away. On his return he saw a cab standing at the door. As he approached, Beppo came out with a portmanteau, handed it up to the driver, jumped in, and was driven off.

"So Beppo has gone, mother," he said, as he joined her in the drawing-room.

"Yes. He came in directly you had left. He said that his feelings had been outraged by a servant being placed at the door. He could not say why she was there, but thought it seemed as if he was doubted. He could not but entertain a suspicion that she was placed there to prevent any one listening at the keyhole; after such an insult as that he could not remain any longer in the house. I said that he was at liberty to leave instantly, as his wages had been paid only three days ago. He made no reply, but bowed and left. Mary came up and told me ten minutes later that he had brought his portmanteau down, left it in the hall, and gone out, she supposed, to fetch a cab. I heard the vehicle drive up just now, and the front door closed half a minute ago."

Signora Forli came into the room as she was speaking. "Mary tells me that Beppo has gone. It is a comfort that he is out of the house. When you once begin to suspect a man, the sooner he is away the better. At the same time,

Frank, there can be no doubt that his going will not increase your chances of reaching Genoa without being searched. I should say that he had made up his mind to leave before you did, and he was glad that the fact of Mary being at the door gave him a pretext for his sudden departure. In the first place, he could conduct the affair better than any one else could do, as he knows your face and figure so well. Then, too, he would naturally wish to get the credit of the matter himself, after being so long engaged in it. Of course, you may as well carry out the plan we arranged, to start in the morning; but you may feel absolutely certain that, whatever you may do, you will not throw him off our track. He must know now that he is suspected of being a Neapolitan agent, and that you will very likely change your route and your time of starting.

"I regard it as certain that the house will be watched night and day, beginning from to-morrow morning, an hour or so before the trains leave. There will be a vehicle with a fast horse close at hand, possibly two, so that one will follow your cab, and the other drive at once to some place where Beppo is waiting. As likely as not he will go *viâ* Calais. If you go that way, so much the better; if not, he will only have to post himself at the station at Paris. It is likely enough that during the last day or two he has had one or two men hanging about here to watch you going in and out, and so to get to know you well, and will have one at each of the railway stations. He may also have written to the agents in Paris to have a look-out kept for you there."

"But how could they know me?"

"He would describe you closely enough for that; possibly he may have sent them over a photograph."

Frank got up and went to a side table, on which a framed photograph that had been taken when he was at home at Christmas, usually stood. "You are right," he said; "it has gone." Then he opened an album. "The one here has gone, too, mother. Are there any more of them about?"

"There is one in my bedroom; you know where it hangs. It was there this morning."

"That has gone, too, mother," he said, when he returned to the room.

"So you see, Muriel, I was right. The one from the album may have been taken yesterday, and a dozen copies made of it; so that, even if you give them the slip here, Frank, you will be recognised as soon as you reach Paris."

"Well, mother, it is of no use bothering any more about it. I have only to travel in carriages with other people, and they cannot molest me; at worst they can but search me, and they will find nothing. They cannot even feel sure that I have anything on me; for now that Beppo knows he is suspected of listening at doors, he will consider it possible that we may have changed our plans about where we shall hide the money. It is not as if they wanted to put me out of the way, you know; you and the signora agreed that that is certainly the last thing they would do, because there would be a tremendous row about it, and they would gain no advantage by it; so I should not worry any further, mother. I do not think there is the slightest occasion for uneasiness. I will just go by Calais, as I had intended, and by the train I had fixed on; that in itself will shake Beppo's belief that I have the money with me, for he would think that if I had it I should naturally try some other way."

"At any rate," Mrs. Percival said, "you shall not go by

the line that we had intended. You would be obliged to travel by diligence from Dole to Geneva, thence to Chambery, and again by the same method over the Alps to Susa. You shall go straight from Paris to Marseilles; boats go from there every two or three days to Genoa."

"Very well, mother; I don't care which it is. Certainly there are far fewer changes by that line; and to make your mind easy, I will promise you that at Marseilles, if I have to stop there a night, I will keep my bedroom door locked, and shove something heavy against it; in that way I can't be caught asleep."

"Well, I shall certainly feel more comfortable, my dear boy, than I should if you were going over the Alps. Of course, the diligence stops sometimes and the people get out, and there would be many opportunities for your being suddenly seized and gagged and carried out."

"They would have to be very sudden about it," Frank laughed. "I do think, mother, that you have been building mountains out of molehills. Beppo may not be a spy, after all; he may have heard you talking of this ten thousand pounds, and the temptation of trying to get it may be too much for him. He will know now that I shall be on my guard, and that, even if I have the money on my person, his chance of getting it is small indeed. I believe that you and the signora have talked the matter over till you have frightened yourselves, and built up a wonderful story, based only on the fact that Mary thought that she caught Beppo listening at the door."

"How about the photographs," Mrs. Percival asked.

"Possibly he has a hidden affection for me," Frank laughed, "and has taken these as mementos of his stay here. Well, don't say anything more about it, mother; I am not in the least nervous, and with a brace of loaded pistols in my pocket and the fair warning that I have had, I do not think I need be afraid of two or three of these miserable Neapolitan spies."

Accordingly, Frank started by the morning mail, as they had arranged. The carriage was full to Dover; and at Calais he waited on the platform until he saw an English gentleman with two ladies enter a compartment, and in this he took a vacant corner seat. On his arrival at Paris he drove across at once to the terminus of the railway to Marseilles, breakfasted there, and sat in the waiting-room reading till the door on the platform opened, and an official shouted, "Passengers for Melun, Sens, Dijon, Macon, Lyons, and Marseilles." There was a general movement among those in the waiting-room. Frank found that there was no fear of his being in a compartment by himself, for only one carriage door was opened at a time, and not until the compartment was full was the next unlocked. He waited until he saw his opportunity, and was the first to enter and secure a corner seat. In a short time it filled up.

He had slept most of the way between Calais and Paris, feeling absolutely certain that he would not be interfered with in a carriage with three English fellow-passengers. It was twelve o'clock now, and he would not arrive at Marseilles until seven the next morning, and he wondered where all his fellow-passengers, who were packed as closely as possible, were going, for although he did not wish to be alone, it was not a pleasant prospect to be for eighteen hours wedged in so tightly that he could scarcely move. Then he wondered whether any of the men who might be following were also in the train. He had quite come to the conclusion that his mother and grandmother had frightened themselves most unnecessarily; but he admitted that this was natural enough, after the losses they had had. At Dijon several passengers got out, but others took their places; and so the journey continued throughout the day. The carriage was generally full, though once or twice there were for a time but five besides himself. He read most of the way, for although he spoke Italian as fluently as English, he could not converse in French. When tired of reading he had several times dozed off to sleep, though he had determined that he would keep awake all night.

At ten o'clock in the evening the train arrived at Lyons. Here there was a stop of twenty minutes, and he got out and ate a hearty meal, and drank two or three cups of strong coffee. He was not surprised to find, on returning to his carriage, that all the passengers with two exceptions had left it. These had got in at Macon, and were evidently men of good circumstances and intimate with each other; he had no suspicions whatever of them, for it was certain that men who had any intention of attacking him would appear as strangers to each other. At Vienne both left the carriage. Frank was not sorry to see them do so.

"If there are really fellows watching me," he said to himself, "the sooner they show themselves and get it over the better; it is a nuisance to keep on expecting something to take place when as likely as not nothing will happen at all." He examined his pistols. They were loaded but not capped, and he now put caps on the nipples, and replaced them in his pocket.

Just before they had left Vienne a man had come to the

window as if intending to enter, but after glancing in for a moment had gone to another carriage.

"That is rather queer," Frank thought. "As I am alone here, there was plenty of room for him. Perhaps he had made a mistake in the carriage. At any rate, they won't catch me napping."

The strong coffee that he had taken at Lyons had sharpened his faculties, and he never felt more awake than he did after leaving Vienne. He sat with his eyes apparently closed, as if asleep, with a warm rug wrapped round his legs. An hour later he saw a face appear at the opposite window. At first it was but for an instant; a few seconds later it appeared again and watched him steadily; then the man moved along to the door and another joined him. Frank without moving cocked the pistol in his right-hand pocket, and took a firm hold of the butt with his finger on the trigger. The door opened noiselessly, and the second man thrust in an arm holding a pistol; so it remained for half a minute. Frank was convinced that there was no intention of shooting if it could be avoided, and remained perfectly still; then the arm was withdrawn, and another man, holding a knife in one hand and a roll of something in the other, entered. In a moment Frank's right arm flew up and his pistol cracked out; his assailant fell back and disappeared through the open door. Frank sprang to his feet as he fired, and stood with his pistol levelled towards the window, where the head of the second man had disappeared as his comrade fell backwards.

"He knows I have the best of him now," Frank muttered to himself; "I don't think that he will have another try."

Advancing cautiously, he pulled the door to, lowered the window, and putting a hand out without exposing his head,

HIS ASSAILANT FELL BACK AND DISAPPEARED.

turned the handle, and then drew up the window again. His foot struck against something as he backed to his seat in the corner. As he still kept his eyes fixed on the window, he paid no attention to this for a minute or two; then he became conscious of a faint odour.

"I expect that is chloroform or ether or something of that sort," he said, as he lowered the window next to him; and then, still keeping an eye on the door opposite, moved a step forward and picked up a large handkerchief, steeped in a liquid of some sort or other. He was about to open the window and throw it out, when an idea struck him.

"I had better keep it," he said: "there may be a beastly row over the business, and this handkerchief may be useful in confirming my story."

He therefore put it up on the rack, lowered the window a few inches, and did the same to the one opposite to it. Then wrapping the handkerchief up in two or three newspapers he had bought by the way, to prevent the liquid from evaporating, he sat down in his corner again. He felt confident that the attack would not be renewed, now he was found to be on the watch and armed. It was probable that the two men were alone, and the one remaining would hardly venture single-handed to take any steps whatever against one who was certain to continue to be vigilant. He had no doubt that he had killed the man he fired at, and that, even if the wound had not been instantly fatal, he would have been killed by his fall from the train.

"It seems horrid," he muttered, "to have shot a man; but it was just as much his life or mine as it would have been in battle. I hope no one heard the shot fired. I expect that most of the passengers were asleep; and if any one did hear it, he might suppose that a door had come open, or had been opened by a guard, and had been slammed to. Of course, the man's body will be found on the line in the morning, and I expect there will be some fuss over it; but I hope we shall all be out of the train and scattered through the town before any inquiries are set on foot. If they traced it to me, I might be kept at Marseilles for weeks. Of course, I should be all right; but the delay would be a frightful nuisance. There is one thing,—the guard looked at my ticket just before the train started from the last station, and would know that I was alone in the carriage."

In a few minutes the speed of the train began to slacken. He knew that the next station was Valence. He closed his eyes and listened as the train stopped. As soon as it did so, he heard a voice from the next carriage shouting for the guard. Then he heard an animated conversation, of which he was able to gather the import.

"The sound of a gun," the guard said. "Nonsense; you must have been dreaming!"

"I am sure I was not," a voice said indignantly. "It seemed to me as if it was in the next carriage."

The guard came to Frank's window. "Ah, bah!" he said. "There is only one passenger there, an Englishman. He was alone when we left Vienne, and he is sound asleep now."

"Perhaps he is dead."

It was possible, and therefore the guard opened the door. "Are you asleep, monsieur?"

Frank opened his eyes. "My ticket?" he asked drowsily. "Why, I showed it you at Vienne."

"Pardon, monsieur," the guard said. "I am sorry that

I disturbed you. It was a mistake," and he closed the door, and said angrily to the man who had called him: "It is as I said. You have been asleep; and I have woke the English gentleman up for nothing."

A minute later the train moved on again.

"So far so good," Frank said. "I should think that I am all right now. We shall be in at seven, and it will not be daylight till half-past six; and I fancy that we must have been about midway between Vienne and Vallence when that fellow fell out, it is not likely that his body will be found for some time. They are sure to have chosen some point a good way from any station to get out of their own carriage and come to mine. Even when they find him, they are not likely to make out that he has been shot for some time afterwards. I hit him in the body somewhere near the heart, I fancy; I did not feel sure of hitting him if I fired at his head, for the carriage was shaking about a good deal. It will probably be thought at first that he has either fallen or jumped out of his carriage. I suppose, when he is found, he will be carried to the nearest station, and put in somewhere till a doctor and some functionaries come, and an inquiry is held; and as he probably has been badly cut about the head and face, his death will be put down to that cause at first. Indeed, the fact that he was shot may not be found out till they prepare him for burial. I suppose they will take off his clothes then, as they will want to keep them for his identification, if any inquiries should ever be made about him. At any rate, I may hope to have got fairly away from Marseilles before the matter is taken up by the police, and even then the evidence of the guard that I was alone will prevent any suspicion falling especially on me."

He had no inclination for sleep, and although he felt certain that he would not again be disturbed, he maintained a vigilant watch upon both windows until, a few minutes after the appointed time, the train arrived at Marseilles. Having only the small portmanteau he carried with him, he was not detained more than two or three minutes there, took a *fiacre* and drove to the Hôtel de Marseilles, which his Bradshaw told him was close to the steamboat offices. After going upstairs and having a wash, he went down again, carefully locking the door after him and putting the key in his pocket. He then had some coffee and rolls, and while taking these, obtained from the waiter a time-table of the departures of the various steamers from the port, and found, to his great satisfaction, that one of the Rubattino vessels would leave for Genoa at twelve o'clock.

As soon as the steamboat offices were open he engaged a berth, walked about Marseilles for an hour, returned at ten to the hotel, took a hearty lunch, and then drove down to the port. On questioning the steward he found that there were not many passengers going, and with a tip of five francs secured a cabin to himself; having done this, he went on deck again and watched the passengers arriving. They were principally Italians; but among them he could not recognise the face of the agent who had levelled a pistol at him. Both men, had, indeed, worn black handkerchiefs tied across their faces below their eyes and covering their chins, and the broad-brimmed hats they wore kept their foreheads and eyes in shadow; and although he watched his fellow-passengers with the faint hope of discovering by some evil expression on his face his last night's assailant, he had no real belief that he should, even under the most favourable circumstances, recognise him again.

Two or three of the men wore beards, and seemed to belong to the sailor class—probably men who had landed from a French ship, after perhaps a distant voyage, and were now returning home. He saw no more of these, as they at once went forward. There were only eight other passengers in the saloon; seven of these were Italians, of whom three were evidently friends. Two of the others had, Frank gathered from their talk, just returned from Brazil; the sixth was an old man, and the seventh a traveller for a firm of silk or velvet manufacturers in Genoa. The three friends talked gaily on all sorts of subjects; but nothing that Frank gathered, either from their conversation on deck or at dinner, gave any clue as to their occupation. They had evidently met at Marseilles for the first time after being separated for a considerable period—one had been in England, one at Paris, and one at Bordeaux; their ages were from twenty-three to twenty-six. Their names were, as he learned from their talk, Maffio, Sarto, and Rubini. Before the steamer had left the port half an hour, one of them, seeing that Frank was alone, said to him as he passed, in broken English,—

"It is warmer and pleasanter here, monsieur, than it is in London."

"It is indeed," Frank replied, in Italian; "it was miserable weather there, when I left the day before yesterday."

"*Per Bacco!*" the young man said, with a laugh, "I took you to be English. Allow me to congratulate you on your admirable imitation of—"

"I am English, signor—that is, I was born of English parents; but I first saw light in Rome, and my grandfather was an Italian."

This broke the ice, and they chatted together pleasantly.

"We are going to Genoa. And you?"

"I also am going to Genoa, and perhaps "—for he had by this time quite come to a conclusion on the subject—" on the same errand as yourselves."

The others looked at him in some little surprise, and then glanced at one another. That this young Englishman should be going upon such an expedition as that upon which they were bound, seemed to be out of the question.

"You mean on pleasure, signor?" one of them said, after a pause.

"If excitement is pleasure, which no doubt it is—yes. I am going to visit an old friend of my father's; he is living a little way out of the town at the Villa Spinola."

The others gave a simultaneous exclamation of surprise.

"That is enough, signor," the one called Rubini said, holding out his hand; "we are comrades. Though how a young English gentleman should come to be of our party, I cannot say."

The others shook hands as warmly with Frank; and he then replied,—

"No doubt you are surprised. My father fought side by side with the man I am now going to see, in the siege of Rome, so also did my grandfather; and both have since paid by their lives for their love of Italy. My name is Percival!"

"The son of the Captain Percival who was murdered while searching in Naples for Signor Forli?" one of them exclaimed.

"The same. So, gentlemen, you can perhaps understand why I am going to the Villa Spinola, and why, young as I am, I am as eager to take part in this business as you yourselves can be."

"Yes, indeed; your father's name is honoured among us as one of our general's friends and companions in South America, and as one of his comrades at Rome; still more, perhaps, for his fearless exposure of the horrors of the tyrant's dungeons. However, it were best that we should say no more on the subject at present. It is certain that the general's presence at Genoa is causing uneasiness both at Rome and Naples. Rumours that he intends to carry out some daring enterprise have appeared in newspapers, and no doubt Neapolitan spies are already watching his movements, and it may be there are some on board this ship. Our great fear is that Victor Emmanuel's government may interfere to stop it; but we doubt whether he will venture to do so—public opinion will be too strong for him."

"No one can overhear us just at present," Frank said. "Certainly the Neapolitan spies are active. My mother's house is frequented by many leading exiles; and we have reason to believe that it has been watched by a spy for some time past. I know that I have been followed, under the idea, perhaps, that I am carrying important papers or documents from the general's friends there. An attempt was made last night to enter the carriage, in which I was alone, by two men, one of whom was armed with a pistol, and the other had a handkerchief soaked with chloroform. Fortunately, I was on my guard, and shot the fellow who was entering with the handkerchief; he fell backwards out of the carriage; I heard nothing more of the other one, and for aught I know he may be on board now."

"You did well indeed!" Sarto said warmly. "I was in the next carriage to you. I did not hear the sound of your pistol shot—I was fast asleep; but we were all woke up by a fellow-passenger who declared he heard a gun-shot. When we reached Valence he called the guard, who said that he must have been dreaming, for there was only a young Englishman in the next carriage, and he knew that when it left the last station he was alone. When the train went on we all abused the fellow soundly for waking us with his ridiculous fancies; but it seems that he was right after all. You say there was another. What became of him?"

"I saw nothing more of him. He may be on board, for aught I know, for they had black handkerchiefs tied over their faces up to the eyes, and as their hats were pulled well down, I should not know him if I saw him."

"Well, you have struck the first blow in the war, and I regard it as a good omen; but you must be careful to-night, for if the fellow is on board he is likely to make another attempt; and this time, I should say, he would begin by stabbing you. Are you in a cabin by yourself?"

"Yes."

"Then one of us will sit up by turns. You must have had a bad night indeed, while we slept without waking, except when I was aroused by that fellow making such a row."

"Oh, I could not think of that!"

"It must be done," Rubini said earnestly. "However, I will lay the mattress of the spare bed of your cabin against the door, and lie down on it—that will do just as well. It will be impossible then to open the door; and if any one tries to do so, I shall be on my feet in a moment. I shall sleep just as well like that as in my berth. I have slept in much more uncomfortable places, and am sure to do so again before this business is over."

"Thank you very much. I will not refuse so kind an

offer, for I doubt greatly whether I could keep awake tonight."

"Now, let us say no more about it, for we may be quite sure that the man is still on your track, and there may be other Neapolitan agents on board. We cannot be too careful. It may be that old man who was sitting facing us at the table, it may be that little fellow who looks like the agent of a commercial house, and it may be one of the two men who say they come from South America; there is no telling. But at any rate, let us drop the subject altogether. We have said nothing at present that even a spy could lay hold of, beyond the fact that you are going to the Villa Spinola, which means to Garibaldi."

They did not go up on deck again after dinner, but sat chatting in the saloon until nine o'clock, when Frank said that he could keep his eyes open no longer. After allowing him time to get into his berth, Rubini came in, took off his coat and waistcoat, pulled the mattress and bedding from the other bunk, and lay down on it with his head close to the door.

"Will you take one of my pistols, Rubini?" for by this time they called each other simply by their surnames.

"No, thank you; if the scoundrel tries to open the door and finds that he cannot do so, you may be sure that he will move off at once. He has been taught that you are handy with your weapons."

Frank was sleeping soundly when he was woke by Rubini's sharp challenge, "Who goes there?" It was pitch dark, and he was about to leap from his bunk, when Rubini said,—

"It is no use getting up. By the time I got this bed away and opened the door, the fellow would be at the other end of the boat. We may as well lie quiet. He is not likely to try again; and, indeed, I should not care about going outside the door, for it is pitch dark, and he might at the present moment be crouching outside in readiness to stab you as you came out. However, he is more likely to be gone now, for directly he heard us talking he would know that his game was up." He struck a match. "It is just two o'clock," he said; "we may as well have four hours' more sleep."

In a few minutes Frank was sound asleep again, and when he awoke it was daylight. Looking at the watch, he found that it was seven o'clock. "Seven o'clock, Rubini!" he said.

The Italian sat up and stretched his arms and yawned. "I have had a capital night. However, it is time to get up; we must turn out at once. We can't be far from Genoa now; we are due there at eight o'clock, so we shall just have comfortable time for a wash and a cup of coffee before going ashore."

Frank dressed hastily, and then ran up on deck, where he stood admiring the splendid coast, and the town of Genoa climbing up the hill, with its churches, campaniles, and its suburbs embedded in foliage. They were just entering the port when Maffio came up to him.

"Coffee is ready," he said. "You had better come down and take it while it is hot. We shall have the custom-house officers off before we land, so there is no hurry."

After making a meal on coffee with an abundance of milk, rolls and butter, Frank went up again. He then, at the advice of Rubini, drew the charges of his pistols and placed them in his portmanteau.

"We must go ashore in a boat," Sarto said. "I have

just heard the captain say that the wharves are so full that he may not be able to take the vessel alongside for a couple of hours."

"Are you going anywhere in particular when you land?" Frank asked.

"We all belong to Genoa, and have friends here. Why do you ask?"

"Could you spare me an hour of your time to-day? I should not ask you, but it is rather important."

"Certainly; we are all at your service," Rubini said in some surprise. "At what hour shall we meet you, and where?"

"I am going to the Hotel Europa. Any time will suit me, so that it is a couple of hours before dusk. I will tell you what it is when you meet me; it is better not to speak of it here."

The young men consulted together. "We will go to our friends," Rubini said, "take our things there and spend an hour, and will call upon you, if convenient, at eleven o'clock."

"Thank you; and you will see, when I have explained my reason for troubling you, that I have not done so wantonly."

They landed at the step of the customs. "Have you anything to declare?" the official asked Frank, after his passport had been examined and stamped.

"I have nothing but this small portmanteau, which contains only clothes and a brace of pistols. I suppose one can land with them on payment of duty."

"Certainly, monsieur; but why should an Englishman want them?"

"I intend to make a walking tour through Italy"—speaking as before in English; "and there are parts of the country where, after dark, I should feel more comfortable for having them in my pockets."

"You are strange people, you Englishmen," the officer said; "but, after all, you are not far wrong, though it seems to me that it would be wiser to give up what you carry about you than to make a show of resistance which would end in getting your throat cut." He glanced at the pistols, named the amount of duty chargeable; and when this was paid, Frank nodded to his companions, who were being much more rigorously examined, took one of the vehicles standing outside the custom-house, and drove to the Hotel Europa.

CHAPTER VI

THE VILLA SPINOLA

AFTER taking a room and seeing his portmanteau carried up there, Frank went out for an hour and looked at the shops in the principal street; then he returned to the hotel, and stood at the entrance until his three friends arrived. He had again loaded his pistols and placed them in his pocket, and had engaged an open vehicle that was now standing at the door.

"Let us start at once," he said; "gentlemen, if you will take your places with me, I will explain the matter to you as we drive along."

They took their seats.

"Drive to the Strada de Livourno," he said to the coachman; "I will tell you the house when we get there. Now, my friends," he went on, as the carriage started, "I will explain what may seem singular to you. My mother has sent out a letter which contained, I may say, a considerable sum to be used by the general for the purposes of this expedition. It had been intended that I should bring it; but when we discovered that there was a spy in the house, and that our cabinets had been ransacked and our conversation overheard, it was thought almost certain that an attempt would be made to rob me of the letter on the way. Finally, after much discussion, it was agreed to send the letter by post to the care of the Countess of Mongolfiere, who is an old friend of

Signora Forli, my grandmother; she was convinced that I should be watched from the moment I landed, and advised me not to go to see the countess until I could take three of Garibaldi's followers with me, and that after accompanying me to her house, they should drive with me to the Villa Spinola. Now you will understand why I have asked you to give up a portion of your first day to come to aid me."

"I think your friends were very right in giving you the advice, Percival. After the two attempts that have been made—I will not say to kill you—but to search you and your luggage, it is certain that Francisco's agents must have obtained information that you were carrying money, and perhaps documents of importance, and that they would not take their eyes off you until either they had gained their object or discovered that you had handed the parcel over to the general. I have no doubt that they are following you now in some vehicle or other.

On arrival at the villa of the Countess of Mongolfiere, Frank sent in his card, and on this being taken in, was at once invited to enter. The countess was a lady of about the same age as Signora Forli.

"I am glad to see you, Signor Percival," she said. "I have received the letter from Madame Forli with its enclosure."

"I have brought you another note from her, Madame la contessa," he said, presenting it, "as a proof of my identity; for the matter is of importance, as you may well suppose, from the manner in which this letter was sent to you, instead of by the post direct to me."

"So I suppose, signor. Signora Forli said that it concerned the good of the cause; and the manner in which she begged me to lock it up at once on my receiving it, was sufficient to show that it either contained money for the cause or secrets that the agents of the foes of freedom would be glad to discover. The mere fact that she gave no particulars convinced me that she considered it best that I should be in the dark, so that, should the letter fall into other hands, I could say truly that I had not expected its arrival, and knew nothing whatever of the matter to which it related."

"It contains drafts for a considerable sum of money, signora, for the use of Garibaldi. The general, being ignorant of my father's death, had written to him, asking him to join him, and recalling his promise to assist with money. My father, unfortunately, could no longer give personal service, but as he had for years put by a certain portion of his income for this purpose, my mother had it in her power to send this money. It was intended that I should bring it; but we found that all our doings were watched, and that, therefore, there was considerable danger of my being followed and robbed upon the way; and Signora Forli then suggested that she should send it direct to you, as possibly a letter addressed to me here might fall into the hands of the Neapolitan agents."

"It was a very good plan," the countess said. "And have you been molested on the way?"

"Attempts have been made on two occasions—once in the train on my way to Marseilles, and once on board the steamer coming here."

"You must be careful even now, signor. If you are watched as closely as it would seem, you may be robbed before you can hand this letter over to the general. There is nothing at which these men will hesitate in order to carry out their instructions. You might be arrested in the streets by two or three men disguised as policemen, and carried away and confined in some lonely place; you might be accused of a theft and given in charge on some trumped-up accusation, in order that your luggage and every article belonging to you might be thoroughly searched, before you could prove your entire innocence. I can quite understand that, when you first started, the object was simply to search for any papers you might be carrying, and if this could be done without violence it would be so effected, although if murder was necessary, they would not have hesitated at it; and even now, guessing as they will that you have come here, directly you have landed, to obtain some important document, they would, if they could find an opportunity, do anything to obtain it, before you can deliver it to Garibaldi."

"I quite feel that, signora, and have three young Garibaldian officers waiting in a carriage below for me, and they will drive with me to the Villa Spinola."

"That will make you perfectly safe," and she then rose from her seat, opened a secret drawer in an antique cabinet, and handed him the letter. "Now, Signor Percival," she said, "this has been a visit of business, but I hope that when you have this charge off your mind you will, as the grandson of my old friend Signora Forli, come often to see me while you are here. I am always at home in the evening, and it will be a great pleasure to me to hear more of her than she tells me in her letters."

Thanking the countess for her invitation, and saying that he should certainly avail himself of it, he went down and again took his place in the carriage.

"Have you found all as you wished?" Sarto asked.

"Yes; I have the letter in my pocket."

"That is good news. Knowing what these secret agents are able to accomplish, I did not feel at all sure that they might not in some way have learned how the money was to be sent, and have managed to intercept the letter."

Having given instructions to the driver where to go, they chatted as they drove along of the proposed expedition.

"None of us know yet," Rubini said, "whether it is against the Papal States or Naples. We all received the telegram we had for some time been hoping for, with the simple word 'Come.' However, it matters not a bit to us whether we first free the Pope's dominions or Francisco's."

"Will you go in with me to see Garibaldi?"

"No; we have already received orders that, until we are called upon, it is best that we should remain quietly with our families. Were a large number of persons to pay visits to him, the authorities would know that the time was close at hand when he intended to start on an expedition of some kind. The mere fact that we have come here to stay for a time with our friends is natural enough; but we may be sure that everything that passes at the Villa is closely watched. It is known, I have no doubt, that an expedition is intended, and Cavour may wait to prevent it from starting, until the last moment; therefore I should say that it is important that no one should know on what date Garibaldi intends to sail until the hour actually arrives. How we are to get ships to carry us, how many are going, and how we are to obtain arms, are matters that don't concern us. We are quite content to wait until word comes to us, 'Be at such a place, at such an hour.'"

"I would give something to know which among the men

we are passing are those who have been on your track," Sarto remarked. "It would be such a satisfaction to laugh in their faces and to shout, 'Have you had a pleasant journey?' or 'We congratulate you,' or something of that sort."

"They feel sore enough without that," Maffio said. "They are unscrupulous villains; but to do them justice, they are shrewd ones, and work their hardest for their employers, and it is not very often that they fail; and you have a right to congratulate yourself that for once they have been foiled. It is certainly a feather in your cap, Percival, that you and your friends have succeeded in outwitting them."

They had now left the city and were driving along the coast road towards the Villa Spinola. There were only a few people on the road.

"You see, it is well that we came in force," Sarto remarked; "for had you been alone, the carriage might very well have been stopped, and yourself seized and carried off, without there being any one to notice the affair. I have no doubt that even now there is a party somewhere behind a wall or a hedge, in waiting for you; they would probably be sent here as soon as you landed, and would not be recalled, as, until you left the house of the countess, all hope that you would drive along this road alone would not be at an end."

"We shall call and see you this evening, and we all hope that you will use our homes as your own while you are staying here," Rubini said. "We can introduce you to numbers of our friends, all of our way of thinking, and will do our best to make your stay at Genoa as pleasant as possible. It may be some time before all is ready for a start, and until that is the case you will have nothing to do, and certainly Garibaldi will not want visitors."

"I shall be pleased indeed to avail myself of your kindness," Frank said. "It will be a great pleasure to me to see something of Italian society, and I should find time hang very heavy on my hands at the hotel, where there are, I know, very few visitors staying at present."

"That is the villa," Rubini said, pointing to a large house surrounded by a high wall.

"Will you take my vehicle back?"

"No; we shall walk. I should advise you to keep the carriage, however long you may stay here. These fellows will be very sore at finding they have failed, after all the trouble they have taken in the matter. I don't say that they will be watching for you; but if they should come across you in a lonely spot, I think it is very probable that they would not hesitate to get even with you with the stab of a knife between your shoulders."

Alighting, Frank rang at the bell. His friends stood chatting with him until a man, after looking through a grill in the gate, came out; and then, feeling that their mission was safely accomplished, they started for their walk back in high spirits.

"I do not know whether the general is in at present, signor," the man said, as Frank was about to enter. "May I ask your business?"

"If you will take this card to him, I am sure that he will see me."

In three minutes the gates were opened. Frank entered on foot, and would have left the carriage outside; but the porter said,—

"It had better come in, signor; carriages standing at a gate attract attention."

Garibaldi was seated in a room with two men, who were, as Frank afterwards learned, Bixio and Crispi. Garibaldi had risen from his seat and was looking inquiringly at the door as the lad entered.

"Welcome, Signor Percival! You have come, doubtless, on the part of my dear friend your father. Has he not come with you? I trust that he is but delayed."

"I come on the part of my mother, general," Frank replied. "I lost my father more than a year ago."

"And I had not heard of it!" the general exclaimed. "Alas! alas! for my friend and comrade; this is indeed a heavy blow to me. I looked forward so much to seeing him. Oh, how many friends have I lost in the past two years! And so your mother has sent you to me?"

"She bade me give you this letter, general."

The letter was not a long one. Mrs. Percival briefly told how her husband had set out to endeavour to find where Professor Forli was imprisoned, how he had been attacked and killed by brigands, and how she, knowing what her husband's wishes would have been, had sent her son. "He is young," she said, "but not so young as many of those who have fought under you. He is as eager and enthusiastic in the cause of Italian liberty as was his father, having, as you may well suppose, learned the tale from my husband and myself, and my father and mother. As you will see, he speaks Italian as well as English, and I pray you, for the sake of my husband, to take him on your staff; or, if that cannot be, he will shoulder a musket and march with you. He does not come empty-handed. My husband has for years laid by a certain amount to be used in the good cause when the time came. He will tell you where it is to be obtained, and how. I wish you success with all my heart, and if the prayers of two widowed women will avail aught, you will have them daily. It is my only son I give you, and a widow cannot give more. The money is from my husband; the boy is from me."

Garibaldi's eyes filled with tears as he read the letter.

"Your mother is a noble woman indeed! How could she be otherwise, as the daughter of Forli and the wife of my brave comrade? Surely you will be most welcome to me; young man—welcome if you came only as your mother's gift to Italy."

Frank opened the envelope, which was directed to himself, and took out five slips of thin paper.

"These are bills, general," he said, handing them to him. "They are drawn upon a bank at Genoa, and are each for two thousand pounds."

"Francs, you must mean, surely?" Garibaldi said.

"No, general; they are English pounds."

Exclamations of surprise and gratification broke from Garibaldi and his two companions.

"This is a royal gift!" the former cried. "My brave comrade is not here to help us; but he has sent us a wonderful proof of his love for the cause. It is noble!—it is superb! This will indeed be aid to us," he went on, holding out his two hands to Frank. "We are strong in men, we are strong in brave hearts, but money is scarce with us, though many have given all that they possess. I know, lad, how you English object to be embraced,—were it not for that, I would take you to my heart; but a hand-clasp will say as much."

The two officers were almost as much excited as Garibaldi

himself, for this gift would remove one of the obstacles that lay in their way. By means of a subscription contributed in small amounts by patriots all over Italy for the purchase of arms, twelve thousand good muskets had been bought and stored at Milan, together with ammunition. When, a few days before Frank's arrival, Crispi, with some other of Garibaldi's officers, had gone to fetch them, they found that Cavour had placed a guard of royal troops over the magazine, with orders that nothing whatever was to be taken out. Heavy though the blow had been, the Garibaldian agents were already at work buying arms, but with no hope of collecting more than sufficient for the comparatively small force that would sail for Sicily. Even this addition of funds would not avail to supply that deficiency, as it was very difficult for the general's agents, closely watched as they now were, to purchase military weapons.

For some time the conversation turned entirely upon the steps to be taken, now that the war-chest had been so unexpectedly replenished. Then Garibaldi put aside the papers on which he had been taking notes, and said,—

"Enough for the time, Signor Percival. I shall, of course, write myself to your good mother, expressing my heartfelt thanks, and telling her that if success attends us, she can be happy in the knowledge that it will be largely due to her. You will, naturally, yourself write home and tell her what joy her gift occasioned, how much it added to our hopes and relieved us of our difficulties. Tell her that I have appointed you as a lieutenant on my staff, and that I shall trust you as I trusted your noble father."

"I thank you greatly, general; I hope to prove myself worthy of your confidence."

"And now, sir, you will advise me as to your own movements?"

"I have put up at the Hotel Europa."

"At present it will be best for you to stay there. We are anxious that there should be no appearance of any gathering here, and my friends will not assemble until all the preparations are completed. How did you come over here?"

"I drove, General; the carriage is waiting for me."

"Then it must wait for awhile; or, better still, it can carry my two friends here to the town, where they have much to do. In future it will be best for you to walk over; 'tis but a short distance, and I know that you English are good walkers. Of course, the authorities know that I am here; there is no concealment about that. As long as they do not see any signs of preparations for a movement, they will leave me alone. As probably your prolonged stay at the hotel may excite curiosity, it is well that you should visit the galleries and palaces, and take excursions in the neighbourhood. It may be as well, too, that you should mention casually at the *table-d'hôte* that you know me, as your father was a great friend of mine when we were together in South America, which will account for your paying visits here frequently. We know that we are being closely looked after by government spies, and must therefore omit no precaution. Now I wish you to take lunch with me, as I have many questions to ask you. I had heard, of course, of Signor Forli being missing, and of the correspondence between your government and that of Naples on the subject."

Frank went out and told the driver that he should not be returning for some time, but that two gentlemen would go back in the carriage in a few minutes. "As I took the carriage from the hotel, the hire will, of course, be charged in my bill; but here are a couple of francs for yourself."

In two or three minutes the Italian officers came out, and thanking Frank for the accommodation, drove away, while the lad himself re-entered the villa.

"The meal is ready," Garibaldi said, when he entered the room where he had left him. "It is very pleasant to me to turn my thoughts for once from the subject of my expedition."

The meal was a very simple one, though the general had ordered one or two extra dishes in honour of his guest.

"Now," he said, when they had sat down, and the servant had retired, "tell me first of all about the loss of my dear friend."

Frank related the story of his father going out to search for Signor Forli, and how he had been captured and killed by brigands. As the general listened, his kindly face grew stern and hard, but he did not speak until Frank brought the tale to an end.

"*Cospetto!*" he exclaimed, "he may have been killed by brigands, but I doubt not the Neapolitan government were at the bottom of it. I would wager any money that they hired the men of the mountains to disembarrass them of one who was exposing the horrible secrets of their prisons. And you say that his body could not be found. Was the search made for it simply by the carabinieri?"

"It was made by them, sir, but the secretary of our legation accompanied them, and wrote that, although he had himself searched everywhere in the neighbourhood of the hut, he could find no traces whatever of a newly made grave. I may say that Signora Forli still believes that my father was not killed, but was, like her husband, carried off to some dungeon."

"It is possible," the general said, "though I would not encourage you to hope; the ways of these people are so dark that there is no fathoming them. Since his grave could not be found, I regard it as certain that he was not buried there, for his captors would not have troubled to carry his body far, but would have dug a hole close by and thrown the earth over the body; and in that case, when the band returned, one or the other of the men who did the work would most likely have carelessly pointed to the spot, and said, 'There lies the Englishman.' But though I believe that he did not die there, he might have died elsewhere. His wounds were evidently very severe, and they may have proved fatal after he was carried off by those who took him away from the brigands; if they were not fatal, he may have been murdered afterwards."

"Signora Forli thought, general, that it was more probable that he had been taken to one of the prisons, and that, just as they hunted down the brigands in order that none of these should have power to betray them, so they might have preferred putting him in prison to having him murdered, because in the latter case the men employed might go to the British legation and accept a large sum for betraying the secret."

"It may have been so," the general said; "and if we succeed, perhaps you will find both your father and grandfather. But do not cherish false hopes. Even if both were once in the Neapolitan dungeons, they may before this have succumbed to their treatment there. You have mourned them as dead; do not buoy yourself up with hope, for if you did so, the chances are all in favour of your suffering a terrible disappointment."

"That is just what my mother impressed upon me, general. She said that from the first she had never allowed herself to think of my father as in prison; and it was not until she received your letter, and thought that at last there was really a chance that the inmost cells of all the prisons would be opened, she would admit a possibility of my father still being alive."

"At least, she and you will have the consolation that if you do not find those dear to you, you will have aided in restoring fathers and husbands to hundreds of other grieving wives, mothers and children.

"May I ask how large a force you are likely to take over with you, general?"

"If the government had remained neutral and not interfered with me, we could have found men for the twelve thousand muskets they have seized; as it is, we have been obliged to write letters to all parts of Italy, stopping the volunteers who were preparing to join us. Some of these letters will doubtless fall into the hands of the authorities, and we have therefore so worded them that it may be supposed that the expedition has been altogether given up. A thousand men is the utmost that we can hope to embark secretly. These will be all picked men and gallant fellows who fought under me in the Alps, or men who have, like myself, been for years living as exiles. These thousand I have chosen, every one; they will die fighting, and will never turn their back to an enemy. Would that I had them all safely landed in Sicily, and had surmounted all the difficulties and dangers that are caused by the hostility of the government, which will, however, be glad enough to take advantage of our work."

"My mother thought that you would probably form the Neapolitan States, if you conquered them, into a republic."

"That was my dream when I was fighting at Rome; but I see now that it is impossible. I am for a republic on principle, but I must take what I can get. I cannot conceal from myself that my experience of Mazzini and other enthusiasts is that they are not practical, they commit terrible blunders, and the matter ends in a dictatorship, as has twice been the case in France. Mazzini would sacrifice the practical to gain his ideal. I care nothing for theory—I want to see Italy free; and this can only be done under Victor Emmanuel. He is popular and energetic. His father suffered for his devotion to the cause of freedom. The son is a stronger man; but at present he is forced by Cavour and the other temporisers who surround him to curb his own impetuosity.

"I don't like Cavour—he gave up my birthplace, Nice, to France; but, at the same time, I respect his great ability, and am sure that as soon as he feels the opportunity has come, he will grasp it, and the king will not hesitate to accept the possessions that I hope to gain for him. With Victor Emmanuel King of Northern and Southern Italy, the rest is simple. Then Italy can afford to wait its opportunity for driving the Austrians from Venezia, and becoming, for the first time since the days of the Romans, a united kingdom. When I hoist my banner in Sicily, it will be as a soldier of Victor Emmanuel, King of Sicily."

Frank was pleased to hear this. His father, though an advanced liberal in matters connected with Italy, was a strong conservative at home; and Frank had naturally imbibed his ideas, which were that the people of a constitutional monarchy, like that under which he lived, were in every respect freer and better governed than under any republic, still more so than they could be under a republic constituted according to the theories of Mazzini or those of the authors of the first and second French revolutions.

"By the way, you must have found it a terrible responsibility carrying so much money with you."

"I did not carry it, general. The bills were, with the letter to you, sent by post to the care of the Countess of Mongolfiere, who was a friend of Signora Forli."

"That was hazardous, too," the general said, shaking his head. "To trust ten thousand pounds to the post was a terrible risk."

"It was the best way that we could think of, general. The courier who was with my father when he was killed came over to see my mother at her request, as she wished to hear every detail about my father's last days. He professed a great fear of returning to Italy, as, having given evidence against the brigands, he would be a marked man."

"There is no doubt that is so," Garibaldi put in. "His life would not have been worth a day's purchase. These scoundrels have their agents in every town, men who keep them informed as to persons travelling, whom it would be worth while to capture, and of any movements of the carabinieri in their direction."

"My mother, therefore, took him into her service," Frank went on; "but two days before I started, she discovered that he had been acting as a spy, had been opening her desk, examining her letters, and listening at the door. She and

Signora Forli had no doubt whatever that he had made himself acquainted with the contents of your letter, and believed that I was going to carry this money to you."

" The villains! " Garibaldi exclaimed, bringing his clenched hand down upon the table: " it is just what they would do. I know that many of my friends enjoyed your father's hospitality; and no doubt it would be a marked house, and the secret police of Francisco would keep an eye over what was being done there, and would, if possible, get one of their agents into it. This man, who had no doubt acted as a spy over your father when he was in Italy, would be naturally chosen for the work; and his story and pretence of fear served admirably to get him installed there. If he had learned that you were about to start to bring me ten thousand pounds, and perhaps papers of importance, it would have been nothing short of a miracle had you arrived safely with them."

" That was what Signora Forli and my mother thought, sir. They were afraid to send the letter directed to me at the hotel where I was to stop, as the man would doubtless telegraph to agents out at Genoa, and they would get possession of it; so instead of doing so, they enclosed it in a letter to the countess. I posted it myself, and there was therefore no chance of the letter being lost, except by pure accident."

" But if the spy did not know that you had sent the letter off by post, it would render your journey no less hazardous than if you had taken it with you."

" My mother and the Signora were both convinced that an attempt would be made to search me and my baggage on the way, but they did not think that they would try to take my life; for after what had happened to my grandfather and father, there would be no question that my murder was the work of Neapolitan agents, and a storm of indignation would thus be caused."

Garibaldi nodded. " No doubt they were right, and if the scoundrels could have got possession of what you carried without injury to you they would have done so. But they would have stuck at nothing in order to carry out their object and had you caught them while they were engaged in searching your clothes or baggage, they would not have hesitated to use their knives. I cannot now understand how you have come through without their having meddled with you. It might have been done when you were asleep in an hotel, or they might have drugged you in a railway carriage, or in your cabin on board the steamer coming here. The secret police of Naples is the only well-organised department in the kingdom. They have agents in London, Paris, and other cities, and from the moment you left your mother's house you must have been watched. Are you sure that, although you may not know it, you have not been searched?"

"I am quite sure, sir. We were so certain I should be watched that I made no attempt to get off secretly, but started by the train I had intended to travel by. I did not stop a night at an hotel all the way, and made a point of getting into railway carriages that contained other passengers. It happened, however, that at Vienne the last of those with me alighted. It was one o'clock in the morning when we left the station, and I felt sure that if an attempt was made, it would be before we stopped, especially as a man looked into the carriage just before we were starting, and then went away. I had a loaded pistol in each pocket and a rug over me, and I sat in the corner pretending to be asleep. An hour later a man came and looked in; another joined him. The door was partly opened, and an arm with an extended pistol pointed at me, but I felt perfectly sure that he had no intention of firing unless I woke.

"Half a minute later his comrade entered the carriage. He had an open knife in one hand, and a cloth in the other; but as he came in I shot him; he fell back through the carriage door. Whether in doing so he knocked his comrade down or not, I cannot say; but, at any rate, I saw no more of him. The man whom I shot had dropped what he held in his hand on to the floor. It was as I had expected—a handkerchief, soaked with chloroform. It was seven when I arrived at Marseilles. Fortunately, a steamer left at twelve. When I went on board I made the acquaintance of three young men, who were, I guessed, on the same errand as myself; their names were Rubini, Sarto, and Maffio. We soon became very friendly, and I found that my conjectures were correct. This being so, I told them what had happened; and as there was no one beside myself in my cabin, Rubini most kindly laid a mattress across the door and slept there. As I had not had a wink of sleep the night before, and only dozed a little the one before that, I should have had great difficulty in keeping awake. In the course of the night some one did attempt to open the door; but he was unable to do so on account of the mattress placed there, and we heard no more of him. I asked these gentlemen to come to the Hotel Europa at eleven, for I was really afraid to come along the road here by myself. They drove with me to the house of the countess, and then here, so that I was well guarded."

"I know them all well," Garibaldi said. "Rubini is a lieutenant in the Genoese company of my cacciatori; the others are in his company. You have done well indeed, my friend; it needed courage to start on such a journey, knowing that Francisco's police were on your track. You have a right to feel proud that your vigilance and quickness defeated their attempt. It is well that you met Rubini and his friends; for as the spies would know directly you entered the palazzo of the countess that you had gone there for some special purpose, probably to obtain documents sent to her, I doubt whether you would have been able to come safely alone, even if the road had been fairly well thronged."

"I should not have gone to the countess's unless I had an escort, general. My intention was to come to you in the first place, and ask that three of your officers might accompany me to get the letter; but, of course, after having found friends who would act as my escort, there was no occasion to do so. I suppose there is no fear of my being further annoyed?"

"I should think not," Garibaldi said; "now they know that your mission has been carried out, you will cease to be of interest to them. But at the same time, it would be well to be cautious. If the fellow you shot was the leader of those charged to prevent the supplies and letter coming to me, we may consider that there is an end of the affair. His death will give a step to some one, and they will owe you no ill will. If, however, the other man was the chief of the party, he would doubtless owe you a grudge. He is sure to be blamed for having been thus baffled by a lad; whereas had he succeeded, he would have received the approval of his superiors. I think, therefore, if I were you, I should abstain from going out after nightfall, unless with a companion, or if you do so, keep in the great thoroughfares and avoid quiet streets. That habit of carrying a loaded pistol in your pocket has proved a valuable one, and I should advise you to continue it so long as you are here. If you see Rubini, tell him that I thank him for the aid he and his friends rendered you. He and the others have all been instructed not to come here until they receive a communication that the time for action has arrived. My followers send me their addresses as soon as they reach Genoa, so that I can summon them when they are needed. It would never do for numbers of men to present themselves here. The authorities know perfectly well that I am intending to make an expedition to Sicily; but as long as they see no signs of activity, and their spies tell them that only some half-dozen of my friends frequent this villa, they may be comtent to abstain from interference with me; indeed, I do not think that in any case they would venture to prevent my sailing, unless they receive urgent remonstrances from Austria or France. Were such remonstrances made, they would now be able to reply that, so far as they can learn, I am remaining here quietly, and am only visited by a few private friends."

CHAPTER VII

THE EXPEDITION SAILS

FRANK spent a pleasant three weeks in Genoa. The three young men did all in their power to make the time pass agreeably to him: they introduced him to their families and friends; one or the other of them always accompanied him to the theatre or opera, or, as much more frequently happened, to gatherings at their own houses or at those of acquaintances. Many of these were, like themselves, members of the Genoese corps; and both as a relative of two men who had sacrificed their lives in the cause of freedom, and especially for the aid that his mother had sent to Garibaldi to enable him to carry out his plans, he was everywhere most warmly received. He himself had not told, even his three friends, the amount that his mother had contributed; but Garibaldi's companions had mentioned it to others, and it soon became known to all interested in the expedition.

Twice a week Frank drove out to Quarto. Matters had been steadily progressing. A thousand rifles, but of a very inferior kind, had been obtained from Farini, and a few hundred of a better class had been bought. These latter were for the use of Garibaldi's own band, while the others would be distributed among such Sicilians as might join him on his landing. These would for the most part come armed, as large numbers of guns and stores of ammunition had been accumulated in the island for use in the futile insurrection a few months previously.

On May 5th all was ready. Frank paid his hotel bill, left his trunk to be placed in the store-room until he should send or return for it, and with a bundle, in which his sword was wrapped up in his blanket, cloak, and a light waterproof sheet, and with a bag containing his red shirts and other small belongings, together with his pistols and a good supply of ammunition, drove to the Villa Spinola. On the previous day he had sent on there a saddle and bridle, valise and holsters. The horses were to be bought in Sicily. Outside all seemed as quiet as usual, but once within the gates there was a great change. A score of gentlemen were strolling in little groups in the garden, talking excitedly; these were almost all new arrivals, and consequently unknown to Frank, who passed on into the house where Garibaldi, the officers of his staff, and other principal officers were engaged in discussing the final arrangements. Most of the staff were known to him, as they had been there for some days. He joined three or four of the younger men, who were sitting smoking in a room on the ground floor while the council was being held.

"So at last the day has arrived, lieutenant," one of them said. "I think everything augurs well for us. I am convinced that the government do not mean to interfere with us, but are adopting the policy of shutting their eyes. Of course, they will disavow us, but they will not dare to stop us. They must know what is going on; there are too many people in the secret for it not to have leaked out. I don't know whether you noticed it, but I could see, when I was in the city this morning, that there was a general excitement;

people met and talked earnestly; every stranger, and there are a good many there to-day, is watched eagerly. You see, there is no ship of war in the port, which there certainly would have been, had they intended to stop us."

"I shall be very glad when we are well at sea," Frank said, "though I agree with you that it is not likely we shall be interfered with."

They chatted for upwards of an hour, and the council broke up. A list was handed round, appointing the boats to which the various officers were told off; and Frank found that he was to go in the third that left the shore, together with Orsini, commander of the second company, and Turr, the first *aide-de-camp* of the general. The hours passed slowly. No regular meals were served, but food was placed on a long table, and each could go in and take refreshments as he pleased. The new-comers, and indeed all the officers, with the exception of two or three of Garibaldi's most trusted friends, were still in ignorance as to how they were to obtain vessels to take them to Messina, and Frank, who was behind the scenes, listened with some amusement to the wild conjectures that they hazarded. He knew that the matter had been privately arranged with the owners of the Rubattino line of steamers that the *Lombardo* and *Piemonte,* both of which were in the harbour, should be seized by the Garibaldians. They were warm adherents of the national cause, but could not, of course, appear openly in the matter. They had already been paid the sum agreed on for any damage or injury that might happen to the vessels; while openly they would be able to protest loudly against the seizure of their ships, and, like the government, profess entire ignorance of what was going on. Only a few hands would be

THE EXPEDITION SAILS 119

left on board. These were to offer a feigned resistance, but were to make no noise.

Among Garibaldi's followers were several engineers, who were to take command of and assist in the engine-rooms. In order to save time, the *Lombardo*, which was much the larger of the two vessels, was to take the *Piemonte* in tow. There was still, however, some anxiety on the part of the leaders lest, at the last moment, the government should intervene, seize the arms, and take possession of the steamers. The seizure of the great magazine of arms at Milan showed that Cavour was in earnest in his endeavour to put a stop to an expedition of whose success he had not the slightest hope; but whether he would risk the ferment that would be excited, were Garibaldi and his followers to be seized at the moment of starting, was doubtful.

This was a question that had been discussed time after time by Garibaldi and his friends. That the minister was well informed as to all the preparations, the purchase of fresh arms, and the arrival of so many men at Genoa, was certain; but he could not know the exact hour at which the expedition was to start, nor even be sure that it might not march down the coast, and take ship at some other port than Genoa.

Ignorant as were the great bulk of those gathered at the Villa Spinola of Garibaldi's plans, they knew that the movement was to begin that night, and there was a general feeling of restlessness and excitement as evening approached. From time to time messengers brought news from the city. All was well; there was no unusual stir among the troops. The police went about their usual duties unconcernedly, and apparently without noticing the suppressed excitement of the population. At nightfall the word was passed round that all were to lie down as they could, as there would be no movement until one o'clock. The order was obeyed, but there was little sleep. It was known that Bixio and some other officers had already left the villa; and a whisper had run round that they were going to seize some ships, and that the embarkation would take place before morning.

At one o'clock all were in motion again. The servants of the villa brought round bowls of coffee and milk, and as soon as these were drunk and some bread hastily eaten, all made ready for a start. Frank had that evening donned his uniform for the first time, and had been at work, with two other members of the staff, serving out rifles and ammunition, from an outhouse which had been converted into a magazine; the men coming in a steady stream through a back entrance into the garden, and passing again with their arms through another door. Another party were at work carrying down boxes of ammunition and barrels of flour and other provisions to the shore. At one o'clock the whole force were gathered there. It was an impressive sight, and Frank for the first time fully realised the singularity and danger of the expedition in which he was to share.

Here were a thousand men, all of whom had fought again and again under Garibaldi in the cause of Italian liberty. They were about to start, against the wishes of the government of their country, to invade a kingdom possessed of strong fortresses and an army of one hundred and twenty-eight thousand regular troops. Success seemed altogether impossible. But Frank had deeply imbibed the conviction of his mother and Signora Forli that the people at large would flock to the standard. He had been carried away with the enthusiasm of the general and those about him, and even the darkness of the night, the mystery of the quiet armed figures and of the boats hauled up in readiness for the embarkation, did not damp the suppressed excitement that made every nerve tingle, and rendered it difficult to remain outwardly impassive.

The men talked together in low tones. Here were many who had not met since they had parted after the events that had laid another stone to the edifice of Italian Unity, by the addition of Tuscany, Parma, and Modena to the Kingdom of Sardinia. The greater part of them were Lombards and Genoese, but there were many from Turin and other cities of Piedmont. Some were exiles, who had received a summons similar to that sent by Garibaldi to Captain Percival. The greetings of all these men, who had been comrades in many dashing adventures, were warm and earnest, though expressed in but few low words.

Hour after hour passed, and expectation grew into anxiety. All knew now that Bixio had gone to seize two steamers, and that they should have been in the roadstead at two o'clock; but at four there were still no signs of them, and the fear that he had failed, that the government had at the last moment intervened, grew stronger. It was not until dawn was beginning to break that the two steamers were made out approaching, and anxiety gave place to delight.

Steadily and in good order the men took their places, under the direction of the officers assigned to each boat, and by the time the steamers arrived as near as they could venture to the shore, the boats were alongside with their crews. The embarkation was quickly effected. It was found that there had been no dangerous hitch in the arrangements, the delay having been caused by the difficulty Bixio had had in finding the two steamers, which were anchored in the extensive roadstead of Genoa among many other ships. The stores were hastily transferred from the boats to the steamers, and these at once started for the spot where two boats, laden with ammunition, percussion caps, and rifles, should have been lying off the coast. Either through misunderstanding of orders or the interference of the authorities, the two boats were not at the rendezvous; and after cruising about for some hours in every direction, Garibaldi decided that no further time could be lost, for at any moment government vessels might start in pursuit. Accordingly the steamers' heads were turned to the south, and the expedition fairly began.

Delighted as all on board the *Lombardo* and *Piemonte* were to have escaped without government interference, the loss of the ammunition was a very serious blow. They had brought with them from the Villa Spinola scarcely sufficient for a couple of hours' fighting for those on board. They had neither a reserve for themselves, nor any to hand over with the guns to those they expected to join them on landing. It was, therefore, absolutely necessary to touch at some port to obtain ammunition, and Garibaldi chose Talamone, at the southern extremity of Tuscany, within a few miles of the boundary of the Papal States. They arrived there early the next morning, and Garibaldi at once went ashore and desired the governor of the fort, in the name of the king, to hand over to him supplies of ammunition and some guns.

Whatever doubts the governor may have had as to Garibaldi's authority, he and the governor of the much larger neighbouring town of Orbetello rendered him all the assistance in their power, and gave him a considerable amount of ammunition and several guns. The vessels filled up with coal, and the inhabitants welcomed the expedition with enthusiasm. For this conduct the governor of Talamone afterwards received a severe reprimand from the government, who were obliged to clear themselves of any participation whatever in the expedition, and had, a few hours after Garibaldi left Genoa, despatched a fast screw frigate, the *Maria*, under the orders of Admiral Persano in pursuit. His official orders were to capture and bring back the steamers and all on board; but there can be little doubt that he received secret instructions in a contrary sense. At any rate, the frigate, after a prolonged cruise, returned to Genoa without having come within sight of the expedition.

Before leaving Talamone, Garibaldi accepted an offer of one of his followers to undertake, with sixty men, to effect a diversion by raising the population in the north of the Papal States. The expedition seemed a hopeless one with so small a force; and it would seem that Garibaldi assented to it in order to rid himself from some whose impetuosity and violent disposition might have led to trouble later. As was to be expected, the little party failed entirely in their object, and were defeated and captured very shortly after crossing the frontier.

All were glad on board the two ships, when they were again under steam, and heading for their goal. As by this time it was certain that the news of their departure from Genoa would have been telegraphed to Naples, and that the ships of war of that country would be on the look-out to intercept them, it was decided, at a council of war held by Garibaldi, that instead of landing near Messina, they should make for the little island of Maregigimo, lying off the northwest corner of Sicily, as by this route they would be likely to escape the vigilance of the Neapolitan ships-of-war, which would be watching for them along the coast from the Straits of Messina to Palermo.

Arriving at Maregigimo late on the evening of the 10th, and learning from the islanders that the coast of Sicily was everywhere patrolled, they decided to take the bold step of sailing into the harbour Marsala. As a large mercantile port, this offered several advantages. The true character of the vessel would not be suspected until they arrived there, and hostile ships cruising near might take them for ordinary merchantmen. There was also the advantage that, being only some seventy miles from Cape Bona, in Africa, it afforded a better chance of escape, should they meet with misfortune after landing, and be obliged to re-embark. As they neared the coast they made out several sailing vessels and steamers near it, and in the roadstead of Marsala two ships-of-war were anchored. To their joy, they were able to make out through a telescope, while still at a considerable distance, that these vessels were flying the British ensign, and so headed straight for the port, which they found full of merchantmen.

They had indeed been attended by good fortune, for three Neapolitan ships-of-war had left the port that morning and were still in sight. Being evidently suspicious, however, of the two steamers entering the port together, they turned and made for Marsala again. Not a moment was lost by the Garibaldians, and the disembarkation at once began. It happened that the British vessels-of-war were in the line of fire, and consequently the whole of the men were landed before the Neapolitans could bring their guns to bear. Two-thirds of them were still on the quay, getting the ammunition and stores into the carts, when the enemy opened fire upon them with shell and grape; fortunately the discharges were ill directed, and the Garibaldians marched off into the town without loss. They were welcomed with lively acclamation by the working classes of the town; but the authorities, while throwing no opposition in their way, received them under protest, as indeed was natural enough, for they could hardly suppose that this handful of men could succeed against the power of Naples, and dreaded the anger of the government should they bestow any warm hospitality upon these adventurers.

Two days were spent at Marsala in gaining information as to the state of the country, making arrangements for the march inland, and for the transport of ammunition and spare rifles, and in obtaining stores of provisions sufficient for two or three days. It was fortunate indeed that no Neapolitan troops were stationed in the town, and that they were therefore able to pursue their work without interruption. During the voyage the force had been divided into eight companies, and a ninth was now formed from the Sicilians who joined them. The enthusiasm, that had been necessarily shown rather in action than in shouts by the people of Marsala, who, with Neapolitan ships in the bay, feared that any demonstration might draw upon themselves a terrible retribution, now showed itself openly. The force was accompanied by great numbers of men and women,—even monks joined in the procession,—while from every village parties of fighting men, many of whom had taken part in the late insurrection, joined the party; and when on the day after leaving Marsala they reached Salemi, the force had been augmented by twelve hundred men.

Here Garibaldi, at the request not only of his own men, but of the authorities of the little town and deputies from villages round, assumed the title of dictator, in the name of Victor Emmanuel, King of Italy—thus proclaiming to the world that he had broken altogether with the republican faction.

Except when on duty, there was a thorough comradeship among the Garibaldians. Fully half of the thousand men who had left Genoa with him belonged to the upper and professional classes, and were of the same rank of life as the officers; consequently, when the march was done or the men dismissed from parade, all stiffness was thrown aside, and officers and men mingled in the utmost harmony. All were in the highest spirits. The first well-nigh insuperable difficulties had been overcome; the hindrances thrown in their way by the Italian government had failed to prevent their embarkation; the danger of falling into the hands of the Neapolitan navy had been avoided, and the reception which they met with showed that they had not overestimated the deep feeling of hostility with which the Sicilians regarded their oppressors.

Frank, while on capital terms with all the officers, who were aware how much the expedition owed to his family, and who saw the almost affectionate manner in which Garibaldi treated him, kept principally with his special friends, Maffio, Rubini, and Sarto.

During the voyage, as an occasional change from the one absorbing topic, they asked him many questions about his school-days, and were intensely interested in his description of the life, so wholly different from that at Italian schools and academies.

"We don't have such good times as you have," Rubini said; "you seem to have done just what you liked, and your masters do not appear to have interfered with you at all."

"No, except when in school, they had nothing to do with us."

"And you went where you liked and did what you liked, just as if you were grown-up men? It is astonishing," Maffio said; "why, with us we are never out of sight of our masters!"

"We might not quite go where we liked: there were certain limits beyond which we were supposed not to pass; but really, as long as we did not get into any rows, we could pretty well go anywhere within walking distance. You see, the big fellows to a certain extent keep order; but really they only do this in the houses where we live—outside there is no occasion to look after us. Though we are but boys, we are gentlemen, and are expected to act as such. I can't see why boys want looking after, as if they were criminals, who would break into a house or maltreat an old woman, if they had the chance. It is because we are, as it were, put on our honour and allowed to act and think for ourselves, instead of being marched about and herded like a flock of sheep, that our public school boys, as a rule, do so well afterwards. Our great general, Wellington—at least I think it was he—said, that the battle of Waterloo was fought in the playing fields of Eton. Of course, though he said Eton, he meant of all our public schools. Certainly we are much less likely to come to grief when we leave school and become our own masters, than we should be, if we had been treated as children up to that time."

"That must be so," Rubini said thoughtfully. "I wish we had such schools in Italy; perhaps we shall have some day. We have many universities, but no schools at all like yours. Of course, your masters are not priests?"

"Well, they are almost all clergymen, but that makes no difference. They are generally good fellows, and take a lot of interest in our sports, which is natural enough, for many of them have been great cricketers or great oarsmen—that is, they have rowed in their university boat. A master who has done that sort of thing is more looked up to by the boys, and is thought more of, than fellows who have never done anything in particular. The sort of fellows who have always been working and reading, and have come out high at the universities, are of course very good teachers, but they don't understand boys half as well as the others do."

"But why should you respect a master who has been, as you say, good at sports, more than one who has studied hard?"

"Well, I don't know exactly. Of course it is very creditable to a man to have taken a high degree; but somehow or other one does have a lot of respect for a fellow who you know could thrash any blackguard who had a row with him in a couple of minutes—just the same as one feels a respect for an officer who has done all sorts of brave actions. I heard, some time ago, that one of our masters had been appointed to a church in some beastly neighbourhood in Birmingham or one of those manufacturing towns, and the people were such a rough lot that he could do nothing with them at first. But one day, when he was going along the street, he saw a notorious bully thrashing a woman, and he interfered. The fellow threatened him; and he quietly turned in, and gave him the most tremendous thrashing he had ever had, in about three minutes. After that he got to be greatly liked, and did no end of good in his parish. I suppose there was just the same feeling among those fellows as there is with us at school."

"It seems impossible," Rubini said, in a tone almost of awe, "that a minister should fight with his hands against a ruffian of that kind."

"Well, I don't know," Frank replied: "if you saw a big ruffian thrashing a woman or insulting a lady, or if even he insulted yourself, what would you do? I am supposing, of course, that you were not in uniform, and did not wear a sword."

"I do not know what I should do," Rubini said gravely. "I hope I should fly at him."

"Yes; but if he were bigger and stronger, and you could not box, what would be the good of that? He would knock you down, and perhaps kick you almost to death, and then finish thrashing the woman."

"Yes; but you say that this man was a priest, a clergyman?" Maffio urged.

The three friends looked gravely at each other.

"Yes; but you must remember that he was also a man, and there is such a thing as righteous anger. Why should a man look on and see a woman ill-treated without lifting his hand to save her, simply because he is a clergyman? No, no, Maffio. You may say what you like, but it is a good thing for a man to have exercised all his muscles as a boy, and to be good at sports, and have learned to use his fists. It is good for him, whether he is going to be a soldier, or a colonist in a wild country, or a traveller, or a clergyman. I am saying nothing against learning; learning is a very good thing, but certainly among English boys we admire strength and skill more than learning, and I am quite sure that as a nation we have benefited more by the one than the other. If there was not one among us who had ever opened a Latin or Greek book, we should still have extended our empire as we have done, colonised continents, conquered India, and held our own, and more, against every other nation by land and sea, and become a tremendous manufacturing and commercial country."

The others laughed. "Well crowed, Percival! No doubt there is a great deal in what you say, still I suppose that even you will hardly claim that you are braver than other people."

"Not braver," Frank said; "but bravery is no good without backbone. If two men equally brave meet, it is the one with most 'last'—that is what we call stamina—most endurance, most strength and most skill, who must in the long-run win."

"But the fault of you English is—I don't mean it offensively—that you believe too much in yourselves."

"At any rate," Frank replied, "we don't boast about ourselves, as some people do, and it is because we believe in ourselves that we are successful. For example, you all here believe that, small as is your number, you are going to defeat the Neapolitans, and I think that you will do it, because I also believe in you. It is that feeling among our soldiers and sailors—their conviction that, as a matter of course, they will in the long-run win—that has carried them through battles and wars against the biggest odds. That was the way that your Roman ancestors carried their arms over Europe.

They were no braver than the men they fought, but they believed thoroughly in themselves, and never admitted to themselves the possibility of defeat. What a mad expedition ours would be if we had not the same feeling!"

"I won't argue any more against you, Percival," Rubini laughed; "and if I ever marry and have sons, I will send them over to be educated at one of your great schools—that is, if we have not, as I hope we may have by that time, schools of the same kind here. Can you fence? Do you learn that at your schools?"

"Not as a part of the school course. A fencing master does come down from London once a week, and some of the fellows take lessons from him. I did among others; but once a week is of very little use, and whenever I was in London during the holidays, I went pretty nearly every day to Angelo's, which is considered the best school for fencing we have. Of course my father, being a soldier, liked me to learn the use of the sword and rapier, though I might never have occasion to use them, for, as I was his only son, he did not want me to go into the army. It is just as well now that I did go in for it."

"I don't expect it will be of much use," Rubini said. "If the Neapolitans do not show themselves to be braver soldiers than we take them for, there will be no hand-to-hand fighting. If, on the other hand, they do stand their ground well, I do not expect we shall ever get to close quarters, for they ought to annihilate us before we could do so. Well, I long for the first trial."

"So do I. I should think that a good deal would depend upon that. If we beat them as easily as I have heard my father say they were beaten near Rome in 1848, it is hardly likely that they will make much stand afterwards. It is not only the effect it will have on the Neapolitan troops, but on the people. We cannot expect that the Sicilians will join us in considerable number until we have won a battle, and we want them to make a good show. Even the most cowardly troops can hardly help fighting when they are twenty to one; but if we are able to make a fair show of force, the enemy may lose heart, even if the greater part of our men are only poorly armed peasants."

To most of those who started from Genoa, fully prepared to sacrifice their lives in the cause they regarded as sacred, the success that had attended their passage, and enabled them to disembark without the loss of a man, seemed a presage of further good fortune, and they now marched forward with the buoyant confidence, that in itself goes a long way to ensure success; the thought that there were fifty thousand Neapolitan troops in the island, and that General Lanza had at Palermo twenty-eight thousand, in no way overawed them, and the news that a strong body of the enemy had advanced through Calatafimi to meet them was regarded with satisfaction.

Calatafimi stood in the heart of the mountains, where the roads from Palermo, Marsala and Trapani met; and on such ground the disproportion of numbers would be of less importance than it would be in the plain, for the cavalry of the enemy would not be able to act with effect. The ground, too, as they learned from peasants, was covered with ruins of buildings erected by Saracens, Spaniards, and Normans, and was therefore admirably suited for irregular warfare. Garibaldi, with a few of his staff, went forward to reconnoitre the position. He decided that his own followers should make a direct attack, while the new levies, working among the hills, should open fire on the Neapolitan flanks and charge down upon them as opportunity offered.

At Marsala the staff had all bought horses, choosing hardy animals accustomed to work among the mountains. It was not the general's intention to hurl his little force directly on the Neapolitan centre, situated in the valley, but, while making a feint there, to attack one flank or the other, the rapidity with which his men manœuvred giving them a great advantage. While, therefore, the six little guns he had obtained at Talamonte were to open fire on the enemy's centre, covered by a couple of hundred men, the rest were to act as a mobile force under his own direction; their movements would be screened by the ruins and broken ground, and he would be able to pass in comparative shelter from one flank to the other, and so surprise the enemy by falling upon them where least expected.

As they approached the scene of action, the Garibaldians left the road, scattering themselves in skirmishing order on either side, and working their way along through the ruins, which so covered their advance, that it was only occasionally that a glimpse of a red shirt or the gleam of the sun on a musket-barrel showed the enemy that their assailants were approaching. On ground like this horses were of little use, and Garibaldi ordered all the junior members of his staff to dismount, fasten their horses in places of shelter, and advance on foot with the troops, as he should not require their services during the fight.

CHAPTER VIII

PALERMO

FRANK'S heart beat fast with the excitement of the moment. Save himself, there was not one of Garibaldi's own men but was accustomed to the sound of artillery, and he could scarcely restrain himself from starting when on a sudden the Neapolitan batteries opened fire, and their missiles struck rocks and walls round him, or burst overhead.

"It is not so bad as it looks," Rubini, whom he joined as he ran forward, said with a laugh.

"It is fortunate that it is not," Frank replied; "it certainly sounds bad enough, but, as I don't think they can see us at all, it can only be a random fire."

He soon shook off the feeling of uneasiness which he could not at first repress, and presently quitted his friend and pushed forward on his own account, keeping close to the road and abreast of Garibaldi, so that he could run up and receive any orders that might be given. It was not long before the enemy opened a musketry fire. The guns had been following Garibaldi, and he now superintended them as they were run into position, three on either side of the road. They were not placed at regular distances, but each was posted where the men would, while loading, be sheltered behind walls, from which the guns could be run out, wheeled round and fired, and then withdrawn. Frank was not long in joining the Garibaldian line, which was lying in shelter at the foot of the declivity.

In front of them was a level space of ground with a few little farmhouses dotted here and there. On the opposite side of this the hills rose much more steeply. Near the summit were the main body of the Neapolitans, who were altogether about two thousand strong; an advanced guard of some five or six hundred had descended into the valley, and were moving across it; they had guns with them, which were now at work, as were others with the main body.

When Garibaldi joined his troops he at once ordered the Genoese company to attack the advancing enemy and if possible to capture the guns they had with them. Followed by a party of Sicilians, and by Frank and several other officers who had no special duties to perform, they dashed forward. At the same moment a number of the peasants, who had made their way round on either flank unobserved, opened fire upon the Neapolitans, who at the order of the officer in command began to fall back. The Garibaldians hurled themselves upon them, and hastened the movement. The guard had no idea of making a frontal attack upon an enemy so strongly posted, and had, as Frank had heard him say before he dismounted, intended to compel them to fall back by flank attacks. He was not surprised, therefore, to hear the trumpet sounding the recall.

The summons was, however, unheard, or at any rate unheeded, by the Genoese, who continued to press hotly upon the Neapolitans; the latter had now been joined by their supporting line, and Garibaldi saw that the small party, who were now almost surrounded, must be destroyed, unless he advanced to their assistance. The trumpet accordingly sounded the charge, and the men sprang to their feet and dashed forward at full speed. The fighting had been hand to hand, and the Garibaldians had only gained the advantage so far from the fact that they were accustomed to fight each for himself, and were individually more powerful men; it was indeed their habit, in all their fights, to rely on the bayonet, and they still pressed forward. Frank was now as cool and collected as he would have been in a football match, and had several times to congratulate himself on the training he had received in the use of his sword, having two combats with Neapolitan officers, and each time coming off victorious.

Presently, in front of him, he saw one of the Neapolitan standards. In the confusion it had been left almost unguarded; and calling to three or four of the men around him, he dashed at it. There was a short, sharp fight: the men standing between him and the flag fell before the bayonets of the Garibaldians. Frank engaged in a tough encounter with the officer who held the flag, and finally cutting him down, seized the staff and carried it back into the Garibaldian ranks.

"Well done, well done, Percival!" He turned and saw Garibaldi himself, who, at the head of his main body, had that instant arrived.

The Neapolitans, although also reinforced, fell back up the hill. The face of the ascent was composed of a series of natural terraces, and as they retreated up these, a storm of fire from the reserve at the top of the hill and the cannon there, was poured upon the Garibaldians. The general halted his men for a minute or two at the foot of the lower terrace, where they were sheltered by the slope from the missiles of the enemy; they were re-formed, and then recommenced the ascent. It was hot work; the ground was very steep, and swept by the enemy's fire. As each terrace was gained the men rushed across the level ground and threw themselves down panting at the foot of the next slope, where they were to some extent sheltered. Two or three minutes, and they made their next rush. But little return to the enemy's fire was attempted, for the wretched muskets with which they had been supplied at Genoa were practically useless, and only the Genoese, who had brought their own carbines, and were excellent shots, did much execution.

Several times the Neapolitans attempted to make a stand, but as often were driven back. On this occasion, however, they fought well and steadily; the terror of Garibaldi's name had ceased to have its effect during the twelve years that had elapsed since Ferdinand's army had fled before him, but the desire to wipe out that disgrace no doubt inspired them, and Garibaldi afterwards gave them full credit for the obstinacy with which they had contested his advance. At last the uppermost terrace was reached; there was one more halt for breath, and then the Garibaldians went forward with a cheer. The resistance was comparatively slight: the Neapolitan troops at first engaged had already exhausted their ammunition, and had become disheartened at their failure to arrest the impetuous assault of their enemies; and when the Garibaldians reached the summit of the hill, they found that the enemy were in full retreat.

Exhausted by their efforts, and having suffered heavy loss, they made a short halt; the horses of the general and his staff were brought up by the small party who had been left with the guns, and who had advanced across the plain at some little distance in the rear of the fighting line. As soon as they arrived the advance continued until the little army halted at Calatafimi, some miles from the scene of battle. The Garibaldians had captured only one cannon, a few rifles, and a score or two of prisoners, for the most part wounded; but by the defeat of the enemy they had gained an enormous advantage, for, as the news spread throughout the country, its dimensions growing as it flew, it created great enthusiasm, and from every town and village men poured down to join the army of liberation.

The Neapolitan governor had indeed made a fatal mistake in not placing a much larger force in the field for the first engagement. The troops fought bravely, and though beaten, were by no means disgraced; and had they been supported by powerful artillery, and by a couple of regiments of cavalry, which could have charged the Garibaldians in the plain, the battle would have had a very different result.

At Calatafimi the Garibaldians halted. The Neapolitan wounded had been left here; their own had, when the fighting ceased, been sent back to Vita. The inhabitants vied with each other in hospitality to them, and although saddened by the loss of many of their bravest comrades, all regarded the victory they had won as an augury of future success. Already the country had risen; the Neapolitans in their retreat had been harassed, and numbers of them killed by the peasants; every hour swelled the force, and next morning they set out in the highest spirits, and with a conviction that success would attend them. And yet there were grave difficulties to be met, for ten thousand Neapolitans were massed in two formidable positions on the road by which it was believed that the Garibaldians must advance, and twelve thousand remained in garrison at Palermo. That evening they reached Alcamo, a large town, where they were received with enthusiasm. The excitement was even more lively when the next day they entered Partinico, where the inhabitants, who had been brutally treated by the Neapolitans in their advance, had risen when they passed through as fugitives, and massacred numbers of them, and pursued them a considerable distance along the road to Palermo. At this point the Garibaldians left the road, and ascended to the plateau of Renne, and thence looked down on the rich plain in which Palermo stands, and on the city itself. Here two days of tremendous rain prevented farther movement.

"You are now seeing the rough side of campaigning, Percival," Rubini said, with a laugh, as the four friends sat together in a little arbour they had erected, and over the top of which were thrown two of their blankets.

"It is not very pleasant, certainly," Frank agreed; "but it might be a good deal worse; it is wet, but it is not cold, and we are not fasting; we each of us laid in a good stock of provisions when at Partinico, but I certainly never anticipated that we should have to rely upon telegraph poles for a supply of fuel; it is lucky that the wires run across here, for we should certainly have had to eat our meat raw, or go without, if it hadn't been for them."

None of the men appeared to mind the discomfort; the supply of wood was too precious to be used except for cooking purposes, and indeed it would be of no use for the men to attempt to dry their clothes until the downpour ceased. Two days later, the enemy having sent out a strong reconnoitring party, Garibaldi determined to cross the mountains and come down upon the main southern road from Palermo. Officers had been sent to the various towns on that road to summon all true men to join. The force started in the evening and performed a tremendous march; the guns were lashed to poles and carried on the men's shoulders, the boxes of ammunition were conveyed in the same manner. The rain continued incessantly, and there was a thick fog which added greatly to the difficulties. It was not until daylight that the head of the column began to straggle into Parco, on the southern road.

They at once seized some commanding positions round the place, and began to throw up entrenchments, but as Parco was commanded by hills, it could not be defended against a determined attack. Two days later two strong columns marched out from Palermo. The first advanced by the road that crossed the valley, and threatened the Garibaldian rear by the passage through the hills known as the pass of Piana dei Greci. Garibaldi at once sent off his artillery and baggage by the road, and with a company of his cacciatori and a body of the new levies, who were known as picciotti, hurried to the pass, which they reached before the Neapolitans arrived there. On their opening fire, the Neapolitans, thinking that they had the whole Garibaldian force in front of them in an extremely strong position retired at once. Finding that the freedom of his movements would be embarrassed by his cannon, which under the most advantageous circumstances could not contend against those of the enemy, he sent them away along the southern road, while he withdrew his force from Parco, and for a short time followed the guns; he then turned off into the mountains and directed his march to Misilmeri, a few miles from Palermo, having completely thrown the enemy off his track. The pursuing column, believing that the whole Garibaldian force was retreating with its guns, pushed on rapidly, while Garibaldi had already turned the strong position of Monreale, and was preparing to attack the town.

His force had here been increased by the volunteers who had arrived from the southern villages. The Neapolitan general, Lanza, soon obtained information as to the invader's position, and prepared with absolute confidence to meet his attack, which must, he believed, be made by the coast road. On the evening of the 26th Garibaldi moved across the country by a little-frequented track, and the next morning appeared on the road entering the town at the Termini gate. The twelve thousand Neapolitan troops who still remained in the town had no suspicion that their foe was near. The day before, the commander of the column that had passed through Parco had sent in the news that he was in hot pursuit of the Garibaldians, who were flying in all directions, and the governor had given a banquet in honour of the rout of the brigands. The military bands had played on the promenade, and the official portion of the population had been wild with joy.

On the other hand, messages had passed constantly between Garibaldi's agents and the leaders of the patriotic party in the town, who had promised that the population would rise as soon as he entered the city. It was upon this promise that the general based his hopes of success; for that three thousand badly armed men could hope to overcome twelve thousand troops, well supported by artillery, and defending the town street by street, seemed impossible even to so hopeful a spirit. No time was lost. The Garibaldians rushed forward, drove in at once an outpost stationed beyond the barriers at the gate, and carried the barricades, before the troops could muster in sufficient force to offer any serious resistance.

But beyond this the opposition became obstinate and fierce; the cacciatori pressed forward by the principal street, the bands of picciotti distracted the attention of the enemy by advancing by parallel streets, and, although the cannon of the Castello Mare thundered, pouring shot and shell broadcast into the quarter through which the Garibaldians were advancing, and though from the large convent of San Antonio, held by a battalion of bersaglieri, a terrible fire was maintained upon the flank of the cacciatori at a distance of a couple of hundred yards, they nevertheless pressed on, clearing the street of the troops who opposed their advance, until they reached the square in the centre of the city.

All this time the guns of the Neapolitan ships-of-war had been pouring a fierce fire into the town, with the apparent object of deterring the populace from rising, for it was upon private houses that the damage was committed, and was, so far as the Garibaldians were concerned, innoxious. For a short time the object was attained: so terrible was the fire that swept the principal streets leading down to the water, so alarming the din of exploding shells and falling walls, that for a short time the populace dared not venture from their houses; but fury succeeded to alarm, and it was not long before the inhabitants flocked out into the streets, and under the direction of Colonel Acerbi, one of the most distinguished officers of the thousand, began to erect barricades. These sprang up with marvellous rapidity; carts were wheeled out from the courtyards and overturned, men laboured with pickaxes and crowbars tearing up the pavements, women threw out mattresses from the windows; all worked with enthusiasm.

Garibaldi established himself at the Pretorio Palace, the central point of the city; and here the members of the revolutionary committee joined him. His staff were sent off in all directions to order all the bands scattered throughout the city to assemble there. The people of Palermo were wholly without firearms, as all weapons of the kind had been confiscated by the authorities; but armed with hatchets, axes, knives fastened to the end of sticks and poles to act as pikes, long spits and other improvised weapons, they prepared to defend the barricades. A few, indeed, brought out muskets which had been hidden away when all the houses had been searched for weapons, but the greatest difficulty was experienced from the want of powder.

Garibaldi now stationed his forces so as to intercept all communications between the various points where the Neapolitan troops were concentrated. Lanza himself, who was at once commander-in-chief and viceroy, was with several regiments at the royal palace.

The Castello Mare was held by a strong force, and there were some regiments at the palace of finance. These points they had only reached after hard fighting; but once there they were isolated from each other, and to join hands they would have to pass along streets blocked by barricades, and defended by a desperate population, and exposed to the fire of the Garibaldians from every window and roof.

That night hundreds of men and women were set to work to grind charcoal, sulphur, and saltpetre, to mix them together to form a rough gunpowder, and then to make it up into cartridges. Such a compound would have been useless for ordinary purposes, but would have sufficient strength for street fighting, where it was but necessary to send a bullet some twenty or thirty yards with sufficient force to kill.

The fire of the fleet, Castello Mare, and the palace was maintained all day. The town was on fire in many places. A whole district a thousand yards in length and a hundred yards wide had been laid in ashes, convents and churches had been crushed by shells, and a large number of the inhabitants had been killed by grape and cannister; but after four hours' fighting there was a lull in the musketry fire: the Neapolitans were gathered in their three strong places and were virtually besieged there. In spite of the continued cannonade, the populace thronged the streets which were not in the direct line of fire, the bells of the churches pealed out triumphantly; bright curtains, cloths and flags were hung out from the balconies, friends embraced each other with tears of joy; while numbers continued to labour at the barricades, the monks and clergy joining in the work, all classes being wild with joy at their deliverance from the long and crushing tyranny to which they had been subjected.

Frank had entered the city with the chosen band, who had led the attack on the Termini gate, and advanced with them into the heart of the city. In the wild excitement of the fight he had lost all sense of danger; he saw others fall around him, his cheek had been deeply gashed by a bullet, but he had scarce felt the pain, and was almost surprised when a man close to him offered to bind up his wound with his sash. One of the first orders that Garibaldi gave, after establishing himself at the Pretorio Palace was to send for him.

"Lieutenant Percival," he said, "I commit to you the honour of leading a party to the prisons, and liberating all the political prisoners you find there. You have won that distinction by having, in the first place, captured the flag of the tyrants at Calatafimi, and also by the gallant manner in which you have fought in the first rank to-day. I marked your conduct, and it was worthy of your brave father. I can give it no higher praise."

Taking twenty men with him, Frank went to the prisons. On entering each, he demanded from the officials a list of all prisoners confined, and the offences with which they were charged, so that no criminals should be released with the political prisoners. He hardly needed the list, however, for the criminals were but few in number, the Neapolitan authorities not having troubled themselves with such trifles as robberies and assassinations, but the prisons were crowded with men of the best blood in the city and the surrounding country, who had been arrested upon the suspicion of holding liberal opinions, and who were treated with very much greater severity than were the worst malefactors. The thunder of the guns had already informed them that a terrible conflict was going on, but it was not until Frank and his men arrived that the prisoners knew who were the parties engaged, and their joy and gratitude was unbounded when they learned that they were free, now and for ever, from the power of their persecutors.

As they marched to the prison, several of the men had shouted to the crowd, "We are going to free the captives." The news had spread like wildfire, and as the prisoners issued from the jail they were met by their friends and relatives, and the most affecting scenes took place. Although Frank considered it unlikely in the extreme that persons arrested on the mainland would be carried across to the island, he insisted on the warders accompanying him over the whole prison and unlocking every door, in spite of their protestations that the cells were empty. Having satisfied himself on this head, he went to the other prisons, where similar scenes took place.

The fire of the Neapolitan ships was kept up until nightfall, and then ceased, rather from the exhaustion of the gunners, who had been twelve hours at work, than from any difficulty in sighting their guns; for in Palermo it was almost as light as day, the whole city being lit up by the tremendous conflagration, and in addition every house save those facing the port was illuminated, candles burning at every window. Throughout the night work was carried on, fresh barricades were erected, and others greatly strengthened. It was all-important that the three bodies of troops, isolated from each other, should not effect a junction. Boats were sent off to the merchant ships in the harbour in order to purchase powder, but none could be obtained; however, by morning so much had been manufactured that with what still remained in the Garibaldian pouches there was enough for the day's fighting.

At Garibaldi's headquarters there was no sleep that night: the revolutionary committee received orders from the general where the armed citizens were to take their posts at the barricades, and how their men were to be divided into sections. They were to impress upon all that, though the fighting must be desperate, it could not last long. At the royal palace there were no provisions of any kind for the troops stationed there, nor were there any in the palace of finance; so that if the struggle could be maintained for another day or two at the most, the troops would be driven to surrender by starvation.

Frank had time, after he returned from the prisons, to have his wound dressed, and he then received the congratulations of his three friends, all of whom were more or less severely wounded.

"You have come out of it rather the best of us, Percival," Maffio said: "I have a bullet through the arm, Rubini has lost two of the fingers of his left hand, and Sarto will limp for some time for he has been shot through the calf of his leg; so we shall have no scars that we can show, while you will have one that will be as good as a medal of honour."

"I am sure I hope not," Frank said; "I can assure you that, honourable as it may be, it would be a nuisance indeed, for I should be constantly asked where I got it, and when I answered, should be bothered into telling the whole story over and over again. However, I think we can all congratulate each other on having come out of it comparatively unhurt; I certainly never expected to do so,—the row was almost bewildering."

"It was almost as bad as one of your football tussles," Sarto laughed.

"You may laugh, but it was very much the same feeling," Frank replied. "I have felt nearly as much excited in a football scrimmage as I was to-day; I can tell you that when two sides are evenly matched, and each fellow is straining every nerve, the thrill of satisfaction when one finds that one's own side is gaining ground is about as keen as anything one is ever likely to feel."

The next day the fighting recommenced, the Neapolitan troops making desperate efforts to concentrate. The fighting in the streets was for a time furious. At no point did the enemy make any material progress, although they gained possession of some houses round the palace and finance offices. The barricades were desperately defended by the armed citizens and the picciotti, and from time to time, when the Neapolitans seemed to be gaining ground, the men of Garibaldi's thousand flung themselves upon them with the bayonet. That morning, under the superintendence of skilled engineers, powder mills were established, and the supply of gunpowder was improved both in quantity and quality, men and women filling the cartridges as fast as the powder was turned out. Fighting and work continued throughout the night, and all **next day.**

CHAPTER IX

HARD FIGHTING

ON the following morning Frank was riding with a message from the general, when he heard a sudden outburst of firing at some distance ahead of him. He checked his horse to listen.

"That must be near the Porto Termini," he said, "and yet there are none of the enemy anywhere near there. It must be either some fresh body of troops that have arrived from the south of the island, or Bosco's column returned from their fool's errand in search of us. If so, we are in a desperate mess. Six thousand Neapolitan troops, under one of their best generals, would turn the scale against us; they must be stopped, if possible, till the general can collect our scattered troops."

Frank's second supposition was the correct one. The two columns that had, as they believed, been in pursuit of Garibaldi, had returned to the town. So unanimous were the country people in their hatred of the Neapolitans, that it was only on the previous day that they had learned that the enemy, who they believed were fugitives, had entered Palermo with their whole force. Furious at having been so tricked, they made a tremendous march, and arriving at the Termini gate early in the morning, made a determined attack on the guard there, who defended themselves bravely, but were driven back, contesting every step.

Frank hesitated for a moment, and then shouted to a soldier near him: "Run with all speed to the palace; demand to see the general at once. Say that you have come from me, and that I sent you to say that the Porto Termini is attacked, I know not with what force, and that I am going on to try to arrest their progress until he arrives with help. As you run, tell every man you meet to hasten to oppose the enemy."

The man started to run, and Frank galloped on, shouting to every armed man he met to follow him. The roar of battle increased as he rode. When he reached the long street leading to the gate, he saw that the enemy had already forced their way in, and that a barricade was being desperately defended by the little force that had fallen back before them. His horse would be useless now, and he called to a boy who was looking round the corner of a house.

"Look here, my lad: take this horse and lead him to the general's headquarters. Here is a five-franc piece. Don't get on his back, but lead him. Can I trust you?"

"I will do it, signor; you can depend upon me."

Frank ran forward. The tremendous roll of fire beyond the barricade showed how strong was the force there, and he felt sure that the defenders must speedily be overpowered. Numbers of men were running along the street; he shouted to them: "The barricade cannot hold out; enter the houses and man every window; we must keep them back to the last. Garibaldi will be here before long."

He himself kept on until within some two hundred yards of the barricade; then he stopped at the door of a house at the corner of a lane at right angles to the street, and ran into it. He waited until a score of men came up.

"Come in here," he said: "we will defend this house till the last."

The men closed the door behind them, and running into the lower rooms, fetched out furniture and piled it against it. They were assisted by five or six women, who, with some children, were the sole occupants of the house.

"Bring all the mattresses and bedding that you have, Frank said to them, to the windows of the first floor. "We will place them on the balconies."

In three or four minutes every balcony was lined with mattresses, and Frank sheltered his men behind them. Looking out, he saw that the fighting had just ceased, and that a dense mass of the enemy were pouring over the barricade; while at the same moment a crackling fire broke out from the houses near, into which its defenders had run, when they saw that the barricade could be no longer defended. Along both sides of the street, preparations similar to those he had ordered had been hastily made; and the men who were still coming up were all turning into the houses. Directly the Neapolitans crossed the barricade, they opened fire down the street, which was speedily deserted; but Frank had no doubt that, as the Garibaldian supports came up, they would make their way in at the back and strengthen the defenders. A hundred yards higher up the street was another barricade; behind this the townspeople were already gathering. Frank ordered his men to keep back inside the rooms until the enemy came along.

"Your powder is no good till they are close," he said, "but it is as good as the best at close quarters."

From time to time he looked out. The roar of musketry was continuous; from every window came puffs of smoke, while the enemy replied by a storm of musketry fire at the defenders. While the column was still moving forward, its officers were telling off parties of men to burst open the doors and bayonet all found in the houses. He could mark the progress made, as women threw themselves out of the windows, preferring death that way to being murdered by the infuriated soldiers. It was not long before the head of the column approached the house; then Frank gave the word, and from every window a discharge was poured into the crowded mass. Stepping back from the balconies to load, the men ran out and fired again as soon as they were ready; while through the upper part of the open windows a shower of bullets flew into the room, bringing down portions of the ceiling, smashing looking-glasses, and striking thickly against the back walls.

Several of the party had fallen in the first two or three minutes, and Frank, taking one of their muskets and ammunition, was working with the rest, when a woman whom he had posted below ran up to say that they were attacking the door, and that it was already yielding. Two or three shots fired through the keyhole had indeed broken the lock, and it was only the furniture piled against it that kept it in its place. Already, by his instructions, the women had brought out on to the landing sofas, chests of drawers, and other articles, to form a barricade there. Frank ran down the stone stairs with six of the men, directing the others to form the barricade on the first floor, and to be prepared to help them over as they returned. It was two or three minutes before the hinges of the door were broken off, by shots from the assailants, and as it fell it was dragged out, and a number of men rushed in and began to pull down the furniture behind.

Now Frank and his party opened fire, aiming coolly and

THE HINGES OF THE DOOR WERE BROKEN OFF.

steadily. But the soldiers rushed in in such numbers that he soon gave the word, and his party ran upstairs, and, covered by the fire of their comrades, climbed up over the barricade on to the landing. Here they defended themselves desperately. The enemy thronged the staircase, those who were in front using their bayonets, while the men in the passage below fired over their heads at the defenders. Momentarily the little band decreased in number, until but two remained on their feet by the side of Frank. The women, knowing that no mercy would be shown, picked up the muskets of the fallen, and fired them into the faces of the men trying to pull down or scale the barricades. But the end was close at hand, when there came a tremendous crash, a blinding smoke and dust. The house shook to its foundations, and for a moment a dead silence took the place of the din that had before prevailed.

Frank and his two companions had been thrown down by the shock. Half stunned, and ignorant of what had happened, he struggled to his feet. His left hand hung helpless by his side. He took his pistol, which he had reserved for the last extremity, from his belt, and looked over the barricade. At first he could see nothing, so dense was the smoke and dust. As it cleared away a little, he gave an exclamation of surprise and thankfulness: the stairs were gone.

"Thank God!" he said, turning round to the women behind him, who were standing paralysed by the explosion and shock. "We are safe: the stairs have gone."

Still he could scarce understand what had happened, until he saw a yawning hole in the wall near the stairs, and then understood what had taken place. The ships-of-war were again at work bombarding the town. One of their shells had passed through the house and exploded under the stairs, carrying them away, with all upon them. Below was a chaos of blocks of stone, mingled with the bodies of their late assailants; but while he looked, a fierce jet of flames burst up.

"What was there under the stairs?" he asked the women.

"The store of firewood, signor, was there."

"The shell which blew up the stairs has set it alight," he said. "We are safe from the enemy; but we are not safe from the fire. I suppose there is a way out on to the roof."

"Yes, signor."

"Then do one of you see that all the children upstairs are taken out there; let the rest examine all the bodies of the men who have fallen; if any are alive they must be carried up."

He looked down at the two men who had stood by him till the last: one had been almost decapitated by a fragment of stone, the other was still breathing; only three of the others were found to be alive, for almost all, either at the windows of the barricade, had been shot through the head or upper part of the body.

Frank assisted the women, as well as he was able, to carry the four men still alive up to the roof. The houses were divided by party walls some seven or eight feet high. Frank told the women to fetch a chair, a chest of drawers, and a large blanket, from below. The chest of drawers was placed against the wall separating the terrace from that of the next house down the lane, and the chair by the side of it. With the aid of this, Frank directed one of the women to mount on to the chest of drawers, and then took his place beside her.

"You had better get up first," he said, "and then help

me a little, for with this disabled arm I should not be able to manage it without hurting myself badly." With her aid, however, he had no difficulty in getting up. There were several women on the next roof, but they had not heard him, so intent were they in watching the fray; and it was not until he had shouted several times that they caught the sound of his voice above the din of fighting.

"I am going to hand some children and four wounded men down to you," he said, as they ran up.

The children were first passed down; the women placed the wounded men one by one on a blanket, and standing on two chairs raised it until Frank and the woman beside him could get hold. Then they lowered it down on the other side until the women there could reach it. Only three had to be lifted over, for when it came to the turn of the fourth he was found to be dead.

"You will all have to move on," Frank said, as he dropped on to the terrace; "the next house is on fire; whether it will spread or not I cannot say, but at any rate you had better bring up your valuables, and move along two or three houses farther. You cannot go out into the street; you would only be shot down as soon as you issued out. I think that if you go two houses farther you will be safe; the fire will take some time to reach there, and the enemy's column may have passed across the end of the street before you are driven out."

The women heard what he said with composure; the terrors of the past three days had excited the nerves of the whole population to such a point of tension, that the news of this fresh danger was received almost with apathy. They went down quietly to bring up their children and valuables, and with them one woman brought a pair of steps, which greatly facilitated the passage of the remaining walls. One of the wounded men had by this time so far recovered himself that he was able, with assistance, to cross without being lifted over in a blanket. A fresh contingent of fugitives here joined them, and another wall was crossed.

"I think that you are now far enough," Frank said: "will you promise me that if the flames work this way"— and by this time the house where the fight had taken place was on fire from top to bottom—"you will carry these wounded men along as you go from roof to roof? I have my duties to perform and cannot stay here longer. Of course, if the fire spreads all the way down the lane, you must finally go down and run out from the door of the last house, but there will be comparatively small danger in this, as it will be but two or three steps round the next corner, and you will there be in shelter."

"We promise we will carry them with us," one of the women said earnestly: "you do not think that we could leave the men who have fought so bravely for us to be burnt?"

Frank now proceeded along the roofs. Two of the women accompanied him, to place the steps to enable him to mount and dismount the walls. There was no occasion to warn those below as to the fire, for all had by this time noticed it. He went down through the last house, opened the door, and ran round the corner, and then made his way along the streets, until he reached the spot where the combat was raging. Garibaldi had, on receiving his message, hurried with what force he could collect to the scene of conflict; but, as he went, he received a letter from General Lanza, saying that he had sent negotiators on board the flag-ship of the British fleet anchored in the roadstead, Admiral Mundy having consented to allow the representatives of both parties to meet there.

The tone of the letter showed how the Sicilian viceroy's pride was humbled. He had, in his proclamation issued four days before, denounced Garibaldi as a brigand and filibuster; he now addressed him as His Excellency General Garibaldi. Garibaldi at once went on board the English admiral's ship, but the fire of the Neapolitan ships and their guns on shore continued unabated. General Letizia was already on board, with the conditions of the proposed convention. To the first four articles Garibaldi agreed: that there should be a suspension of arms for a period to be arranged; that during that time each party should keep its position; that convoys of wounded, and the families of officials, should be allowed to pass through the town and embark on board the Neapolitan war-ships; and that the troops in the palace should be allowed to provide themselves with daily provisions. The fifth article proposed that the municipality should address a humble petition to his majesty the king, laying before him the real wishes of the town, and that this petition should be submitted to his majesty.

This article was indignantly rejected by Garibaldi. Letizia then folded up the paper and said, "Then all communications between us must cease."

Garibaldi then protested to Admiral Mundy against the infamy of the royal authorities in allowing the ships and forts to continue to fire upon his troops while a flag of truce was flying. Letizia who could hardly have expected that the article would be accepted, now agreed to its being struck out, and an armistice was arranged to last for twenty-four hours. Garibaldi returned on shore, and at a great meeting of the citizens explained the terms to them, and stated the condition that he had rejected. It was greeted with a roar of approval, and the citizens at once scattered with orders to increase the strength of the barricades to the utmost. The work was carried on with enthusiasm; the balconies were all lined with mattresses, and heaped with stones and missiles of all kinds to cast down upon the enemy, and the work of manufacturing powder and cartridges went on with feverish haste. Now that the firing had ceased, officers from the British and American vessels off the town came ashore, and many of them made presents of revolvers and fowling-pieces to the volunteers. The sailors on a Sardinian frigate almost mutinied, because they were not permitted to go ashore and aid in the defence.

Before the twenty-four hours had passed, General Letizia called upon Garibaldi and asked for a further three days' truce, as twenty-four hours was not a sufficient time to get the wounded on board. This Garibaldi readily granted, as it would give time for the barricades to be made almost impregnable, and for him to receive reinforcements, while it could not benefit the enemy. Volunteers arrived in companies from the country round, and Orsini landed with the cannon and with a considerable number of men who had joined him.

Such was the report given by Letizia, on his return to the royal palace, of the determined attitude of the population and of the formidable obstacles that would be encountered by the troops directly they were put in motion, that General Lanza must have felt his position to be desperate. He

HARD FIGHTING

accordingly sent Letizia back again to arrange that the troops at the royal palace, the finance office, and the Termini gate should be allowed to move down towards the sea and there join hands. To this Garibaldi willingly assented, as, should hostilities be renewed, he would be able to concentrate his whole efforts at one point, instead of being obliged to scatter his troops widely to meet an advance from four directions.

All idea of further fighting, however, had been abandoned by Lanza, and before the end of the armistice arrived, it was arranged that all should be taken on to their ships, and the forts, as well as the town, evacuated. The general also bound himself to leave behind him all the political prisoners who had been detained in the Castello Mare.

The enthusiasm in the city was indescribable, as the Neapolitans embarked on board their ships. The released prisoners were carried in triumph to Garibaldi's headquarters. Every house was decorated and illluminated, and the citizens, proud of the share they had taken in winning their freedom, speedily forgot their toils and their losses. The men who had marched with Garibaldi from Marsala were glad indeed of the prospect of a short time of rest. For nearly three weeks they had been almost incessantly marching or fighting, exposed for some days to a terrible downfall of rain, without shelter and almost without food. Since they had entered Palermo, they had only been able to snatch two or three hours' sleep occasionally. They had lost a large number of men, and few of them had escaped unwounded; but these, unless absolutely disabled, had still taken their share in the fighting, and even in the work of building the barricades.

For Garibaldi's staff there was little relaxation from their labours. In addition to his military duties, Garibaldi undertook with his usual vigour the reorganisation of the municipal affairs of the town. The condition of the charitable establishments were ameliorated; schools for girls established throughout the island; a national militia organised; the poorer part of the population were fed and employed in useful work; the street arabs, with whom Palermo swarmed, were gathered and placed in the Jesuit College, of which Garibaldi took possession, to be trained as soldiers. The organisation of the general government of the island was also attended to, and recruiting officers sent off to every district evacuated by the enemy.

This Garibaldi was able to do, as over £1,000,000 sterling had been, by the terms of the convention, left in the royal treasury when it was evacuated by the enemy. Contracts for arms were made abroad; a foundry for cannon established in the city, and the powder mills perfected and kept at work. Increasing reinforcements flocked in from the mainland; Medici with three steamers and two thousand men arrived the evening before the Neapolitan troops had finished their embarkation; Cosenz shortly afterwards landed with an equal number; other contingents followed from all the Italian provinces. Great Britain was represented by a number of enthusiastic men, who were formed into a company. Among these was a Cornish gentleman of the name of Peard, who had long been resident in Italy, and had imbibed a deep hatred of the tyrannical government that ground down the people, and persecuted, imprisoned, and drove into exile all who ventured to criticise their proceedings. He was a splendid shot, and the coolness he showed, and his success in picking off the enemy's officers, rendered him a noted figure among Garibaldi's followers.

The army was now organised in three divisions: one under General Turr marched for the centre of the island; the right wing, commanded by Bixio, started for the south-east; and the left, under Medici, was to move along the north coast; all were finally to concentrate at the Straits of Messina.

It was now the middle of July. Wonders had been accomplished in the six weeks that had passed since the occupation of Palermo. Garibaldi, who had been regarded as almost a madman, was now recognised as a power. He had a veritable army, well supplied with funds—for in addition to the million he had found in the treasury, subscriptions had been collected from lovers of freedom all over Europe, and specially England—and although there still remained a formidable force at Messina, it was regarded as certain that the whole of Sicily would soon become his.

One of the Neapolitan war-ships had been brought by her captain and crew into Palermo and placed at the disposal of Garibaldi; two others had been captured. Cavour himself had changed his attitude of coldness, and was prepared to take advantage of the success of the expedition, that he had done his best to hinder. He desired, however, that Garibaldi should resign his dictatorship, and hand over the island to the King of Sardinia. The general, however, refused to do this. He had all along declared in his proclamations that his object was to form a free Italy under Victor Emmanuel, and now declared that he would, when he had captured Naples, hand that kingdom and Sicily together to the king, but that until he could do so he would remain dictator of Sicily.

There can be no doubt that his determination was a wise one, for, as afterwards happened at Naples, he would have been altogether put aside by the royalist commissioners and generals, his plans would have been thwarted in every way, and hindrances offered to his invasion of the mainland, just as they had been to his expedition to Sicily.

Cavour sent over Farina to act in the name of the king. Admiral Persano, who, with a portion of the Italian navy, was now at Palermo, persuaded Garibaldi to allow Farina to assume the position of governor; but, while allowing this, Garibaldi gave him to understand that he was to attend solely to financial and civil affairs. Farina's first move, however, was to have an enormous number of placards that he had brought with him stuck all over the city, and sent to all the towns of the island, with the words, "Vote for immediate annexation under the rule of Victor Emmanuel." The Sicilians neither knew now cared anything for Victor Emmanuel, whose very name was almost unknown to the peasants. It was Garibaldi who had delivered them, and they were perfectly ready to accept any form of government that he recommended. Garibaldi at once told Farina that he would not allow such proceedings. The latter maintained that he was there under the authority of the king, and should take any steps he chose; whereupon the general sent at once for a party of troops, who seized him and carried him on board Persano's ships, with the advice that he should quit the island at once. This put an effectual stop to several intrigues to reap the entire fruits of Garibaldi's efforts.

Frank had passed a weary time. His wound had been a serious one, and at first the surgeons had thought that it would be necessary to amputate the limb. Garibaldi, however, who, in spite of his many occupations, found time to come in twice a day for a few minutes' talk with him, urged them, before operating, to try every means to save the arm; and two weeks after Frank received the wound, the care that had been bestowed upon him, and his own excellent constitution enabled them to state confidently that he need no longer have any anxiety upon that account, as his recovery was now but a question of time. The general thanked Frank for the early information sent by him of Bosco's arrival, and for his defence of the house, and as a reward for these and his other services promoted him to the rank of captain. A fortnight later, he was so far convalescent that he could move about with his arm in a sling. He had already regained most of his bodily strength, and by the end of the second week in July he was again on horseback.

He was, then, delighted when, on July 17th, he heard that Garibaldi was going to start at once to assist Medici, who, with Cosenz, had advanced to within some twenty miles of Messina, and had had some skirmishes with a force of six thousand five hundred picked troops with a powerful artillery. The Neapolitans, who were commanded by General Bosco, had now taken up a very strong position near the town and fortress of Milazzo.

Colonel Corti arrived at Palermo on that day with nine hundred men in an American ship. He had left Genoa at the same time as Medici, but the vessel was captured by Neapolitan men-of-war, and towed into Naples, where she was anchored under the guns of the fort. She lay there for twenty-two days, when the strong remonstrances of the American minister forced the government of Naples to allow her to leave. She now arrived just in time for those on board to take part in the operations. Garibaldi embarked a portion of them on a British merchantman he had chartered, and proceeded on board with his staff. The next day he landed at the port of Patti, some twenty miles from Milazzo, and on the 19th joined Medici's force.

A strong brigade that had been sent by land had not yet arrived, but Garibaldi determined to attack at once. The position of the Neapolitan force was a very strong one. Their right extended across the front of the fortress of Milazzo, and was protected by its artillery; its approaches were hidden by cactus hedges, which screened the defenders from view, and could not be penetrated by an attacking force, except after cutting them down with swords or axes. The centre was posted across the road leading along the shore. Its face was defended by a strong wall, which had been loopholed. In front of this the ground was covered with a thick growth of canes, through which it was scarcely possible for men to force their way. The Neapolitan left were stationed in a line of houses lying at right-angles to the centre, and therefore capable of maintaining a flanking fire on any force advancing to the attack.

The Garibaldians suffered from the very great disadvantage of being ignorant of the nature of the ground and of the enemy's position, the Neapolitans being completely hidden from view by the cactus hedges and cane brakes. Garibaldi had intended to attack before daylight, but the various corps were so widely scattered that it was broad day before the fight began. As soon as the force had assembled they advanced across the plain, which was covered with trees and vineyards, and as they approached the enemy's position they were received with a heavy fire by the unseen foe. For hours the fight went on. In vain the Garibaldians attempted to reach their hidden enemies, for each time they gathered and rushed forward, they were met by so heavy a fire that they were forced to retire. The left wing, indeed, gave way altogether and fell back some distance from the battle-field, but the centre and right, where Garibaldi himself, with Medici and many of his best officers were fighting, still persevered.

At one o'clock Garibaldi sent off several of his officers to endeavour to rally and bring up some of the scattered detachments of the left wing. After a lot of hard work they returned with a considerable force. Garibaldi, at the head of sixty picked men, made his way along the shore, until, unobserved, they reached a point on the flank of the enemy's left wing; then, pouring in a heavy volley they dashed forward, captured a gun, and drove the Neapolitans from their line of defence. Suddenly, however, a squadron of the enemy's cavalry fell upon the Garibaldians and drove them back in disorder. Garibaldi himself was forced off the road into a ditch; four troopers attacked him, but he defended himself with his sword, until Missori, one of his aides-de-camp, rode up and shot three of the dragoons.

The other troops, who had been following at a distance, now came up; and together they advanced, driving before them the defenders of the enemy's entrenchments, until these, losing heart, broke into flight towards the town. The panic spread, and at all points the Garibaldians burst through the defences, in spite of the fire of the guns of the fortress, and pursued the flying enemy into the town. Here a sanguinary contest was maintained for some hours, but at last the Neapolitan troops were all driven into the fortress, which, now that the town had been evacuated by their own men, opened fire upon it. The gunners were, however, much harassed by the deadly fire maintained by Peard and his companions; all of whom were armed with rifles of the best pattern, while the guns of the Garibaldian frigate played upon the sea face of the fortress. The position was, in fact, untenable. General Bosco knew that no assistance could reach him, for the greater portion of the Neapolitan troops had already withdrawn from the island. The little fortress was crowded with troops, and he had but a small supply of provisions.

Three days later, he hoisted the white flag, and sent one of his officers into the town to negotiate terms of surrender. These were speedily concluded. All artillery, ammunition, and the mules used by the artillery and transport, were left behind, and the troops were to be allowed to march, with their firearms, down to the wharf; there to be conveyed on board the ships in the harbour, and landed on the mainland.

Frank had not taken part in the battle of Milazzo, which had cost the Garibaldians over a thousand in killed and wounded; for he had been despatched by Garibaldi, when the latter went on board ship at Palermo, to General Bixio, who was in the centre of the island, to inform him of the general's advance, and to state that probably he would be in Messina in a week. He said that some little time must elapse before the arrangements for the passage across to the mainland could be effected; and that Bixio was to continue to stamp out the communistic movement, that had burst out in several of the towns there, and to scatter the bands of brigands; and was, a fortnight after Frank's arrival, to march with his force to Messina.

Frank would have much preferred to accompany the general, but the latter said: "No doubt, Percival, you would have liked to go with me, but someone must be sent, and my choice has fallen upon you. I have chosen you because, in the first place, you are your father's son. You have already distinguished yourself greatly, and have fought as fearlessly and as steadily as the best of my old followers. Surely it would be impossible for me to give you higher praise than that. In the next place, you are not yet fit for the hard work of the campaign. Mantoni tells me that it will be some weeks before your arm will be strong again; though the bone has healed better than he had expected, after the serious injury you received in your gallant defence of that house, when Bosco entered the town.

"But even had it not been for that, I think that you have done more than your share. There are many ardent spirits who have arrived from the mainland, who have not yet had a chance of striking a blow for their country; and it is but fair that they should have their opportunity. Moreover, your mother sent you out on a special mission, first to hand to me her noble gift, and secondly to search the prisons in the towns we might occupy, for her father, and possibly her husband. She knew that, going with me, you must share in the perils and honours of the campaign. You have done so gloriously, but in that way you have done enough. Grievous indeed would it be to me had I to write to your good mother to say that the son she had sent me had been killed. Her father has been a victim for Italian liberty. Her husband has, if our suspicions are well founded, sacrificed himself by the fearlessness with which he exposed the iniquities of the tyrants' prison-houses. It would be too cruel that she should be deprived of her son also.

"I regard it as certain that you will not find those you seek in the prisons of this island. As you saw when we opened the doors here, there were no prisoners from the mainland among those confined there. You will be with me when we cross the straits: it is there that your mission will really begin, and it is best that you should reserve yourself for that. The battle I go to fight now will be the last that will be needed, to secure at least the independence of Sicily. And I doubt much whether, when we have once crossed, we shall have to fight as hard as we have done. Here we landed a handful; we shall land on the mainland over twenty thousand strong; the enemy despised us then—they will fear us now."

"Thank you, general; I should not have thought of questioning your orders, whatever they might have been, but I felt for a moment a little disappointment that I was not to take part in the next battle. I will start at once to join General Bixio. Will it be necessary for me to stay with him till he marches to Messina, or can I ride for that city when I have delivered your orders?"

"In that you can consult your own wishes, but be assured that I shall not attempt to cross the straits until Bixio joins me; and I should say that you would find it more interesting with him than doing routine work at Messina; moreover, you must remember that the population there are not all united in our favour, as they are here. They are doubtless glad to be free, but the agents of the revolutionists have been at work among them, and, as you know, with such success that I have been obliged to send Bixio with a division to suppress the disorders that have arisen. I have not freed Sicily to hand it over to Mazzini's agents, but that it shall form a part of United Italy under Victor Emmanuel. Still there is enough excitement existing there to render it somewhat hazardous for one of my officers to ride alone through the country, and I think that it would be much better for you therefore to remain with Bixio."

CHAPTER X

WITH BIXIO

JUST as the ship carrying Garibaldi and his followers weighed anchor, Frank rode out from Palermo. The road was the best in the island, and he arrived late that evening at Polizzi, a distance of some forty miles from Palermo. On the following day he halted at Traina; here he found a detachment of Bixio's brigade, which was commanded by Rubini, who welcomed him most cordially.

"Who would have thought of seeing you, Percival! Surely the general is not coming this way?"

"He started yesterday to join Medici, and give battle to Bosco, who has some seven thousand picked troops at Milazzo. He has sent me here with an order for Bixio."

"It is enough to make one tear one's hair," Rubini said, "to think that we are out of it."

"Well, we have done our share, Rubini, and although I was disappointed at first, I admit that it is only fair that the men who have done no fighting should have a turn. We have lost about a third of our number, and most of us have been wounded. Medici's corps have never fired a shot yet, nor have those of Cosenz; we shall have our share again when we cross to Calabria. Now, what are you doing here?"

"We are scattered about in small detachments, giving a sharp lesson, whenever we get the chance, to the revolutionists."

"But who are the revolutionists?"

"They are agents of the revolutionary committee—that is, of Mazzini and his fanatics—and it seems that several parties of them were landed on the east coast to get up a row on their own account; and just as Farina has been trying to induce the country to throw over Garibaldi, and declare for Victor Emmanuel, of whom the people know nothing, and for whom they care less, these agents have been trying to get them to declare for a republic, and they have certainly had more success than Farina had. There is nothing tangible in the idea of a king, while, when the poor fools are told that a republic means that the land and property of the rich are to be handed over to the poor, the programme has its attractions. At any rate, it has its attractions for the brigands, of whom, at the best of times, there are always a number in the forests on the slopes of Etna; and I have no doubt that money was freely distributed among them to inflame their zeal. Several houses of well-to-do citizens and country proprietors had been looted, and something like a reign of terror had begun, before Bixio's brigade marched to restore order.

"You see there are a great many more of these bands in the forests than usual. After the rising in the winter was suppressed, very many of those who took part in it dared not return to their homes, and so fled to the hills; the better class of these men came in as soon as our capture of Palermo made it safe for them to do so. A company of them has been formed, and is now with Bixio, and I believe that others have enlisted with Medici; still there are a good many of the lower class who joined in the rising, still among the hills. In a rebellion like this the insurgents would be divided into two classes—the one true patriots, the other men who join, in the hope of plunder, the discontented riffraff of the towns. A life in the mountains offers great attractions to these: in the first place they don't have to work for a living, and in the next there is always the chance of carrying off some rich proprietor and getting a large ransom for him. These therefore go to swell the ranks of the men who have for years set the authorities of the island at defiance, and have terrorised all the people dwelling on the plains at the foot of Etna.

"Just at present all these men call themselves republicans, and had it not been for Bixio's arrival they would have established a perfect reign of terror. We here have shot a good many, and I believe Bixio has also given them some sharp lessons; at any rate, our presence here has effectually stopped the game of the revolutionists in the towns and villages on the plain, but it will be a long time indeed before brigandage can be suppressed, and of course there is no intention of attempting such a business now; that will be a work that must be undertaken by government, when Italy has achieved her freedom, and feels in a position to turn her attention to putting down these bands which have for years past—I may almost say for centuries—been a disgrace to our land. We are here solely to put a stop to the revolutionary movement, just as Garibaldi put a stop to the royal movement by sending Farina out of the island."

"And where is Bixio?"

"He has been sweeping through the small towns and villages round the foot of the mountains, and will this afternoon, I believe, arrive at Bronte, which has been the headquarters of this revolutionary business. I expect he will put his foot heavily on the men who have been foremost in stirring the people up there. Bixio is just the man for this work. He knows that one sharp lesson impresses the minds of people like these Sicilians, and has far more effect than lenient measures or verbal reproofs. They have to be taught that it is not for them to meddle in the affairs of state. All these matters must be left to their representatives in parliament and the government of the country. The petty authorities of these little towns come to regard themselves as important personages, and indulge themselves in prating on public affairs instead of minding their own business, which, in this case, is to do their best to give protection to the people in their districts against the incursions of bands of brigands. I suppose you go on to-morrow?"

"Yes; I shall start at daybreak; it is not many hours' ride."

"I have about a score of mounted men here, Percival. I will send four of them with you."

"Surely there is no occasion for that," Frank said.

"Well, I don't know: I think there is. There are no large bands, so far as I know, down in the plain at present; but some of these gangs have broken up, especially those that came from the mainland, and have not as yet taken to the mountains. They go about perpetrating crimes at detached houses or on any traveller they meet. I need not say that at present their animosity to the red shirts is bitter, and that in revenge for their comrades who have been shot or hanged, they would certainly kill any of us on whom they could lay hands; so it would be better for you to have four men as an escort. They might as well be doing that as anything else, for just at present there is nothing going on about here, and it is as dull as it would be in a small garrison town in Northern Italy. How long do you suppose it will be before we join Garibaldi at Messina?"

"Not for some little time, I think. If he and Medici defeat Bosco at Milazzo, as I suppose they will, he will at once go on to Messina; but his message to Bixio was that it must take some time to make the preparations for crossing to the mainland, and that until he sends word to the general to join him, he is to continue his work of stamping out this movement in restoring order, in reorganising the municipal authorities, and in placing the administration of the towns and villages in the hands of well-affected men, so that there can be no chance of Mazzini's party causing any serious disturbances again, after he has left."

"I see you still wear your arm in a sling?"

"Yes; Mantoni told me that it would not be safe to take it out of the splints for another month, but he had every hope that when I did so I should be able to use it, though I must not put too much strain on it. Of course it is a nuisance, but I have every reason to be thankful, for I was afraid for a time that I was going to lose it altogether."

"It was a grand thing, the defence of that house, Percival."

"It was a grand thing that that shell struck the stairs just when it did, for another minute would have seen the end of the defence and of our lives. As it was, that explosion saved four of us, for the wounded men we carried off are all convalescent,—and also the lives of five women and eight children, for, exasperated as the Neapolitans were, they would assuredly have shown no more mercy there than they did in the other houses they entered. I have been well rewarded, for Garibaldi has made me captain."

Sarto and Maffio returned at this moment, and the three heartily congratulated Frank on his promotion. They had been away with a small detachment to a village three miles distant, in search of a man who had been one of the most prominent in stirring up the peasantry, but he had left before they got there. They spent a pleasant evening together, and in the morning Frank started with the four mounted men and rode to Bronte. Just as he approached the town he heard several volleys of musketry, and on inquiry found that thirty men who had been captured on the march or caught in hiding in the town had been shot. All were strangers—either revolutionary agents or brigands. On inquiring for the general, he found that he had just gone to the town hall, where he had ordered the municipal authorities and the principal citizens to meet him. Putting up his horse, he went there first. Bixio had just begun to speak.

"If I had done my duty," he said, "you as well as the men who have been stirring up riot and revolution would be lying dead outside the town. It is scandalous that you, men who have been elected by your fellows for the maintenance of order and good government in this town and district, should allow yourselves to be terrified into obedience by a handful of agitators, instead of calling out all the men capable of bearing arms and suppressing the sedition at once. You have failed miserably in your duty. The man who came as your deliverer is now, in the hour of battle, weakened by being compelled to send part of his army to suppress the disorder at which you have connived. You private citizens are scarcely less to blame: when you saw that these men were allowing brigandage and robbery to go on unchecked and making speeches subversive of order instead of doing their duty, you should have taken the matter into your own hands, expelled them from the offices they disgraced, and appointed worthier men as your representatives."

He spoke to an officer standing by him, who went out and returned with twenty soldiers who had been drawn up outside the hall. Bixio remained silent during his absence, and now said: "Captain Silvio, you will arrest the syndic and these municipal councillors, and march them off to prison. They may think themselves fortunate that I do not order them to be shot for conniving at sedition, and permitting these brigands to carry on their work of crime with impunity."

The soldiers surrounded the men pointed out, and marched away with them.

"Now, sirs," Bixio then went on to the private citizens, "you will at once placard the town with notices that the most worthy and loyal man in the town, whoever he may be, is nominated by me as syndic, and that twelve others, all of them loyal and true men, are appointed municipal councillors. I leave it to you to make the choice, but mind that it be a good one. Of course I wish men of standing and influence to be appointed, but the one absolute qualification is that they shall be men who have shown themselves opposed to the conduct of those who will pass the next six months in prison; who can be trusted to maintain law and order with a strong hand, to punish malefactors, and to carry out all orders they may receive from General Garibaldi, Dictator of the Island of Sicily. Let me have the names of the men you have chosen in the course of an hour. I shall have inquiries made as to the character and reputation of each before confirming their appointment. I have nothing more to say."

The men retired, looking greatly crestfallen; and Bixio, turning round, saw for the first time Frank, who had quietly taken up his place behind him. The young fellow had been a great favourite of his ever since he saw him on the occasion of his first visit to Garibaldi.

"Ah, Percival, I am glad to see you, and that you should be here is a proof that your arm is getting stronger. I suppose you are here on duty?"

"Yes, sir; knowing that rumours of various kinds might reach you, the general has sent me to tell you that he has started with a portion of Cosenz's men to reinforce Medici, and to attack Bosco at Milazzo. He considers that he will have sufficient force for the purpose, but if not, he will, in a couple of days after he arrives there, be joined by the rest of Cosenz's command, who are proceeding by land. After beating Bosco, he will go on to Messina. It will take him a considerable time to make all the preparations needful for the expedition to the mainland, and he wishes you to continue your work here, to put down all disorder, and to organise and establish strong and loyal municipal and district councils in this part of the island, so that when he advances, he need have no cause for any anxiety whatever for the state of affairs here. He will send you ample notice when all is in readiness for the invasion of Calabria."

"I should like to be at Milazzo," Bixio said, "but as that is now impossible I should prefer remaining here until Garibaldi is ready to start, to hanging about Messina for weeks: that sort of thing is very bad for young troops. Here they get plenty of marching, and a certain amount of drill every day, and in another month or six weeks even the latest recruits, who arrived before we left Palermo, will be fit to take part in a battle by the side of our veterans. Are you to stay with me, or to go on to Messina?"

"I had no explicit order, sir, but from what the general said, I gathered that he thought it better for me to stay, at any rate for the present, with you. The doctor said that I must keep my arm in a sling for some time to come, and although I did not ride here at any great speed, I feel some sharp twinges in it, and think I should wait a few days before I mount again. After that I shall be happy to carry out any orders, or perform any duty, with which you may think fit to intrust me."

"Quite right, Percival. You will, of course, be attached to my staff while you are with me, and I will set you to easy work when I consider you fit to undertake it. Now that I have put things in train here, I shall make it my headquarters for a time, but shall be sending parties to the hills. I know that the villages there are all terrorised by the brigands, and although it is hopeless to try to stamp these fellows out, I may strike a few blows at them. The worst of it is, that half the peasantry are in alliance with them, and the other half know that it as much as their lives are worth to give any information as to the brigands' movements, so that to a large extent I shall have to trust to luck. When you are able to ride again, I will send you off with one of these parties, for I am sure that the air of the slopes of Etna would do an immense deal towards setting you up again, while the heat in the plains is very trying, especially to those who are not in robust health, and are unaccustomed to a climate like this."

"It is hot," Frank said. "I started my journeys very early in the morning, and stopped for five or six hours in the middle of the day; but I think that, even in that way, the heat has taken a good deal more out of me than the fatigue of riding."

"I have no doubt that is so; and I could recommend you, for the next week, to rise at daybreak, lie down, or at any rate keep within doors, between ten or eleven and five in the afternoon, and then take gentle exercise again, and enjoy yourself until eleven or twelve o'clock at night. Even the natives of the island keep indoors as far as possible during the heat of the day, at this time of year, and if they find it necessary, it is still more so for you. I suppose you came through Traina last night?"

"Yes, sir; and was very glad to find Rubini and my other two friends there."

The next week passed pleasantly. Bixio himself was often away, making flying visits to the towns and villages where he had left detachments; but as there were several of the officers of the force at Bronte, who had crossed in the same ship with him from Genoa, and by whose side he had fought at Calatafimi and Palermo, Frank had very pleasant society. Indeed, as the majority of the force were men of good family and education, there was, when off duty, little distinction of rank, and with the tie of good comradeship, and of dangers and fatigues borne in common, there was none of the stiffness and exclusiveness that necessarily prevail in regular armies. All of the original thousand knew Frank well, had heard how largely the expedition was indebted for its success to the aid his mother had sent, and how he had distinguished himself in the fighting, and they welcomed him everywhere with the utmost cordiality.

Early in the morning he always went for a walk, and was usually accompanied by one or two of his acquaintances who happened to be off duty. After taking a meal, he generally spent the evening sitting in the open air in front of the principal *café*, eating ices, drinking coffee, and chatting with the officers who gathered there. At the end of a week he no longer felt even passing pains in his arm, and reported to Bixio that he was ready for work again.

"Not hard work," the general said; "but I can give you employment that will suit you. I am calling in Rubini's detachment from Traina, where things are settling down, and shall send fifty men under his command to the village of Latinano. It is some three thousand feet above the sea, and you will find it much more cool and pleasant there than it is here. Other villages, on about the same line, will also be occupied. The brigands have found that it is no longer safe to come down into the plains, and I am going to push them as far up the slopes as I can: possibly we may then be able to obtain some information from the peasants below that line as to the principal haunts of these fellows in the mountains. At present these villages that I am going to occupy are all used by the brigands, whom the people regard as good customers; and though they ill-treat and murder without mercy any they suspect of being hostile to them, it is of course to their interest to keep well with the majority, and to pay for what they want. Terror will do a great deal towards keeping men's mouths shut; but anything like the general ill-treatment of the population would soon drive somebody to betray them.

"Of course, hitherto the brigands have had little fear of treachery. The commanders of the Bourbon troops had no disposition to enter upon toilsome expeditions, which offered small prospect of success, merely to avenge the wrongs of the peasants; but now matters have changed. We are not only willing, but eager, to suppress these bands; and, seeing that we are in earnest, some of the peasantry may pluck up heart enough to endeavor to get rid of those who at present hold them at their mercy.

"However, I own I have no very great hopes that it will be so. There exists, and has existed for many years, an association called the Mafia, which extends over the whole island. It comprises men of all classes, from the highest to the lowest, and exercises a terrible power. No one, save the leaders, know who are its members, and therefore each distrusts his neighbour. A murder is committed. Every one may be perfectly well aware who is its author, and yet no one dare say a word. If by some chance the carabinieri, knowing the assassin had a standing feud with the victim, lay hands upon him, the organisation sets to work. The judge himself may be a member; if not, he speedily receives an intimation that his own life will be forfeited if the murderer is condemned. But it is seldom that this is necessary. The jailors are bribed or terrorised, and when the time comes for him to be brought to trial, it is found that he has mysteriously escaped; and, in the few cases where a man is brought into court, no witnesses dare appear against him, and he is certain to be acquitted. It is a scandalous state of things, and one which, we may hope, will be changed when Italy is free, and able to attend to its domestic affairs. But at present the organisation is all-powerful, so that you see it is not only the vengeance of the brigands, but the power of the Mafia, which seals men's mouths, and enables criminals to carry on their proceedings with but little fear of the arm of the law."

"I am much obliged to you for sending me up with Rubini," Frank said; "and I shall greatly enjoy the mountain air, but I hardly see that I can be of much service there."

"Not much, perhaps; but it will fit you to do duty when we land in Calabria. Rubini's corps is, like the rest, composed partly of men who have seen service before, with a few of the thousand; but with them are a large proportion of fresh arrivals, as brave, no doubt, as the others, but without their experience. He will at times make excursions if he can obtain news of a party of brigands being in the neighbourhood, in which case he will naturally take the men he can most rely upon; and I shall request him when he is away to intrust the command of those left in the village to you, who are one of the thousand. You are a captain, as I heard with much pleasure in a letter from Garibaldi, and on the general's staff; and as you showed how stoutly you could defend a house against an overwhelming force, you could certainly hold a village with fifteen or twenty men against any number of brigands who might try to take advantage of the absence of a portion of the force to attack those that remained there. However, it is not likely that anything of the sort will take place; the brigands are not fond of fighting unless there is ample booty to be obtained, though they might endeavour to avenge the losses they have sustained by a sudden attack, if they thought they could take you wholly unawares. Rubini will arrive here with his corps to-morrow afternoon, and will start the next day with half his detachment; the other half will go to Malfi, a village ten miles from Latinano."

"You are looking better," Rubini said, as Frank met him, when the company piled arms in the principal square in the town. "You said you were all right when I saw you the other day, but you were not looking so."

"No; I was feeling the ride, and my arm was hurting me a bit. However, ten days' rest has set me all right again, and I am quite equal to moderate work. Do you know what you are going to do?"

"No, I have only orders to march in here to-day."

"Well, I can tell you. Several detachments, of fifty men each, are going up to the villages some three thousand feet up the slopes of Etna. Your company is to be divided into two. You with half of them are to go to Latinano, and the other half to Malfi, a place ten miles from it. Your lieutenant, Pasco, will take the other wing to Malfi. I am going with you."

"Well, in that case I shall not mind it, though it will not be lively there unless we have a brush with the brigands. It will at any rate be a great deal cooler than Traina, which was an oven for six hours every day. Are you going as second in command?"

"To a certain extent, yes. Bixio said that, as I should be no good for fighting at present, I was to take command of the village when you were away brigand-hunting. He said that naturally you would take your best men for that work, and leave some of those who have had as yet no experience in fighting to take care of the village."

"Well, they could not be left in better hands than yours," Rubini said heartily. "I shall be very glad to have you with me."

At daybreak the next morning Rubini's little column got

into motion. Frank was the only mounted officer, and he took his place by the side of Bixio, who marched at the head of the column. The rise was steady, and though occasionally they came to steeper places, there was no pause, with the exception of a couple of halts for a few minutes, and they reached Latinano at eleven o'clock, having been nearly seven hours on the way. There was no demonstration of welcome when they arrived, nor did they expect it. Doubtless such of the villagers as felt glad to see them march in would be afraid to show it openly, as they would assuredly suffer, were they to do so, when the troop marched away again. Rubini at once quartered his men in twos and threes among the houses. He himself, with Frank as his lieutenant, accepted the invitation of the priest, whose house was the best in the village, to stay there.

"It is not like the Palazzo at Palermo, Percival," Rubini laughed; "but you can scarcely expect that on Mount Etna; at any rate, it is a vast improvement on our camping ground on the plains."

The priest set before them what provisions he had in the house, and assured them that he would provide better for them in the future. Rubini, however, knowing how poor were the priests of these mountain villages, told him that, although they thankfully accepted his hospitality on that occasion, they would in the future cater for themselves.

"We have," he said, "two waggons following us; they will be up by the evening. We have no idea of imposing ourselves, or our men, upon the inhabitants of this village, who assuredly could hardly fill fifty additional mouths. We have brought with us flour, wine, and other necessaries, and no doubt we shall be able to purchase sheep and goats from your people, who, by the way, did not appear to be very much pleased at our arrival."

"You must not blame them, signor. In the first place, they are poor; and once, when a detachment of Bourbon troops came up here, they devoured everything, and paid for nothing: happily they only stayed for a week, or the village would have been ruined. After the tales that have been spread of the lawlessness of Garibaldi's troops, they must have feared that even worse than what before happened was about to befall them."

"They do nothing but tell lies of us," Rubini said angrily. "Never since we landed at Marsala have we taken a mouthful of food without paying for it, unless it has been spontaneously offered to us, as it was when we were fighting at Palermo."

"I have no doubt that what you say is true, signor; but the poor people have been taught to believe otherwise, so they are hardly to blame if they did not evince any lively joy at our arrival. Moreover, they do not know how long you are going to stay here, and are well aware that any who show satisfaction at your coming, or who afford you any aid or hospitality beyond that which they dare not refuse, will be reported to the brigands, who will take a terrible revenge after you have left the village."

"I can understand that their position is not a comfortable one," Rubini said; "but the people of these districts have largely brought it upon themselves. I do not say that they are in a position to resist large parties of brigands, but their sympathy seems to be everywhere with these scoundrels; they afford them every information in their power, screen them in every way, give false information to the carabinieri, and hinder the course of justice. People who act thus must not be surprised if they are regarded as allies of these bands, and they must put up with the inconvenience of having troops quartered upon them, and may think themselves fortunate that the consequences are no worse. At present we are not here to act against the brigands alone, as that work must be postponed until other matters are settled, and the government has time to turn its attention to rooting out a state of things that is disgraceful to the country. We are here now as the agents of General Garibaldi, Dictator of Sicily, to suppress—not crime—but the stirring-up of insurrection and revolt against the existing government of the island."

"I heartily wish that it could be rooted out," the priest said. "I can assure you that we, whose work lies in these mountain villages, feel the evil consequences to the full as much as those who work in the towns and villages lying round the foot of the mountains. It is not that our people suffer so greatly in pocket—for the most part they are too poor to be robbed; the few that are better off pay a yearly contribution, and as long as they do so are left in peace, while the better class down in the plains are liable at any time to be seized and compelled to pay perhaps their all to save their lives. The harm is rather to their souls than to their bodies; as you say, their sympathies are wholly with the brigands, they come to regard them as heroes, and to think lightly of the terrible crimes they commit upon others; and not infrequently some young man more enterprising than the rest, or one who has perhaps stabbed a rival in love or has been drawn for service in the army, takes to the hills and joins them, and for so doing he incurs no reprobation whatever. 'Tis a sad state of things, and I trust that when your general has settled all other matters in the island he will employ his whole force in a campaign against the brigands. It is not a work to be taken up by small parties; the evil has grown to such dimensions that nothing short of an army would root it out, and indeed it could only then be accomplished by months of patient work, so extensive are the forests, so great the facility for concealment."

"It will fall to other hands than Garibaldi's father. His mission is to deliver Sicily and the mainland from the Bourbon rule, and then to hand them over to Victor Emmanuel, who, a free king over a free nation, will be able to remove all these abuses that have flourished under the Bourbons. As for us, we are soldiers without pay, fighting for love of our country. When we have done our work and freed it from its oppressors, we shall return to our homes, and leave it to the king, his parliament, and the regular army to put down such abuses as this brigandage. I suppose, father, it would hardly be fair to ask you if there are many of these fellows in the neighbourhood?"

The priest smiled. "I do not mind telling you that there was a band of some fifty of them within five miles of this place yesterday. This morning it was known that several detachments of troops would march from Bronte at daybreak, and that their destination was the mountains. I have no doubt whatever that the news was carried to the band half an hour later; and by this time they are probably twenty miles away up in the forests, but in which direction I have no idea, nor do I know what their plans are. It may be that so long as these villages are held they will move round to the other side of Etna. It may be that several of the bands will unite and attack one or other of your parties, not for what they think they would get, but as a lesson that it would be better to leave them alone. I should say that, except by pure accident, you are not likely to catch sight of a brigand—unless, indeed, one comes down here as a shepherd from the hills, to make some small purchases, and to gather news."

"I think that is likely to be the result of our journey," Rubini laughed; "but, nevertheless, our being here will have served its purpose. So long as we and the other detachments are up here, the brigands will not care to venture into the plain; nor will the agents of the revolution who are with them. If they do, they are not likely to get safely back again. I may tell you that signals have been arranged by which smoke from the hill-tops near Bronte will give us information that some of these bands have passed down the mountain, the direction in which they have gone, and that in which they are retiring; and I fancy they will hardly regain the mountains without being intercepted by one or other of our parties. It is true that we shall not remain here very long; but by the time we go, there will be a very different system established throughout the island; and they will find in future that they can no longer get friends and abettors among the local authorities, but will have to meet an active resistance, that plunder cannot be obtained without fighting, and that even when obtained it will not be carried off to the hills without a hot pursuit being maintained."

"I shall be glad indeed if it is so," the priest said. "If the people of the towns and villages will but combine, and are actively supported by small bodies of troops in all the towns, it will deal a far heavier blow to brigandage than can be effected by sending flying expeditions into the mountains."

CHAPTER XI

A HAZARDOUS EXPEDITION

"I FANCY, Percival, that the brigands are far more likely to find us than we are to find them," Rubini said on the following morning, when he and Frank strolled out into the village. "We can expect no information from these people; and as to marching about on the off chance of lighting upon them, it would be simply absurd. On the other hand, the brigands will know, by this time, where all our detachments are quartered, and what is their strength. They must be furious at the losses they have had down in the plains; some forty or fifty of them have been killed in fights, and over a hundred shot, at Bronte and other towns. They must be burning for vengeance. I cannot help thinking that some of these bands are likely to unite, and attack some of our posts. Even if they came a couple of hundred strong, we might feel pretty safe of beating them off if they ventured by daylight; but a sudden attack at night might be extremely serious."

"Very serious indeed," Frank agreed. "Scattered as the men are, through the village, they would be shot down as they came out of the houses."

"It is an awkward position, certainly," Rubini said, "and one that I don't see my way out of."

"I should say, Rubini, the best thing we could do would be to quarter ourselves in the church."

"It would be a very serious step," Rubini said gravely. "We know that one of the great weapons the Neapolitans have used against us is, that we are heretics and atheists; and were we to occupy the church, reports would circulate through the island that we were desecrators."

"They spread that sort of reports whether there is any foundation for it or not, Rubini; besides, at Palermo we used several of the churches as hospitals for the wounded. But there would be no occasion for us to live and take our meals in the church, or to interfere with the services. If we keep half a dozen sentries round the village, we need not fear any surprise during the daytime, but could go on as usual in the houses where we are quartered, taking our meals there, and so on; then at night we could retire to the church, and sleep there securely with a couple of sentries posted at the door."

"I think that is a very good idea; at any rate, we will tell the priest when we go in to breakfast, and hear what he says. He is a good fellow, I think—though, of course, his hands are very much tied by the position he is placed in."

After they had eaten their breakfast, Rubini went with Frank to the priest's room.

"Padre," he said "we don't like our position here. It is certain that the brigands have no reason to love us, and that after the numbers who have been put out of the way down below, they must be thirsting for revenge."

"That is certainly to be expected," the priest said gravely.

"Therefore we think it is by no means unlikely that several of these bands will unite in an attack on one of our posts."

"I hinted as much as that to you last night."

"You did, padre; and the more I think of it, the more

probable it seems to me that this is what they will do. It may be this post, or another; but I feel that, although we could beat off any attack in the daytime, it would be most serious were they to fall upon us at night, when we are scattered throughout the village."

"It would certainly be so, signor. The consequences would, I think, be most grave."

"Therefore, padre, we intend to retire to the church every evening."

"Between ourselves, Captain Rubini, I am not sorry that you have made that proposal, or rather, have announced to me your intention of doing so. You will understand that it was a suggestion that could not come from me, and that I bow to your decision, having no means of resisting it; that being understood, I can say, frankly, that I think the plan a wise one. I hope that you do not intend to occupy it during the day, nor to eat and drink there, but simply to pass the night in the shelter of its walls, and that at all other times our services can be held as usual?"

"Certainly; that is our intention. We wish to put the people to no inconvenience, and to abstain, as far as possible, from doing aught that would hurt their feelings, by, as they would consider it, desecrating the church. Things will simply go on as they do now in the daytime, but at nightfall we shall march into the church, and place two sentries at the door; and in the morning we shall leave it, after placing everything in order, as far as we can, at a quarter to six—so that you can hold your morning mass at the usual hour."

"I am well pleased with the arrangement. Should my people or others complain of your thus using the church,

I can say that it was no proposal of mine, and that you did not ask my opinion on the subject; but simply informed me of your intention, which, of course, I have no power to combat. I may tell you that I have no sure intelligence whatever that the brigands meditate such an attempt, either here or at other villages, where parties of your troops have gone; but knowing the people as I do, I think it very likely that such an attack may be made. I myself, a well-wisher of your general and of his great movement, am convinced that the people can never be raised from their present condition, so long as we are subject to the government of Naples. I believe that, with freedom, the island would advance, not only in prosperity, but in orderly life and all the blessings of civilisation; and none will hail more heartily than I the establishment of a constitutional government, such as is enjoyed by that portion of Italy under the rule of Victor Emmanuel. Still, so long as things exist as they do in the mountains, it would do more harm than good, were I to declare my feelings. I speak not of personal danger, but I should lose all power and influence over my flock; therefore, though heartily wishing you well, I cannot openly aid you. I shall on Sunday speak from the pulpit, pointing out that the conduct of your soldiers shows that the reports that have been circulated regarding them are untrue; that they come here with no evil intentions towards us, and that I trust when they retire they will carry with them the good wishes of all; that I hope above all things, nothing will occur that will cause trouble, still less evil to our guests, for not only have they given no occasion for animosity, but if any harm befall them here, we may be sure that their general at Bronte will send up a strong body of troops, who will probably burn the village to the ground, and shoot every man they catch. I should say, signor, that my words would be more likely to have effect were some of your soldiers, and perhaps one of yourselves, to attend mass daily; this would show that you were not, as they have been told, despisers of all religion, and go far to remove the unfavourable impression with which I cannot deny that you are regarded."

"The suggestion is a good one, sir," Rubini said, "and I will see that it is carried out. I will come each morning. Captain Percival is an Englishman, and what you would call a heretic, so he will, I know, undertake to be on duty about that hour."

"Then we quite understand each other, padre: openly you protest against our using the church, privately you approve of our doing so?"

"My protest will not be a strong one," the priest said, with a smile; "indeed, I shall tell my people that, although I have thought it my duty to protest formally, I cannot but see that it is best that it should be so, as it will ensure peace and tranquillity in the village, and will do away with the risks of broils when men sit drinking after dark in wine-shops."

When the church bell rang for the midday mass, the villagers were surprised to see Rubini enter the edifice, and that some twenty of his men straggled in, not as a body ordered to take part in a service, but as if it was their regular custom as individuals to attend service. Before the bell ceased ringing, Frank also went in, and sat down by Rubini; when they left together at the close of a short service Rubini said, "I did not expect to see you, Percival."

"Why not?" Frank replied: "if there were a Protestant

church, of course I should go to it, but as there is not, I come here. Surely it is better to say one's prayers in a church of a religion that on all its main points differs but slightly from our own, than to abstain from going to church at all. And now, what are we to do with ourselves? I suppose we can hardly start for a long walk?"

"I should think not," Rubini said grimly—"at least, not without taking twenty men with us. It is as likely as not that we are watched from the forest, and if we were to go out alone, we might be pounced upon by fellows lying in ambush for us, or at best get a bullet through our head."

"At best?" Frank laughed.

"Certainly at best," Rubini replied gravely. "It would be better to die with a bullet through one's head than to fall into the hands of these vindictive scoundrels, who would certainly select some much slower and more painful way of putting an end to our existence. No, there must be no walking about beyond the edge of the village."

"Then, in fact, Rubini, our journey up here is to be a mere useless promenade?"

"I am afraid so. There is only one hope. It may be taken as a fact that in every band of scoundrels—whether they are robbers or conspirators or bandits—there are sure to be one or two discontented spirits, men who think that they ought to have been chosen as chiefs, that their advice has been slighted, or that their share of the plunder is insufficient; and should an opportunity occur, men like these are always ready to turn traitors, if they think that they can do so with safety. I do not suppose that the bands in these mountains are any exception; indeed, the chances of dissent are larger than usual, for we may be sure that both the brigands and these men who have been sent over from the mainland to foment discontent and create a counter-revolution in favour of a republic are greatly dissatisfied with the result of their joint undertaking. The prompt step Garibaldi took in sending Bixio's division here must have upset all their plans. The guerillas, no doubt, have taken a considerable amount of booty; but this could have been done without the aid of the strangers. The latter counted on doing great things with the assistance of the brigands. They have failed altogether. A good many of both sections have been killed; and I should imagine, at the present time, that there is not much love lost between them.

"It is therefore quite possible that some of these men are perfectly ready to betray the rest; and I regard it as on the cards that I may get a message to the effect that one of them will, if promised a pardon and a handsome reward, conduct us to the rendezvous where the band is gathered. In that case we should not return empty-handed. In some respects it is better that we should get at them that way than in any other; for the knowledge that one of their bands had been destroyed by treachery on the part of a member would cause a feeling of distrust and uneasiness in every gang in the mountains. Every man would begin to suspect every other man of being a traitor; and although the fear of being either followed or killed, or of being denounced as a traitor and murdered, perhaps days, perhaps weeks, perhaps even months afterwards, but certainly some day or other, would keep the bands together, yet they would lose all heart in the business; quarrels would break out, desperate fights would take place, and many of their parties would finally break up; while the others would, for a considerable time at least, undertake no fresh enterprises."

Four days passed without incident. An hour after sunset the men marched to the church, the muskets were piled inside, and they were then permitted to sit on the steps outside smoking and talking until nine o'clock, when sentries were posted, and the men lay down inside. Late on the following afternoon, as Rubini with a sergeant was at the end of the village, a woman, standing half-hidden in some bushes a short distance away, motioned to him that she wanted to speak to him.

"There might be half a dozen men hidden in that bush," Rubini said. "Let us turn off and go to that shed, and beckon to her to come to us. If we stand close to it, no one will see her speaking to us."

The woman hesitated for some time, evidently afraid to leave the shelter of the bushes. Then, making a sign to Rubini that she would join them presently, she went back into the wood. In a short time she came out on the other side and walked a couple of hundred yards away; then she turned and made a wide circuit, keeping as much as possible in shelter, and at last joined them. She was a wild-looking creature: her hair was in disorder; her face bore signs of tears; her clothes were torn in several places, as if she had run recklessly through a thick wood. She might have cried as she came; but at present her flushed face, her fierce eyes, her tightly compressed lips, and her quick breathing, spoke of passion rather than grief.

"What do you want with me?" Rubini asked.

"I have come to ask for vengeance," the woman panted. "Prato has this afternoon shot my husband; and for what? Merely because he said that if the band were not going to do anything, he would return home. That was all; and Prato

IN HER EXCITEMENT SHE FELL ON HER KNEES.

drew his pistol and shot him. My Antonio! I cannot bring him to life again, but I can avenge him. Signor, the band of Prato, the most merciless and most famous of our chiefs, lies but five miles away! I will lead you to the place, but you must swear to me that you will show him no mercy. If you take him prisoner, he will escape: no judge in the island dare convict him, no jailor would dare keep his door shut. I must have his life-blood; unless you will swear this I will not take you to him. As for the others, I care not, but I should like them all to be killed, for they laughed when Prato shot my Antonio like a dog; but I bargain not for them. Do as you will with them, but Prato must die. I ask no reward— I would not touch blood money; I ask only for vengeance," and in her excitement she fell on her knees, and waving her arms above her head, poured down a string of maledictions upon the brigand chief.

"I can promise you that he shall not be taken prisoner," Rubini said. "The villain has committed a score of murders; but he might escape."

"He will fight to the last," the woman said; "he is a devil, but he is no coward. But he would find it difficult to escape. His fires are lit at the foot of a crag, and if you approach him on both sides and in front, he must fight."

"How many men has he?"

"Thirty-seven, counting himself, signor; but you will take them by surprise, and can shoot down many before they can fire a shot."

"What do you think, Zippo?" Rubini asked, drawing his comrade two or three paces aside. "The man is one of the most notorious brigands in the mountains. There has been a big reward offered for him, dead or alive, for years past;

it would be a grand service if we could destroy him and his band, and we should earn the gratitude of all the towns and villages below there."

"Yes, it would be a grand exploit," the sergeant said eagerly, "for us to accomplish what the Neapolitan troops and carabinieri have so long failed to do. Per Baccho, 'tis a glorious stroke of luck."

"That is what I think," Rubini said. Then he went to the woman. "We are ready to aid you to avenge your husband," he said. "You know your way through the forest in the dark?"

"I know it well. Prato's band has been in this neighbourhood for months past, and I have been in here scores of times to buy provisions. There are two or three paths by which you might go, and I know all of them; if you like you can carry a lantern until you are within half a mile of them. The forest goes well-nigh up to the cliff."

"I will not start till nine o'clock," Rubini said. "At that time my men withdraw into the church; but we can move out by the door of the vestry behind, and no one in the village will dream that any of us have left the place. Will you be at that door five minutes after the clock strikes?"

"I will be there," the woman said fiercely, turning and shaking her fist in the direction from which she had come.

As Frank was strolling up the street he met the two friends, for Zippo was a cousin of the captain.

"I have some very important news to give you, Percival," Rubini said, as they met him; " but I won't tell you here, for the people loitering about might notice that I was talking seriously, and suspect that something out of the way had occurred. Let us walk down quietly to the other end of the village, and out of earshot of any of the houses; until we get there let us chat of other matters. Your arm still goes on well?"

"It could not be better. Five or six days of this mountain air has done me no end of good. I have not felt a single twinge in my arm, and I believe I could use it for all ordinary purposes now with perfect safety."

"That is a pretty little child, isn't she, if her face were but clean? I should doubt if it has ever been really washed. I should certainly say that her hair has never been combed. There: the little beggar knows we are speaking of her. Did you see how she scowled? She has evidently picked up the popular sentiment concerning us."

When fairly beyond the village Rubini told his story. "It will be splendid," he said. "Why, the capture of Prato would cause almost as much sensation in Sicily as the taking of Palermo!"

"Yes, it would be a grand thing," Frank agreed; "but are you quite sure, Rubini, that her story is a true one, and not a feint to draw you into an ambush?"

"I am perfectly convinced of the woman's earnestness, Percival, and so would you have been had you seen her. Do you not agree with me, Zippo?"

"Certainly. I have not the slightest doubt in my mind as to the fact that she was speaking the truth."

"Well, if you are both perfectly satisfied," Frank said, "there can be no doubt that it would be a great service to destroy this fellow's band. How many men do you propose to take with you?"

"I should certainly take as strong a force as possible. These brigands are desperate fellows when cornered."

"Well, there would be no occasion to leave many men with me," Frank said; "as you would no doubt get away unnoticed, it would be supposed that the whole force is as usual in the church. If you leave me five good men I shall be quite satisfied, and when you have gone we will barricade the doors, and could hold out stoutly for a long time. There is very little woodwork about the place, and if we were driven into the belfry they could not burn us out. However, it might be a wise precaution if you were to tell three or four of your men to buy a couple of loaves apiece and a skin of wine; as it will be dusk before they go as usual to the church steps, they could bring these with them without being noticed."

"I will do as you suggest, Percival, but I really think that you are carrying precaution beyond what is necessary."

"It will not be an expensive precaution," Frank replied, with a smile.

"Then you think five men would be sufficient?" Rubini asked.

"So far as I am concerned, I do not see why you should not take them all. I was ordered to assume the command of any men left here, but that did not imply that your force was always to be broken up; certainly I am willing to remain here by myself. I would infinitely rather go with you, but a night march through a dark forest would be more serious for me than going into a pitched battle, for if I were to trip and fall, I should certainly smash my arm again. I do not see why you should leave any here: five men or even ten would be of no great use, and for a business like yours every musket may be of advantage. I shall certainly feel very anxious about you while you are away. I can quite believe that, as you say, the woman was perfectly in earnest; but when she was missed from that camp, after the murder of her husband, the suspicion that she had come here to tell us where they were encamped might very well occur to them, and you might find them vigilant and prepared for you."

"That may be so," Rubini agreed. "Well, then, as the villagers here will not know that we have left until we are back again, I think I will take forty-five men and leave you with five. You shall pick the men."

"I should like to have Sarto and Maffio, if you can spare them; as to the other three I leave it to you entirely."

"Yes; you can have those two. They are both thoroughly good men as well as good fellows; as for the others, I will pick you out three of the best of those who last joined us. I should like as many of the old hands with me as possible, for I know that they will keep their heads, whatever happens."

It was not until the men were all gathered round the church door, as usual, that Rubini told them of the expedition on which they were about to start. The news excited general satisfaction. There had been little doing since Palermo was taken, and the old hands were all eager for the fray, while those who had more recently joined burned to show that they were worthy to be comrades of Garibaldi's first followers.

At nine o'clock all came into the church as usual, and ten minutes later the detachment, with the exception of Frank's little command, moved silently out through the vestry door.

"So we are to stay behind with you?" Sarto said, as he and Maffio joined Frank, who had taken a seat and was thinking over the course that should be pursued if Rubini's enterprise turned out badly. "Rubini said that you specially asked for us, which was no doubt a compliment, but one which, if you don't mind our saying so, we would gladly have dispensed with. It will be a nuisance indeed watching here all night, while the others are engaged in a business quite after our own heart."

"I was sure that you would feel rather annoyed," Frank said; "but I should not have liked to be here without at least two men on whom I know I can rely to the last."

"But what can there be for us to do?" Sarto asked, in some surprise at the tone in which Frank spoke.

"I don't know; that is just what I don't know, Sarto. I acknowledge that I by no means like this expedition. Rubini and Zippo are both certain that this woman is acting in perfect good faith. I did not see her, and therefore I can only take their opinion, but she may have been only acting. You know how passionate these women are; and it seems to me possible that, thinking what she would have done had her husband been shot by Prato, she might have worked herself up into such a state that no one could doubt the reality of her story. Of course, I do not say that it was so—I only say that it was possible. In the next place, even if her story is perfectly true, she may have been seen to leave the camp, or, if she passed out unobserved by any of them, her absence would be noticed, and she might be followed and her interview with Rubini observed; and in that case the band may either have moved away when they got the news, or, what is more likely, be prepared to attack Rubini's column on its way. I mentioned the possibility to Rubini that the woman's absence might have been noticed and the band be uneasy in consequence, and on the look-out; and although it in no way shook his determination to take advantage of her offer, he would, I am sure, take every precaution in his power.

Still, there is no saying how things will turn out. It may be that, if the brigands anticipate an attack, they may by this time have sent to another party to tell them that the greater part of our detachment will be away, and invite them to come and finish with the men left here, while they themselves tackle those who have gone out against them."

"It certainly looks possible in the way you put it," Maffio said, "though I hope it may not turn out so. However, I see that we shall, at any rate, have something to think about while they are away. So that is what that bread and wine you brought in was for? Rubini asked us, and two others, to bring in a couple of loaves each, and the other to bring in a skin of wine; of course, we thought that it was for the use of the expedition."

"I asked him to do so, Maffio. He rather laughed at the idea, but it seemed to me possible that they might be of use here while he was away; and at any rate I will guarantee that the food shall not be wasted."

"Six of us, including yourself, could not hold this church long?"

"Not against a great effort. But even if they should take advantage of the absence of part of our force to attack us, they would not know how strong a party had been left behind, and would be cautious for a bit; but I do not suppose that we should be able to resist a determined onslaught. I thought that we might take to the tower: we could hold that for hours."

"Yes; we could do that," Sarto said confidently. "Well, I don't at all suppose that we are going to be disturbed, but it is a satisfaction to feel that we are not altogether out of the affair."

As usual, a dozen candles had been lighted in different parts of the church as soon as it was dark. The three Genoese, who had joined the company after the capture of Palermo, looked sulky and downcast at being left behind, and Frank called to them.

"I have no doubt that you are disappointed, gentlemen," he said; "but you should really take it as a compliment. I asked Captain Rubini to leave me, in addition to my two friends here, the three best men he could pick out from those who had not formed part of the original force, and I have no doubt that he has done so. I may tell you that I consider it possible, I do not say probable, that we may be attacked, and we will first see what steps should be taken in that case. I have not been up to the tower: have any of you?"

None of them had mounted there.

"Then let us investigate," he said.

The campanile stood at the north-west corner of the church; it had an exterior door, and another opening into the church. Taking a couple of candles, they entered by the latter, and mounted a stone staircase leading to the lower story of the tower; beyond this a wooden staircase led to the rough wooden floor under the bells, and another to the flat terrace above.

"The first thing to do," Frank said, "is to block up the outside door; at any rate, let us have a look at it." It was roughly made, but very strong. "The door is well enough, but I doubt whether this lock would not give under heavy blows."

"We might pile chairs behind it," Sarto suggested.

"I would rather not do that, if we can help it," Frank replied. "They may burn the door down, and the less combustibles there are the better; however, if we can find nothing else we must use them."

Nothing could be found, and Frank then said, "I think that we can manage with one chair."

The others looked puzzled.

"We will cut up the legs and back into six-inch pieces, sharpen them into wedges, and drive them in all round the door: I think that would withstand any battering until the door itself splintered."

They all fell to work at once, and in a quarter of an hour a score of wedges were driven in.

"Now we will do the same at the bottom of the church door itself, and put in a few as high as we can reach on each side; that will detain them some time before it yields."

When this was done, Sarto said, "What next, Percival?"

"The only other thing to be done in the way of defence is to carry all the chairs upstairs to the first story of the tower, to make a barricade there," Maffio remarked.

"Yes, we might make a barricade of them half way up the stairs, but my main object is to get rid of them here. If they found they could not storm the stairs, they might pile all the chairs in the middle of the church and set them on fire—they are the only things that will burn; and although the flames would scarcely mount to the roof, sparks would fly up, and as there is sure to be a lot of dust and soot on the beams there, which might catch fire, we should be burnt out."

"Well, at any rate there would be no great trouble in doing that" Sarto said; "though I should hardly think that they would attempt to burn the church down. The brigands have no respect for life, but they are not without their superstitions, and might be afraid to burn a church, though they would cut half a dozen throats without a scruple."

"Yes; but a portion of the band are no doubt composed of revolutionists from the mainland—fellows who have no scruples of any sort, and who, as the men of the same kind did in Paris seventy years ago, would desecrate a church in every conceivable manner, for, as a rule, they hate religion as they hate authority."

The chairs were accordingly carried up and stowed on the wooden floor beneath the bells.

"Now," Frank said, "I should like to see how this ladder is fastened, and if we can move it."

This, however, they found would be well-nigh impossible. It was over thirty feet from the stone floor to the next story, while that in which the bells hung was but some twenty feet. The ladder was very solid and heavy, and as only two could get at it from above, it could not be lifted up that way.

"We can manage it," Frank said, after thinking for a minute. "We can pull the bell ropes up through their holes, and fasten them somewhere above the middle of the ladder; then, with three of us pulling on each, we could certainly raise it without much difficulty. We should not have to pull it very high—six feet would be ample. If they want to smoke us out, they must bring wood from outside, which will not be easy to do under our fire. Now we will leave one on watch above. He shall be relieved every hour. Do you take the first watch, Pedro. If you hear any stir in the village below, come down and tell us at once; but, above all, listen for distant firing. It is five miles to the spot where the bandits are, but on a still night like this it would certainly be heard here."

He and the other four men then descended to the first floor. Here those who were to take the next turn of duty said, "If you do not want us further, captain, we will sit here and light our pipes, if you have no objection."

"No objection at all. I don't think that I should like to smoke myself in the church below, but that is a matter of opinion; but certainly no one could object to its being done in this detached tower."

Then, with Sarto and Maffio, he went down into the church.

CHAPTER XII

AN AMBUSCADE

"THE others will have the laugh at us when they come back," Sarto said.

"That will in no way trouble me," Frank said. "It has given us a couple of hours' work, and it has passed the time away. If all has gone well, we should hear the firing very soon; we may be sure that they won't be able to go fast through the wood, especially as they will have to be careful not to make any noise. Of course, it is all up hill too, and will be as dark as pitch under the trees; they will have almost to crawl along the last mile. I should not be surprised if it were another hour before they are in a position to attack. And now that we are prepared to repel any attack upon us, and to hold out if necessary, for three days or even more on the provisions we have got, we ought to consider another alternative."

"What other alternative can there be?" Maffio asked.

"Let us suppose—and it is as well to suppose the worst —that Rubini falls into an ambush. It makes no difference whether the woman leads him into one, or whether she has been trapped and the ambush laid without her knowledge. Suppose that they are ambushed and that none of them get back here?"

An exclamation broke from the others.

"I said that we will suppose the worst," Frank went on.

"This man Prato, who is an old hand at such matters, would not improbably, if he expected that Rubini would come to attack him, have at once sent off to another band, or to men who sometimes act with him, and instead of their meeting thirty-eight men, they may meet sixty. In that case we might calculate that a third of Rubini's force would fall at the first volley; there they would be in the forest, without a guide, in the dark, surrounded by twice their number of men well acquainted with the place, and accustomed to traversing it at night. Now I ask you frankly, do you think that many of them, or, indeed, any of them, would be likely to get back here? They might not all be killed; some might hide in the woods, and make their way down the mountain to-morrow, but the chance of any of them returning here seems to me to be small indeed, if things turn out as I have been saying."

"But you don't think, you can't think, Percival——" Sarto said, in a tone of horror.

"I don't say that I think so, Sarto. I only say that it seems to me to be possible; and, situated as we are, it is always as well to see what, if even the most unlikely thing takes place, could be done. Let us suppose that the detachment has been cut to pieces: what is our look-out here? We can defend the place, or rather we can defend ourselves, for three or four days; but what would be the benefit of that? If the news got down to Bronte, it would be necessary to send two or three companies up here to rescue us. If, as is very probable, no news got down there, we should have to surrender; and we know what that would mean, especially as, assuredly, we should have killed a good many of the brigands in the course of the fighting. Thus, then, nothing would be gained by our resistance. I was appointed to command that portion of troops left here, in case of Rubini going away in pursuit of brigands with the rest. I do not suppose that it was ever contemplated that only five men would be left behind, still that does not alter the case. The idea was, that the village might be attacked during the absence of part of the force, and that those here should maintain themselves until Rubini returned. But in the event of such a disaster as we are supposing, so far from there being any advantage in holding this church, it would be a serious disadvantage; for we should risk our lives without any point whatever in our doing so."

"That is certainly true; but in that case, why should we have made these preparations for defence?"

"Simply because we hope, and have every reason to hope, that Rubini will return, and we are prepared to hold out until he does so. But, once assured that the detachment will not come back, the whole matter is changed."

"But how are we to be assured?"

"Ah! that is a very difficult question to answer. As long as there is the slightest possibility of any part, however small, of the detachment returning, we are bound to hold on here. But, when we can feel certain that this will not be the case, our duty would be to consult our own safety by retreating if possible to Bronte."

At this moment the sentry on the campanile ran in.

"I heard a sudden outburst of firing, Captain Percival, and it is continuing."

Followed by all the others, Frank ran up to the top of the tower. There was no doubt that a tough fight was going on: the reports of the muskets came in quick succession; sometimes there would be a short pause, and then half a dozen shots would ring out close together.

For three or four minutes not a word was spoken; then, as the reports became less frequent, Sarto exclaimed, "It is nearly over: Rubini has done his work."

Frank was silent, and Sarto added, "Do you not think so, Percival?"

"I hope so," Frank replied, "but I am very much afraid that it is not so. Had Rubini taken the brigands completely by surprise, there would have been one crashing volley, then he would have rushed in with the bayonet, and it would have been all over in two minutes. Some of the brigands might have escaped, but there can have been no pursuit, for in the darkness in the forest there would have been no chance whatever of overtaking men perfectly familiar with it. No, I think that they have failed in taking them by surprise, and if they did fail to do so, the brigands would either have moved off, in which case there would have been no fight at all, or have laid an ambush for our party, which would account for the heavy firing we have heard. Whether the ambush was successful, or whether Rubini has beaten his assailants off, is uncertain."

The others saw the justness of his reasoning, and remained silent. An occasional shot was still heard.

"What do you think that means?" Maffio asked—for both he and Sarto were beginning to feel a profound respect for the opinion of their companion.

"It means, of course, that one party or the other is pursuing fugitives, and I am afraid that it is a bad sign, for, as I have just said, our men would hardly try and chase these brigands through the wood they know very well."

They waited another five minutes. Still shots were occasionally heard.

The conviction that Frank's worst anticipations had been but too surely verified, forced itself upon the others.

"Will you stay here a short time longer?" Frank said to the others; "I will go down into the church. I should like to think over quietly what we had best do."

He walked up and down the church. It was a tremendous responsibility for a lad not yet seventeen to bear. Some of Rubini's party had escaped, and might be making their way back in hopes of finding shelter and safety. What would be their feelings if they arrived and found the party gone? On the other hand, defend themselves as well as they might, six men must finally succumb before a determined attack by a large party of ruffians exulting over their victory and thirsting for complete vengeance. But by the time his companions returned from above he had made up his mind as to the plan that had best be adopted.

"We will take a middle course," he said. "We will leave the church, and conceal ourselves within a short distance of the door into the vestry. One of us must hide close to it, so that if any of our comrades come up and knock at the door for admission, he can bring them to us. We can then learn what has happened. If even eight or ten have escaped, we will return to the church and hold it; if only one or two, we will, when the brigands arrive and there is no chance of others coming, start for Bronte."

"That is a capital plan," Sarto exclaimed; and a murmur from the others showed that they too warmly approved.

"There is no hurry," Frank went on. "We will eat a good meal before we start, then there will be no occasion to burden ourselves with provisions. Before leaving, we will light fresh candles: there are four or five pounds in the vestry.

We will leave four alight in each floor of the tower, and the rest in different parts of the church, so that, when the brigands do arrive, they will think that we are watchful and well prepared for them. It is not likely they will know exactly what strength Rubini had with him, but will think that we have at least ten or twelve men with us, and will be sure to hesitate a little before they make an attack. They will take some little time to burst in the great doors; and even the door of the vestry is strong enough to bear a good deal of battering before they break that in, so that we shall get a good long start of them. Of course they may pursue, but we can keep on the road for the first half-mile, and then turn off and make our way through the forest. We can't go very far wrong, as it is always a descent; besides, for aught they will know, we may have been gone a couple of hours before they get here. I think in that way we shall have done our duty to our comrades, and at the same time secured our own safety, for we have no right to throw away our lives when we can still do some work for Italy."

"It could not be better," Maffio said. "In that way we shall have the consolation of knowing that none of our friends, who have been wounded, have dragged themselves here after we had left only to find that they were deserted; while on the other hand it does away with the necessity of our throwing away our lives altogether uselessly. I revert to my former idea, Percival. If ever I have sons, I will send them to one of your great schools in England. It is clear that the life there and your rough games make men of you."

They first sat down and ate a hearty meal of bread and wine, and then fresh candles were lighted and placed as Frank had directed. Then they left the church, locking the vestry door behind them. Sarto lay down behind a tombstone ten yards from the door, and the others took their places behind the low wall that ran round the church-yard. After waiting an hour Frank returned to Sarto.

"I am going," he said, "to conceal myself at the end of the village, close enough to the road to hear anything that is said by people coming along. If, as I hope, they may be some of our men, I will join them and bring them on here, if not I will make my way here at once, and will give a low whistle. Directly you hear me, retire and join us. It will give us a few minutes' extra time, for you may be sure that when they see the church lighted up, those who first arrive will wait for the rest before running the risk of a shot from the tower. When all are gathered no doubt there will be a good deal of talk as to how they had best attack it."

Leaving Sarto, Frank made his way through the gardens until he arrived at the end of the village, and then sat down behind a low wall, close to the road. In half an hour he heard footsteps, and judged that six or eight men were coming from the forest.

"There is no doubt they are on the watch there," one of them said; "the windows in the tower are lit up,—we shall have some work to do before we finish with them. They fought bravely—I will say that for them; and although half their number fell at our first volley, they killed eight or ten of our men, and wounded as many more, before, when there were only about half a dozen of them left, they broke through us and ran. It was lucky that Phillipo's band arrived in time, for notwithstanding the surprise, I doubt whether we should have beaten them, had we been alone. It was a good thought of Prato to send young Vico to follow that woman, and that he saw her talking to the officer."

Frank could hear no more, but rising quietly, he retraced his steps at a run, and as soon as he joined his companions gave a low whistle, which in a minute brought Sarto to his side.

"It is as I feared," he said: "they laid an ambush for Rubini, and shot down half his men at once; the rest kept together and fought till all but six or seven were killed, and these burst through them and took to flight; and I am afraid that those shots we heard told that some even of these were overtaken and killed. Now let us be going; there were only about eight men in the party who first came along, and we may be sure that nothing will be attempted until the rest arrive. The men had noticed our lights in the tower, and evidently expected that we should sell our lives dearly; at any rate, we can calculate upon at least half an hour before they break into the church and find that we have left."

They were obliged to go cautiously before they gained the road beyond the village, and then they broke into a trot.

"Half an hour will mean something like four miles," Frank said; "and as it is not likely that they can run much faster than we are going, we may safely calculate that they will not overtake us for over an hour after they do start, and by that time we shall be well within five miles of Bronte. Indeed, with the slope in our favour, I am not sure that we may not calculate upon reaching the town itself; they certainly ought not to be able to run fifteen miles while we are running eleven."

"If they do we should deserve to be caught," Maffio said; "but I should think that they would not follow us far, as, for anything they can tell, we may have left the church a couple of hours ago."

There were few words spoken as they ran steadily along. The thought of the slaughter of so many of their friends oppressed them all, and the fact that they had personally escaped was, at present, a small consolation. Frank had not been long enough with the company to make the acquaintance of many of the men, but he felt the loss of Rubini extremely. At Genoa, during the voyage, and on the march to Palermo, they had been constantly together, and the older man had treated him with as much cordiality and kindness as if he had been a younger brother. Frank regretted now that he had not even more strongly urged his doubts as to the expediency of the expedition, though he felt that, even had he done so, his remonstrances would have been unavailing, so convinced were Rubini and Zippo of the sincerity and good faith of the woman. As it seemed, in this respect they had been right, and he had not pressed more strongly upon them the probability of her being followed when she left the brigands after the murder of her husband. It was so natural a thing that this should be so, that he wondered it had not struck him at once. Had he urged the point, Rubini might have listened to him, and his fatal expedition might not have taken place.

It seemed to him a heartbreaking affair, and as he ran he wiped away more than one tear that ran down his cheeks. After keeping on at the same speed for three or four miles, Frank heard, by the hard breathing of his companions, that their powers were failing; he himself was running quite easily, his school training being of good service to him, and after the long runs at hare and hounds across country, four miles down hill was a trifle to him. He had, too, the advantage of not having to carry a musket and ammunition.

"We had better walk for a few hundred yards and get our breath again," he said. And the order was thankfully obeyed.

"Are you ready to trot on?" he asked, five minutes later; and on a general assent being given, they again broke into a run.

The more he thought of it, the more persuaded Frank was that no pursuit would be set on foot. Doubtless, the first step of the brigands would be to surround the church, and to place strong parties at both doors; they would therefore know that the church must have been deserted for at least half an hour before they obtained an entry, while possibly it might have been two or three hours before; so on finding the place empty their impulse would be to go to the wine-shops and celebrate their victory, rather than to start upon a pursuit which offered small prospects indeed of success. Every few minutes they halted for a moment to listen for the sound of pursuing feet, but everything was still and quiet; and so confident did they become as to their safety, that the last three or four miles down into Bronto were performed at a walk.

"I must go and report to Bixio," Frank said, as they entered the town. "You had better find a shelter somewhere."

"There is no occasion for that," Maffio replied. "The sky has been getting lighter for some little time, and it must be nearly five o'clock. It was past two when we started."

"I will wait for another half-hour," Frank said, "before I rouse Bixio; he is always out by six, and bad news will keep."

Shortly before that hour he went to the general's quarters. The house was already astir.

"The general will be down in a few minutes, captain," an orderly said. "I called him a quarter of an hour ago."

In two or three minutes Bixio came down.

"Have you any news?" he asked hastily, when he saw Frank, whose downcast face struck him at once.

"Yes, general; and very bad news."

"Come in here," Bixio said, opening the door of a sitting-room. "Now, what is it?"

"I grieve to have to report, sir, that I have arrived here with only Sarto, Maffio, and three other men of the detachment, and that I fear Captain Rubini and the whole of the rest of the men have been killed."

Bixio started. "All killed!" he repeated, almost incredulously. "I trust that you are mistaken. What has happened?"

Frank briefly related the circumstances.

"This is sad indeed—terrible," the general said, when he had brought his story to a conclusion. "Rubini's loss is a grievous one; he was a good officer, and was greatly liked and trusted by us all; there were good men, too, among his company. He had fifteen men of the thousand among them. And you say this woman did not betray them?"

"No; the men I overheard, distinctly said that she was a traitress, and as soon as she was missed by them she was followed and her meeting with the officer observed."

"But what took you out beyond the village, Captain Percival? You have told me the main facts of this most unfortunate expedition: please give me the full details of what you did after they had left, and how you came to escape."

"I felt uneasy from the first," Frank said. "Directly Rubini told me about the woman, I suggested that she might be merely acting a part, in order to lead them into an ambuscade; but both Rubini and Zippo, who was with him when he met her, were absolutely convinced of her good faith.

"I also suggested that, even if they were right, the woman might possibly have been followed. Her disappearance after the murder of her husband would be almost certain to excite suspicion that she intended to avenge herself by bringing our detachment down upon them. I communicated this suspicion to Sarto and Maffio, and we at once set to work to make the church defensible."

He then related in detail the measures they had taken, and how he became convinced, by the sound of the distant conflict, that Rubini and his party had fallen into the ambuscade and been destroyed.

"For some time I could not make up my mind what course to adopt, sir: we might have defended the tower for two or three days; but it was by no means certain—in fact, it was very improbable—that anything of what was going on would reach your ears. On the other hand, I could not withdraw my little party, as, even if my worst suspicions were correct, some of Rubini's men might have escaped and might make their way back to the church." He then proceeded to explain the plan he had adopted, and how it had been carried out. "I do not know whether I have acted rightly," he concluded. "It was a terrible responsibility, but I can only say that I consulted with Sarto and Maffio, who have had far more experience than I, and that they both approved of my plan. I hope, general, you do not think that I was wrong."

"Certainly not—certainly not. Your position was a most difficult one, and your preparations for defence were excellent; the alternatives that you had to choose between when you became convinced that Rubini had been defeated were equally painful. If you stayed and defended the place, I may almost say you would have thrown away the lives of yourself and the five men with you. If you went, any wounded men straggling back from the forest would have found neither friends nor refuge. The middle course you adopted was admirable. You would at once have saved any poor fellows who might arrive, while you ensured the safety of your little party. By illuminating the church you secured for yourself a long start; and by going out so as to overhear the conversation of the first party of brigands who entered the village, you were able to assure yourself that it was useless staying longer in hopes of any survivors of the expedition coming in.

"I have received a message from Garibaldi, ordering me to move to Taormina, on the sea-coast. He has defeated Bosco at Milazzo; and the Neapolitan general and his troops have been permitted to take ship for Naples. He said that if I had not concluded my work here I could remain for another week, as it would probably be a considerable time before the preparations made for invading Calabria were completed. I was intending to send off some messages this morning to recall all the outlying detachments. That I shall do still; but I shall certainly remain here three or four days longer, in the hope that some of Rubini's party may have escaped. If I thought there was the smallest chance of laying hands on this scoundrel Prato and his band, I would march with a couple of hundred men into the mountains. But we may be sure that he did not stop more than an hour or two at the village, after he learned that your party had escaped; and by to-morrow morning they may be fifty miles away, on the other side of

Etna. However, as soon as our affair is over, I shall urge upon Garibaldi the necessity for sending a strong force into the mountains to put down brigandage, and especially to destroy Prato's band."

The disaster that had befallen Rubini's column cast a great gloom over the brigade: not a man but would gladly have undergone any amount of fatigue to avenge his comrades; but all felt the impossibility of searching the great tract of forest which extended over the larger part of the slopes of Etna. Bixio however, determined to send off a strong party to find and bury the dead, and two hours later a detachment a hundred strong left Bronte. Their orders were to attack the brigands if they found them in the village; if they had left, however, they were not to pursue. They were to sleep there, and in the morning to compel two or three of the villagers to guide them to the scene of conflict, where they were to find and bury the dead. Every precaution was to be observed, although it was regarded as certain that the brigands would not have remained so near the village, but would only stop there a few hours, and then place as great a distance as possible between it and them.

Frank had offered to accompany the party, but Bixio refused to allow him to do so.

"You have had a sleepless night, and the anxiety you have suffered is quite sufficient excitement for a convalescent. You could do no good by going there, and had best lie down and take a few hours' sleep."

Before the party started Frank asked the captain in command to see if his horse had been carried off. "It was in a shed adjoining the priest's house," he said; "and it may still be there. The brigands would not be likely to make many inquiries; and when they discovered that we had gone, probably made off directly they had eaten their supper; for had we, as might have been the case so far as they knew, started for Bronte soon after Rubini left, it would have been possible for reinforcements to reach the village within an hour of daybreak. Even if one of the villagers told them that the horse was there—which is not likely, for the whole place must have been in a ferment at the news—the brigands may not have cared to carry it off, as it would be useless to them in a journey over ground covered with forest and broken up by ravines and gorges."

The detachment returned two days later, bringing with it, to Frank's satisfaction, his horse and saddlery. They had been to the scene of the conflict, and had found and buried all the bodies with the exception of a few, who must either have escaped or have been killed at a considerable distance from the spot where they were attacked. The brigands had, as Frank had expected, left the village before daybreak. They had on arriving opened fire at the windows of the church; and a quarter of an hour later, finding that no reply was made, had endeavoured to force an entry. The great door, however, had defied their efforts, and when at last they obtained access by breaking in the door of the vestry, more than an hour had been wasted. The discovery that the church was untenanted had greatly disappointed and disquieted them, and after carousing for a short time they hastily left.

Early on the day after the return of Frank and his comrades, one of the missing party reached the town: he was utterly worn out and broken down, having apparently wandered for thirty-six hours in the forest in a state of semi-delirium. He had at last quite accidentally stumbled upon a small village, and after being fed and cared for, had been brought down to Bronte in a cart. He was, he said, convinced that he was the only survivor of the fight. The party had arrived within, as they believed, a quarter of a mile of the brigand's lurking-place, when a whistle was heard, and from the trees on both sides of a narrow path a volley was fired, and half at least of the party dropped. Rubini, he believed, was among those who fell; at least he did not hear his voice afterwards. Zippo had rallied the men, who, gathering together, endeavoured to fight their way through their assailants.

What the effect of their fire was, he could not tell, but his comrades dropped fast, and when there were but a few left, they threw down their muskets and rushed headlong into the forest. They scattered in various directions, but were hotly pursued; several shots were fired at him, but they all missed. After running for half an hour he flung himself down in a clump of undergrowth. He had heard, as he ran, other shots, and had no doubt that his companions were all killed. He lay where he was until morning, and then tried to find his way down to Bronte, but he had no distinct recollection of what had happened after he left the bushes, until he found that wine was being poured down his throat, and that he was surrounded by a group of pitying women.

The fury of the Garibaldians, on their arrival from the various villages at which they had been posted, when they heard of the slaughter of their friends, was extreme; and many of the officers begged the general to allow them to make one effort to find and punish the brigands, but Bixio refused.

"We have a far greater business on our hands," he said. "Italy has to be freed. The first blow has been struck, and must be followed up at once; brigandage can wait—it is an old sore, a disgrace to a civilised country; but Italy once freed, this can be taken in hand. We might spend weeks, or even months, before we could lay hands on Prato's band; the villagers and woodmen would keep them informed of every movement we made, while not only should we gain no information, but all would be interested in putting us upon the wrong track. It is not to be thought of. Moreover, I have Garibaldi's orders to march to Taormina, and if we had lost five hundred men instead of fifty, I should obey that order, much as I should regret being obliged to march away and leave the massacre unavenged."

The day after the fugitive had arrived, the force left Bronte. The mountainous nature of the country to the north prevented a direct march towards Taormina. They therefore took the road round the foot of Etna, through Bandazza to Gairre, which lay nearly due east of Bronte, and then followed the line along the coast to Taormina. Here the troops were halted, while Bixio, with Frank and a small escort, rode on to Messina, as the general wished to confer with Garibaldi, and to ascertain how the preparations for the invasion of Calabria were proceeding.

CHAPTER XIII

ACROSS THE STRAITS

GARIBALDI had, on entering Messina, been received with tremendous enthusiasm, and at once, while waiting for the reinforcements now pouring in, set himself to work to improve the condition of affairs in the town. He had taken up his abode in the royal palace, where he retained all the servants of the former viceroy, considering that it would be unjust to dismiss them. He ordered, however, that his own dinner was to consist only of some soup, a plate of meat, and some vegetables. The large subscriptions that flowed in from Italy and other countries were entirely devoted to public service, as had been the money taken in the treasury at Palermo; the general allowed himself only, as pay, eight francs a day, and this was always spent before breakfast; for although at Messina, as at Palermo, he endeavoured to clear the streets of beggars, he himself was never able to resist an appeal, and no sooner had he sauntered out in the morning than his eight francs melted away among the children and infirm persons who flocked round him.

He received Frank on his arrival with real pleasure, and congratulated him upon having so completely recovered from the effects of his wound.

"There is plenty for you to do," he said; "almost every hour ships bring me volunteers from all parts. Arrangements have to be made for bestowing and feeding these.

We found a considerable supply of tents here, but they are now occupied, and all arrivals henceforth will have to be quartered on the citizens or in the villages near the town. A list will be given to you, every morning, of persons who are willing to receive them, and a mark will be made against the names of those of a better sort, among whom the officers will be quartered. I beg that you will act in concert with Concini and Peruzzi, and as the troops land give them their billets, and in the case of officers conduct them to the houses where they are to be lodged. Of course you yourself will take up your abode here; there is an abundance of room, and I will order the servants to set aside a comfortable chamber for you. All who are in the palace take their early breakfast here, the rest of their meals they take in the town. I have enemies enough, and I do not wish it to be said that we are spending the funds so generously subscribed for us in feasting in the palace. In the evening, you know, you will always be welcome here."

It was, of course, too late in the day for Frank's work to begin; but later on he again went to the room where Garibaldi was chatting with several of his staff.

"Bixio has been telling me of your adventure," Garibaldi said: "it was a sad business. The death of Rubini is a grievous loss to me. He fought most gallantly in the Alps, and distinguished himself greatly since we landed here; he was a true patriot, and I shall miss him sorely. Others there were who died with him, whom I also greatly regret. The one redeeming point in the affair is, as Bixio has been telling me, the admirable way in which you succeeded in saving the little party of whom you were in command. He has detailed the matter in full to me, and the oldest head could not have made better preparations for defence, or better hit upon a plan by which you might at once save any stragglers of Rubini's detachment who might return, and at the same time ensure the safety of the five men with you. There will be a steamer going to Marseilles in the morning, and it will be a pleasure to me to again write to your mother, saying how well you have done, and how completely you have recovered from your wound. The last time I wrote, although I had as warm a praise to give of your conduct, I abstained from telling her that you were seriously wounded. No doubt you will give her full particulars in your own letters."

Frank's duties, in the way of billeting the troops as they arrived, were of short duration. So rapidly did crowds of volunteers arrive from the north of Italy, that it was found impossible to house them in Messina. Many were sent off to outlying villages; thousands bivouacked on the sandy shore. Garibaldi himself went across to Sardinia, and returned with two thousand five hundred men who had been gathered there for a descent upon the coast of the Papal States. The Italian government had, however, vetoed this movement, and had promised that their own troops should, when the time came, perform this portion of the operations. The port was crowded with shipping. By the convention that had been agreed upon between Garibaldi on his entrance to Messina, and the Neapolitan general who commanded the force that occupied the citadel, it was arranged that the sea should be open to both parties; and the singular spectacle was presented of the Neapolitan navy looking quietly on while ships arrived loaded with troops for Garibaldi, while the Sardinian ships-of-war viewed with equal indifference the arrival of reinforcements to the garrison of the citadel.

Garibaldi's force had now increased to over twenty-five thousand men; of these but five thousand were Sicilians, the rest, with the exception of a few French and English volunteers, coming from Northern Italy. Here the enthusiasm caused by the conquest of Sicily was unbounded. The universities had all closed their doors, the students having left in a body; and among the volunteers were hundreds of boys of from thirteen to fifteen years old. Garibaldi had, with the aid of the Municipality of Palermo, raised a loan of nearly three million pounds, and obtained, not only rifles for his own force, but a large number for distribution among the peasants of Calabria.

Five days after his arrival, Garibaldi sent for Frank, and said:

"I am going to bestow on you an honour which will, I am sure, be one after your own heart. I am going to send Missori with two hundred men across the straits; Nullo goes with him. They are to choose the men, and the competition for the honour of being among the first to set foot in Calabria will be a keen one indeed; I have spoken to Missori, and he will gladly take you as his staff officer. Of course it is not intended that he should fight. His mission will be to travel about the country, inciting the population of the Calabrian villages to prepare to join us when we land; to confuse the commanders of the Neapolitan troops by his rapid movements, and to cause alarm at Naples by the news that the invasion of Calabria has begun."

"I should enjoy that greatly, general, and I feel very much obliged to you for your kindness in choosing me."

As Major Missori had been on Garibaldi's staff from the time Frank joined him at Genoa, he was well known to him;

and when Frank visited him, and placed himself under his orders, he received him with great cordiality.

"The general could not have made a better choice," he said. "It is a great satisfaction to have an officer with me on whose activity and energy I can so confidently rely. I have just got through the hardest, and I may say the most trying part of my work, for I have had to refuse the applications of scores of old comrades, who, almost with tears in their eyes, have begged me to enroll them among my party. But I am limited to two hundred, and when I had once selected that number I was obliged to say no to all others. I think that every man of my band is well suited for the work: all are young, active men, capable of long marches and the endurance of great fatigue; all are men of tried bravery, and should we have a brush with the Neapolitans can be trusted to hold their own. We hope to seize the fortress of Alta Fiumara; we have opened communication with some soldiers of the garrison, and have hopes that we may take it by surprise. If we can do so, it will greatly facilitate the passage of the army across the straits.

"Here is a list of the stores we are to take in the boats. Of course the men will each take eighty rounds of ammunition; we can carry no reserve, for if we have to take to the mountains it would be impossible to transport it. Therefore, you see, we practically take with us only a day's provisions. These will be carried down before sunset to the boats, and I wish you would see them so divided that each man will carry approximately the same weight. Thus one can take four pounds of bread, another four pounds of meat, a third two bottles of wine and so on; once in the hills we can purchase what we require at the villages. There will, at any rate, be no difficulty in obtaining meat, nor, I should say, bread. Beyond that nothing is necessary.

"Three Calabrians, who know the country well, crossed yesterday, and will act as our guides. We shall probably have to maintain ourselves for a week or ten days before the main body crosses. A cart will go down at four o'clock with the stores. I will order six men to accompany it, and to place themselves under your orders. In the cart you will find two hundred haversacks, in which the provisions will be placed, after you have seen to their division, together with forty rounds of spare ammunition. By the way, you had better sell your horse. Across such a country as we shall have to traverse, it would be impossible to ride, and you will probably be able to buy another on the mainland for the sum that you will get for him. There are a good many men on the staff of some of the late arrivals, who are on the lookout for horses."

Frank, indeed, had several times been asked by officers if he could tell them where they could procure mounts; and, in the course of a day, he had no difficulty in disposing of his horse and saddlery, for the same amount as he had given for them at Marsala. He took with him only a spare shirt and pair of socks rolled up in a large blanket, that, with a hole cut in the middle, served as a cloak by day and a cover by night. Hitherto this had been strapped on his saddle; he now rolled it up in the fashion followed by most of the Garibaldians, so as to carry it slung over one shoulder. This, with his sword, a brace of pistols, and a small haversack, was his only encumbrance. At the appointed hour he went down with the cart and escort to the point, some two miles from the town, where the boats were lying. It took an hour to make the division of the stores, and then there was nothing to do until, at half-past nine o'clock in the evening, Missori with his two hundred men marched down.

There were fourteen boats, and as these were sufficient to carry the men in comfort, no time was lost in embarking. It was a long row, for although the water was perfectly calm there was a strong current through the straits, and they had to row head to this while crossing; but two hours after starting they landed at a short distance from the fort. They soon had evidence that the commandant here was watchful, for they had gone but a hundred yards when they suddenly came upon a small outlying picket, who, after challenging, fired, and then ran off towards the fort, where the beating of a drum showed that the garrison were already falling in to repel any attack. Their hopes of a surprise were therefore at an end, and as it was by surprise alone that the little force had the slightest chance of capturing so strong a fortress, orders were given, after a hasty consultation between Missori and Nullo, to turn off at once and make for the mountains, while the boats were directed to start back for Messina.

Headed by their guides, they mounted the slopes of Aspromonte. When they had gained a height of some four or five hundred feet, they came upon a wooden shed; this was hastily pulled down and a great bonfire lighted, to inform their friends on the other side of the straits that they had safely landed and were on their way to the hills. They had, as they ascended, heard a sharp fire break out at the water's edge, and knew that a portion of the garrison of the fortress had sallied out and opened fire on the retreating boats.

The march was continued for some hours. The cannon of

the fort had also opened fire—the object doubtless being to inform the large bodies of troops, gathered at various points along the coast to oppose the Garibaldians should they cross, that a force of the enemy had landed in the darkness. However, the little party made their way unobserved past the enemy's outposts, who remained stationary, as the officers were ignorant of the strength of the force that had thus evaded the vigilance of the ships-of-war, and thought it probable that Garibaldi himself with some thousands of men might be at hand.

This portion of Calabria was admirably suited for guerilla warfare. The Garibaldians were received with enthusiasm at the first village at which they arrived. The news of the easy conquest of Sicily had at first filled all hearts with the hope that their day of liberation was at hand; but the concentration of troops in South Calabria had damped their spirits, for, accustomed for centuries to be treated like cattle by the soldiers of their oppressors, it seemed to them wellnigh impossible that Garibaldi would venture to set foot on the mainland in the face of so imposing a gathering. The presence, then, of this band of men in red shirts seemed to them almost miraculous. The inhabitants vied with each other in their hospitality, and the able-bodied men of the place declared their readiness to take up arms the moment that Garibaldi himself crossed the straits. Many of them, indeed, at once joined the party, while others started, some among the mountains and some by the roads leading to other villages, in order to bring in early news of the approach of any body of Neapolitan troops, and the Garibaldians were therefore able to lie down for a few hours' sleep.

For the next week they continued their march, visiting

village after village, gathering recruits as they went, crossing mountains, winding up ravines, and constantly changing their course so as to throw the Neapolitan troops off their track. Several times from lofty points they caught sight of considerable bodies of the enemy moving along the roads. Once a Neapolitan officer rode into a village where they were halting with a despatch from General Briganti, containing a demand for their surrender. Missori simply replied that they were ready to give battle whenever the supporters of tyranny chose to meet them; but, although he thus answered the summons, he had no idea of encountering an overwhelming force of Neapolitans. Failing the capture of the fortress on first landing, his mission was to arouse the population, not to fight; and he continued his work among the mountains in spite of the efforts of the enemy to surround him.

Cavalry were useless in so mountainous a country, and the Garibaldians, free from all weight of equipment, and unencumbered by baggage carts, were able to move with a rapidity that set at defiance the efforts of the soldiery hampered by knapsacks and belts, and with their movements restricted by their tightly-fitting uniforms. Although their course had been devious, the Garibaldians had been gradually working their way south, skirting the heights of Montalto. Before starting, Missori had been informed by Garibaldi that he intended to land near Reggio eight or nine days after he crossed, and that he was to place his band in that neighbourhood in order to join him in an attack on that town.

When he reached a point within ten miles of Reggio, Missori said to Frank. "I must keep moving about, and cannot leave my men; but I will send twenty of them under your command down to Melito. There are, as we have learnt from the peasants, none of the Neapolitan troops there; but at the same time do not on any account enter the town. Were you to do so, some of the inhabitants might send word to Reggio; and it might be suspected that you were there for some special purpose. Therefore hide yourself among the hills a short distance from the town; and after nightfall send one of your men in. He had better take one of the peasants' cloaks and hats: it will be ample disguise for him. It will be his duty to watch on the shore; and then, if he sees two or three steamers—I cannot say what force Garibaldi will bring over—approach the shore, tell him to come up to you at once; and you can then lead your men down to cover, if necessary, the landing of the troops, and to give them any aid in your power. Tell the general that I have now eight hundred men with me, and am ready to move to any point he orders."

These instructions Frank carried out, except that he obtained two peasants' cloaks and hats instead of one. He halted late in the afternoon two miles behind the town, and when it became quite dark took down his men within a quarter of a mile of it; then, assuming one of the disguises, he proceeded with one of the party similarly habited into the town. He posted his follower by the shore, and then re-entered the place. A good many peasants in their high conical hats, with wide brims adorned with ribbons—a costume which is now generally associated with Italian brigands, and differs but slightly from that of the Savoyards—were wandering about the town. All sorts of rumours were current. It was reported that the Neapolitan war-ships were on the look-out for vessels in which it was said Garibaldi was about to cross from Messina and the Cape of Faro. Others reported that Garibaldi himself was with the small corps that had been, for the past week, pursued among the mountains, and whose ever-increasing numbers had been greatly exaggerated by rumour.

Frank seated himself in front of a wine-shop where several of these men were drinking. He could with difficulty understand their patois; but he gathered that all wished well to the expedition. An hour later he heard a tumult, and going to see what was the matter, he found that one of the police officers of the town had accosted the man he had left upon the sea-shore, and finding that he was ignorant of the patois of the country, had arrested him. Four or five other agents of the municipality, which consisted of creatures of the Neapolitan government, had gathered round the captive; and the inhabitants, although evidently favourably disposed towards the prisoner, were too much afraid of the vengeance of their masters to interfere. After hesitating a moment, Frank ran back to the wine-shop where he had been sitting. His great fear was that the Neapolitan agents would at once send news to Reggio that a spy had been taken, and that the garrison there would be put on their guard. He therefore entered, and throwing aside his cloak, addressed the eight or ten peasants present.

"My friends," he said, "I am one of the officers of Garibaldi, who will soon come to free you from your tyrants. As true Italians, I doubt not that your hearts are with him; and you now have it in your power to do him a real service."

All rose to their feet. "We are ready, signor. Tell us what we have to do, and you can rely upon us to do it."

"I want you to post yourselves on the road to Reggio a

hundred yards beyond the town, and to stop any one who may try to leave the place, no matter whether he be a police officer of the syndic. We have a large force near; but we do not wish to show ourselves till the proper moment. It is all-important that no news of our being in the neighbourhood should reach the commander of the troops at Reggio."

"We will do it, signor; be assured that no one shall pass along."

"Simply turn back the first that comes," Frank said; "if more come, kill them; but I want these agents of your tyrant to know that the road is closed. I could place our own men to do this, but I do not wish it known that there are troops near."

The men hurried away, and Frank went off and followed the little crowd that accompanied the prisoner and his captors to the house of the syndic. He watched them go in, and in a short time several of the police left the house, and ere long returned with some eight or ten persons whom Frank judged to be the municipal council. He waited for a minute or two, and then went to the door.

"Stand back," he said, to two men who barred the entrance. "I am one of Garibaldi's officers. I have hundreds of my peasants round the town, ready to lay it in ashes if I but give the word."

They slipped back, confounded by the news; and entering, he went into a room of which the door was standing open. The man who had been left on watch was standing between four policemen; his cloak had been torn off, and he stood in the red shirt, blue breeches and gaiters, that had now become the uniform of the greater portion of Garibaldi's followers. Some ten or twelve men were seated by a large

"SILENCE, SIGNORS!" HE SAID IN A LOUD VOICE.

table, and were talking eagerly. Frank again threw back his cloak, walked up and struck the table with his fist.

"Silence, signors!" he said in a loud voice. "I am the master of this town for the present: it is surrounded by armed peasants who are instructed to cut the throats of any one who attempts to leave it. I am an officer of Garibaldi, as you may see by my attire. I have but to give the word, and in ten minutes the whole of you will be strung up from the balcony of this house; therefore, if you value your lives, retire at once to our houses, and, agents though you be of the Neapolitan tyrant, no harm will befall you; but if one of you attempts to leave the town, or to send any one out with a message, his life will be forfeited. That will do, sirs: leave at once."

The astounded men filed out from the room. When they had all left, Frank went out with the late prisoner, locked the door, and put the key in his pocket.

"Put on your hat and cloak again," he said, "and go down to the road by the sea; watch if any one goes along, and stay a quarter of an hour to see if he returns."

Then, without putting on his own disguise, he went to the spot where the townspeople, among whom the report of what had happened had spread rapidly, were assembled, and mounting on the steps of a large building there, addressed them.

"Calabrians," he said, "the moment when your freedom will be attained is at hand. You have heard that a party of troops of that champion of freedom, General Garibaldi, has crossed to the mainland. The officer in command has sent me to tell you that they are everywhere joined by the brave Calabrians, and will speedily have a force capable of giving battle to the armies of your tyrants. It may be that before many days they will come down here from the mountains, and he hopes to find every man capable of bearing arms ready to join him; it will be a bad day for those who, in spite of the wishes of the people, and the certainty that Garibaldi will shortly be freed from the presence of the troops at Naples, strive to check the tide.

"For your own sakes watch the men who have acted as the agents of the government of Naples, station armed men on every road by which they could send a message to Reggio, for should they do so troops might be sent here, and then, when the soldiers of freedom come down from the hills, a battle will be fought in your streets, and many innocent persons might suffer. I do not ask any to come forward now, to declare himself for the cause of freedom; I only ask you to hold yourselves in readiness, so that when we come down from the hills you will welcome us, as men welcome those who come to strike the fetters from their limbs. It may be that you will not have long to wait, and that in eight-and-forty hours Missori with a portion of his army will be here. But this I do ask you: keep an eye on your syndic and his council, on the police, and all others who represent the authority of Naples, and see that no one on any pretence leaves the town for the next forty-eight hours."

The town was a very small one, and a large portion of its population were fishermen; these latter shouted loud approval of Frank's words, and declared themselves ready to carry out the instructions he had given them, but the trading class was silent. They had something to lose, and had been so long accustomed to the tyranny of the government that they feared to make any demonstration whatever of liberal opinions until they saw how matters went. It was upon them that the taxes pressed most heavily, and they had far more reason than the fishing class to hail a release from these exactions; but they had more to lose, and they felt that it was best to hold themselves aloof from any manifestation of their feelings. The fishermen, however, thronged round Frank, and announced themselves ready at once to obey his orders.

"Divide yourselves into four parties," he went on; "let each choose a leader and take it in turn to watch the roads and see that none passes."

At this moment Frank's follower returned. "Two of the police went out along the road," he said, "but have just come back."

"I am not surprised at what I have just heard," he went on, addressing the fishermen. "The police have already endeavoured to send word to Reggio that our friends from the hills are shortly coming here, but they have been stopped on the way by some brave peasants whom I stationed on the road for the purpose. How many police are there here?"

"Only eight, signor," one of the men said.

"Come with me, and I will warn them that if any attempt is again made to send word of what is going on here they will be at once hanged."

Followed by forty or fifty fishermen, he went at once to the police quarters. The sergeant who was in command came out with his detachment.

"Men," Frank said, "we bear no ill-will to those who serve the Neapolitan government. It has been the government of this country, and none are to be blamed for taking service with it; and I doubt not that when, like Sicily, Calabria is free, those who have done their duty, without undue oppression and violence, will be confirmed in their appointments. But woe be to those who oppose the impulse of the country! There are thousands of peasants in the mountains already in arms. The Neapolitan soldiers, who were powerless to oppose the people of Sicily, will be equally powerless to oppose the people of Calabria, aided as these will be, when the time comes, by the great army from the other side of the straits. Already, as you know, sir," he said to the officer, "the roads leading from here are guarded. You have made an effort, as was perhaps your duty, to send word to Reggio that the heart of the people here beats with those of their brethren among the hills. Let there be no further attempts of the sort, or it will be bad, alike for those who go and for those who stay, and when Colonel Missori arrives you will be treated as the enemies of freedom and punished accordingly.

"Already I have a detachment close at hand, and the sound of a gun will bring them here at once; but if all is quiet these will not enter the place until the main body arrives. I have come on before to see whether the people here are to be regarded as friends or as enemies. I already know that they are friends; and in the name of Colonel Missori, and in the cause of freedom, I order you to remain quiet here, to take no steps either for or against us, and I doubt not that, when the time comes, you will be as ready as the brave fellows here to join the army of freedom. At present my orders are that you remain indoors. I will have no going out, no taking notes as to the names of those who join our cause. I do not order you to give up your arms; I hope that you will use them in the cause of freedom."

"Your orders shall be obeyed, signor," the sergeant said. "I am powerless to interfere one way or another here, but I promise that no further attempt shall be made to communicate with Reggio."

"I accept your word, sergeant. And now you will send a man round to the houses of all the town council and all functionaries of the Neapolitan government, and state that, by the orders of the representative of Colonel Missori, they are none of them to leave their houses for the next forty-eight hours; and that they are not to attempt to communicate with each other, or to send any message elsewhere. Any attempt whatever to disobey this order will be punished by immediate death. Which man do you send?"

"Thomasso," the sergeant said. "You have heard the order. Will you at once carry it round?"

"Let four of your men," Frank said to the fishermen, go with this policeman. See that he delivers this message, and that he enters into no communication whatever with those to whom he is sent, but simply repeats the order and then goes to the next house."

Four men stepped forward, and at once started with the policeman. The sergeant and the others withdrew into the house.

"Now, my friends," Frank went on to the fishermen, "do as I told you, and let the first party take up at once the duty of watching the roads, and remain there for six hours. It is now ten; at four the second party will relieve them, and so on at intervals of six hours. It will not be long ere the necessity for this will be at an end. Each party will detach eight men in pairs to patrol the streets till morning and arrest any one they find about, and conduct him to the hotel where I shall take up my quarters. Those not on duty had best retire quietly to their homes, as soon as it is settled to which section they are to belong. I shall not go to bed, and any question that may arise must at once be referred to me."

The fishermen went off to the shore to choose their leaders.

"Rejoin your comrades," Frank said to his follower. "Tell them that everything is going on well, and that while two of them are to come down at once to keep watch on the beach, the rest can wrap themselves in their cloaks and lie down until they receive orders from me."

Frank now went to the one hotel in the town and ordered supper to be prepared for him. The landlord, who had been among the crowd when he addressed them, said humbly,—

"I have already ordered supper to be got ready, signor, thinking that when you had arranged matters you would yourself come here. Pray do not think that because many of us did not at once come forward and offer to join you, it was because we were indifferent to your news; but you see it is not with us as with the fishermen. If things go badly, they can embark their families and goods in their boats, cross the straits, and establish themselves in the villages there, and earn their living as before. But with us who have something to lose it is different. Our property would be confiscated, we should be driven from home, many of us would be shot, and others thrown into their dungeons."

"I quite see that, landlord; and I can hardly blame you for hesitating a little, though you must remember that the men who have been the champions of freedom have been almost wholly men who have had much to lose, but have risked all for their principles, and that Garibaldi's army is very largely composed of such men."

"Ah, signor, but we have never seen any chance of success. When Garibaldi once lands, we shall not hang back; but at present it is but a revolt of the peasants. They tell us that France and other powers are endeavouring to prevent him from invading Calabria; and if he should not come, what can a few thousand peasants do against a hundred thousand trained troops?"

"Well, I do not think that Garibaldi will be restrained from crossing, whatever pressure is put upon him: they tried to prevent him from sailing from Genoa—now he is Dictator of Sicily; he will land somewhere on the coast, never fear."

"In that case, signor, I shall shout as loud as any one, and I shall send my son to carry a musket in his ranks."

Frank smiled.

"Well landlord, let me have my supper; to-morrow we may talk over the affair again. Bring me a bottle of good wine, and when supper is served you can close the house for the night. I shall not require a bed, but shall remain here till morning. Do not fasten up the front door, as I shall have men call frequently. I hope there are plenty of provisions in the town in case three or four thousand men should march in here to-morrow."

"For a day, signor, we might feed them; but I doubt if it would go beyond that."

CHAPTER XIV

A DISCOVERY

AT one o'clock one of the men on the look-out brought to Frank the news that he could make out two steamers approaching. Frank ran down to the shore. The man's eyesight had not deceived him: the two steamers were certainly making their way towards Melito, and, from the direction of their course, they had almost certainly come from some port in Sicily, and did not belong to the Neapolitan squadron that were constantly parading the straits. These, indeed, were for the most part lying twenty miles away, while some were anchored off Reggio. Demonstrations had been made for some days both at Messina and the Cape of Faro, in order to attract their attention, and lead to the belief that it was intended to land near the spot where Missori had disembarked, or at some point north of the entrance to the straits.

Stores had been ostentatiously placed on board steamers at Messina and Faro; men had embarked in considerable numbers every evening, and smoke pouring from the funnels showed that steam was being got up. These preparations were keenly watched by the Neapolitans, and served their purpose by concentrating all their attention upon these points. Garibaldi, on arriving from Sardinia with the troops which had been collected there, had despatched the *Torino* and *Franklin*, carrying a thousand of these men, round the island with instructions to them to put in at Giardini, the port of Taormina. He himself proceeded to Messina, and then, after seeing that all was going on well there, rode down to the port, having previously sent forward seven hundred men.

This detachment was so small that its departure attracted little attention, and it was supposed that it had only gone down to reinforce Bixio's brigade; thus Messina was as ignorant of the fact that an expedition was about to start from Giardini as were the Neapolitan commanders. On arrival at Giardini, on the evening of August 18th, Garibaldi found that Bixio had already embarked a thousand men on board the *Torino*, which was a steamer of seven hundred tons, and that he was prepared to send another thousand on board. The *Franklin* was a small paddle steamer of two hundred tons, and she was reported to be leaking so badly that no troops had been embarked on her. Garibaldi at once went on board with his staff, and found that she was making water fast. The leak could not be discovered, but Garibaldi, as an old sea captain, knew what should be done to check the inrush of water, at least for a time, as it was all-important that she should be able to carry her complement of men across the sixteen miles of water between Giardini and Melito. Several of his officers could swim, and he ordered these to dive overboard, and to find, if possible, the position of the leaks.

In the meantime, he sent ashore for a boat-load of a mixture of manure and chopped straw. When this arrived, lumps were thrust down at the end of poles, to the points where leaks had been discovered; particles of the composition were drawn into the leaks by the inrush of water, and in a short time the leakage almost entirely ceased, and the work of embarkation recommenced. Three thousand men were carried by the *Torino*, and twelve hundred on the *Franklin*, where Garibaldi himself took his place, while Bixio commanded on the *Torino*. Both vessels were crowded to a dangerous extent; men were packed on deck as closely as they could stand, and were even clustered on the shrouds. Had there been any wind, it would have been dangerous in the extreme to put to sea overloaded as they were, but fortunately there was not a breath of air, and the water was perfectly calm. At ten o'clock the two vessels started on their eventful voyage, but owing to the difficulties caused by the strong currents, they did not arrive off Melito until two in the morning.

As soon as Frank had assured himself that the approaching vessels were those he expected, he sent off one of his two men to fetch down the party that had for twelve hours been lying outside the place, while he despatched the other to the huts of the leaders of the three parties of fishermen not engaged in watching the roads, to tell them to call up all their men as quietly as possible and to get their boats in the water. In a short time, therefore, after the *Franklin's* anchor had been dropped, Frank arrived alongside the *Torino* with half a dozen fishing boats; he had rowed to her both as being the larger craft and being nearest to the shore, and thought that Garibaldi would be on board her. On reaching her he found Bixio. Several lanterns had been placed near the gangway, and the general at once recognised him.

"Welcome, Captain Percival!" he said heartily, as he shook hands with him. "We were glad indeed when we saw the boats putting off, and knew that a detachment of Missori's men must be there. Have you more boats coming out?"

"Yes, sir; there will be a dozen more off in a few minutes. I set off as soon as I had assembled a sufficient number of fishermen to man those alongside."

"I am sorry to say," Bixio said, "that we have run aground and I fear badly. I have just sent a boat to the *Franklin,* where Garibaldi is, to tell him what has happened. You had better go at once and report to him. What force have you?"

"Only fifty men, sir. The colonel sent only a small party, as he was afraid that, were he to come with all his force, he would bring the enemy down here at once."

"There is no fear of trouble in the town?"

"No, sir; I have arranged all that. You will be entirely unopposed; there are no Neapolitans nearer than Reggio, and they have no suspicions of our being here."

Frank at once returned to the boat in which he had come off, and rowed to the *Franklin.*

"Ah, it is you, Percival!" Garibaldi exclaimed when he saw him. "Then all is well. We will begin to land at once, and you can tell me as we go ashore what Missori has been doing. How many boats have you with you?"

"I have brought six, sir; but there will be at least a dozen more in a few minutes."

Garibaldi descended into the boat, and was followed by as many men as could be crowded into her.

"Now, first about the state of things here. Is there any chance of our being disturbed before the men are all ashore?"

"I should think not, sir. With the exception of the fishermen, whom I have roused to man the boats, no one in the place knows anything of what is going on. The great bulk of the people are in your favour. The syndic and all the authorities are prisoners in their houses, and even if they were conscious of your landing, they could not send the news to Reggio, as I have armed parties on all the roads. You have therefore certainly six or eight hours before there is any chance of interruption."

"That is good news. Indeed, everything has gone well with us so far, except this misfortune of Bixio's steamer running aground. Unless we can succeed in getting her off, I fear that the Neapolitans will capture her. However, that is a minor matter. Now, what can you tell me about the position of the enemy?"

"There are about thirty thousand men under General Viale in and around Monteleone; there are twelve thousand at Bagnara, and the towns between it and Reggio, where there are but fifteen hundred men under General Galotta; eighteen hundred men are in Aspromonte, in pursuit of Missori, who has now about eight hundred men with him."

"They could hardly be disposed better for our purpose," Garibaldi remarked. "We shall take Reggio before supports can arrive to the garrison, and our success there will be worth ten thousand men to us."

Garibaldi remained on shore watching the disembarkation of the men. Every boatman in Melito was soon employed in the work, and, by four o'clock the whole of the troops were on the shore. While the disembarkation had been going on, Garibaldi had sent for the syndic and other authorities, and had informed them that they must now consider themselves under his authority, and obey promptly all orders that he gave them; that he should require bread, meat, and wine, for a day's consumption for the whole of his force; that he was prepared to pay for the food, but that they must obtain it from the inhabitants.

Except among the fishermen, the arrival of the force was regarded with an appearance of apathy. The townspeople had been told by the authorities that there was no fear whatever of Garibaldi and his freebooters coming near them, and believing that he must speedily be crushed, they regarded his arrival with fear rather than pleasure. There were many there who were well-wishers of the cause, but they feared to exhibit any sign of their friendship, lest they should suffer terribly for it when he and his followers had been destroyed by the troops. In Sicily there had been previous insurrections and risings, and the people had long hoped that some day they would shake off the yoke of Naples; but no such hope had been entertained on the mainland, where the reign of oppression had been so long unbroken that no thought that it could ever be thrown off had entered the minds of the great majority of the ignorant people. At daybreak the war-vessels at Reggio could be seen getting up steam, and the greatest efforts were made to get the *Torino* afloat again.

Unfortunately the reduction effected in her draught of water by the removal of her passengers and a certain amount of stores had been counteracted by the force of the current, which, as fast as she was lighted, carried her up higher on the shoal. The little *Franklin*, which was an American vessel chartered for the occasion, hoisted the stars and stripes as soon as the Garibaldians had landed, and steamed across to the island. The *Torino's* Italian flag remained flying until three Neapolitan steamers came up and opened fire upon the Garibaldians on shore. Three men were wounded by a shell; when the rest, forming up, marched out of the town, taking the path (it could scarcely be called a road) towards Reggio.

Four men had, soon after the landing had been effected,

been sent to Missori with orders that he should join at Reggio. As soon as the Garibaldians were out of range, the Neapolitan commanders turned their guns on the *Torino,* and after keeping up a heavy fire upon her for some hours, they sent parties in boats to board her and set her on fire.

The first part of the march towards Reggio was an extremely toilsome one. For the first eight miles, from Melito to Cape D'Armi, the slopes of the mountains extend to the very edge of the water, and the troops were continually mounting the steep spurs or descending into ravines. They had with them four mountain guns, and as the path could only be traversed by the men in single file, the difficulty of taking the guns along was immense.

The men were in the highest spirits. The fact that, in case of disaster, the destruction of the *Torino* had cut off all means of return to Sicily, in no way troubled them. Similarly they had thrown themselves on shore at Marsala, and the ships in which they had come had been captured by the enemy. Their confidence in Garibaldi was absolute, and no thought of disaster was for a moment entertained. Once past the Cape, they halted. It was already evening, and although the distance in miles had been short, the fatigue had been very great, and none had closed an eye on the previous night. It was therefore impossible to go farther. They were received with enthusiasm by the people of the villages scattered here and there on the mountain-side. A Greek colony had very many years before settled there, and retained many of their own customs, and even their language; but although conversation with the North Italian Garibaldians was difficult, and often impossible, there could be no mistake as to the heartiness of their welcome.

A DISCOVERY 251

Everything in the way of provisions was given to the soldiers, and each cottage took in as many men as it could hold; and from the moment, indeed, when the Garibaldians set foot in Calabria, they met with a far deeper and heartier welcome than had been the case in Sicily. In the latter they had been joined by a comparatively small body of volunteers, and the people had contented themselves with shouting and cheering, but had given little else; and even in Messina the appeals of Garibaldi for aid in the hospitals, and lint and bandages for the wounded, had met with little response: the Sicilians had, in fact, fallen to the level of the Neapolitans. In Calabria, on the other hand, the population was manly, hardy and hospitable—possessing the virtues of mountaineers in all countries; and as the news of Garibaldi's landing spread, the whole population took up arms.

Here communications were received from Missori, who stated that he was pushing forward with all haste; but that, from the ruggedness of the mountains along which he was travelling, he could not hope to be at Reggio until late the following evening. The next day the Garibaldians advanced along the mountain-side; a detachment sent out from Reggio retiring along the road as they advanced. The force halted for the night six miles from the town. A messenger from Missori announced that, in spite of his efforts, he was still far distant; Garibaldi, therefore, determined to attack the next morning without waiting for him. Communications had been opened with the townsfolk, and a message was sent back that the national guard would support him.

Few towns are more beautifully situated than Reggio. It lies on the lowest slope of a spur of Aspromonte. Behind it rises the castle, with its guns commanding the town, whose scattered suburbs and gardens, stretch far away up the mountain-side; while across the straits lies the Bay of Catania, with numerous towns and villages up the slopes of Etna, which forms a background, with wreaths of smoke ascending from the volcano on its summit. Away to the right lies Messina, and the coast stretching along to Cape Faro. The intervening strait is dotted with shipping: steamers on their way to the East, or returning to Italy and France; sailing-ships flying the flags of many nations, fishing and rowing-boats.

It was settled that Bixio with his brigade was to enter the town by the main road, and effect a junction with the national guard in the piazza lying below the castle; and that, when the junction was made, a battalion was to descend to the shore and attack a small fort near the marina.

As soon as the news of Garibaldi's landing had reached the town, the principal people and the officers of the national guard had called upon Galotta, and begged him, if he intended to fight Garibaldi, to go outside the town to do so, and so save the place from the injury that would be effected by a desperate struggle in the streets. The request was a strange one; but the general, who no doubt considered that he would do better in a fight in the open than in the streets, where possibly the inhabitants might take part against him, agreed to do this, and on Garibaldi's approach marched out of the fortress with eight hundred men in two detachments, one of which took post at the bridge just outside Reggio, while strangely enough, the other four hundred men took up a position on the opposite side of the town.

In order to confuse the Italian troops, who would be marching from all the towns on the coast towards Reggio, Garibaldi had sent orders to Cosenz to cross during the night from Cape Faro with twelve hundred men in boats, and to land near Bagnara. Expecting some hard fighting, the Garibaldians moved on at midnight. When they approached the town the scouts went forward, and found to their surprise that the bridge was unoccupied. Bixio at once crossed it; and, reaching the piazza, joined the national guard there without a shot having been fired. Similarly, Garibaldi with the rest of the force entered the suburbs. They came upon a small outpost, which was at once driven back; and Gallotta, who, not dreaming of a night attack, had withdrawn most of his troops into the castle, now beat a hasty retreat with the remainder, and a cannonade was at once opened by its guns upon the town.

The Neapolitan force on the other side of Reggio retreated at once, fearing that they would not be able to enter the castle, and retired along the road, hoping to meet General Braganti, who was advancing with a column to reinforce the garrison. Bixio's battalion took the little fort on the marina without difficulty. Barricades were at once thrown up across all the streets leading to the castle, in order to prevent the garrison from making a sortie, or any relieving force reaching it. It was daylight now, and Missori and his column arrived, as arranged, upon the hill-side above the castle, and at once opened so heavy a musketry fire upon its defenders, that the artillery were unable to serve the guns. Feeling that the castle could not hold out long, Garibaldi despatched a battalion to hold the relieving column in check; but Bragnati had already heard from the fugitives that the town and seaside fort were in the hands of the Garibaldians, and the castle invested upon all sides: he therefore fell back to await further reinforcements, being ignorant of the force under Garibaldi's command.

At twelve o'clock a loud cheer broke from the Garibaldians round the castle, for the white flag of surrender was hoisted. The general granted the same terms that were given to Bosco's force at Milazzo—namely, that the garrison might march down to the shore, and there embark on board the Neapolitan war-ships for conveyance to Naples, leaving all munitions of war, money, and all prisoners who might be confined there, behind them. Thus, with the loss of only seven men killed and wounded, a castle which had been considered capable of resisting a long siege was captured, and the first blow struck at the Bourbon dynasty of Naples. The success in itself was a striking one; its consequences were far-reaching. The news that Reggio had been captured by the Garibaldians, almost without fighting, spread like wild-fire. Cosenz's landing had also been successful; and this, added to the news that all southern Calabria has risen in arms, created such consternation among the commanders of the various bodies of troops in the towns facing the straits, that all prepared to march at once to join the main force at Monteleone.

As soon as the castle surrendered, Garibaldi despatched boats across the straits, with orders to the troops at Messina and Cape Faro to cross at once in any craft they could get hold of. No advance from Reggio was made that afternoon, as the troops required some rest after their exertions. As evening came on the scene was a striking one; every town and village on the other side of the straits from Cape Faro to Giardini being illuminated. The lights twinkled, and bonfires blazed, far up the sides of Etna.

As soon as Garibaldi had entered the castle, he said to

Frank, who had been near him all day: "Take ten men and search the castle thoroughly, and release all political prisoners. There are sure to be many here."

Frank obeyed the order eagerly. At Palermo he had not expected to find any prisoners from the mainland; and he had read through the list of those found and released at Messina without emotion—for there, as at Palermo, all were men, for the most part of good family, belonging to the city; but now he was on the mainland, and prisoners taken in any part of the Neapolitan dominions might be found here. First he obtained the list of those detained from the officer in special charge of them. No familiar name met his eye as he glanced hastily down it.

"You are sure that this is the entire list?" he asked the officer.

"There are none others," the latter replied; "but if you are searching for a friend you may find him here, though bearing another name. The majority of the prisoners are registered under their real names, but in some cases, where there are particular reasons for secrecy, another name is given when they are brought here, and I myself am ignorant of what their real designations may be."

"You had better accompany me round, sir," Frank said, "and see that the jailors open all the doors and give me every facility."

The officer willingly assented: he felt that his appointment under the Neapolitan government was at an end, and was anxious to please those who were likely to be his masters in the future. As a rule some fifteen or twenty men were confined together; these were first visited, but no familiar face was found among them.

"Those you have seen," the officer said, "are, I believe, all confined here under their own names; as you see, a number are kept together. All are allowed at certain hours of the day to go out into the courtyard and to converse with each other freely. There are four prisoners who are kept apart from the rest, and each other; these are the four who bear I believe, other names than those given on the list. They go out for four or five hours at a time on to the walls, but each has his separate place for exercise, and they can hold no communication with each other, or with the rest of the prisoners. In all other respects they have the same food and treatment.

The scene in each of the rooms that he had hitherto entered had been very painful; the prisoners had heard the sound of firing, but were in ignorance of what it meant. No news from the outside world ever reached them; they had heard nothing of the events in Sicily, and the only explanation that they could imagine for the firing was that there had been a revolution in the province, and that the castle had been attacked by a party of insurgents. Their hopes had fallen when the firing ceased; and during the hour that had passed while the negotiations were being carried on, had altogether faded away. They had heard no cannon from without; and that a body of insurgents should have captured the fortress seemed out of the question. There had been an attack, but the assailants had evidently fallen back. When, therefore, Frank entered, attended by their chief and followed by eight men in red shirts, broad-brimmed hats, and carrying muskets, they were too astonished even to guess at the truth until Frank said:

"Gentlemen, in the name of General Garibaldi, who has

captured this castle, I have the pleasure to announce to you that from this moment you are free men."

For the most part the announcement was received in silence. They could scarce believe the possibility of what he said. The name of Garibaldi was known to all. It was he who had commanded at the defence of Rome; it was he who, as those who had been longest there had learned from comparatively late comers, had done such signal service in the Alps with his volunteers, when, by the aid of France, Milan and part of Lombardy was wrested from the Austrians. They looked at one another almost incredulously; then, as the meaning of Frank's words dawned upon them, some fell into each other's arms, murmuring incoherent words, others burst into tears, while some again dropped on their knees to thank God for their deliverance. Frank had to wait for a few minutes in each room until they had recovered themselves a little, and then sent out each batch with two of his soldiers to see for themselves that they were really free, and to thank Garibaldi for their rescue.

"Now, signor," the officer said, when they had left the last of the large rooms, "there are only the four special prisoners to visit."

The first of these was a man in the prime of life, although with long unkempt hair and beard. As Frank repeated the words he had used before, the man looked at him with an unmeaning smile. Again and again he spoke to him, but a low childish laugh was the only answer. Frank turned angrily to the officer.

"The poor fellow's mind has gone," he said. "How long has he been a prisoner here?"

"About eight years, signor; for some time his mind has been getting weaker."

"The brutes!" Frank exclaimed passionately. "Here men, take this poor fellow out to the courtyard, and remain with him: I will ask the general presently what had best be done with him. Are the others like this?" he asked the officer, with a thrill of fear that overpowered the hope that he had lately been feeling.

"One of them is silent, and seldom speaks, but he is, I believe, quite sensible; the other two are well. The man we shall next see is perfectly so; he never speaks to us, but when alone here, or when upon the wall for exercise, he talks incessantly to himself: sometimes in Italian; sometimes, as one of the officers who understands that language says, in English; sometimes in what I have heard our priests say is Latin; sometimes in other languages."

"Before you open the door, tell me what age he is," Frank asked, in a low strained voice.

"I should say that he was about sixty, signor; he has been here nearly three years," the man said.

"Now open the door."

Frank entered almost timidly. A tall man rose from a palette, which was the sole article of furniture in the room.

"Is it treason, lieutenant," he asked quietly, "to ask what has been going on?"

Frank with an exclamation of joy stepped forward: "Grandfather," he said, "thank God I have found you!"

The prisoner started, looked at him searchingly, and exclaimed, "Frank! yes, it is Frank: is this a miracle, or am I dreaming?"

"Neither, grandfather. Garibaldi has landed; we have taken the castle, and, thank God, you are free."

The professor sank back on his bed and sat for a minute

A DISCOVERY 259

or two with his face buried in his hands; then he rose, put his hands upon Frank's shoulders, and then clasped him in his arms, bursting as he did so into tears, while Frank's own cheeks were wet. The professor was the first to recover himself.

"I had fancied, Frank," he said, "that I was a philosopher, but I see I am not; I thought that all emotion for me was over, but I feel now like a child. And can I really go out?"

"Yes," Frank said; "but I have two more doors to open, and then I will go with you."

"I will wait here for you, Frank: I shall be glad to be for a few minutes alone, to persuade myself that this is not a dream, and to thank God for His mercy. One moment, though, before you leave me: is my wife alive and well, and my daughter?"

"Both are well," Frank said; "it is five months since I saw them, but I had letters from both four days ago." Then he left the cell.

"This is the silent man," the officer said, as he opened the next door. Frank repeated his usual speech to the dark-bearded man who faced him when he entered.

"You are young to lie, sir," the man said sternly. "This, I suppose, is a fresh trick to see whether I still hate the accursed government that has sent me here."

"It is no lie, signor," Frank said quietly. "I am an officer of General Garibaldi's. He has conquered all Sicily, and with some four thousand men crossed the straits three days ago to Melito, and has now captured this place."

The man burst into a wild fit of laughter and then, with another cry of "You lie!" he sprang upon Frank, and had it not been for the officer and the two Garibaldian soldiers, who still accompanied them, would assuredly have strangled him; for, strong as he was, Frank was but an infant in the man's hands. After a desperate struggle, he was pulled off, and forced down on his bed.

"Leave him," Frank said: "he will be quiet now.—Signor, I can understand your feelings; you think what I have said is impossible. You will soon see that it is not. As soon as you calm yourself, one of my men will accompany you to the courtyard, which is, you will find, full of Garibaldians; and the general himself will assure you that you are a free man, and can, if you choose, quit this place immediately."

The man's mood changed. "I am calm," he said, rising to his feet. "Perhaps this man will take me out to execution, but it will be welcome to me. I have prayed for death so long that I can only rejoice if it has come." Then he quietly walked out of the cell, followed by one of the soldiers, who, being by no means satisfied that the prisoner had ceased to be dangerous, slipped his bayonet on to his musket before following him.

The fourth prisoner was very feeble, but he received the news with tranquillity. "It does not make much difference to me now," he said; "but it will be some satisfaction to know that I shall be buried outside the prison."

"You must not look at it in that light, signor," Frank said. "No doubt you will pick up health and strength when you rejoin your friends, and find that the tyranny and oppression you struggled against are at an end."

Leaving the last of his men to give the poor fellow his arm and lead him out, Frank returned to Professor Forli. The latter rose briskly as he came in.

"I am myself again," he said. "Your coming here so strangely, and the news you brought, were so great a surprise, that everything seemed confused, and I was unable to grasp the fact. I have heard that a good swimmer, if he falls suddenly into deep water, behaves for a few moments like one who is ignorant of the art, striking out wildly, swallowing much water before he fairly grasps the situation and his skill returns to him. So it was with me: my equanimity has never been shaken since I was first seized. I perceived at once that what was to come was inevitable. I reflected that I was vastly better off than most; that my mind was stored with knowledge accumulated by the great thinkers of all ages, and that, so fortified, I could afford to be indifferent to imprisonment or persecution. But you see the suddenness of the knowledge that I was free, did what captivity, even as hopeless as mine, had failed to do. Now, Frank, let us go out: you shall take me down to the seashore, and then tell me by what marvel you come to be here. If it had been your father, I should not have been so surprised; but that you, whom I had thought of as a boy at Harrow, should throw open my prison-door, is past my understanding at present. Of course, your father is here with you?"

"I am sorry to say that he is not," Frank said quietly; "but I will tell you all about it when we get down to the shore. I must, before we start, tell the general that all the prisoners have been freed, and that I have found you, and ask if he will require me just at present."

Going into the courtyard, Frank left his grandfather to look on at a scene so novel to him, and went into the room where Garibaldi and Bixio were examining, with the syndic, a map of the district. He stood at the door till the general looked round.

"Pardon me, sir, for interrupting you, but I wish to report to you that among the other prisoners I have found Signor Forli, and that he is in good health."

Garibaldi rose from his seat, and holding out both hands grasped those of Frank.

"I am glad—I am glad indeed, lad," he said with deep feeling, "that my old friend is rescued; glad that the sacrifice that your mother made in parting with you has not been in vain, and that your own bravery and good conduct have been thus rewarded. I pray God that that other that you are seeking for, still nearer and more loved, may also be found."

"Excuse me," he said to Bixio and the syndic: "I must shake Signor Forli by the hand before I go farther into this."

As he hurried out, Frank said,—"I have not told him about my father yet, sir. He suggested himself that we should go down together to the sea-shore, where we could talk matters over quietly; and I came in partly to ask you if you would require my services for the next hour or two?"

"Certainly not, Percival. Yes, I will be careful; it would be a shock to him to be told suddenly that your father had lost his life in his search for him."

Led by Frank, he hurried to the spot where the professor was standing, quietly regarding the Garibaldians laughing and chatting, and the groups of the Neapolitan troops, who, now disarmed, were standing talking together with disheartened and sombre faces.

"Ah, professor," he exclaimed, as he came up to him; "glad indeed am I that you have been found and rescued.

Your friends were right in not despairing of you. It seems an age since we parted twelve years ago at Rome. You are little changed. I feared that if found you would be like so many of the others whose prison doors we have opened—mere wrecks of themselves."

"Nor have you changed much," Signor Forli said, as he stood holding the general's hand; "a line or two on the forehead, but that is all. And so you have taken up again the work that seemed postponed for another century at Rome?"

"Yes; and this time I hope that all Italy will be freed. Now, old friend, you must excuse me for the present—I am full of business; this evening we must have a long talk together; much has happened in the three years that have passed since you disappeared. You can keep this youngster with you. He has well earned a day's holiday." So saying, Garibaldi hurried off.

CHAPTER XV

THE ADVANCE FROM REGGIO

PROFESSOR FORLI was silent until he and Frank had passed out through the gate of the castle, then he took a long breath.

"The air of freedom," he said, "is no different from that I have breathed daily on the walls there, for wellnigh three years, and yet it seems different. It is a comfort that my prison lay in this fair spot, and not in some place where I could see but little beyond the walls. Often and often have I thanked God that it was so, and that, even as a free man and with the world before me, I could see no more lovely scene than this. There was change, too: there was the passage of the ships; I used to wonder where each was sailing; and about the passengers, and how hopefully many of these were going abroad to strange countries in search of fortunes, and how few were returning with their hopes fully satisfied. I smiled sometimes to think of the struggle for wealth and advancement going on in the world round me, while I had no need to think of the future; but my needs, always, as you know, few and simple, were ministered to; and though cut off from converse with all around me, I had the best company in the world in my cell. How thankful I was that my memory was so good—that I could discourse with the great men of the world, could talk with Plato and argue with Demosthenes; could discuss old age with Cicero, or travel with either

Homer or Virgil; visit the Inferno with Dante, or the Heavens with Milton; knew by heart many of the masterpieces of Shakespeare and Goethe, and could laugh over the fun of Terence and Plutarch: it was a grand company."

So the professor continued to talk until they reached the shore. Frank was not called upon to speak. The professor was talking to himself rather than to him, continuing the habit of which the officer of the prison had spoken. As yet his brain was working in its old groove. Once on the strand, he stood silently gazing for two or three minutes, then he passed his hand across his forehead, and with an evident effort broke the chain of his thoughts and turned to Frank.

"Strange talk, no doubt you are thinking, Frank, for a man so suddenly and unexpectedly released from a living grave; but you see, lad, that the body can be emancipated more quickly than the mind from its bonds, and I am as one awaking from a deep sleep and still wondering whether it is I myself, and how I came to be here, and what has happened to me. I fear that it will be some time before I can quite shake off my dreams. Now, lad, once more tell me about my wife and your mother. But no, you have told me that they are well. You have said naught of your father, save that he is not here. Where is he? and how is he?"

"I can answer neither question, grandfather. He, like you, has been lost to us; he disappeared a few months after you did, and we were led to believe that he was killed."

The professor was himself again in an instant. The mood that had dominated him was shaken off, and he was keen, sharp, and alert again, as Frank remembered him.

"He is lost?" he repeated: "you heard that he was killed? How was it? tell me everything. In the early days of my imprisonment, when I thought of many things outside the walls of my gaol, one thing troubled me more than others. My wife had her daughter; no harm would come to her, save the first grief at my loss and the slow process of hope dying out. My daughter had everything that a woman could wish to make her happy; but your father, I knew him so well, he would not rest when the days passed and no news of me came —he would move heaven and earth to find me; and a man in this country who dares to enquire after a political prisoner incurs no small danger. Is it so that he was missing? Tell me all, and spare no detail; we have the rest of the day before us. We will sit down on this seat. Now begin."

Frank told, at length, how, on the news of the professor's disappearance, his father had interested the English government in the matter, and how to all enquiries made the government of Naples had replied that they knew nothing whatever concerning his disappearance; and how, at last, he himself started with an order obtained from Naples for him to search all the prisons of southern Italy.

"It was just like him; it was noble and chivalrous," the professor said; "but he should have known better. An Englishman unacquainted with Italy might have believed that with such an order he might safely search for one who he suspected was lying in a Neapolitan prison, but your father should have known better. Notice would assuredly be sent before he arrived; and had he come here, for example, I should a week before have been carried away up into the mountains, till he had gone. He would have been shown the register of prisoners, he would not have found my name among them, he would have been told that no such person as he described had ever been confined here,—it was hopeless. But go on with your story."

Frank told how his father had visited several prisons, and how he wrote letters, exposing their horrors, that had appeared in the English papers, and had created an immense impression throughout the country.

"It was mad of him," the professor murmured; "noble, but mad."

Then Frank told how the news came of his being carried off by brigands, of the steps that had been taken, of the evidence of the courier who saw him fall, and of some of his effects being found in the hut on the mountain when this was captured and the brigand chief killed, of the report given by one of the prisoners that his father had died and been buried shortly after he was taken there, and of the vain search that had been made for his body.

"And was this tale believed?" Signor Forli exclaimed, leaping to his feet. "No Italian would for a moment have thought it true—at least, none who had the misfortune to be born under the Neapolitan rule. Surely my wife never believed it?"

"In her heart I know now that she did not," Frank said, "but she kept her doubts to herself for the sake of my mother. She thought that it was far better that she should believe that father was dead than that she should believe him buried in one of the foul prisons he had described."

"She was right—she was right," the professor said: "it was certainly better. And your mother—did she lose hope?"

"She told me that she would not allow herself to believe that he might still be alive, and I believe she and the signora never said one word on the subject to each other until just before I started." He then related how the courier had been brought over, how he had been installed in the house in Cadogan Place, and how no suspicion of his being a spy had been entertained until after the receipt of Garibaldi's letter, and how they were convinced at last that he had overheard all the arrangements made for his leaving for Italy.

"And you are alive, Frank, to tell me this! By what miracle did you escape from the net that was thrown around you?"

This part of the story was also told.

"It was well aranged and bravely carried through, Frank. So you took up the mission which had cost your father either his life or his liberty? It was a great undertaking for a lad, and I wonder indeed that your mother, after the losses she had suffered, permitted you to enter upon it. Well, contrary to all human anticipations, you have succeeded in one half of it, and you will, I trust, succeed in the other. What seemed hardly possible—that you should enter the castle of Reggio as one of its conquerors, and so have free access to the secrets of its prison—has been accomplished; and if Garibaldi succeeds in carrying his arms farther, and other prison doors are opened, we may yet find your father. What you have told me has explained what has hitherto been a puzzle to me: why I should have been treated as a special prisoner, and kept in solitary confinement. Now I understand it. England had taken the matter up; and as the government of Naples had denied all knowledge of me, it was necessary that neither any prisoner, who, perhaps, some day might be liberated, nor any prison official should know me, and be able to report my existence to the British representative. You may be sure that, had your father come here, and examined every prisoner and official, privately, he would have obtained no intelligence of me. Giuseppe Borani would not have been here, he would have been removed, and none would dream that he was the prisoner for whom search was made. And now tell me briefly about this expedition of Garibaldi. Is all Europe at war, that he has managed to bring an army here?"

"First of all, grandfather, I must tell you what happened last year."

He then related the incidents of the war of 1859, whereby France and Sardinia united and wrested Milan and Lombardy from the Austrians; the brilliant achievements of the Garibaldians; the disappointment felt by Italy at Nice and a part of Savoy being handed over to Napoleon as the price of the services that he had rendered; how Bologna and Florence, Palma, Ferrara, Forli, and Ravenna, had all expelled their rulers and united themselves with Sardinia; and how, Garibaldi having been badly treated and his volunteers disbanded he himself had retired disappointed and hurt to Caprera.

Then he related briefly the secret gathering of the expedition; the obstacles thrown in its way; its successful landing in Sicily, and the events that had terminated with the expulsion of the Neapolitan forces from the island.

"Garibaldi began with but a thousand men," he said in conclusion. "He is now at the head of twenty thousand, and it will grow every hour; for we have news of risings throughout southern Calabria. If a thousand sufficed for the conquest of Sicily, twenty thousand will surely be sufficient for that of the mainland. The easy capture of this place will strike terror into the enemy, and raise the enthusiasm of the troops and the Calabrians to the utmost. Garibaldi has but four thousand men with him now; but by this time tomorrow ten thousand at least will have crossed, and I think it is possible that we shall reach Naples without having to fight another battle. At any rate, one pitched battle should be enough to free all Southern Italy. The Papal States will come next, and then, as Garibaldi hopes, Venice; though this will be a far more serious affair, for the Austrians are very different foes from the Neapolitans, and have the advantage of tremendously strong fortifications, which could only be taken by siege operations with heavy artillery, and certainly could not be accomplished by troops like Garibaldi's.

"Now about my father. Supposing him to be alive where do you think he would most probably be imprisoned?"

"There is no saying. That he is alive, I feel confident—unless, indeed, he died in prison from the effect of the wound given him when he was captured. That he did not die when in the hands of the brigands, we may take to be certain, for his grave must in that case have been discovered. He must have been handed over to a party of police sent to fetch him by previous agreement with the brigands, and would have been confined in some place considered especially secure from search. I should fancy that he is probably in Naples itself,—there are several large prisons there. Then there would be the advantage that, if the British government had insisted upon a commission of their own officers searching these prisons, he could be removed secretly from one to another, so that before the one in which he was confined could be examined he would have been taken to another which had been previously searched.

"His case was a more serious one than mine. Although I was a naturalised British subject, I had gone of my own free will to Italy, in the vain belief that I should be unmolested after so long an absence; and probably there would have been no stir in the matter had not your father taken it up so hotly, and by the influence he possessed obtained permission to search the dungeons. But, as I said, his case was a far more serious one. He went out backed by the influence of the British government; he was assisted by the British legation; he held the order of the Neapolitan government for admission to all prisons. Thus, had it been found that he had, in spite of their own so-called safe-conduct, been seized and imprisoned, the British fleet would have been in the Bay of Naples in a very short time—especially as his letters, as you tell me, created so much feeling throughout the country. Therefore it would be an almost vital question for the government to maintain the story they had framed, and to conceal the fact that, all the time they were asserting that he had been captured and killed by the brigands, he was in one of their own prisons.

"I may say frankly that they would unhesitatingly have had him killed, perhaps starved to death in a cell, were it not that they would have put it in the power of some official or other to betray them: a discovery that would have meant the fall of the government, possibly the dethronement of the king. Had he been an Italian, he would assuredly have been murdered, for it would not have paid any prison official to betray them; whereas, being an Englishman of distinction, in whose fate the British government had actively interested itself, any man who knew the facts could have obtained a reward of a very large amount indeed for giving information. That is the sole reason, Frank, that leads me to believe that he may still be alive. He was doubtless imprisoned under another name, just as I was; but at least it would be known to the men that attended upon him that he was an Englishman, and these could scarcely have avoided suspecting that he was the man about whom such a stir had taken place. The government had already incurred a tremendous risk by his seizure; but this would have been far greater had foul means been used to get rid of him in prison.

"In the former case, should by any extraordinary chance his existence have become known to the British legation, they would have framed some deliberate lie to account for their ignorance of his being Captain Percival. They might, for instance, assert that he had been taken prisoner in the mountains, with a party of brigands; that his assertions that he was an Englishman had been wholly disbelieved, for he would naturally have spoken in Italian, and his Italian was so good that any assertions he made that he was an Englishman would have been wholly discredited. That is merely a rough guess at the story they might have invented, for probably it would have been much more plausible; but, however plausible, it would not have received the slightest credit had it been found that he had been foully done to death.

"It is difficult, Frank, when one is discussing the probable actions of men without heart, honour, or principle, and in deadly fear of discovery, to determine what course they would be likely to take in any particular circumstances. Now, the first thing that I have to do is to cross to Messina, and to telegraph and afterwards to write to my wife. Can I telegraph?"

"Yes, but not direct: the regular line is that which crosses the straits to this town and then goes up through Italy. That, of course, we have not been able to use, and could not use it now. All messages have been sent by the line from Cape Passaro to Malta, and thence through Sardinia and

Corsica to Spezzia. You can send a message by that. There will be no difficulty in getting a boat across the straits. You see the war-ships have steamed away. As soon as the castle was taken they found that their anchorage was within range of its guns. They fired a few shots into the town when the castle was bombarding it, and then retired. I believe that all through the men of the navy have been very reluctant to act against us, except, of course, at Palermo."

"Then I will go at once. It is strange to me to be able to say I will go."

"Very well, grandfather. Of course you have no money, but I can supply you with as much as you like. I have plenty of funds. I can't say where you will find me when you come back, but you will only have to enquire where Garibaldi himself is: I am sure to be with him."

"I shall stay a couple of days there. After that hard pallet and prison fare I cannot resist the temptation of a comfortable bed, a well-furnished room, and a civilised meal, especially as I am not likely to find any of these things on the way to Naples."

"By the way, I should think you could telegraph from here," Frank said. "Garibaldi sent off a message to Messina directly the castle was taken."

"Then let us do so by all means."

They went at once to the telegraph office, and from there the professor sent the following message: "Dearest wife, Frank has found and released me. Am well and in good health. Shall write fully this evening. Shall accompany him and aid in his search for Leonard. Love to Muriel.—FORLI."

Having handed this in they went down to the shore again,

and had no difficulty in hiring a boat. Frank took twenty sovereigns from his belt.

"You will want all this, grandfather, for indeed you must have an entirely new fit-out."

"I suppose I must. There has not been much wear-and-tear in clothes, but three years is a long time for a single suit to last, and I have lately had some uneasiness as to what I should do when these things no longer hung together; and I certainly felt a repugnance to asking for a prison suit. I must decidedly go and get some clothes fit to be seen in before I present myself at an hotel. No respectable house would take me in as I am."

"Will you have more, sir? I can let you have fifty if you would like it."

"No, my boy, I don't want to be encumbered with luggage. A suit besides that I shall wear, and a change of under-clothes, will suffice. These can be carried in a small hand-bag, and whether we walk, or ride, I can take it with me."

After seeing Signor Forli off, Frank returned to the castle.

"Where is the professor?" Garibaldi asked, when he reported himself as ready for duty.

"I have just sent him off to Messina, general. He is sorely in need of clothes, and he wants to write a long letter home, and he could scarcely find a quiet room where he could do so in Reggio. He will rejoin us as we advance."

"That is the wisest thing he could do; for although he looks wonderfully well, he could hardly be capable of standing much fatigue after taking no exercise for three years. He will have a great deal to learn as to what has taken place since he has been here, for I don't suppose the prisoners heard a whisper of the great changes in Northern Italy."

THE ADVANCE FROM REGGIO

"I told him in a few words, sir, but I had no time to give him any details."

At Reggio twenty-six guns, five hundred muskets, and a large quantity of coal, ammunition, provisions, horses, and mules were captured. On the following morning, Major Nullo and the Guides with a battalion were thrown out towards San Giovanni. There was no other forward movement. The general was occupied in receiving deputations from many towns and villages, and there were arrangements to be made for the transport of such stores and ammunition as were likely to be required. The Garibaldians had crossed in large numbers. Cosenz and Medici, with a considerable portion of their commands, were already over, and the former had gone up into the hills. The next morning Garibaldi with two thousand men and six captured field-pieces moved forward. It was possible that they would meet with opposition at San Giovanni, and they had scarcely started when a messenger arrived from Nullo. Believing from the reports of the countrymen that the Neapolitans were retiring, he had ridden on with six of the Guides, till to his astonishment, at a bridge crossing a ravine close to that town, he came upon two squadrons of Neapolitan Lancers. With great presence of mind, he and his men had drawn their revolvers and summoned the officers in command to surrender.

"Surrender to whom?" the latter asked.

"To Garibaldi; he is ready to attack at once, if you refuse."

"I will take you to the general," the officer said.

To him Nullo repeated his command.

"I have no objection to confer with Garibaldi himself," the general said, "and will go with you to him."

"I cannot take you," Nullo said: "my instructions are simply to demand your surrender; but I will go myself and inform him of your readiness to meet him. In the meantime, I demand that you withdraw your lancers from the bridge, which must be considered as the boundary between the two forces. You can leave two men on your side, and I will leave two on mine."

To this the general agreed; and posting two of his men at the bridge, another was sent back to beg Garibaldi to hurry up the troops. Messengers went backward and forward between General Melendis and Garibaldi, who was marching forward with all haste. But, as the terms the latter laid down were that the troops should give up their arms and then be allowed to march away, no agreement was arrived at, and the Neapolitans evacuated the town and took up a very strong position on the hillside above it. They were two thousand five hundred strong, with five guns. In the evening Garibaldi with two thousand men arrived near the place, and sending forward two companies to the bridge, made a circuit through the hills, and took up a position above and somewhat in rear of the Neapolitans. A messenger was sent to Cosenz, who was seventeen miles away, ordering him to start at once, and, if possible, arrive in the morning. A body of Calabrian peasantry undertook to watch the enemy, and the Garibaldians, wrapping themselves in their blankets, lay down for the night.

Before daybreak they were on their feet, and moved down the hill. The enemy opened fire with shell, but only two or three men fell, and the fire was not returned. On arrival at a spot where they were sheltered from the fire, Garibaldi sent in a messenger with a flag of truce, renewing the offer of terms. The Neapolitans shot the bearer of the flag as he approached them, but afterwards offered to treat. Garibaldi, however, greatly angered at this violation of the laws of war, replied at first that he would now accept nothing but unconditional surrender. An armistice was however granted, to enable the general to communicate with General Braganti. This afforded time, too, for Cosenz to arrive from Salerno, and for Bixio, whose brigade had remained at Reggio, to bring up some guns; these were posted so as to entirely cut the Neapolitan line of retreat.

At five o'clock Garibaldi sent an order to the Neapolitans to lay down their arms within a quarter of an hour, or he would advance. Their general, seeing, that he could not now hope to be reinforced, and that he was completely surrounded, assented to the demand. His soldiers piled their arms and soon fraternised with the Garibaldians, many of them showing unconcealed pleasure that they had not been called upon to oppose those who had come to free their country. The greater portion of them threw away their accoutrements, and even their caps, and then dispersed, a few starting to join the main force under Viarli, the greater portion scattering to their homes. The fort by the water's edge below the town had also surrendered.

This was an important capture, as it possessed several heavy guns; and these, with those of Faro on the opposite shore, commanded the Straits, consequently the Neapolitan ships could not pass on their way up towards Naples, but were forced to retire through the other end and to make their way entirely round the island, thus leaving the passage between Messina and the mainland entirely open. At daybreak Garibaldi started at the head of Cosenz's column for

Alta-fiumara, which the first party of Garibaldians that landed had failed to capture. This, after a short parley, surrendered on the same terms as those granted the day before, and the men, throwing away their shakos and knapsacks, started for their various homes. Three miles farther, the castle of Scylla surrendered, the national guard of the town having taken up arms and declared for Garibaldi as soon as they heard that he was coming. Bagnara had also been evacuated, Viarli having withdrawn with his force and marched to Monteleone.

A halt was made here. The strictest orders had been given by Garibaldi against plundering or in any way giving cause for hostility among the peasantry. Sentries were posted and one of the soldiers found stealing grapes was shot—an example which prevented any repetition of the offence.

That evening Frank, who was down on the shore, watching the men from Messina being landed from several steamers, saw Signor Forli.

"It is lucky indeed that I was down here," he said, "for every house in the town is full of troops, and you might have searched all night without finding me. It is quite useless to look for a bed now, and, indeed, the houses are so crowded that I had made up my mind to sleep here, and I should recommend you to do the same. I see you have got a blanket with you. It will be much cooler and more pleasant than indoors."

"I will do so gladly, Frank. It will be a fresh luxury for me to see the stars overhead as I lie, and the sand is quite as soft as any of these Italians' beds are likely to be."

Frank had indeed slept out every night since the Garibaldians first landed. It saved the trouble of endeavouring to find accommodations, and enabled him to have a swim every morning to refresh him for his day's work.

Day after day the Garibaldians marched on without encountering resistance. It was indeed a procession rather than a military advance. The country was lovely, the weather superb. At each village they were saluted by numbers of the country people, who had come down to greet them. They were all armed, and numbers of them joined the Garibaldians. They were, for the most part, of fine physique, with handsome faces, and the women of this coast were famous for their beauty. The Greek element was still predominant, and in many of the villages no other language was spoken. In the towns, the national guard was drawn up to receive their deliverers with all honour, and the inhabitants of all classes vied with each other in their hospitality. Frank had been unable to buy a horse, but had succeeded in purchasing a donkey, on which the professor sat placidly smoking as they went along, with one marching column or another. Cosenz's division generally led the way, followed by those of Medici and Ebers, while Bixio followed in the rear, his division having already had their share of glory in Sicily and at Reggio.

The main Neapolitan army, retiring from Monteleone, passed through each town only a few hours ahead of the Garibaldians. The people reported that great insubordination existed among them. General Braganti had been shot by his own men at Bagnara; the other generals were accused by their men of treachery, and great numbers of these had deserted; and the Garibaldians felt that if they could but overtake the retreating foe victory was certain. Orders had been sent round by Garibaldi to all the villagers that the men were to meet him at Maida; and leaving the army at two o'clock in the morning, he, with a few of his staff, rode across the mountain to that town. The Calabrians, eager to fight, had obeyed the order, but with some disappointment; for had they been left to themselves they would have occupied the terrible gorges through which the retreating Neapolitans would have to pass, and taking their posts among inaccessible hills, would have almost annihilated them. But Garibaldi was on all occasions most anxious to prevent bloodshed, and would never fight unless his foes forced him to do so; and it was for this reason that he had ordered the Calabrians to meet him at Maida, thereby preventing them from occupying the pass.

Frank, as one of his aide-de-camp, rode with him, the professor preferring to move forward at the more comfortable pace of the marching column. Ordering the Calabrians to follow, Garibaldi went on from Maida to Tyrola, situated on the backbone of the Apennines, and commanding a view of the sea on either hand. Arriving there, he found that the Neapolitans were but a mile ahead. He therefore halted for an hour, and then rode seven miles farther to Samprotro, where he saw the rearguard of the enemy not more than half a mile ahead. Leaving a few armed peasants to watch them, Garibaldi and his staff went quietly to bed. In the morning they again started in pursuit, at the head of two thousand Calabrians. The peasants brought in news that the enemy had halted at a village seven miles ahead, and were endeavouring to obtain food. The Calabrians, when they approached the place, were sent forward as skirmishers; the head of Cosenz's column was now but a short distance in the rear. Colonel Peard, who had ridden with Garibaldi, was in advance, with three Calabrians, when, at a turn of the road, he came upon seven thousand infantry, cavalry, and artillery, huddled together without any appearance of regularity.

He rode up at once to the nearest officers, and called upon them to surrender. They took him to Ghio, their general, who, saying to Peard that it was not customary to talk so loud before the soldiers, asked him to step aside; and on being told that he was surrounded, and had no choice between surrendering and being annihilated, he agreed at once to send an officer to Garibaldi. While the officer was absent, the disposition of the troops manifested itself: many of them at once threw down their arms and accoutrements and started on the road, or made their way up the hill. In a few minutes the officer returned with Garibaldi's conditions, which were surrender and disarmament, when the troops would be allowed to leave, on their promise not to serve again. In an hour there was not a Neapolitan left in the place; and the Garibaldians, who had marched thirty miles that day, halted to allow the rest of the troops to come up.

There was, indeed, no further occasion for haste. It was morally certain that no battle would be fought before they reached Naples. The Neapolitan troops were hopelessly dispirited, and the greater part would gladly have thrown away their arms and returned to their homes; the minority, who were still faithful to their oath, were bitterly humiliated at the manner in which large bodies of men had surrendered without striking a blow, and at the way in which the main force fled, as hastily as if it had suffered a disgraceful defeat, at the approach of the Garibaldians. Already Naples was almost in a state of insurrection; and in the other towns the whole populace had risen, and the Neapolitan authorities were powerless.

"It is wonderful," Signor Forli, who arrived on the following morning, said to Frank, "that the Calabrians should have remained passive for a couple of centuries under the rule of a people so much inferior to themselves. That Sicily should do so, I am not surprised. Its population is not to be compared in physique with these grand fellows. Among the mountains of Sicily, no doubt, there may be a finer type of people than those of the plains and sea-coast; but, as you have told me, although as pleased as a crowd of children at a new game, they did little to aid Garibaldi to free them, and Messina once taken, the number that enlisted with him was small indeed. Here the population have joined to a man; and what splendid men they are! Had they all risen together before, there would have been no need for a Garibaldi. What could an army, however numerous, of the frivolous population of Naples have done against them?

"There are hundreds of passes and ravines. We have ourselves marched through a score that might have been held by a handful of determined men against an army. I believe that it is the fear of cannon rather than of soldiers that has enabled a decaying power, like that of Naples, to maintain its hold. Cannon would be useful in a mountainous country for those who have to defend the passes, but it is of little avail to an invader: it is notorious that, even on the plains, vastly more men are killed by bullets than by shell. One thing that no doubt has kept the Calabrians from rising, as a body, is that blood feuds exist among them, as in Corsica. The number of crosses that you have seen by the roadside mark the number of the victims of these quarrels. Each little village stands apart from the rest, and there has been no centre round which the country could gather. There has been, in fact, a community of interest, but no community of feeling; and the consequence is, risings have been always partial, and there has been nothing like one determined effort by all Calabria to win its freedom."

CHAPTER XVI

NAPLES

THE resemblance between Colonel Peard and Garibaldi was so great that, being similarly dressed, the Englishman, pushing on so far in advance, was everywhere taken for the general, and he utilised this likeness to the utmost. The news of his rapid approach hastened the retreat of the Neapolitans. He sent fictitious telegrams to their generals as from private friends, magnifying Garibaldi's forces, and representing that he was taking a line that would cut them off from Naples, and so sent them hurrying away at full speed and adding to the alarm and confusion of the government.

"I suppose we had better push on with Garibaldi, grandfather?" Frank said one day, as they finished an unusually long march.

"Certainly, Frank," Signor Forli said, somewhat surprised; "we shall be in Naples in another three or four days. I am sure Garibaldi will not wait for his troops; he was saying to me yesterday that he was most anxious to enter the city, as he had notice from a friend that Cavour's party were hard at work trying to organise a general rising of the city before he arrives, and the issue of a manifesto declaring Victor Emmanuel king of Italy and inviting him to come at once. This Garibaldi is determined not to allow. He has from the first always declared that he came in the name of the king, and that when his work was done he would hand over Southern Italy to him. You know his loyalty and absolute disinterestedness; and the idea that he would endeavour to obtain any advantage for himself is absurd.

"If he had chosen, instead of accepting the dictatorship of Sicily he could have been elected king; and assuredly it is the same thing here. He is the people's hero and saviour; the very name of the King of Sardinia is scarcely known in Sicily, and excites no interest whatever. It is the same thing in Calabria: the enthusiasm is all for Garibaldi, and had he consented to accept the crown he would have been elected unanimously. His wish and hope is to present to Victor Emmanuel Southern Italy cleared of all enemies, complete and undivided; and yet, rather than so receive it, Cavour, Farina, and the rest of them are intriguing at Naples, as they intrigued in Sicily, in order that the king should appear to take this wide accession of territory as the expression of the will of the people, and not from the hand of Garibaldi.

"It is pitiful to see such mean jealousy. In time, no doubt, even had there not been a Garibaldi, this would have come about, but it might have been fifteen or twenty years hence; and had it been done by means of a royal army, France and Austria would probably both have interfered and demanded compensation, and so left Italy still incomplete. It is the speed with which the change has been effected, and I may say the admiration with which Europe has viewed it, and the assurance of the government at Turin that it has had no hand in this business, but has taken all means in its power to prevent it, that has paralysed opposition. I trust that all these intrigues will fail, and that Garibaldi may have the sole honour that he craves—namely, that of presenting the kingdom of the two Sicilies to Victor Emmanuel. Should Cavour's intrigues succeed, and Garibaldi be slighted, it will be the blackest piece of ingratitude history has ever recorded. However, why do you ask 'shall we go on to Naples?' I thought that you were burning to get there."

"I am! but you see we are passing, without time for making any investigations, many places where my father, if alive, may be in prison. At Potenza, for example, I know that a large number of political prisoners are confined, and doubtless it is the same at many other towns. I cannot bear to think of the possibility that he may be in one of these, and that we have passed him by."

"I can quite understand your feelings, Frank; but you know we are agreed that it is at Naples, we shall most probably find him, if he is still alive. Bad as the prisons may be in other places, they are more loosely managed; there would be fewer conveniences for keeping one prisoner apart from the others, while there are ample opportunities in those of Naples for many to be kept in secret confinement. Certainly I was so kept myself at Reggio; but that was a royal fortress, and though used as a prison for political offenders, there were no malefactors there. In the jails in the provincial towns this could not be so, and I know that prisoners are all mixed up together, save those who can afford to pay, who can live in comparative comfort, while the rest are herded together anyhow, and can scarcely exist upon the rations allowed to them. The more I think of it, the more I am convinced that it is at Naples that we must look for your father. Now that we have arrived at Salerno, and that, as we hear, the Neapolitan troops are falling back from the capital, and taking up their position round Capua and Gaeta, there can be little doubt that Garibaldi will, in a day or two, go forward. There is, indeed, nothing to prevent you and me from going by train there to-morrow, if you lay aside that red shirt and scarf, and dress in clothes that will attract no attention. But I do not see that anything would be gained by it; you will still have to wait until Garibaldi is supreme there, and his orders are respected, and you may be sure that, as soon as he is in power, his first step will be to throw open the prisons and release all who are charged with political offences, to order these hideous dungeons to be permanently closed, and to thoroughly reorganise the system. You have told me that he did this at Palermo, and he will certainly do the same at Naples."

Four days later the king issued a farewell notice to the people, and left Naples for Gaeta; and three hours afterwards Romano, his minister, who had drawn up his farewell, addressed the following telegram to Garibaldi:—

"To the Invincible Dictator of the two Sicilies.—Naples expects you with anxiety to confide to you her future destiny.—Entirely yours, LIBORIO ROMANO."

A subsequent letter informed him that at a meeting of the ministers it had been decided that the Prince of Alessandria, Syndic of Naples, should go to Salerno, with the commander of the national guard, to make the arrangements for his entry into the capital. Garibaldi, however, did not wait. Were he to arrive at the head of his troops, the Neapolitan garrisons of the castle and other strong places in the city might oppose him by force; and, as ever, wishing to avoid bloodshed, he determined to rely solely upon the populace of Naples. He at once ordered a small special train to be prepared,

"I am only taking with me," he said to Frank, "a few of my staff. You will be one of the number: you have a right to it, not only as the representative of your mother, to whose aid we are largely indebted for our being now here, but for your own personal services. Signor Forli shall also go: he stood by me on the walls of Rome twelve years ago, he has suffered much for his principles, he is your mother's father, therefore he too shall come."

There were but four carriages on the little train that left at nine o'clock in the morning on the 7th of September for Naples. Cosenz, and thirteen members of the staff, represented the national army; the remaining seats being occupied by various personal friends and two or three newspaper correspondents.

"'Tis an affair not without risk," Signor Forli said to Frank, as they walked towards the station. "That the people will receive Garibaldi with enthusiasm is certain, but the attitude of the troops is very doubtful. Certainly the flower of the Neapolitan army will have been left in garrison at Naples; and if but a score of these remain faithful to the Bourbons, Garibaldi's life may be sacrificed. However, I cannot believe that Providence will permit one who has done so great and mighty a work to perish, just at the moment of the completion of his enterprise."

The station-master at Salerno, as soon as the train had started, flashed the news to the various stations on the road; and the consequence was, that at every village the people assembled, and when half the journey was done the crowds were so vast, that they overflowed on to the line, and the train was brought to a standstill. National guards climbed on to the roofs of the carriages, and decorated them with flags and evergreens. At Torre del Greco, Resina, and Portici, progress became almost impossible, and the train had to proceed at a snail's pace to Naples. Here the authorities had prevented all access to the station, but outside the scene was an extraordinary one: horses and carriages, men and women of the highest and of the lowest classes; national guards and gendarmes, members of Bertani's and the Cavourian committees, were all crowded in confusion together. The houses were decorated with flags and tapestry, and thronged with eager spectators from basement to roof; and as Missori and three others rode out from the station on horseback, followed by Garibaldi in an open carriage with Cosenz, and by a dozen other carriages containing his staff and those who had arrived with him, the roar of welcome was overpowering.

It was with the greatest difficulty that the horsemen cleared the way; for all along the road the crowd was as great as at the station. The attitude of the troops, however, at the various points where they were massed, was sullen and threatening. At Castle Nuovo the guns were pointed on the road; the troops stood ready to fire. One shot, and the course of history might have been changed. Garibaldi ordered his coachman to drive slower, and sat in his carriage calmly, with his eyes fixed upon the troops. One officer gave the order to fire; but he was not obeyed. The calmness and daring of the lion-like face filled the soldiers with such admiration that, for the moment, their hostility evaporated; and while some of them saluted as if to a royal personage, others took off their hats and burst into a cheer. Garibaldi acknowledged it by lifting his hat, and by a cheery wave of his hand, and drove on as calmly as before.

In the carriages behind, all had held their breath at the critical moment.

"What an escape! What an escape!" Signor Forli murmured to Frank, who was sitting next to him. "Had but one musket been fired, we should all have been dead men in a minute or two; and, what is of more consequence, the freeing of Italy must have been postponed for twenty years."

"It was horribly close," Frank said. "I would rather go through ten hand-to-hand fights, than another time like the last three minutes; it has made me feel quite queer, and I own that what you say about putting back Italian freedom for twenty years never entered my mind. The one thought I had was, that we were all going to be smashed up without having the chance of striking a single blow. I went through some pretty sharp fighting at Palermo, but I was always doing something then, and did not think of the danger. I don't mind saying that I was in a blue funk just now."

Garibaldi drove straight, as was the custom of kings on first entering Naples, to the palace of the archbishop. Here the Te Deum was sung; and he then went on to the palace of Angri, where he and his staff took up their quarters. Vast crowds assembled outside the palace, and the general had to appear again and again on the balcony in reply to the roars of acclamation from the enthusiastic population. General Cosenz, who was himself a Neapolitan, was appointed to organise a government. This he did to the general satisfaction—moderate men only being chosen. Garibaldi requested Admiral Persano in the name of Victor Emmanuel to take command of the Neapolitan navy, decreeing that it should form part of the Sardinian squadron; and appointed to the pro-dictatorship the Marquis of Pallavicini, a staunch friend of the king. He had offered Signor Forli an apartment in the palace, and as soon as the first excitement had ceased the latter said to Frank, who had at Salerno received the portmanteau he had left at Genoa:—

"Let us go out and see the state of the city. But before we do so, you had best put on your ordinary clothes: we should simply be mobbed if you were to go out as one of Garibaldi's officers."

"Yes; we have had quite enough of that as we came along," Frank said. "It will really be a comfort to go about for once in peace and quiet."

They started in a few minutes, leaving the palace by one of the side entrances, and soon mingled in the crowd. The people seemed half mad with delight. As soon as the news of Garibaldi's arrival spread through the town every house was decorated, and the whole population poured out into the streets. Among the better classes the joy that the government of the Bourbons had come to an end, and that the constitutional government, which had done so much for Northern Italy, would succeed the despotism which had pressed so heavily on all with anything to lose, was deep and sincere. Among the lower classes the enthusiasm manifested was but the excitement of some few minutes, and had Francesco returned a month later, at the head of his victorious troops, they would have shouted as lustily.

It was a fête, a special fête, and it mattered but little to the fickle and excitable population what was its cause. But here, as on all occasions when Italian people give way to bursts of enthusiasm, foreigners were struck with the perfect good-temper, the orderly behaviour, and the entire absence of drunkenness, among the population. In Paris the first step of people excited by a change of government would have been to fall upon those whom they considered to be the agents of their oppressors. The gendarmes, who had so long been feared, would not have dared show themselves in the streets; the emblems of royalty would have been torn down in the public buildings; the members of the last government would have been forced to fly for their lives. There was a little of this in Naples, but, as in Venice, six years later, this feeling of animosity for the past speedily passed away.

But how faint was the feeling of real patriotism in the minds of the Neapolitans is shown by the fact that only one inhabitant of the city joined Garibaldi's army; that not a single house was open for the reception of his officers or soldiers; that after the battle of Volturno hundreds of wounded men were left lying all day on the pavements without aid or nourishment, without a single mattress being found for them to lie upon, by the inhabitants. Never, except by the King of Italy and the civil and military authorities of Piedmont to Garibaldi and his followers, who had won a kingdom for them, was such national ingratitude displayed as by the people of Naples.

"It is pleasant to see," Signor Forli said, as he and Frank wandered about; "but it would be far more pleasant if one did not know that it means absolutely nothing. You have told me that it was the same thing at Messina: that, in spite of Garibaldi's appeal to the ladies of the place, they did nothing whatever to aid the wounded in the hospitals— never contributed so much as a piece of lint or material for bandages; and, frivolous as the people there are, these in Naples are worse. If all Italy were like the Neapolitans, the country would not be worth shedding a drop of blood for. However, one must make some allowances for them. For centuries they have been slaves rather than free people; they have had no voice as to their own disposal, they could not express even an opinion on public affairs, without risking imprisonment or death; there has been nothing left for them but to amuse themselves; they have been treated like children at school, and they have become children. We can only hope that in time, under a free government, they will grow worthy of freedom, worthy of forming a part of an Italy to which the Lombards, the Piedmontese, and the Calabrians belong."

It was already late in the afternoon, and until some of the troops arrived it would be impossible to take any steps with relation to public buildings. The castle of St. Elmo, and the prison of Santa Maria, with many other places, were still in the hands of the Neapolitan soldiers, whose attitude continued to be hostile, and until these retired nothing could be done; and it was by no means certain that the guns at St. Elmo, which completely commanded the town, might not at any moment open fire.

"I can well understand your impatience to get rid of these troops from the city," Garibaldi said the next morning. "I do not forget, Percival, the main object that you had in view, and I too long for the time when I may clasp the hand of my old comrade of South America and Rome. I promise you that the moment the prisons are evacuated you shall go with the party who will search them, and search them strictly. You know what these jailors are: they are the creatures of the worst men of Francesco's government. By years of cruelty and oppression they have earned for themselves the hatred of every one within the walls of the prisons and of their friends and relatives. Our victory means their dismissal—that is, as soon as the prisons are cleaned from the lowest dungeons to the roofs. That they shall superintend: it is they who are responsible for it, and they themselves shall be engaged in the work of purification. It may well be that they will try to hide the lowest and worst dungeons from our search, partly from fear that the natural and righteous indignation excited by the discoveries may end in their being promptly punished with death for their accumulated crimes, partly in hopes that the royal troops may yet overcome us and restore Francesco to his throne; in which case they would receive approval for still retaining some of the worst victims of the tyranny of his government."

"You may be sure that I shall search them thoroughly, general."

On going out, they found the streets were still thronged by an almost frenzied populace. These invaded the hotels and cafés, and pressed all they could lay hands on to join in the demonstrations. A few murders were perpetrated; the state of things prevailing affording an excellent opportunity for satisfying private revenge, as it needed only a cry that the victim was a spy of the government to justify it in the eyes of the bystanders.

In the quarter nearest to St. Elmo the enthusiasm had a good deal cooled down, as the fear that the guns of the castle might at any moment open fire for the time dissipated any desire for marching about and acclaiming Garibaldi. At four o'clock, however, it was known that two officers of the castle had gone down to the palace, and at six the welcome news spread that the garrison had capitulated, and would march out on the following morning.

Frank had little sleep that night. All along his hopes had been high that he should find his father here; but now that the question would be so soon decided, his fears were in the ascendant. He remembered that the evidence in favour of his father's death was extremely strong, the only hopeful fact being that his body had not been discovered. So slight did even his mother and Signora Forli deem the chance of his being alive, that for two years neither had breathed a word to the other as to the existence of a possibility that he might be still living. Undoubtedly the release of his grandfather had increased his own hope, but he felt now that there was but small ground for the feeling. Had his father been hidden away in a fortress, he might also have survived; but the probabilities seemed altogether against this. It was not until midday that St. Elmo was evacuated, and several companies of the national guard marched in. A colonel of the staff had, with Frank, been charged with the duty of searching the dungeons. They had brought with them fifty lazzaroni, who had been engaged for this repulsive work. A dozen of the Garibaldian troops were to accompany them; the prison officials were all ordered to go with the party, and they, as well as the lazzaroni, were told to bring pails and brooms.

The castle of St. Elmo covers an area of no less than four acres; it was cut out of the solid rock, and is surrounded by a sunken ditch, sixty or seventy feet deep, and fifty wide. This great mass of stone is honeycombed in every direction with a network of corridors and subterranean apartments, and there is ample space to hold several thousand prisoners. The upper tiers of chambers were fairly clean; these were, in fact, the barracks of the troops. The guns looked out from embrasures. Several batteries of field artillery, with waggons and all fittings, still remained there, and the chambers were littered with rubbish of all kinds, discarded by the troops before leaving. It was not here that prisoners were to be found. The national guard had already opened the doors of the cells and chambers in the stage below, and had liberated those confined there; the work of searching those still lower began at once. The extent was so vast and the windings were so intricate that the work seemed interminable. In order to make sure that each passage had been searched, a pail of whitewash was sent for, and a splash made at each turning. Each story was darker, and the air more stifling, than that above it, for they were now far below the level of the castle itself.

Frank had taken the advice of Signor Forli, and had bought several bundles of the strongest cigars, and he and the officer in command, the officer of the national guard who attended them and the soldiers all smoked incessantly. At the worst places the lazzaroni and turnkeys set to work with their buckets and brooms. It was not until late in the evening that they came to the conclusion that every cell and chamber had been searched. About a hundred and fifty prisoners had been found and released, but among them Frank looked in vain for his father. The lowest dungeons of all had been found empty; and this, and the solemn assurances of all the prison officials, who had been threatened with instant death should further search discover any prisoners, convinced him that at any rate his father was not there.

The next day the neighbouring prison of Santa Maria was searched. It had formerly been a monastery, and the upper cells were lofty and capacious. The jailors declared, indeed, that these were the only cells, but a careful search showed a door in the rock. This was burst open, and a series of subterranean passages was discovered. The jailors declared that these had never been used in their time, and, they believed, never before. That they had been used, however was evident, from the marks where lamps had been hung on the walls, and by many other signs. No prisoners were found there, all having been released directly it was known that the garrison of the castle had capitulated. The search occupied the whole day, so extensive were the underground galleries; and a passage was discovered that evidently at one time formed a communication between St. Elmo and this prison. As he came out into daylight Frank staggered, and would have fallen had not one of the soldiers caught him. He had been ill the night before; and the effects of the close air, noxious smells and the work, which had been even more trying than on the previous day, and his bitter disappointment, had now completely overcome him. After some water had been dashed in his face and he had taken a draught of some wine which one of the prison officials fetched, he partially recovered. He was assisted by two of the Garibaldians down the road to the town, and then, obtaining a vehicle, was driven to the palace, and managed with assistance to get up to his apartment. A minute or two later Signor Forli joined him, one of the attendants having summoned him as soon as Frank arrived.

"Do not trouble to speak, my dear boy," he said. Frank was lying on the bed sobbing convulsively. "You have failed—that I can well understand; but you must not altogether lose heart. We had thought this the most likely place; but there are still other prisons, and we will not give up hope until every one of these has been ransacked. I am sorry now that I did not accompany you, but I am afraid, after what I have gone through myself, that only a few minutes in one of those places would overpower me! and I wonder how you, young and strong as you are, were able to spend two days in such an atmosphere."

"I shall be better to-morrow," Frank said. "That last place was awful; but I think that it was as much the strong tobacco as those horrible stinks, which upset me. It was a choice of two evils; but I would smoke even worse tobacco if I could get it, if I had to go through it again."

"I will get you a glass of brandy and water. Frank; that will do you more good than anything."

The next morning Frank was still too unwell to be able to get up; his failure had completely broken him down, and he felt indisposed to make the slightest exertion. At twelve o'clock, however, Signor Forli came in.

"I have a piece of news to give you," he said, "news which affords us some shadow of hope that you have not failed altogether. Last night I was talking with the general and one or two of his staff. Garibaldi is, as you know, intensely interested in your search, and sympathises with you most warmly. Suddenly he said, 'Is it not possible that he may have been removed before the king and his court retired?' Had Percival been found in the prisons, it would have rendered the bad faith and mendacity of the government more glaring than ever, and would have deprived it of any little sympathy that was felt for it in England. Therefore, feeling sure that the prisons would be searched as soon as I entered, Percival, had he been here, may with other special prisoners, have been sent to Capua, which is so strongly fortified a place that they may well believe it to be impregnable to anything but a long siege by troops possessing a battering train."

Frank sat up. "That is indeed a good idea," he exclaimed. "How stupid of me not to have thought of questioning the prison people! Yes; it is quite likely that if any of the prisoners were removed, he would be one of them."

"I have no doubt you would have thought of it, Frank. if it had not been that you were completely upset by that strong tobacco. Mind, I don't blame you for taking it: it is better to be poisoned with nicotine than by the stenches of a Neapolitan prison. The thought only struck Garibaldi after we had chatted over the matter for some time. I went over there this morning with Colonel Nullo. Although the officials at first asserted that no prisoners had been taken away, they soon recovered their memories when he said that he would interrogate every one of the warders separately, and if he found that any prisoners had been sent away he would have them taken out into the courtyard and shot for lying to him. They then remembered that four prisoners had been taken away, but all declared with adjurations to all the saints that they did not know who they were: they were delivered over to them under numbers only. One had been there seven years, and two had been there five years, and one two years. Again threatening to examine all the turnkeys, he learned that the last prisoner received had been confined in one of the lower dungeons, where they yesterday asserted that no one had for years been imprisoned; the other three were also kept in the most rigid seclusion, but in the upper cells.

"I insisted on seeing the man who had attended on the prisoner kept in the lower cell. He was a surly ruffian, and it was not until Nullo ordered four men to load, and to put the fellow with his back to the wall, that he would answer my questions. He said then that the prisoner was, he should say, between forty and fifty, but it was not easy to judge of age after a man had been below there for a few months. He had never said more than a few words to him, and it had never struck him that he was not an Italian. I questioned him more closely as to this, and he admitted that he had sometimes, when he went down, heard the prisoner singing. He had listened, but could not understand the words, and they might have been in a foreign language. He had no more interest in that prisoner than in any other. He supposed, by his being sent down below there, that it was hoped he would die off as soon as possible. They seldom lived many months in those dungeons, but this man seemed tougher than usual, though his strength had failed a good deal lately. He was able to walk up from his cell to the carriage when he was taken away. Now we mustn't feel too sanguine, Frank, but although there is no proof that this prisoner is your father, the evidence, so far as it goes, is rather in favour of such a supposition than against it."

"It is indeed," Frank said eagerly. "The fact that they put him down into the cells where, as the man says, it was almost certain he would soon die, and that when it was found that he had not done so, he was at the last moment taken away, shows that there was some very strong motive for preventing the fact that he was a prisoner becoming public; and we know that they had the very strongest reason in the case of my father. The age would be about right, and the fact that he was singing would show, at any rate, that it was some one who was determined not to give in, but to keep

IT WAS NOT UNTIL NULLO ORDERED FOUR MEN TO LOAD
THAT HE WOULD ANSWER.

up his spirits till the very last, and I am sure my father would have done that. Well, I will get up now. I could not lie here quietly; it would be impossible, after what you have been telling me."

"I think you are right, Frank. I will have a basin of soup sent in for you. When you have eaten that, and dressed, we will take a carriage and go for a long drive by the road along the shore to Pompeii. The sea-breeze will do you more good than anything, and the lovely view, and a stroll through Pompeii itself, will distract your thoughts. There is nothing to be done until Capua is taken, which may not be for a long time yet. However, events are moving. We hear that Victor Emmanuel and his government, alarmed at the success of Garibaldi, and feeling that if they are to have any voice in the matter they must not be content to rest passive while he is carrying all before him, have resolved upon taking some part in the affair. Under the pretext that in order to restore peace and order it is necessary that they should interfere, they are about to despatch an army to Ancona by sea; and, landing there, will advance into Central Italy, and act, as they say, as circumstances may demand. All of which means, that now Garibaldi has pulled the chestnuts out of the fire for them they will proceed to appropriate them."

"It is too bad!" Frank exclaimed angrily.

"No doubt it is mean and ungracious in the extreme, but Garibaldi will not feel it as other men would; he is human, and therefore he would like to present the Kingdom of Naples and the States of Rome, free from the foreigner, to Victor Emmanuel. But that feeling, natural as it is, is but secondary to his loyalty to Italy. He desires to see her one under

Victor Emmanuel, and so long as that end is achieved he cares comparatively little how it comes about. Moreover, he cannot but see that, though he has accomplished marvels, that which remains to be done would tax the power of his army to the utmost. The Neapolitans have still some seventy thousand men, who are encouraged by their king being among them. They have in Capua a most formidable fortress, which could defy the efforts of irregular troops, wholly unskilled in sieges and deficient in heavy guns, for many months. Moreover, it would no longer be mountain warfare, but we should have to fight in plains where the enemy's cavalry would give them an enormous advantage. There is another thing: the intrigues of Cavour's agents here are already giving him very serious trouble, and this will doubtless increase; therefore I can well understand that he will be glad rather than otherwise that Sardinia at last should do her part towards the freeing of Italy, from which she will benefit so vastly."

CHAPTER XVII

THE BATTLE OF THE VOLTURNO

BEFORE starting for his drive Frank telegraphed to his mother: "Have not found him here. I do not yet despair. Have a faint clue that may lead to something."

That evening he wrote a long letter, acknowledging that he had been bitterly disappointed, but saying that Signor Forli had found out that some of the prisoners had been sent away to Capua before Garibaldi entered the town, and that he still hoped his father might be among the number. He gave no detail as to these prisoners, for he was anxious not to raise hopes that might not be fulfilled; indeed, he had in all his letters said little on the subject. He knew his mother had refused to allow herself to cherish any hope, and he had written almost entirely of matters concerning the events of the march, the country through which he had travelled, and the scenes in which he had taken a part. He and Signor Forli had at Salerno received long letters from home full of the delight which the news of the discovery and re-release of the latter had given them. His mother had said:—

"This is a joy indeed, my boy—one that I had never expected, or even hoped for. But do not let yourself anticipate for a moment that because this unlooked-for happiness has been given to us our other dear lost one will similarly be recovered. That my father had been thrown into a Neapolitan prison we never doubted for a moment; and I believed that, should he have survived, Garibaldi's success would open his prison doors. But it is not so in the case of your father. The evidence is almost overwhelming that he died in the hands of the brigands who carried him off, and nothing short of knowing that he is alive will induce me to abandon the conviction I have all along felt that this was so. I pray you not to indulge in any false hopes, which can but end in bitter disappointment. You will, of course, search until absolutely convinced that he is not in any of the prisons of the country. The search will at least have been useful, for it will remove the last dread which, in spite of myself, I have occasionally felt ever since he has been missing, that he had been wearing his life out in one of these horrible dungeons."

The next ten days passed slowly. Frank and the other members of the staff had bought fresh horses a few days after the capture of Reggio; and he was now constantly in the saddle, carrying messages between Garibaldi's headquarters and the army. Garibaldi himself had been distracted by the intrigues going on around him, and had been obliged to go to Sicily. Depretis, who had been appointed head of the government there, was inclined to the annexational policy, which was opposed by Crispi and the other Garibaldians, and the consequence was that an alarming state of affairs existed there. Garibaldi was therefore obliged to hurry over there himself, and having appointed Mordeni, a determined partisan of his own, pro-dictator, and arranged affairs generally, he returned to Naples, where his presence was urgently required.

The Neapolitan army at Capua had been very largely reinforced, and had taken post along the river Volturno. Turr,

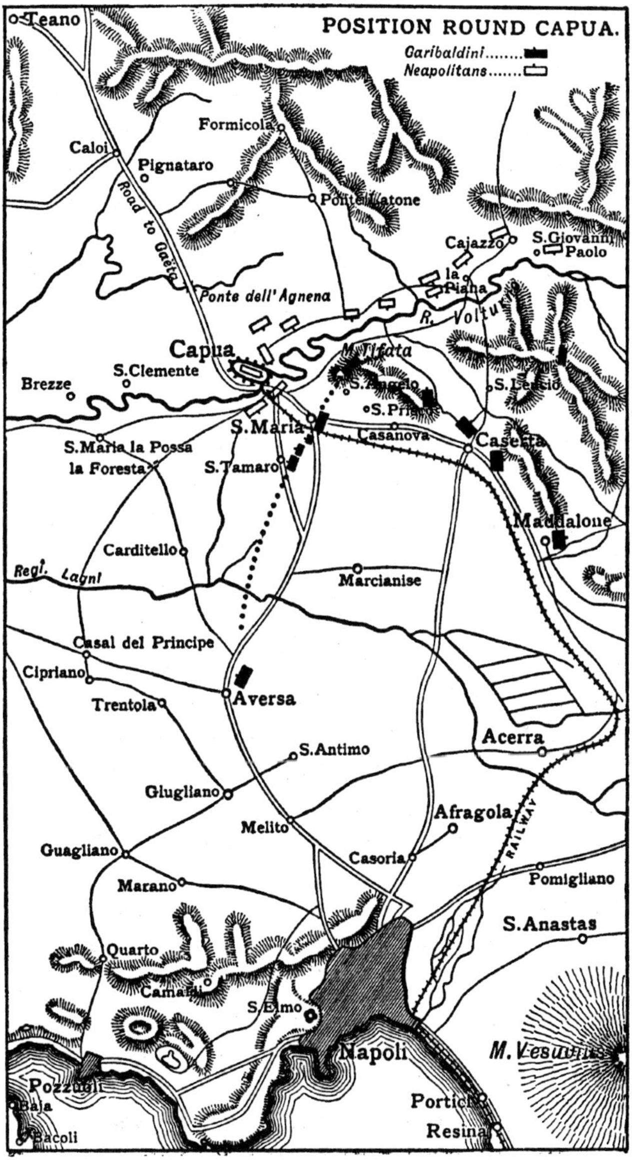
POSITION ROUND CAPUA.
Garibaldini
Neapolitans
Teano
Caloi
Pignataro
Formicola
Ponte Latone
Road to Gaeta
Ponte dell' Agnena
Cajazzo
S.Giovanni
Paolo
la Piana
R. Volturno
Capua
M. Tifata
S.Angelo
S.Clemente
Brezze
S.Prisco
S.Leucio
S.Maria
Casanova
Caserta
S.Maria la Fossa
la Foresta
S.Tamaro
Maddalone
Carditello
Regi. Lagni
Marcianise
Casal del Principe
Cipriano
Trentola
Aversa
Acerra
S.Antimo
Giugliano
Afragola
Melito
Railway
Guagliano
Casoria
Marano
Pomigliano
S.Anastas
Quarto
Camaldi
S.Elmo
Napoli
M.Vesuvius
Pozzuoli
Baja
Bacoli
Portici
Resina

who was in command of the Garibaldian army, had in consequence, taken up a defensive position at Madalone, Caserta and Aversa, thereby barring any advance on the part of the royal army. The latter's position was an extremely formidable one: its right rested on Gaeta near the sea, and forty thousand men were massed on the right bank of the Volturno, a river which was here from fifty to a hundred yards in width, their left was at Cajazzo, in the mountains of the Abruzzi, where the inhabitants were favourable to the royal cause.

Capua itself, on the left bank of the river, afforded them a means of moving forward to the attack of the Garibaldians. Three sides of its fortifications were surrounded by the river, which here makes a great loop, and around the town twenty thousand men were massed, one half of whom were in position in front of it. The only bridge across the river was at Capua, but there was a ferry near Caserta. The position was so threatening that Turr, who had under him about seventeen thousand men, pushed a force up to the town of Santa Maria and the heights of Sant' Angelo, both of which points were occupied after a skirmish.

On the 17th, six hundred men were sent off to march far up the river, to cross it, and to throw themselves into the mountains above Cajazzo, which was occupied by two thousand two hundred men with four guns. Garibaldi arrived at Caserta on the night of the 18th, but did not interfere with Turr's command. In order to attract the attention of the enemy, and keep them from sending reinforcements to Cajazzo, it was arranged that a feint should be made against Capua: two battalions were to advance from Aversa to menace the southwest of that town, six battalions were to advance directly against it from Santa Maria, and Ebor's brigade was to march to Sant' Angelo, and then to drive the Neapolitans on their left into Capua, and to extend on the right along the hills as far as the road to Cajazzo.

The movement was completely successful. Cajazzo was captured, and the force in front of Capua obliged to retire under the guns of the citadel. Some loss, however, was sustained, owing to the division from Santa Maria, instead of returning as soon as the work was done, being kept for four hours under the fire of the guns of the fortress, owing to a misconception of orders. The positions now taken were occupied in strength. The next day, six hundred and fifty men were sent off to Cajazzo to strengthen the small force of three hundred there, as the place was attacked by no fewer than twelve thousand Neapolitan troops. Although without artillery, the town was desperately defended for four hours. The barricades at the end of the main streets were held, in spite of repeated attacks and the fire from eight guns. Not until two hundred of the little force had fallen, did the Garibaldians fall back, and they succeeded in crossing the river at the ferry, covered by two companies and a couple of guns, which had been posted at that point to prevent the Neapolitans from crossing.

There was an interval now: the Garibaldians were far too weak to attack their numerous enemy, posted in an almost impregnable position. Garibaldi was so much harassed by the political intriguers, that he left Caserta every morning long before daybreak, and remained the whole day at a cottage on the heights of San Antonio. He had already done all in his power to satisfy the royal party that he had no intention of favouring a republic. Bertrani, who had done so much for him as chief organiser and agent, was requested to leave Rome. Mazzini also was sent away, and other appointments were made, showing how bent he was on handing over his conquest to Victor Emmanuel. There can be no doubt now that it would have been far better had he from the first abandoned his wish not to present his conquests to the king until they were completed. Had he, on his arrival at Messina, at once declared Victor Emmanuel king of the island, and requested him to take possession, he would have allayed the jealousy and suspicion with which his movements were viewed by Cavour and the Piedmontese ministry.

A similar course, as soon as Naples was occupied, would have had a still greater effect, and both Garibaldi himself and his brave followers would have been spared the bitter humiliations and the gross display of ingratitude, which, however, disgraced those who inflicted them far more than those so undeservedly treated.

Turr remained idle during the next six days, and beyond throwing up two or three small intrenchments, did nothing to strengthen the position. In fact, it was daily becoming more probable that there would be no further fighting. Cialdini's division had landed near Alcona, had defeated the army of Lamoriciere, and was advancing westwards without opposition. Fanti, with another army, had crossed the northern frontier of the Neapolitan territory, and was marching south. Thus, in a short time, the Neapolitans would be surrounded by three armies, and would be forced to lay down their arms.

On the 29th it became evident that a considerable movement was in progress on the other side of the river and fort. Forty thousand men were being concentrated at Capua and Cajazzo.

Garibaldi's force, available in case of attack, was about twenty-four thousand men, of whom thirteen thousand were Northern Italians, eleven thousand Calabrians and Sicilians, and one inhabitant of Naples. Of these, two thousand five hundred were with Conti at Aversa, and over seven thousand at Caserta; the remainder being at Santa Maria, Sant' Angelo, the village of Santa Lucia, and Madalone. The position occupied was nearly thirty miles long, but the reserves at Caserta and Madalone, lying beind the centre, could be despatched speedily to any point required. Frank had come out with Garibaldi to Caserta, and spent the whole of his time riding between the different points occupied, with communications from Garibaldi to his generals.

At three o'clock on the morning of October 1st, Garibaldi started as usual for the front. Frank, with two or three of the younger staff-officers, rode, and three carriages carried the general and the older members of the staff. They had scarcely left the town when a scattered fire of musketry was heard near Santa Maria. This rapidly increased in volume; and soon afterwards the guns at Sant' Angelo opened vigorously. When approaching the town, a mounted soldier, riding at a furious gallop, overtook them. He was the bearer of a message that a telegram had just been received from Bixio, who was in command at Madalone, saying that he was being assailed in great force. This was even more serious than the attack in front, for, if successful, it would have cut the communication between the Garibaldians and Naples.

Galloping on to Santa Maria, Garibaldi sent a telegram to Sartori, who commanded at Caserta, to tell him to hold a brigade in readiness to support Bixio if the latter was pressed; and that Turr, with the rest of the reserves, was to hold himself in readiness to move to the front, but was only to send forward a single brigade, till quite assured of Bixio's success. At Santa Maria were the greater part of the old cacciatori, with four thousand other good troops, and Garibaldi felt confident that the town was in no danger of being taken. He accordingly started at once for Sant' Angelo, which was the key of his position. Morning had broken now, but a heavy mist, rising from the low ground near the river, rendered it impossible to see more than a few yards. The din of conflict was prodigious. The Garibaldian guns at Santa Maria kept up a desultory fire, answered by those of the Neapolitans, and the rattle of musketry was incessant ahead, and, as it seemed, the fight was raging all round; but it was impossible to tell whether Santa Lucia and other posts to the right were also attacked. Suddenly a volley was fired from an invisible enemy within a hundred yards. The balls whistled overhead.

"This is uncomfortable," Frank said to the officer riding next to him. "They have evidently broken through our line connecting Sant' Angelo with Santa Maria. If we had had a few earthworks thrown up this would not have happened. Now they will be able to take Sant' Angelo in rear; and, what is much more important, we may at any moment run right into the middle of them, and the loss of Garibaldi would be more serious than that of all our positions put together."

The Neapolitans had indeed issued out in three columns. One of them, pushing out under cover of the deep watercourses, had broken through the weak line, had captured a battery of four guns and a barricade, and had then mounted one of the spurs of Tifata and taken Sant' Angelo in rear;

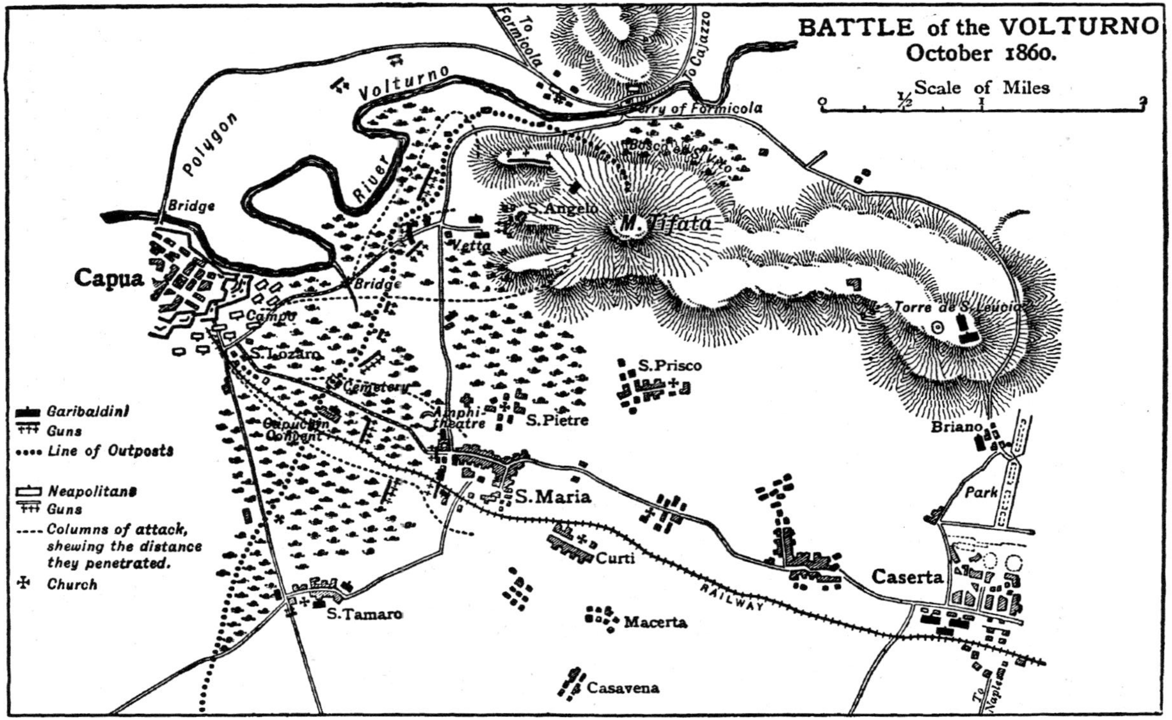
BATTLE of the VOLTURNO
October 1860.
Scale of Miles
0
½
1
2
To Formicola
To Cajazzo
Ferry of Formicola
Bosco di S. Vito
Volturno
Polygon
River
Bridge
Capua
Bridge
Campo
S. Lozaro
Cemetery
Capuchin Convent
S. Angelo
M. Tifata
Vetta
Amphi-theatre
S. Pietre
S. Prisco
Torre de S. Leucio
Briano
Park
S. Maria
Curti
Caserta
RAILWAY
S. Tamaro
Macerta
Casavena
To Naples
Garibaldini
Guns
Line of Outposts
Neapolitans
Guns
Columns of attack, shewing the distance they penetrated.
Church

while a second column, attacking it in front, had captured another four-gun battery and a barricade two hundred and fifty yards below the village on the Capua road, and had taken two or three hundred prisoners, the rest of Medici's division taking up their position in and around the abbey, which stood on the hillside above the village.

Three of the guides, who had accompanied Garibaldi to carry messages, and the three mounted staff officers, took their place in front of the carriages in readiness to charge, should they come suddenly upon the enemy, and so give time to their occupants to escape. The horses were all galloping at full speed; and though occasionally caught sight of by the enemy, and exposed to a fire, not only of musketry but of round shot, they remained uninjured until two-thirds of the distance to Sant' Angelo, which Garibaldi believed to be still in possession of his troops, had been covered. Presently, however, they saw, but sixty or seventy yards away, a strong body of Neapolitans on the road.

"Turn off to the right!" Garibaldi shouted. As the carriage left the road a round shot struck one of the horses. Garibaldi and the other occupants at once jumped out, and shouting to the carriages behind to follow them, ran across the fields. Fortunately there was a deep watercourse close by; and the others, leaving their carriages, all ran down into this. The mist was too thick for the movement to be observed, and the Neapolitans kept up a heavy fire in the direction in which they had seen the carriages through the mist. As soon as they entered the watercourse Garibaldi told Frank and his companions to dismount, as, although the bank was high enough to conceal the men on foot, those on horseback could be seen above it. All ran along at the top of their speed. As they did so, Frank told his companions and the guides, if they came upon any force of the enemy, to throw themselves into their saddles again and charge, so as to give time to the general to turn off and escape.

They had gone but a few hundred yards when a party of the enemy, who were standing on the left bank of the watercourse, ran suddenly down into it. Frank and the others sprang into their saddles, and with a shout rode at them; there was a hurried discharge of musketry, and then they were in the midst of the Neapolitans. These were but some twenty in number. They had already emptied their muskets, but for a minute there was a hand-to-hand contest. The horsemen first used their revolvers with deadly effect, and then fell on with their swords so fiercely that the survivors of their opponents scrambled out of the watercourse and fled, just as Garibaldi and his staff ran up to take part in the conflict. It was well for the general that he had found the road to the village blocked, for, had he ridden straight on, he must have been captured by the enemy, who were already in full possession of it, with the exception of the abbey church and a few houses round it, and the slope of the hill.

Two of the mounted party were missing. One of the guides had fallen when the Neapolitans fired, and an officer had been killed by the thrust of a bayonet. One of Garibaldi's party was also missing; but whether he had been killed by a chance shot or had fallen behind and been taken prisoner none knew. As they ascended the slope of the hill they got above the mist, and could now see what had happened. A part of the column that had broken through the line of outposts had pressed on some distance, and then moved to its left, until in the rear of Sant' Angelo, where its attack had taken the defenders wholly by surprise. The force had then mounted the hill, and from there opened fire upon the defenders of the abbey and the houses round it.

These were stoutly held. The houses were solidly-built structures in which resided the priests and servitors of the church, and the only road leading up from the village to it was swept by two twenty-four-pounders, while from the windows of the houses and from the roof of the abbey a steady muskethy fire was maintained. Garibaldi ordered Frank to gallop to the pass, a short distance behind the village, where two companies of Genoese carbineers and two mountain howitzers were posted, and to direct them to mount the hill and take up a position on the heights above that occupied by the enemy. With a cheer the men ran forward as soon as they received the order. Ignorant of what was taking place in front, but certain from the roar of battle that it was raging round the village, they had been eager to advance to take part in the struggle; but their orders to hold the pass had been imperative, as their presence here was indispensable to cover the retreat of the Garibaldians in Sant' Angelo, and to check pursuit until reinforcements came up from the rear.

The movement was unobserved by the enemy, who were fully occupied in their attempts to capture the abbey; and it was not until the two companies were established on a ridge well above that occupied by the Neapolitans, and opened a heavy musketry fire, aided by their two guns, that the latter were aware that they had been taken in rear. Their position was altogether untenable, as they were unable to reply effectively to the fire of their opponents, and, descending the slopes, they joined their comrades in the village.

THE BATTLE OF THE VOLTURNO 315

Several desperate attacks were made upon the abbey, but each was repulsed with heavy loss; and as the carbineers had now moved lower down, and their guns commanded the village, the Neapolitans lost heart and fell back.

A battalion of Garibaldi's bersaglieri now came up. They were commanded by Colonel Wyndham, and occupied the village as the Neapolitans fell back, quickened their retreat, and then, descending to the four-gun battery that had first been taken, turned the guns, which the enemy had forgotten to spike, upon them.

In the meantime the fighting had been fierce round Santa Maria. At first the Garibaldians had been hard pressed, and the Neapolitans had carried all before them, until they came under the fire of the batteries placed on the railway and in front of the gate facing Capua. These were well served, and although the assailants several times advanced with both cavalry and infantry, they never succeeded in getting within a hundred yards of the guns. The left wing, however, swept round the town, and captured all the out-buildings, except a farmhouse, which was gallantly defended by a company of Frenchmen.

On the right the Neapolitans fared still more badly, for when their attack upon the battery failed, the Garibaldian force at San Tamaro, nearly three thousand five hundred strong, advanced and took them in flank, and drove them back with heavy loss. By eight o'clock the attack had ceased all along the line; but as the enemy, while falling back, preserved good order, no attempt was made to follow them.

The battle had lasted four hours, and the Garibaldians were now strengthened by the arrival of a brigade with four guns from Caserta, where the news had just arrived that

Bixio was confident of being able to hold his ground at Madalone. Two of the newly-arrived regiments were ordered to endeavour to reopen communications with Sant' Angelo, and fighting on with the force still threatening Santa Maria; these, after suffering heavy loss, the Garibaldians, at ten o'clock, drove some distance back, and captured three guns and many prisoners.

At eleven a fresh attack was made, Count Trani, one of the King's brothers, having brought some fresh battalions from the town. This attack was also repulsed, the Garibaldians maintaining their strong positions. But the Neapolitan troops were still full of spirit, and at a quarter-past one made another determined effort: their field batteries advanced within three hundred yards of the town, and their cavalry charged almost up to the railway battery, but were received with so heavy an infantry fire by the troops protecting the guns, that they were forced to fall back. The infantry, however, pressed on, covered by a storm of fire from their field artillery, while the guns of Capua aided them by firing shell into the town. The Garibaldians serving the guns at the gate and at the railway suffered very heavily, but volunteers from the infantry regiments took their place, although at one time their fire was arrested by the explosion of a magazine which killed many of the men, and dismounted two or three of the guns.

All this time, fighting was going on fiercely round Sant' Angelo. The two regiments that had been sent out from Santa Maria to open communications with the village had been unable to effect their object, the enemy's force being too strong for them to move far from the town. At eleven o'clock, the Neapolitans being largely reinforced, made a fresh attack on the battery and barricades in front of Sant' Angelo, and an obstinate struggle took place here; but superior force triumphed, and the royal troops again captured the battery, killing or taking prisoners almost the whole of the force that defended it.

Infantry and cavalry then advanced against the village; but the Garibaldians, having their leader among them, fought with extraordinary bravery, and for three hours maintained themselves, as did those in the abbey, although the enemy brought up their cannon and rocket batteries to within a short distance of it. The walls of the abbey were, however, so massive that even the artillery failed to make much impression upon them. Seeing that the assault upon Santa Maria had been repulsed, Garibaldi sallied out with his entire force, retook the houses that had been captured by the enemy, drove them back to the battery, and at last captured this also. Knowing that some of the reserve would soon be up, Garibaldi at half-past two rode out from the rear of Sant' Angelo, and making a wide détour, entered Santa Maria, and at once ordered a general advance. Ebor's brigade sallied out by the Capua gate, and advanced against the Carthusian convent and cemetery on the Capuan road, while a brigade moved out to endeavour once more to clear the way to Sant' Angelo.

The former attack was successful. A small squadron of Hungarian Hussars charged three squadrons of the enemy's dragoons, defeated them, and captured the two guns that accompanied them. The infantry went on at a run, but it required an hour's hard fighting to gain possession of the convent and cemetery. By this time five thousand men with thirteen guns had arrived from Caserta, and the advance became general. Medici issued out from Sant' Angelo, and the whole force from Santa Maria advanced, the Neapolitans falling back from all points; and by five o'clock the whole had re-entered Capua, abandoning all their positions outside it, and the Garibaldian sentries were posted along the edge of a wood half a mile from the ramparts. Until the arrival of the five thousand men of the reserve, the Garibaldians had throughout the day, although but nine thousand five hundred strong, maintained themselves successfully against thirty thousand men supported by a powerful artillery.

At Madalone Bixio had routed seven thousand men who had advanced against his position, and had captured four guns. The only reverse sustained was at Castel Morone, which was garrisoned by only two hundred and twenty-seven men of one of Garibaldi's bersaglieri regiments. They held out for some hours against a Neapolitan column three thousand strong, and then, having expended all their ammunition, were obliged to surrender. The battle of the Volturno cost the Garibaldians one thousand two hundred and eighty killed and wounded, and seven hundred taken prisoners, while the enemy lost about two thousand five hundred killed and wounded, five hundred prisoners, and nine guns. At two o'clock a detachment of Sardinian artillery, which, with a regiment of bersaglieri, had been landed a few days before at Garibaldi's request, had arrived at Santa Maria, and did good service by taking the places of the gunners who had been almost annihilated by the enemy's fire. The bersaglieri did not arrive at Caserta till the battle was over. Wearied by the day's fight, the Garibaldians, as soon as the long work of searching for and bringing in the wounded was over, lay down to sleep.

THE BATTLE OF THE VOLTURNO 319

Frank and the two other aides-de-camp of Garibaldi were, however, aroused, within an hour of their lying down. The news had arrived that the Neapolitan column, which had captured Castel Morone had suddenly appeared on the heights above Caserta: their number was estimated at three thousand. Orders were sent to Bixio to occupy a strong position. Columns were directed to start from Sant' Angelo and Santa Maria for Caserta, while another brigade was to reinforce the garrison of Santa Lucia. At two in the morning Garibaldi himself started for Caserta, and moved out with two thousand five hundred Calabrians and four companies of Piedmontese bersaglieri. The latter soon found themselves obliged to take off their knapsacks, hats, and useless accoutrements, finding themselves, picked men as they were, unable to keep up with the Garibaldians, clad only in shirt and trousers, and carrying nothing but ninety rounds of ammunition.

There was but little fighting. The Garibaldians lost but seven or eight men, among whom were three Piedmontese, who were the first men of the Sardinian army to shed their blood for the emancipation of Naples. By evening over two thousand five hundred prisoners were taken, and this number was doubled in the course of the next few days by the capture of a large portion of the force which, after being defeated by Bixio in their attempt to seize Madalone, had scattered over the country pillaging and burning. Thus, including the fugitives who escaped, the Neapolitan army was weakened by the loss of nearly ten thousand men The explanation of the singular attack upon Caserta, after the defeat of the Neapolitan army, was that, after capturing Castel Morone, their commander had received a despatch stating that a complete defeat had been inflicted on Garibaldi, and urging him to cut off the retreat of the fugitives by occupying Caserta.

Now that the work was over, and that there was nothing to be done until the royal army advanced from Ancona, and, brushing aside all opposition, arrived to undertake the siege of Capua, Frank broke down. He had not fully recovered from the effects of the two long days spent in the pestilential atmosphere of the prisons; but had stuck to his work until the Neapolitans surrendered; then he rode up to Garibaldi, and said,—

"General, I must ask you to spare me from my duties, for I feel so strangely giddy that I can scarce keep my seat."

"You look ill, lad. Hand your horse over to one of the guides. I have sent for my carriage; it will be up in a few minutes. Sit down in the shade of that tree. I will take you down to Caserta with me, and one of Bixio's doctors shall see you at once."

On arriving at Caserta, the doctor at once pronounced that it was a case of malarial fever, the result of the miasma from the low ground, increased, no doubt, by over-fatigue. Garibaldi immediately ordered another carriage to be brought round, instructed two of his men to take their places in it with Frank, and despatched a telegram to Professor Forli at Naples, telling him to have four men in readiness to carry him up to his room as soon as he reached the palace, and to have a doctor in waiting. Frank was almost unconscious by the time he arrived at the city. Everything was ready, and he was soon undressed and in bed, ice applied to his head, and a draught of medicine poured down his throat. In a week the fever left him, but he was so much weakened that it was another fortnight before he could move about again unassisted.

"You have lost nothing: things have been very quiet," his grandfather said. "To-day the voting takes place. Of course that is a mere farce, and the country will declare for Victor Emmanuel by a thousand votes to one. Medici has been occupied in putting down an insurrection in the mountains, and Cialdini has won two battles on his way west; and a large Piedmontese force has landed here, and undertaken the work of the garrison."

"How long will it be before Cialdini arrives with his army before Capua?"

"I should think that it would be another week."

"I must be able to go forward again by that time," Frank said. "I must be at Capua when it is taken."

"I quite understand your feelings, and I am eager to be there myself; but we must have patience. The Neapolitans have withdrawn their forces from Cajazzo, and the country round, into the town. There are now some nine thousand men there, and if the commander is obstinate he ought to be able to defend the place for some months. Still I grant that obstinacy has not been the strong point of the Neapolitan generals hitherto; though it must be said that their troops fought gallantly the other day, coming back again and again to the attack. But the commander of the town, however brave he may be, must see that even if he can hold out for the next ten years he would not benefit Francesco. The game is already hopelessly lost. The Garibaldians, single-handed, have proved themselves capable of defeating the Neapolitan troops; and with the army that Cialdini has brought from Ancona, and that which has marched down from the north, the cause is beyond hope. The army now in Gaeta and the garrison of Capua alone remain in arms; and I should say that, ere another fortnight has passed, Francesco is likely to have left this country for ever."

"Quite so, grandfather," Frank replied; "that is what I have been thinking for the last week, and that is why I am so anxious to go forward again as soon as possible."

"That you shall certainly do; at any rate you have a few more days to stay here, then we will get a carriage and go to Santa Lucia, lying high in the mountains. The change to the splendid air there will benefit you, while a stay at Santa Maria or Caserta would at once throw you back."

CHAPTER XVIII

CAPUA

GARIBALDI had been remaining quietly at Caserta when, on the 24th, he received a message from Cialdini inviting him to cross the river and be in readiness to co-operate in a general action, which might possibly be brought on the next day. A bridge had to be thrown over the Volturno, but at five the following morning he crossed with five thousand men. He found that a strong Neapolitan force had fallen back, in the direction of Gaeta, on the previous evening. Missori was sent on with the guides to reconnoitre, and at Teano found the escort of the Neapolitan general, who had gone on to hold a conference with Cialdini. At five in the evening Garibaldi advanced eight miles farther in that direction, and bivouacked in the open air for the night. Scarcely had he resumed his march, at daybreak the next morning, when he met the advance-guard of the Piedmontese. The force marched off the road and encamped while Garibaldi and his staff rode on to meet the king and his general.

The latter was first encountered, and the heartiest greeting was exchanged between him and Garibaldi, for they were old friends. They then rode together to meet Victor Emmanuel, whose greeting with Garibaldi was extremely cordial. They rode together till the afternoon; Garibaldi went with his column to Calvi, and on the 28th retired to Caserta. On the news reaching Naples, Frank, who by this time had almost recovered, drove to Santa Lucia. The Piedmontese and Garibaldians had now taken up their position on the south side of Capua, the former occupying their old positions at Santa Maria and Sant' Angelo, while the Piedmontese occupied the ground between the former town and La Forresta; the Piedmontese general, Della Rocca, being in command of the whole. The troops were at once set to work to construct batteries, and a strong chain of outposts was pushed forward to within five hundred yards of the fortifications, to check the frequent sorties made by the Neapolitans. The latter were still resolute, and several fierce fights took place. At four o'clock in the afternoon of November 1st the batteries opened fire, and the guns of the fortress replied vigorously, the bombardment being maintained until dark. Preparations were made for an assault on the following morning. In the evening, however, the Swiss general, Du Cornet, sent in to capitulate, and his surrender was accepted on the condition that he and his garrison should be allowed to march out with the honours of war. Frank and the professor had driven early that morning from Santa Lucia, and had taken up their post high up on Mount Tifata, whence they could obtain a view of the city and surrounding country.

They drove back when the bombardment ceased. Early the next morning they set out again, and, meeting an officer, were informed that Capua had surrendered. Signor Forli had two days previously gone down to Caserta and seen Garibaldi, and had asked him to give Frank a letter of introduction to General Cialdini, requesting him to allow him to enter with the first party to search the prisons of Capua.

"That I will do right willingly," Garibaldi said. "Indeed, as I rode with him two days ago, we naturally talked over the past; and I mentioned to him that I in no small degree owed the success of my expedition to the large sum of money sent to me by Madame Percival, the wife of the gentleman whose murder by brigands had created so much stir two and a half years ago. He remembered the circumstances perfectly; and I told him that her son had accompanied me throughout, and had greatly distinguished himself, even among the gallant men who accompanied me. I mentioned to him that he had still hopes that his father had not been murdered, and might be found in a Neapolitan prison, and gave him his reason for hoping that he might yet be found in Capua. I need not, therefore, write a long letter."

The general at once sat down and wrote a note to Cialdini, introducing Frank to him, and asking that he might be nominated to accompany the officer charged with the duty of examining the prisons of Capua. As soon, therefore, as they learned that the garrison had capitulated, Signor Forli and Frank drove to La Fortuna, where Cialdini's headquarters were. Frank sent in his card and Garibaldi's letter, and after waiting a few minutes was shown into his room.

"I am glad to see you, Captain Percival," the governor said warmly. "Garibaldi was speaking to me of you in the highest terms and interested me much in the quest you are making for your father. A party of our troops will enter the town to take possession of the magazines, and see that order is maintained until the evacuation of the town by the garrison, which will indeed commence this afternoon. I shall myself be entering in a couple of hours' time; and the best way will be for you to ride in with me. I will provide you with a horse; and it will save time and relieve you of your anxiety if I send an officer with you to the prisons, ordering that you shall at once have every facility given you for ascertaining whether your father is among those confined there."

"I thank you greatly, general," Frank said. "I will not trouble you about the horse, but will, with your permission, drive in in the carriage I have outside. My mother's father, whom I found in prison at Reggio, is with me; and should I be happy enough to find my father, we can then take him away at once."

"Very well, we will arrange it so. Colonel Pasta, please write out an order to the governor of the state prisons in Capua to offer every facility to Captain Percival to visit the jails and inspect the prisoners, with power to liberate his father at once should he find him there. It will save trouble altogether if when we enter the town you at once ride with his carriage to the prisons, and see that this order is complied with. You will also, before you set out, give orders to the officer commanding the escort to allow the carriage to follow him.

"I heartily wish you success in your search," he said, turning to Frank, and again shook him warmly by the hand.

Signor Forli was much pleased when Frank told him the result of his interview. "However, my dear Frank," he said, "I pray you not to allow yourself to be buoyed up with any strong hope: if you do you may only be bitterly disappointed. You must remember, too, that even should we not find him here, we may discover him at Gaeta."

"I will try not to let myself hope too much," Frank replied; "but at the same time I own that the description you obtained of one of the prisoners sent on here from Naples has given me a strong hope that it is my father. Should it not be so, I will not despair altogether, but will look forward to the search at Gaeta. If that does not succeed I fear that it will be no good to hope any longer, for all the prisons south of Naples have been opened long before now, and had my father been confined in one of them, I feel sure that, if able, he would at once have made his way to Naples to see Garibaldi, and obtain from him funds to enable him to return home."

Leaving the carriage, they endeavoured to obtain some food, for they had only taken some coffee and milk and a piece of bread before starting. They found it, however, almost impossible to do so—everything in the place had been eaten up; but after some search they succeeded in getting a bottle of wine and a small piece of bread at one of the cafés. Having taken this, they went back to the carriage, and sat there until they saw the general and his staff come out from headquarters and mount. Just as they were starting, an officer rode up to the carriage.

"I have orders, sir, to permit you to follow in rear of the escort, and to enter the city with them. Will you please drive on at once?"

An hour later they entered Capua. Shortly before an Italian brigade had marched in, placed guards at the gates and all the public buildings, and relieved the Neapolitan sentries on the ramparts. Cialdini dismounted at the palace of the governor, and ten minutes later Colonel Pasto rode up to the carriage. He was accompanied by a gentleman on foot, who introduced himself to Signor Forli as a member of the Municipal body, and, taking a seat, directed the driver to the state prison, Colonel Pasto riding by the side of the carriage. When they arrived at the gate, where two of the bersaglieri were on guard, they alighted, and Colonel Pasto knocked at the gate, which was at once opened.

"I wish to see the governor of the jail," he said.

The warder at once led the way to the governor's residence, followed by the colonel, Frank, and Signor Forli. The governor bowed, with evident trouble in his face, as they entered.

"This officer," the colonel said, "is the bearer of an order from General Cialdini, to search the prison thoroughly for the person of Captain Percival, a British subject, believed to be confined here, and to free him at once if he is so. I also require a full list of all prisoners confined here, with a statement of the charges on which they have been imprisoned. To-morrow the place will be searched from top to bottom, and all prisoners—I believe that no criminals are confined here—will be released."

"I have no such person as Captain Percival here," the official said humbly.

"Not under that name, perhaps," Frank said. "I demand, sir, in the first place, to see the four prisoners who were brought here from Naples on the 5th or 6th of September. If Captain Percival is not one of the four, though I am convinced that he is so, I will postpone a general search until I make it with the Royal officials to-morrow."

The governor looked somewhat surprised at the knowledge possessed by the young officer; however, he only said, "I will take you to them at once, sir; they are together, and as you will see, comfortably lodged."

"I can believe that they are so at present," Frank said sternly, "and have been, perhaps for the past twenty-four hours"; for he felt sure that as soon as it was known that the general was about to capitulate, all the prisoners from the lower dungeons would be hastily removed to better quarters.

"I will accompany you so far, Captain Percival," Colonel Pasto said, "in order that I may inform General Cialdini if you have met with success in your search."

Led by the governor, they left the apartment, entered the prison itself, and followed him down several corridors. One of the warders, by his orders, followed him with a bunch of keys: Frank was very pale, his face was set, and he was evidently trying to nerve himself to bear disappointment. Signor Forli walked with his hand on his shoulder, as if to assure him of his sympathy, and to aid him to support joy or disappointment. Colonel Pasto, deeply interested in the drama, walked a pace or two behind them. At last the turnkey stopped before a door, inserted a key in the lock, and opened it. The governor entered, with the words, " These are the four prisoners, sir."

Frank paused for a moment, took a long breath, and then entered. Three men were lying on the pallet-beds; the fourth, who had been seated, rose as they entered. It was on him that Frank's eyes first fell, and then paused in doubt; the man's hair was long and streaked with grey, he wore long whiskers, beard and moustache, his face was very white and his figure somewhat bent. He was very thin, and his eyes seemed unnaturally large in the drawn, haggard face. As his eyes fell upon the uniforms of the Piedmontese and Garibaldian officers, he held out his arms and cried hoarsely: "I was right, then; we heard the firing yesterday, and knew that the town was attacked, and when we were taken from our foul dungeons and brought up here, I felt sure that deliverance was at hand. Ah, Forli," he broke off, as his eyes fell on the professor, " this is all that was wanted to complete my joy. You too are rescued!" and bursting into tears he sank back upon his pallet and covered his face with his thin hands.

The professor laid his hand on Frank's shoulder, as the latter was about to dart forward.

"Stay a minute or two, lad," he whispered—"it may be too much for him," and he went up to Percival and put his hand on his shoulder. "It is a joyful occasion indeed, Leonard," he said. "You are free. Save for the Papal States and Venice, all Italy is free. I have other good news for you. Muriel, your boy and my wife are all well, and will soon be able to rejoin you."

"A minute, Forli—give me a minute," Captain Percival said, in a low voice. "I should not have broken down thus. It is almost too much, coming all at once, after so long a time of waiting."

Two of the other prisoners had half risen at Signor Forli's words; the other was too weak to do more than turn his face towards them.

"The news is true, gentlemen," Colonel Pasto said. "To-morrow, you and all within this prison will be free men. Capua has surrendered, and we have but just entered the town. As there are still nine thousand of the Neapolitan troops here, there are many arrangements to be made, and we must find some place for you all until you can be sent to your homes. It is impossible to search the jails until to-morrow, but you need not regard yourselves any longer as prisoners. I have orders from General Cialdini to the governor here, that you shall in the meantime be well and plentifully fed, so as to prepare you for leaving this place.

"You hear, sir," he said, turning to the governor. "You will procure, regardless of expense, every luxury possible,

HE WENT UP TO PERCIVAL AND PUT HIS HAND ON HIS
SHOULDER.

with a proper supply of good wine; and see that all have a thoroughly good meal this afternoon, and another this evening. I request that you will, without delay, have every prisoner informed of what has happened, and that he will tomorrow be released."

"I will see that it is done, colonel," the governor said. "I will at once give the necessary orders.

"Perhaps it will be better, sir," he went on, speaking to Signor Forli, "that your friend should take something before he leaves. I have pleasure in placing my private room at your disposal, and will order some refreshment to be served there immediately."

Captain Percival now rose to his feet with an effort. "I am afraid I shall have to be carried, Forli," he said with an attempt at a smile. "I was able to walk across the room this morning, but your news has, for the present, demolished what little strength I had left."

"You had better sit down, Captain Percival," the colonel said. "The governor will doubtless send some men with a stretcher at once, and I need hardly assure you how great a pleasure it has been to me to be employed on so successful a mission. I shall tell General Cialdini that you have been found." And so saying, after shaking hands with Captain Percival and the other prisoners, he left the room with the governor.

Frank also went outside, as, seeing how weak his father was, he quite recognised the wisdom of Signor Forli's advice that he should not be told too much at once; and, indeed, he felt that he could no longer suppress his own emotions. Leaning against the wall in the passage, he cried like a child.

Assisted by Signor Forli, Percival went round and shook hands with the other three prisoners.

"I was right, you see," he said: "I told you last night, when we were all brought up here, that our deliverance was at hand, but I hardly thought that it could be so near. Soon you too will see your friends, from whom you have been kept a much longer time than I have.

"We have only met once before," he said to the professor, "when nearly two months ago we were all brought out and placed in a vehicle together, and driven here. On the way we told each other what our real names were, and the addresses of our friends, so that if by some miracle one of us should issue alive from our horrible dungeons, we might let the friends of the others know how and where they had died. Thank God, we shall now all be bearers of good news."

"I fear that I shall never be so," the weakest of them said, feebly.

"Do not think that," Signor Forli said cheerfully: "good food, fresh air, and, more than all, freedom, will do wonders for you. I, like yourselves, have been a special prisoner in a fortress for upwards of three years, and you see me now as strong and as well as I was when I entered it. Make up your mind that you will get well and cheat these tyrants, who had thought to kill you by inches."

Four of the jailors now entered; one of them carried a stretcher, another had a bottle of excellent wine and four large glasses, which he filled and handed to the prisoners.

"This is the first taste of freedom," one said, as he emptied his glass. "There, friend," he went on, as one of the jailors partly lifted the sick man and placed the glass to his lips, "that is your first step towards health and strength. I can feel it already tingling in my veins, which years ago a glass of pure spirit would hardly have done. No, we will take no more now," he said, as one of the men was about to refill his glass. "Leave it here; another glass now would intoxicate me, after five years on water alone and starvation diet."

Captain Percival was now placed on the stretcher and carried out; Frank fell in with Signor Forli as he followed the party. "Unless you are going to tell him soon," he said, "I must go; I cannot stand it, being so close to him."

"I will tell him as soon as we are alone," the professor said: "he has calmed down, and that glass of wine will do him a world of good."

On arriving at the governor's room, Captain Percival was placed in an easy chair, and the jailors left. Frank went to the window and looked out.

"I can hardly believe that it is not all a dream, Forli. The strangest part is that, while I had hoped to open your prison doors, you have opened mine."

"You are wrong, Leonard: the same person who opened my doors has opened yours; as you set out to find me, so another set out to find us both,"

Captain Percival looked at him wonderingly.

"Of whom are you speaking, Forli? My head is not very clear at present. But who could have been looking for us both? You don't mean Garibaldi?"

"No, no, Leonard; truly he has opened the doors to all prisoners, but he was not searching for any one in particular. When I tell you that Muriel sent out to Garibaldi the sum that you had put aside for that purpose, and that she and my wife had never altogether lost hope that you and I were both still alive, whom should she send out with it, and to search for you, but——"

"You don't mean Frank? You cannot mean him: he is only a boy at school."

"He is nearly seventeen now, and there are hundreds of younger lads who, like him, have done their duty as men. Yes, it is Frank. I would not tell you at first; one shock was enough at a time. Frank, my boy, you have your reward at last."

Frank turned and ran towards his father. The latter rose from his seat.

"My boy, my dear lad!" he cried, as he held out his arms, "this is too much happiness!"

It was some minutes before either father or son could speak coherently; and fortunately, just as Frank placed his father in the chair, one of the attendants brought in a basin of clear soup, two cutlets, an omelette, and a bottle of wine, saying that the governor had sent them from his own table, with his compliments.

Captain Percival smiled faintly when the man left the room.

"It is my last meal in prison, and if it had been sent to me a week ago I should have declined to eat it, for I should have made sure that it was poisoned; however, as it is, I will take it with thankfulness."

"Yes, and you must eat as much as you can," Forli said. "You have got a drive before you: we shall take you straight up to Santa Lucia, where we have rooms; the mountain air has done wonders for Frank, who has had a touch of these marsh fevers. It would be difficult to find a place in Capua now, so the sooner you are out of it the better."

Captain Percival took a mouthful or two of soup and then stopped.

"That won't do, Leonard—that won't do; you really must make an effort. Do it in Italian fashion: pour a glass of wine into it; if you will take that, I will let you off the meat."

"I could not touch it whether you let me off or not. I have not touched meat for two years and a half, and I shall be some time taking to it again."

He finished the soup, and then, upon the insistence of Signor Forli, took some of the omelette.

"Now," the latter said, "we will be off. When we came in here, we told the driver to find some place where he could take the horses out and feed them, and then come here and wait for us. I suppose we must get somebody to let us out of the prison."

Frank rang the bell. When the attendant came in, he said, "Please tell the governor that we are now leaving, and that we shall be obliged if he would send down an official to the gate to let us out."

The governor himself came in two minutes later; the gate was close by the entrance to his house; and Signor Forli said,—"I will go out first, sir, and fetch our carriage round, if you will be good enough to give orders that the gate is to be kept open until I return, and to order the warder there to allow Captain Percival to pass out with us." Ten minutes later they were on their way. Captain Percival would not be laid on a stretcher again, but leaning upon his father-in-law and son, was able to walk to the carriage.

"I have a flask of brandy-and-water in my pocket, Leonard, and if you feel faint you must take a little."

Very few words were spoken on the journey. Frank sat by the side of his father and held his hand in his own, and it was not long before Captain Percival fell asleep. The excitement of the past thirty-six hours had for a time given him a fictitious strength; and now the sense of happiness and of freedom, aided, no doubt, by the unaccustomed meal and the wine he had taken, took the natural effect, and after trying in vain to question Frank as to what had taken place, he dozed off.

"That is the best thing for him," Signor Forli said in low tones, when he saw that Captain Percival was asleep. "I hope he will not wake up till we arrive at Santa Lucia. He has borne it better than I expected. It has, of course, pulled him down a great deal more than it did me. A strong and active man must naturally feel solitary confinement much more than one who seldom takes any exercise beyond half an hour's walk in the streets of London; who is, moreover, something of a philosopher, and who can conjure up at will from his brain many of his intimate friends. I have no doubt he will sleep soundly to-night, and I trust—though of this I do not feel quite sure—that he will be a different man in the morning. Of course it may be the other way, and that when the effect of the excitement has passed off he will need a great deal of careful nursing before he begins to gain strength. At any rate, I shall go into Naples to-morrow and send a telegram to your mother, and tell her to come over with my wife at once. It would be of no use going down to Caserta; the wires will be so fully occupied by the military and royal telegrams that there will be little chance of a private message getting through. They are sure to start directly they get my message, and may be here in three or four days. I shall advise them to come *viâ* Marseilles; for, as the train service is sure to be upset, they might be a good deal longer coming by land, besides the annoyance of long detentions and crowded trains; for you may be sure that there will be a rush from the north to come down to witness the king's entrance into Naples."

"I think that will be a very good plan indeed," Frank agreed; "and the knowledge that they are coming will, I should think, do a great deal of good to my father."

Darkness had fallen long before they reached Santa Lucia. The village was still full of soldiers. As he leapt out from the carriage Frank called to four of them standing near to help in carrying his father upstairs; and so soundly was Captain Percival sleeping, that this was managed and he was laid on the bed without his fairly waking, though he half opened his eyes and murmured something that Frank could not catch.

"We will not try to take his things off," Signor Forli said, "but just throw a blanket lightly over him now. I will remain here while you go down and get some supper. You had better stay in the room with him all night; there is no getting hold of another bed, but——"

"I shall do just as well without a bed," Frank said; "since I landed at Marsala I have hardly slept in one; besides, I don't fancy that I shall sleep much, anyhow. I have plenty to think about and to thank God for, and if my father moves I shall be at his bedside in a moment. It is likely enough that he will not have the least idea where he is."

"Quite so, Frank. When you come up from supper bring an extra candle with you: you had better keep a light burning all night."

Captain Percival, however, did not wake up until it was broad daylight. He looked round in a bewildered way until his eyes rested upon Frank, who was seated close to his bedside.

"That settles it," he said with a smile, holding out his hand to him. "I could not make out where I was. I remember leaving Capua in a carriage, and nothing more; I must have slept like a log, as you got me out of the carriage and up here without my waking."

"I think it was the professor's fault chiefly, father, in making you take that second glass of wine in your soup. You see you were altogether unaccustomed to it, and being so weak, that and all the excitement naturally overpowered you. However, I think it a capital thing that it did. You had twelve hours' good sleep, and you look all the better for it. I will tell Signor Forli you are awake. He has peeped in three or four times to see how you are going on."

He went out for a minute, and a little later the professor came in with a large cup of hot milk.

"You are looking fifty per cent. better, Leonard," he said. "You had better begin by drinking this, and then I should recommend you to get rid of those rags you have on, and to have a good wash. I am going into Naples, and will bring you some clothes. You certainly could not get into my coat, but I will lend you a shirt, and that is all that you will want, for you had better lie in bed to-day and listen to Frank's account of his adventures, having a nap occasionally when you feel tired, and taking as much soup as you can get down, with perhaps a slice of chicken."

"What are you going to Naples for?"

"I am going to send the good news to Muriel, and to tell

her and my wife to come over at once and help you to build up your strength again. I won't say come over to nurse you, for I think you can do without that,—all you want is building up."

Before he started the professor showed them the telegram he had written out.

"It is rather long," he said, "but a pound or two one way or the other makes little difference." It ran: "Prepare yourself for good news, and don't read farther till you have done so. Thank God, Frank's search has been successful. I dared not tell you when I last wrote that I had found a clue lest it should only give rise to false hopes. However, it led us to our goal. Leonard is recovered and free. He is weak, but needs nothing but good food and your presence. Start with Annetta at once; come straight to Marseilles and take the first steamer to Naples. You will find us at the Hotel d'Italie, where I shall have rooms ready for you."

After Signor Forli left, Frank told the story of his adventures bit by bit, insisting upon his father taking rest and food three or four times.

The professor returned late in the evening. "I have got rooms at the hotel," he said; "and it is lucky that I did not put off going down till to-morrow, for telegrams are coming in from all parts of Italy to secure accommodation. However, fortunately there were still some good rooms left when I arrived there, and I need not say that I did not haggle over terms, outrageous as they were on the strength of the coming crowd. Your father is going on all right, I hope?"

"Very well indeed, I think. I only talked for about half an hour at a time, he has slept a good deal, and he has eaten well, his voice is stronger, and there is a little colour in his cheeks; he was terribly white before."

"That was from being kept in the dark, Frank, as much as from illness."

They went upstairs together. "I hear a good account of you, Leonard," the professor said, "so I will give you what I have in my pocket, which I should otherwise have kept till to-morrow morning." He took out a piece of thin paper, handed it to Captain Percival, and held the candle close, so that he should read the contents. It was but a few words, but it took some time in the reading, for the invalid's eyes were blinded with tears. When he had read it, he dropped it on the coverlet and put his hands over his face, while the bed shook with his deep sobs. Frank took up the paper and ran his eye over it.

"The good God be praised for all His mercies! Oh, my husband, I can say no more now. Mother and I start to-night for Marseilles.—Your most happy and loving wife."

Two days later the party left for Naples. That morning Garibaldi, to whom Frank had sent a message on the morning after his return from Capua, drove up to Santa Lucia to see his old friend.

"I am almost as pleased, Percival," he said, after a silent hand-grip had been exchanged, "to have freed you as I am to have freed Italy, a matter in which the money your wife sent me in your name had no slight share. You have reason to be proud of your son: he has shown throughout the expedition a courage and coolness equal to that of any of my veterans. He captured the first Neapolitan standard that was taken, and has rendered me innumerable services as my aide-de-camp. You are looking better than I expected."

"I should be an ungrateful brute, if I were not getting better, after all my son has gone through to rescue me, and the feeding up that I have had since I came here."

"You must have suffered intensely, Percival?"

"It has been pretty hard. I have all the time been in solitary confinement in filthy holes, where scarce a ray of daylight penetrated. I have had nothing but either the blackest of bread or roasted maize to eat, but I have been kept up throughout by the conviction that ere very long there must be an upheaval: things could not go on as they were. I knew that my own letters had excited a general feeling of horror at the accounts of the dungeons in which political prisoners were confined, and I determined to make the best of matters. A year ago—at least, I suppose that it is about a year, for I have lost count of time—a fresh hope was given me, when one of my jailors, who was at heart a good fellow, and occasionally ventured to say a few words to me, told me that the Sardinians, with the help of France, had recovered Lombardy from Austria, and that Tuscany and other Papal States had all revolted and joined Sardinia. That gave me fresh hope and courage. I felt that things could not long remain so, and that the south would soon follow the example of the north. I felt sure that you had borne your part in the struggle with the Austrians, and that, just as you headed the Roman insurrection, you would certainly throw yourself heart and soul into a rising in the south. I hear now, from my son, that in fact the whole has been entirely your work."

"I have done what I could," Garibaldi said, "and well have I been rewarded by the gratitude of the people. But I see already that the jealousy of the Piedmontese is carrying them beyond all bounds, and that I shall soon be back in Caprera. But that matters not; I shall be happy in the thought that I have earned the gratitude of all Italy, and that the work I have done can never be undone. The king is a brave and gallant gentleman, but he is prejudiced by the lies of the men round him, who cannot forgive me for having done what should have been their work. It is a pity, but it matters but little. I fought for the cause and not for myself, and my only regret is that my brave companions should suffer by the jealousy and ill-humour of a handful of miserables. I shall be in Naples in a few days, and hope to find still further improvement in your condition."

The long drive to Naples had no ill effect whatever, and Captain Percival was able to walk from the carriage up to his room, leaning upon Frank's arm. They learned that it would be two days before the next steamer from Marseilles arrived, and these were passed by Captain Percival in the carriage, driving slowly backwards and forwards along the promenade by the sea, sometimes halting for an hour or two, while he got out and walked for a time, and then sat down on a seat, enjoying intensely the balmy air and the lovely view. He was now able to dispense altogether with Frank's assistance. His hair had been cut short, and his face clean-shaved with the exception of his moustache, for, as he said, " he hardly knew his own face with all that hair on, and he wanted his wife to see him again as he was when he left her. His cheeks were still very thin and hollow, but the sun and sea air had removed the deadly pallor, and the five days of good feeding had already softened the sharpness of the outlines of his face.

On the day when the steamer was due he remained down at the sea until she was sighted. Then he returned to the hotel with Signor Forli, leaving Frank to meet the ladies when they landed and to bring them up to the hotel. Garibaldi had run down to Naples on the previous day, and spent some hours in endeavouring to smooth matters between the contending factions, and had given Frank an order to the officers of the custom-house to pass the baggage of Signora Forli and Mrs. Percival unopened. The greeting between Frank and his mother and the Signora was a rapturous one. Not many words were spoken, for both ladies were so greatly affected that they hurried at once into the carriage. Frank saw the small amount of baggage that they had brought handed up, and then jumped in.

"How is he looking?" Mrs. Percival asked anxiously.

"Of course he is looking thin, mother. He was very weak when we found him, five days ago, but he has picked up a good deal since then, and in another fortnight he will be walking about with you just as of old."

"You are looking thin yourself, Frank—very thin. My father mentioned in his letter that you had had a touch of fever."

"Yes, it was rather a sharp touch; but, as you see, I am all right now, though I have not yet returned to duty. I was able to take a part in the battle of Volturno, but collapsed after it was over."

"And your grandfather has not changed much, you said?" the Signora asked.

"He has borne it marvellously," Frank said. "As I told you in my letter, he has kept himself up by going through all the authors he knew by heart. You know what a marvellous memory he has, and of course that helped him immensely. Of all the prisoners we have released, there was not one who was so well and strong as he was. I really don't think that you will find any change in him since you saw him last—except that, of course, his hair is rather greyer. Father is a good deal greyer, mother. I think that, perhaps, it is the result of there being so little light in the places where he has been kept. Here is the hotel. Now I will take you up to them, and will leave you there while I come down and see after your traps. I should doubt whether any English ladies ever arrived at Naples before with so little luggage."

He spoke cheerfully, for both his mother and the Signora were so much agitated that he was afraid of their breaking down before they got upstairs. On reaching the door he opened it, and, closing it quickly behind him, went away. It was a quarter of an hour before he returned to the room. All had now recovered from the effects of their first meeting.

"We have already settled, Frank, that we will start for home at once. Your grandfather says that he has ascertained that a steamer will leave to-morrow for England; and we mean to go all the way by sea. It will do your father good, and you too, for your grandfather says the doctor told him that, although you have got rid of the fever altogether, you need change to set you up thoroughly, and that a sea voyage would be the best thing for you. And, as we are all good sailors, it will be the pleasantest way as well as the best. Fortunately your work is done here. The fighting is over, and even if it were not, you have done your share. You have not told us much about that in your letters, but Garibaldi spoke of you in the highest terms to your father; and your grandfather learned from some of your comrades, what you really did at Calatafimi and Palermo."

"I did just what the others did, mother, and was luckier than most of them, though I was laid up there for a month with the wound I got; but I don't see how I could start to-morrow without leave, and, at any rate, without thanking Garibaldi for his kindness."

"Well, then, you must run over to Caserta and see him this evening. The railway is open, is it not? It is only a run of half an hour or so."

"Very well, mother, I will do that; and very likely he will be over in the morning. He comes here nearly every day, and if he had not intended doing so to-morrow, I am sure he would come, if only to see you and the signora, and to say good-bye to father and the professor. About what time does the steamer start?"

"At one o'clock."

"Oh, that will leave plenty of time; the general is always up at three in the morning."

Frank was not mistaken: at eight o'clock Garibaldi arrived at the hotel and spent half an hour with them. He delighted Mrs. Percival by the manner in which he spoke of Frank, saying that no one had distinguished himself more during the campaign.

The voyage to England was pleasant and uneventful, and by the time they arrived at home, Captain Percival was almost himself again, while Frank had entirely shaken off the effects of his illness. It had been agreed that he should not return to Harrow; six months of campaigning had ill-fitted him for the restrictions of school life, and it was arranged that he should be prepared for Cambridge by a private tutor. He finally passed creditably, though not brilliantly, through the University. He and his family had the pleasure of meeting Garibaldi when the latter paid a visit to London, four years after the close of the campaign; and the general, in spite of his many engagements, spent one quiet evening with his friends at Cadogan Place.

Four years later Frank married, and his father settled

upon him his country estate, to which, since his return to England, he had seldom gone down, for, although his general health was good, he never sufficiently recovered from the effects of his imprisonment to be strong enough again to take part in field sports. He lived, however, to a good old age, and it is not very long since he and his wife died within a few days of each other. The professor and Signora Forli had left them fifteen years before.

THE END

Additional Books and Educational Materials

When our family began home schooling 20 years ago, it was never our intention to produce books and CD-ROMs for children. The death in 1988 of our wife and mother, Laurelee, when the children were 12, 10, 8, 6, 6, and 1 1/2-years-old, markedly changed our lives. From then on, our home school became a project in self-teaching, which required, more than ever before, the very best books and educational materials because the children had no teacher.

From this experience has grown the Robinson Self-Teaching Curriculum on 22 CD-ROMs that is now used by more than 60,000 children. These CDs provide the best books, vocabulary exercises, reference works, and examinations that we have been able to find or produce – all in printable form. Also, to supplement the teaching of history, we have collected the complete works of G. A. Henty on a similar 6 CD-ROM set.

These CDs, including digitizing more than 150,000 pages of text, were produced by the Robinson family themselves, with special help in various ways from colleagues at the Oregon Institute of Science and Medicine.

Now, in order to make these materials even more widely available, we have embarked on a project to offer these books and educational materials in printed form. The following pages describe some of these products.

Arthur B. Robinson – May 2002
Oregon Institute of Science and Medicine

Superb Educational Results

ROBINSON SELF-TEACHING CURRICULUM
VERSION 2.2

The Robinson children teach themselves (as do the 60,000 other children now using the Robinson Curriculum) – so well that their 11th- and 12th-grade work is equivalent to high quality 1st- and 2nd-year university instruction.

They also teach themselves study habits that do not depend upon planned workbooks, teacher interaction, and other aids that will not be available later in life.

They teach themselves to think.

Many home schools are limited by the burden of teaching that is placed upon parents. Dr. Robinson has spent less than 15 minutes each day teaching all six children at ages 6 through 18. Yet his students have achieved very high SAT scores and received years of advanced placement in college. Teach your children to teach themselves and to acquire superior knowledge, as did many of America's most outstanding citizens in the days before socialism in education.

Give children access to a good study environment and the best books in the English language and then – get out of their way! Entire curriculum, including the books, can be viewed on the computer screen or printed (better for the children) with included software. One caution: Do not use this curriculum unless you are willing for your children to be academically more learned than you.

With Far Less Teacher Time

CURRICULUM FOR GRADES 1-12
ORIGINAL SOURCE LIBRARY
COMPLETE 12-YEAR CURRICULUM $195

- Outstanding course of study
- 120,000-page library resource
- 1911 Encyclopedia Britannica
- 1913 Noah Webster's Dictionary
- 2,000 historic illustrations
- 6,000-word vocabulary teacher
- Progress exams keyed to books
- Outstanding science program
- 20% discounts on Saxon math books
  (the only additional materials required)

❏ Please send _____ copies of the Robinson Self-Teaching Curriculum, Version 2.2. Enclosed is $195 for each 22 CD-ROM set.

❏ Please send _____ copies of both the Robinson Curriculum and the Henty Collection. Enclosed is $275 (a $19 savings) for each 28 CD-ROM set.

Name _____
Address _____
City/State/Zip _____

My computer is ❏ IBM ❏ MAC

Send to: Oregon Institute of Science and Medicine, 2251 Dick George Road, Cave Junction, OR 97523

An Outstanding Resource for Home Education

Complete 12-Year Education

If you could have only one home school resource, this would be the one. It includes all of the books and other materials for an academically superior education, except for Saxon math books, delivered to you it an extraordinarily economical CD-ROM format.

Including the curriculum, Saxon books, and supplies for your computer printer, the entire cost of high quality home schooling is about $100 per year - for your entire family, since all of your children can use the same materials. Moreover, the children teach themselves, so very large amounts of parent time are saved as well.

The child works from materials that you print with your computer – not from the computer screen. (The entire curriculum is screen usable, but printed materials are better for the student.) This includes books, exercises, examinations, and other study aids.

Developed by an outstanding scientist and his coworkers, this curriculum teaches children to think and learn independently – and prepares them with the basic skills and knowledge that must be learned early in life.

While effectively teaching basic skills, the Robinson Curriculum is also by far the most academically superior curriculum available today. Robinson students routinely complete one or two years of college work by age 18.

Four Keys to Learning

The keys to learning are study environment, study habits, course of study, and high quality books.

The Robinson Curriculum carefully integrates the student's habits and study materials into a single system of learning, so that the four keys to learning work together.

The Course of Study included with the curriculum carefully explains all aspects of the Robinson method, including the placement of students who have been previously using other study materials.

Independent of Parent Time and Skills

This teaching program is not dependent upon the teacher's individual education because it requires almost no teacher interaction. It routinely allows children to acquire skills and knowledge beyond those of their parents.

This is not merely a convenience for the parents. A child who teaches himself develops superior skills. This is especially important in problem solving in math, science and engineering and in independent thought about history, literature, economics, and general studies.

The special abilities and self-confidence produced by self-study using the Robinson method are extraordinary. Students often finish calculus by the age of 14 and are frequently able to pass by examination many freshman and sophomore college science courses by age 18.

Yet, slower students excel, too, because the curriculum matches learning rate to ability. After a building a firm foundation at their own pace, students that initially work more slowly can frequently achieve a very high level.

120,000 Pages of Outstanding Materials

Provided with 250 of the greatest science, history, literature, economics, reference, and general education books in the English language, an integrated planned course of study, and appropriate study aids, each child proceeds at his own pace.

With encyclopedic reference works, all science books, thousands of beautiful illustrations, printable flash cards for phonics, math, and vocabulary, and SAT-style examinations, the curriculum is complete in every way.

Very special attention is paid to verbal ability, with an extensive system of instruction that enables the student to master a carefully selected 6,400 word vocabulary. This is especially important today, since students have more difficulty in vocabulary because they are often in contact with government schooled students who have very poor skills.

Outstanding Results

Although no prediction can be made as to the progress of an individual student, results with the Robinson Curriculum are generally extraordinary. Dr. Robinson's two oldest students, after using this curriculum, completed college with BS degrees in chemistry in only two years and have gone on to distinguished graduate programs. Their SAT and GRE exam scores ranged between 95 and 99 percentile, with some perfect scores. The younger Robinson children are also performing in an outstanding manner.

The Robinson Curriculum has been created by a Christian family for Christian students. It is by far the most easy to use and yet academically advanced educational program available – and, it is very economical.

99 Books by G.A. Henty

In addition to the book that you hold in your hand, G. A. Henty wrote 98 other books. All 99 of Mr. Henty's books are available from Robinson Books in the original unedited printed formats.

The pages that follow contain an alphabetic listing of these books and also content summaries of each. These books can be ordered by mail from Robinson Books, 2251 Dick George Road, Cave Junction, OR 97523. Telephone (541) 592-4142 and Fax (541) 592-2597.

The most convenient ordering is available at the Robinson Books Internet site:

www.robinsonbooks.org

At the time of this printing, these books were available in both soft bound and hard bound versions. In order to learn the prices and availability, you will need to look at the above Internet web site or call the telephone number given above.

Note: Some of these same Henty books have appeared under other titles. Other than short stories, however, all of his books are listed here. No other full length books by G. A. Henty are known to exist.

Adventure, Character, and History – in

99 BOOKS (all that he wrote) and 53 SHORT STORIES BY

G. A. Henty

WITH 216 ADDITIONAL HENTY-ERA SHORT STORIES BY OTHER AUTHORS

On 6 CD-ROMS for $99

Children learn by example, and the examples set by Henty's heroes of honesty, integrity, hard work, courage, diligence, perseverance, personal honor, and strong Christian faith are unsurpassed. And, each hero is at the center of fast-moving adventures that capture the reader's interest and will not let go – adventures that take place during great historical events.

From the French Revolution to the Great Plague of London, from the Crusades to the American Civil War, Henty readers learn in-depth history, superior vocabulary and literary techniques, and the advantages of high personal character – while they are being entertained by a master storyteller.

This 42,000-page Robinson Books Henty Collection is an excellent supplement to the Robinson Curriculum and is also outstanding reading for any person – young or old, regardless of educational background.

Books that Children Love to Read!

❏ Please send _____ copies of the Robinson Books Henty Collection. Enclosed is $99 for each 6 CD-ROM set including 99 books and 269 short stories.

❏ Please send _____ copies of both the Henty Collection and the Robinson Curriculum. Enclosed is $275 (a $19 savings) for each 28 CD-ROM set.

Name _____
Address _____
City/State/Zip _____

My computer is ❏ IBM ❏ MAC

Send to: Oregon Institute of Science and Medicine, 2251 Dick George Road, Cave Junction, OR 97523

G. A. Henty's Books

Title	ISBN - Paper Cover	ISBN - Hard Cover
A Chapter of Adventures	1-59087-000-X	1-59087-001-8
A Final Reckoning	1-59087-002-6	1-59087-003-4
A Hidden Foe	1-59087-004-2	1-59087-005-0
A Jacobite Exile	1-59087-006-9	1-59087-007-7
A Knight of the White Cross	1-59087-008-5	1-59087-009-3
A March on London	1-59087-010-7	1-59087-011-5
A Roving Commission	1-59087-012-3	1-59087-013-1
A Search for a Secret	1-59087-014-X	1-59087-015-8
A Woman of the Commune	1-59087-016-6	1-59087-017-4
All But Lost Volume I	1-59087-018-2	1-59087-019-0
All But Lost Volume II	1-59087-020-4	1-59087-021-2
All But Lost Volume III	1-59087-022-0	1-59087-023-9
At Aboukir and Acre	1-59087-024-7	1-59087-025-5
At Agincourt	1-59087-026-3	1-59087-027-1
At the Point of the Bayonet	1-59087-028-X	1-59087-029-8
Beric the Briton	1-59087-030-1	1-59087-031-X
Bonnie Prince Charlie	1-59087-032-8	1-59087-033-6
Both Sides the Border	1-59087-034-4	1-59087-035-2
By Conduct and Courage	1-59087-036-0	1-59087-037-9
By England's Aid	1-59087-038-7	1-59087-039-5
By Pike and Dyke	1-59087-040-9	1-59087-041-7
By Right of Conquest	1-59087-042-5	1-59087-043-3
By Sheer Pluck	1-59087-044-1	1-59087-045-X
Captain Bayley's Heir	1-59087-046-8	1-59087-047-6
Colonel Thorndyke's Secret	1-59087-048-4	1-59087-049-2
Condemned as a Nihilist	1-59087-050-6	1-59087-051-4
Dorothy's Double	1-59087-052-2	1-59087-053-0
Facing Death	1-59087-054-9	1-59087-055-7
For Name and Fame	1-59087-056-5	1-59087-057-3
For the Temple	1-59087-058-1	1-59087-059-X
Friends Though Divided	1-59087-060-3	1-59087-061-1
Gabriel Allen M.P.	1-59087-062-X	1-59087-063-8
Held Fast For England	1-59087-064-6	1-59087-065-4
In Freedom's Cause	1-59087-066-2	1-59087-067-0
In Greek Waters	1-59087-068-9	1-59087-069-7
In the Hands of the Cave Dwellers	1-59087-070-0	1-59087-071-9
In the Heart of the Rockies	1-59087-072-7	1-59087-073-5
In the Irish Brigade	1-59087-074-3	1-59087-075-1
In the Reign of Terror	1-59087-076-X	1-59087-077-8
In Times of Peril	1-59087-078-6	1-59087-079-4
Jack Archer	1-59087-080-8	1-59087-081-6
John Hawke's Fortune	1-59087-082-4	1-59087-083-2
Maori and Settler	1-59087-084-0	1-59087-085-9
No Surrender!	1-59087-086-7	1-59087-087-5
On the Irrawaddy	1-59087-088-3	1-59087-089-1
One of the 28th	1-59087-090-5	1-59087-091-3
Orange and Green	1-59087-092-1	1-59087-093-X

Title	ISBN - Paper Cover	ISBN - Hard Cover
Out on the Pampas	1-59087-094-8	1-59087-095-6
Out With Garibaldi	1-59087-096-4	1-59087-097-2
Queen Victoria	1-59087-098-0	1-59087-099-9
Redskin and Cow-Boy	1-59087-100-6	1-59087-101-4
Rujub, the Juggler	1-59087-102-2	1-59087-103-0
St. Bartholomew's Eve	1-59087-104-9	1-59087-105-7
St. George for England	1-59087-106-5	1-59087-107-3
Sturdy and Strong	1-59087-108-1	1-59087-109-X
The Bravest of the Brave	1-59087-110-3	1-59087-111-1
The Cat of Bubastes	1-59087-112-X	1-59087-113-8
The Cornet of Horse	1-59087-114-6	1-59087-115-4
The Curse of Carne's Hold	1-59087-116-2	1-59087-117-0
The Dash for Khartoum	1-59087-118-9	1-59087-119-7
The Dragon and the Raven	1-59087-120-0	1-59087-121-9
The Lion of St. Mark	1-59087-122-7	1-59087-123-5
The Lion of the North	1-59087-124-3	1-59087-125-1
The Lost Heir	1-59087-126-X	1-59087-127-8
The March to Coomassie	1-59087-128-6	1-59087-129-4
The March to Magdala	1-59087-130-8	1-59087-131-6
The Plague Ship	1-59087-132-4	1-59087-133-2
The Queen's Cup	1-59087-134-0	1-59087-135-9
The Sovereign Reader	1-59087-136-7	1-59087-137-5
The Tiger of Mysore	1-59087-138-3	1-59087-139-1
The Treasure of the Incas	1-59087-140-5	1-59087-141-3
The Young Buglers	1-59087-142-1	1-59087-143-X
The Young Carthaginian	1-59087-144-8	1-59087-145-6
The Young Colonists	1-59087-146-4	1-59087-147-2
The Young Franc-Tireurs	1-59087-148-0	1-59087-149-9
Those Other Animals	1-59087-150-2	1-59087-151-0
Through Russian Snows	1-59087-152-9	1-59087-153-7
Through the Fray	1-59087-154-5	1-59087-155-3
Through the Sikh War	1-59087-156-1	1-59087-157-X
Through Three Campaigns	1-59087-158-8	1-59087-159-6
To Herat and Cabul	1-59087-160-X	1-59087-161-8
True to the Old Flag	1-59087-162-6	1-59087-163-4
Under Drake's Flag	1-59087-164-2	1-59087-165-0
Under Wellington's Command	1-59087-166-9	1-59087-167-7
When London Burned	1-59087-168-5	1-59087-169-3
Winning His Spurs	1-59087-170-7	1-59087-171-5
With Buller in Natal	1-59087-172-3	1-59087-173-1
With Clive in India	1-59087-174-X	1-59087-175-8
With Cochrane the Dauntless	1-59087-176-6	1-59087-177-4
With Frederick the Great	1-59087-178-2	1-59087-179-0
With Kitchener in the Soudan	1-59087-180-4	1-59087-181-2
With Lee in Virginia	1-59087-182-0	1-59087-183-9
With Moore at Corunna	1-59087-184-7	1-59087-185-5
With Roberts to Pretoria	1-59087-186-3	1-59087-187-1
With the Allies to Pekin	1-59087-188-X	1-59087-189-8
With the British Legion	1-59087-190-1	1-59087-191-X
With Wolfe in Canada	1-59087-192-8	1-59087-193-6
Won by the Sword	1-59087-194-4	1-59087-195-2
Wulf the Saxon	1-59087-196-0	1-59087-197-9

G. A. Henty's
Historical Adventures
Published by Robinson Books
2251 Dick George Road
Cave Junction, OR 97523
www.robinsonbooks.org

AT AGINCOURT
A Tale of the White Hoods of Paris

The story begins in a grim feudal castle in Normandie, on the old frontier between France and England, where the lad Guy Aylmer had gone to join his father's old friend Sir Eustace de Villeroy. The times were troublous and soon the French king compelled Lady Margaret de Villeroy with her children to go to Paris as hostages for Sir Eustace's loyalty. Guy Aylmer went with her as her page and body-guard. Paris was turbulent and the populace riotous. Soon the guild of the butchers, adopting white hoods as their uniform, seized the city, and besieged the house where our hero and his charges lived. After desperate fighting, the white hoods were beaten and our hero and his charges escaped from the city, and from France. He came back to share in the great battle of Agincourt, and when peace followed returned with honor to England.

WITH FREDERICK THE GREAT
A Tale of the Seven Year's War

The Hero of this story while still a youth entered the service of Frederick the Great, and by a succession of fortunate circumstances and perilous adventures, rose to the rank of colonel. Attached to the staff of the king, he rendered distinguished services in many battles, in one of which he saved the king's life. Twice captured and imprisoned, he both times escaped from the Austrian fortresses.

The story follows closely the historical lines, and no more vivid description of the memorable battles of Rossbach, Leuthen, Prague, Zorndorf, Hochkirch, and Torgan can be found anywhere than is here given. Woven in this there runs the record of the daring and hazardous adventures of the hero, and the whole narrative has thus, with historic accuracy, the utmost charm of romance.

WITH WOLFE IN CANADA
Or, The Winning of a Continent

Mr. Henty here gives an account of the struggle between Britain and France for supremacy in the North American continent. The fall of Quebec decided that the Anglo-Saxon race should predominate in the New World; and that English and American commerce, the English language, and English literature, should spread right round the globe.

THROUGH RUSSIAN SNOWS
A Story of Napoleon's Retreat from Moscow

The hero, Julian Wyatt, after several adventures with smugglers, by whom he is handed over a prisoner to the French, regains his freedom and joins Napoleon's army in the Russian campaign, and reaches Moscow with the victorious Emperor. Then, when the terrible retreat begins, Julian finds himself in the rear guard of the French army, fighting desperately, league by league, against famine, snow-storms, wolves, and Russians. Ultimately he escapes out of the general disaster, after rescuing the daughter of a Russian Count; makes his way to St. Petersburg, and then returns to England. A story with an excellent plot, exciting adventures, and splendid historical interests.

BERIC THE BRITON
A Story of the Roman Invasion

This story deals with the invasion of Britain by the Roman legionaries. Beric, who is a boy-chief of a British tribe, takes a prominent part in the insurrection under Boadicea; and after the defeat of that heroic queen (in A. D. 62) he continues the struggle in the fen-country. Ultimately, Beric is defeated and carried captive to Rome, where he is trained in the exercise of arms in a school of gladiators. Such is the skill which he there acquires that he succeeds in saving a Christian maid by slaying a lion in the arena, and is rewarded by being made librarian of the palace, and the personal protector of Nero. Finally he escapes from this irksome service, organizes a band of outlaws in Calabria, defies the power of Rome, and at length returns to Britain, where he becomes a wise ruler of his own people.

WHEN LONDON BURNED
A Story of the Plague and the Fire

The hero of this story was the son of a nobleman who had lost his estates during the troublous times of the Commonwealth. Instead of hanging idly about the court seeking favors, Cyril Shenstone determined to maintain himself by honest work. During the Great Plague and the Great Fire, which visited London with such terrible results, Sir Cyril was prominent among those who brought help to the panic-stricken inhabitants. This tale has rich variety of interest, both national and personal, and in the hero you have an English lad of the noblest type – wise, humane, and unselfish.

THE LION OF THE NORTH
A Tale of Gustavus Adolphus and the Wars of Religion

In this story Mr. Henty gives the history of the first part of the Thirty Year's War. The issue had its importance, which has extended to the present day, as it established religious freedom in Germany. The army of the chivalrous King of Sweden was largely composed of Scotchmen, and among these was the hero of the story.

A MARCH ON LONDON
A Story of Wat Tyler's Rising

The Story of Wat Tyler's Rebellion is but little known, but the hero of this story passes through that perilous time and takes part in the civil war in Flanders which followed soon after. Although young he is thrown into many exciting and dangerous adventures, through which he passes with great coolness and much credit. Brought into royal favor he is knighted for bravery on the battlefield, and saving the lives of some wealthy merchants, he realizes fortune with his advancement and rank. New light is thrown on the history of this time and the whole story is singularly interesting.

WITH MOORE AT CORUNNA
A Story of the Peninsular War

A bright Irish lad, Terence O'Conner, is living with his widowed father, Captain O'Conner of the Mayo Fusiliers, with the regiment at the time when the Peninsular war began. Upon the regiment being ordered to Spain, Terence received a commission of ensign and accompanied it. On the way out, by his quickness of wit he saved the ship from capture and, instead, aided in capturing two French privateers. Arriving in Portugal, he ultimately gets appointed as aid to one of the generals of a division. By his bravery and great usefulness throughout the war, he is rewarded by a commission as Colonel in the Portuguese army and there rendered great service, being mentioned twice in the general orders of the Duke of Wellington. The whole story is full of exciting military experiences and gives a most careful and accurate account of the various campaigns.

UNDER WELLINGTON'S COMMAND
A Tale of the Peninsular War

The dashing hero of this book, Terence O'Connor, was the hero of Mr. Henty's previous book, "With Moore at Corunna," to which this is really a sequel. He is still at the head of the "Minho" Portuguese regiment. Being detached on independent and guerilla duty with his regiment, he renders invaluable service in gaining information and in harassing the French. His command, being constantly on the edge of the army, is engaged in frequent skirmishes and some most important battles.

TRUE TO THE OLD FLAG
A Tale of the American War of Independence

A graphic and vigorous story of the American Revolution, which paints the scenes with great power, and does full justice to the pluck and determination of the soldiers during the unfortunate struggle. [This description and this book are especially interesting because they are written from the British point of view of the Revolution.]

WITH COCHRANE THE DAUNTLESS
The Exploits of Lord Cochrane in South American Waters

The hero of this story, an orphaned lad, accompanies Cochrane as midshipman, and serves in the war between Chili and Peru. He has many exciting adventures in battles by sea and land, is taken prisoner and condemned to death by the Inquisition, but escapes by a long and thrilling flight across South America and down the Amazon, piloted by two faithful Indians. His pluck and coolness prove him a fit companion to Chochrane the Dauntless, and his final success is well deserved.

THE TIGER OF MYSORE
A Story of the War with Tippoo Saib

Dick Holland, whose father is supposed to be a captive of Tippoo Saib, goes to India to help him escape. He joins the army under Lord Cornwallis, and takes part in the campaign against Tippoo. Afterwards, he assumes a disguise, enters Seringapatam, the capital of Mysore, rescues Tippoo's harem from a tiger, and is appointed to high office by the tyrant. In this capacity Dick visits the hill fortresses, still in search of his father, and at last he discovers him in the great stronghold of Savandroog. The hazardous rescue through the enemy's country is at length accomplished, and the young fellow's dangerous mission is done.

THE DASH FOR KHARTOUM
A Tale of the Nile Expedition

In the record of recent British history there is no more captivating page for boys than the story of the Nile campaign, and the attempt to rescue General Gordon. For, in the difficulties which the expedition encountered, in the perils which it overpassed, and in its final tragic disappointments, are found all the excitements of romance, as well as the fascination which belongs to real events.

BONNIE PRINCE CHARLIE
A Tale of Fontenoy and Culloden

The adventures of the son of a Scotch officer in the French service. The boy, brought up by a Glasgow bailie, is arrested for aiding a Jacobite agent, escapes, is wrecked on the French coast, reaches Paris, and serves with the French army at Dettingen. He kills his father's foe in a duel, and escaping to the coast, shares the adventures of Prince Charlie, but finally settles happily in Scotland.

THE PLAGUE SHIP
A Story of a Ship and a Tragedy

The ship, *The Two Brothers*, survives adventures with Malay pirates and a hurricane – only to succumb to tragedy when it meets a ship that is infected with the plague.

UNDER DRAKE'S FLAG
A Tale of the Spanish Main

A story of the days when England and Spain struggled for the supremacy of the sea. The heroes sail as lads with Drake in the Pacific expedition, and in his great voyage of circumnavigation. The historical portion of the story is absolutely to be relied upon, but this will perhaps be less attractive than the great variety of exciting adventure through which the young heroes pass in the course of their voyages.

BY PIKE AND DYKE
A Tale of the Rise of the Dutch Republic

In this story Mr. Henty traces the adventures and brave deeds of an English boy in the household of the ablest man of his age – William the Silent. Edward Martin, the son of an English sea-captain, enters the service of the Prince as a volunteer, and is employed by him in many dangerous and responsible missions, in the discharge of which he passes through the great sieges of the time.

BY ENGLAND'S AID
Or, The Freeing of the Netherlands

The story of two English lads who go to Holland as pages in the service of one of "the fighting Veres." After many adventures by sea and land, one of the lads finds himself on Board a Spanish ship at the time of the defeat of the Armada, and escapes only to fall into the hands of the Corsairs. He is successful in getting back to Spain, and regains his native country after the capture of Cadiz.

IN THE HEART OF THE ROCKIES
A Story of Adventure in Colorado

From first to last this is a story of splendid hazard. The hero, Tom Wade, goes to seek his uncle in Colorado, who is a hunter and gold-digger, and he is discovered after many dangers, out on the plains with some comrades. Going in quest of a gold mine the little band is spied by Indians, chased across the Bad Lands, and overwhelmed by a snowstorm in the mountains.

ST. GEORGE FOR ENGLAND
A Tail of Cressy and Poitiers

No portion of English history is more crowded with great events than that of the reign of Edward III. Cressy and Poitiers; the destruction of the Spanish fleet; the plague of the Black Death; the Jacquerie rising; these are treated by the author in "St. George for England." The hero of the story, although of good family, begins life as a London apprentice, but after countless adventures and perils becomes by valor and good conduct the squire, and at last the trusted friend of the Black Prince.

BY RIGHT OF CONQUEST
Or, With Cortez in Mexico

With the Conquest of Mexico as the ground-work of his story, Mr. Henty has interwoven the adventures of an English youth. He is beset by many perils among the natives, but by a ruse he obtains the protection of the Spaniards, and after the fall of Mexico he succeeds in regaining his native shore, with a fortune and a charming Aztec bride.

THROUGH THE FRAY
A Story of the Luddite Riots

The story is laid in Yorkshire at the commencement of the present century [in G. A. Henty's time], when the price of food induced by the war and the introduction of machinery drove the working-classes to desperation, and caused them to band themselves in that wide-spread organization known as the Luddite Society. There is an abundance of adventure in the tale, but its chief interest lies in the character of the hero, and the manner in which he is put on trial for his life, but at last comes victorious "through the fray."

THE LION OF ST. MARK
A Tale of Venice in the Fourteenth Century

A story of Venice at a period when her strength and splendor were put to the severest tests. The hero displays a fine sense and manliness which carry him safely through an atmosphere of intrigue, crime, and bloodshed. He contributes largely to the victories of the Venetians at Porto d'Anzo and Chioggia, and finally wins the hand of the daughter of one of the chief men of Venice.

THE YOUNG CARTHAGINIAN
A Story of the Times of Hannibal

There is no better field for romance-writers in the whole of history than the momentous struggle between the Romans and Carthaginians for the empire of the world. Mr. Henty has had the full advantage of much unexhausted picturesque and impressive material, and has thus been enabled to form a striking historic background to as exciting a story of adventure as the keenest appetite could wish.

FOR THE TEMPLE
A Tale of the Fall of Jerusalem

Mr. Henty here weaves into the record of Josephus an admirable and attractive story. The troubles in the district of Tiberias, the march of the legions, the sieges of Jotapata, of Gamala, and of Jerusalem, form the impressive setting to the figure of the lad who becomes the leader of a guerrilla band of patriots, fights bravely for the Temple, and after a brief term of slavery in Alexandria, returns to his Galilean home.

IN GREEK WATERS
A Story of the Grecian War of Independence

Deals with the revolt of the Greeks in 1821 against Turkish oppression. Mr. Beveridge and his son Horace fit out a privateer, load it with military stores, and set sail for Greece. They rescue the Christians, relieve the captive Greeks, and fight the Turkish war vessels.

WITH CLIVE IN INDIA
Or, The Beginnings of an Empire

The period between the landing of Clive in India and the close of his career was eventful in the extreme. At its commencement the English were traders existing on sufferance of the native princes; at its close they were masters of Bengal and of the greater part of Southern India. The author has given a full account of the events of that stirring time, while he combines with his narrative a thrilling tale of daring and adventure.

CAPTAIN BAYLEY'S HEIR
A Tale of the Gold Fields of California

A frank, manly lad and his cousin are rivals in the heirship of a considerable property. The former falls into a trap laid by the latter, and while under a false accusation of theft foolishly leaves England for America. He works his passage before the mast, joins a small band of hunters, crosses a tract of country infested with Indians to the California gold diggings, and is successful both as digger and trader.

IN THE REIGN OF TERROR
The Adventures of a Westminster Boy

Harry Sandwith, a Westminster boy, becomes a resident at the chateau of a French marquis, and after various adventures accompanies the family to Paris at the crisis of the Revolution. Imprisonment and death reduced their number, and the hero finds himself beset by perils with the three young daughters of the house in his charge. After hair-breadth escapes they reach Nantes. There the girls are condemned to death in the coffin ships, but are saved by the unfailing courage of their boy-protector.

THE DRAGON AND THE RAVEN
Or, The Days of King Alfred

In this story the author gives an account of the fierce struggle between Saxon and Dane for supremacy in England, and presents a vivid picture of the misery and ruin to which the country was reduced by the ravages of the sea-wolves. The hero, a young Saxon thane, takes part in all the battles fought by King Alfred. He is driven from his home, takes to the sea, and resists the Danes on their own element, and being pursued by them up the Seine, is present at the long and desperate siege of Paris.

CONDEMNED AS A NIHILIST
A Story of Escape from Siberia

The hero of this story is an English boy resident in St. Petersburg. Through two student friends he becomes innocently involved in various political plots, resulting in his seizure by the Russian police and his exile to Siberia. He ultimately escapes, and, after many exciting adventures, he reaches Norway, and thence home, after a perilous journey which lasts nearly two years.

A JACOBITE EXILE
Being the Adventures of a Young Englishman in the Service of Charles XII. of Sweden

Sir Marmaduke Carstairs, a Jacobite, is the victim of a conspiracy, and he is denounced as a plotter against the life of King William. He flies to Sweden, accompanied by his son Charlie. This youth joins the foreign legion under Charles XII., and takes a distinguished part in several famous campaigns against the Russians and Poles.

IN FREEDOM'S CAUSE
A Story of Wallace and Bruce

Relates the stirring tale of the Scottish War of Independence. The hero of the tale fought under both Wallace and Bruce, and while the strictest historical accuracy has been maintained with respect to public events, the work is full of "hairbreadth 'scapes" and wild adventure.

HELD FAST FOR ENGLAND
A Tale of the Siege of Gibraltar

This story deals with one of the most memorable sieges in history – the siege of Gibraltar in 1779-83 by the united forces of France and Spain. With land forces, fleets, and floating batteries, the combined resources of two great nations, this grim fortress was vainly besieged and bombarded. The hero of the tail, an English lad resident in Gibraltar, takes a brave and worthy part in the long defense, and it is through his varied experiences that we learn with what bravery, resource, and tenacity the Rock was held for England.

FOR NAME AND FAME
Or, Through Afghan Passes

An interesting story of the last war in Afghanistan [at G. A. Henty's time]. The hero, after being wrecked and going through many stirring adventures among the Malays, finds his way to Calcutta and enlists in a regiment proceeding to join the army at the Afghan passes. He accompanies the force under General Roberts to the Peiwar Kotal, is wounded, taken prisoner, carried to Cabul, whence he is transferred to Candahar, and takes part in the final defeat of the army of Ayoub Khan.

ORANGE AND GREEN
A Tale of the Boyne and Limerick

The record of two typical families – the Davenants, who, having come over with Strongbow, had allied themselves in feeling to the original inhabitants; and the Whitefoots, who had been placed by Cromwell over certain domains of the Davenants. In the children the spirit of contention has given place to friendship, and though they take opposite sides in the struggle between James and William, their good-will and mutual service are never interrupted, and in the end the Davenants come happily to their own again.

MAORI AND SETTLER
A Story of the New Zealand War

The Renshaws emigrate to New Zealand during the period of the war with the natives. Wilfrid, a strong, self-reliant, courageous lad, is the mainstay of the household. He has for his friend Mr. Atherton, a botanist and naturalist of herculean strength and unfailing nerve and humor. In the adventures among the Maoris, there are many breathless moments in which the odds seem hopelessly against the party, but they succeed in establishing themselves happily in one of the pleasant New Zealand valleys.

BY CONDUCT AND COURAGE
A Story of Nelson's Days

This is a rattling story of the battle and the breeze in the glorious days of Parker and Nelson. The hero is brought up in a Yorkshire fishing village, and enters the navy as a ship's boy. In the course of a few months after joining he so distinguishes himself in action with French ships and Moorish pirates that he is raised to the dignity of midshipman. His ship is afterward sent to the West Indies. Here his services attract the attention of the Admiral, who gives him command of a small cutter. In this vessel he cruises about among the islands, chasing and capturing pirates, and even attacking their strongholds. He is a born leader of men, and his pluck, foresight, and resource win him success where men of greater experience might have failed. He is several times taken prisoner: by mutinous negroes in Cuba, by Moorish pirates who carry him as a slave to Algiers, and finally by the French. In this last case he escapes in time to take part in the battles of Cape St. Vincent and Camperdown. His adventures include a thrilling experience in Corsica with no less a companion than Nelson himself.

AT ABOUKIR AND ACRE
A Story of Napoleon's Invasion of Egypt

The hero, having saved the life of the son of an Arab chief, is taken into the tribe, has a part in the battle of the Pyramids and the revolt at Cairo. He is an eye-witness of the famous naval battle of Aboukir, and later is in the hardest of the defense of Acre.

A FINAL RECKONING
A Tale of Bush Life in Australia

The hero, a young English lad, after rather a stormy boyhood, emigrates to Australia and gets employment as an officer in the mounted police. A few years of active work on the frontier, where he has many a brush with both natives and bush-rangers, gain him promotion to a captaincy, and he eventually settles down to the peaceful life of a squatter.

THE BRAVEST OF THE BRAVE
Or, With Peterborough in Spain

There are few great leaders whose lives and actions have so completely fallen into oblivion as those of the Earl of Peterborough. This is largely due to the fact that they were overshadowed by the glory and successes of Marlborough. His career as General extended over little more than a year, and yet, in that time, he showed a genius for warfare which has never been surpassed.

A CHAPTER OF ADVENTURES
Or, Through the Bombardment of Alexandria

A coast fishing lad, by an act of heroism, secures the interest of a ship owner, who places him as an apprentice on board one of his ships. In company with two of his fellow-apprentices he is left behind, at Alexandria, in the hands of the revolted Egyptian troops, and is present through the bombardment and the scenes of riot and blood-shed which accompanied it.

FACING DEATH
Or, The Hero of the Vaughan Pit

"Facing Death" is a story with a purpose. It is intended to show that a lad who makes up his mind firmly and resolutely that he will rise in life, and who is prepared to face toil and ridicule and hardship to carry out his determination, is sure to succeed. The hero of the story is a typical British boy, dogged, earnest, generous, and though "shamefaced" to a degree, is ready to face death in the discharge of duty.

THE CAT OF BUBASTES
A Story of Ancient Egypt

A story which will give young readers an unsurpassed insight into the customs of the Egyptian people. Amuba, a prince of the Rebu nation, is carried with his charioteer Jethro into slavery. They become inmates of the house of Ameres, the Egyptian high-priest, and are happy in his service until the priest's son accidentally kills the sacred cat of Bubastes. In an outburst of popular fury Ameres is killed, and it rests with Jethro and Amuba to secure the escape of the high-priest's son and daughter.

BY SHEER PLUCK
A Tale of the Ashanti War

The author has woven, in a tale of thrilling interest, all the details of the Ashanti campaign, of which he was himself a witness. His hero, after many exciting adventures in the interior, is detained as a prisoner by the king just before the outbreak of the war, but escapes, and accompanies the English expedition on their march to Coomassie.

STURDY AND STRONG
Or, How George Andrews made his Way

The history of a hero of everyday life, whose love of truth, clothing of modesty, and innate pluck, carry him, naturally, from poverty to affluence. George Andrews is an example of character with nothing to cavil at, and stands as a good instance of chivalry in domestic life.

ST. BARTHOLOMEW'S EVE
A Tale of the Huguenot Wars

The hero, Philip Fletcher, is a right true English lad, but he has a French connection on his mother's side. This kinship induces him to cross the Channel in order to take a share in that splendid struggle for freedom known as the Huguenot wars. Naturally he sides with the Protestants, distinguishes himself in various battles, and receives rapid promotion for the zeal and daring with which he carries out several secret missions. It is an enthralling narrative throughout.

REDSKIN AND COW-BOY
A Tale of the Western Plains

The central interest of this story is found in the many adventures of an English lad who seeks employment as a cow-boy on a cattle ranch. His experiences during a "roundup" present in picturesque form the toilsome, exciting, adventurous life of a cow-boy; while the perils of a frontier settlement are vividly set forth in an Indian raid, accompanied by pillage, capture, and recapture. The story is packed full of breezy adventure.

WITH LEE IN VIRGINIA
A Story of the American Civil War

The story of a young Virginian planter, who, after bravely proving his sympathy with the slaves of brutal masters, serves with no less courage and enthusiasm under Lee and Jackson through the most exciting events of the struggle. He has many hairbreadth escapes, is several times wounded, and twice taken prisoner; but his courage and readiness and, in two cases, the devotion of a black servant and of a runaway slave whom he had assisted bring him safely through all difficulties.

THROUGH THE SIKH WAR
A Tale of the Conquest of the Punjaub

Percy Groves, a spirited English lad, joins his uncle in the Punjaub, where the natives are in a state of revolt. When the authorities at Lahore proclaim war Percy joins the British force as a volunteer, and takes a distinguished share in the famous battles of the Punjaub.

WULF THE SAXON
A Story of the Norman Conquest

The hero is a young thane who wins the favor of Earl Harold and becomes one of his retinue. When Harold becomes King of England Wulf assists in the Welsh wars, and takes part against the Norsemen at the Battle of Stamford Bridge. When William of Normandy invades England, Wulf is with the English host at Hastings, and stands by his King to the last in the mighty struggle. Altogether this is a noble tale. Wulf himself is a rare example of Saxon vigor, and the spacious background of stormful history lends itself admirably to heroic romance.

A KNIGHT OF THE WHITE CROSS
A Tale of the Siege of Rhodes

Gervaise Tresham, the hero of this story, joins the Order of the Knights of St. John, and leaving England he proceeds to the stronghold of Rhodes. Subsequently, Gervaise is made a Knight of the White Cross for valor, while soon after he is appointed commander of a war-galley, and in his first voyage destroys a fleet of Moorish corsairs. During one of his cruises the young knight is attacked on shore, captured after a desperate struggle, and sold into slavery in Tripoli. He succeeds in escaping, however, and returns to Rhodes in time to take part in the splendid defense of that fortress. Altogether a fine chivalrous tale of varied interest and full of noble daring.

ONE OF THE 28TH
A Tale of Waterloo

The hero of this story, Ralph Conway, has many varied and exciting adventures. He enters the army, and after some rough service in Ireland takes part in the Waterloo campaign, from which he returns with the loss of an arm, but with a substantial fortune.

A HIDDEN FOE
A Romantic Adventure of Inheritance

Constance Corbyn, with the aid of Robert Harbut, searches for evidence of her true father, aided also by the erstwhile heir to his estates, Philip Clitheroe. After many intrigues, her inheritance is proved. During the search, she falls in love with Philip, and they ultimately share the estate together.

WITH THE ALLIES TO PEKIN
A Tale of the Relief of the Legations

In this book the writer tells the story of the Siege of Pekin in a way that is sure to grip the interest of his young readers. The experience of Rex Bateman, the son of an English merchant at Tientsin, and of his cousins, two girls whom Rex rescues from the Boxers just after the first outbreak, offer a variety of heroic incident sufficient to fire the loyalty of the most indifferent lad.

THROUGH THREE CAMPAIGNS
A Story of Chitral, Tirah, and Ashanti

The exciting story of a boy's adventures in the British army. Lisle Bullen, left an orphan, is to be sent home by the colonel of the regiment on the eve of the Chitral campaign. The boy's patriotism compels him, instead, to secretly join the regiment. He early distinguishes himself for conspicuous bravery. His disguise is discovered and his promotions follow rapidly.

THE TREASURE OF THE INCAS
A Tale of Adventure in Peru

Peru and the hidden treasures of her ancient kings offer Mr. Henty a most fertile field for a stirring story of adventure in his most engaging style. In an effort to win the girl of his heart, the hero penetrates into the wilds of the land of the Incas. Boys who have learned to look for Mr. Henty's books will follow his new hero in his adventurous and romantic expedition with absorbing interest. It is one of the most captivating tales Mr. Henty has written.

WITH KITCHENER IN THE SOUDAN
A Story of Atbara and Omdurman

Mr. Henty has never combined history and thrilling adventure more skillfully than in this extremely interesting story. It is not in boy nature to lay it aside unfinished, once begun; and finished, the reader finds himself in possession, not only of the facts and the true atmosphere of Kitchener's famous Soudan campaign, but of the Gordon tragedy which preceded it by so many years and of which it was the outcome.

A ROVING COMMISSION
Or, Through the Black Insurrection at Hayti

This is one of the most brilliant of Mr. Henty's books. A story of the sea, with all its life and action, it is also full of thrilling adventures on land. So it holds the keenest interest until the end. The scene is a new one to Mr. Henty's readers, being laid at the time of the Great Revolt of the Blacks, by which Hayti became independent. Toussaint l'Overture appears, and an admirable picture is given of him and of his power.

WITH THE BRITISH LEGION
A Story of the Carlist Uprising of 1836

Arthur Hallet, a young English boy, finds himself in difficulty at home, through certain harmless school escapades, and enlists in the famous "British Legion," which was then embarking for Spain to take part in the campaign to repress the Carlist uprising of 1836. Arthur shows his mettle in the first fight, distinguishes himself by daring work in carrying an important dispatch to Madrid, makes a dashing and thrilling rescue of the sister of his patron, and is rapidly promoted to the rank of captain. In following the adventures of the hero the reader obtains, as is usual with Mr. Henty's stories, a most accurate and interesting history of a picturesque campaign.

TO HERAT AND CABUL
A Story of the First Afghan War

The greatest defeat ever experienced by the British Army was that in the Mountain Passes of Afghanistan. Angus Cameron, the hero of this book, having been captured by the friendly Afghans, was compelled to be a witness of the calamity. His whole story is an intensely interesting one, from his boyhood in Persia; his employment under the government at Herat; through the defense of that town against the Persians; to Cabul, where he shared in all the events which ended in the awful march through the Passes from which but one man escaped. Angus is always at the point of danger, and whether in battle or in hazardous expeditions shows how much a brave youth, full of resources, can do, even with so treacherous a foe. His dangers and adventures are thrilling, and his escapes marvelous.

WITH ROBERTS TO PRETORIA
A Tale of the South African War

The Boer War gives Mr. Henty an unexcelled opportunity for a thrilling story of present-day interest which the author could not fail to take advantage of. Every boy reader will find this account of the adventures of the young hero most exciting, and, at the same time a wonderfully accurate description of Lord Roberts's campaign to Pretoria. Boys have found history in the dress Mr. Henty gives it anything but dull, and the present book is no exception to the rule.

NO SURRENDER
The Story of the Revolt in La Vendée

The revolt of La Vendée against the French Republic at the time of the Revolution forms the groundwork of this absorbing story. Leigh Stansfield, a young English lad, is drawn into the thickest of the conflict. Forming a company of boys as scouts for the Vendéan Army, he greatly aids the peasants. He rescues his sister from the guillotine, and finally, after many thrilling experiences, when the cause of La Vendée is lost, he escapes to England.

AT THE POINT OF THE BAYONET
A Tale of the Mahratta War

One hundred years ago the rule of the British in India was only partly established. The powerful Mahrattas were unsubdued, and with their skill in intrigue, and great military power, they were exceedingly dangerous. The story of "At the Point of the Bayonet" begins with the attempt to conquer this powerful people. Harry Lindsay, an infant when his father and mother were killed, was saved by his Mahratta ayah, who carried him to her own people and brought him up as a native. She taught him as best she could, and, having told him his parentage, sent him to Bombay to be educated. At sixteen he obtained a commission in the English army, and his knowledge of the Mahratta tongue combined with his ability and bravery enabled him to render great service in the Mahratta War, and carried him, through many frightful perils by land and sea, to high rank.

IN THE IRISH BRIGADE
A Tale of War in Flanders and Spain

Desmond Kennedy is a young Irish lad who left Ireland to join the Irish Brigade in the service of Louis XIV. of France. In Paris he incurred the deadly hatred of a powerful courtier from whom he had rescued a young girl who had been kidnapped, and his perils are of absorbing interest. Captured in an attempted Jacobite invasion of Scotland, he escaped in a most extraordinary manner. As aid-de-camp to the Duke of Berwick he experienced thrilling adventures in Flanders. Transferred to the Army in Spain, he was nearly assassinated, but escaped to return, when peace was declared, to his native land, having received pardon and having recovered his estates. The story is filled with adventure, and the interest never abates.

OUT WITH GARIBALDI
A Story of the Liberation of Italy

Garibaldi himself is the central figure of this brilliant story, and the little-known history of the struggle for Italian freedom is told here in the most thrilling way. From the time the hero, a young lad, son of an English father and an Italian mother, joins Garibaldi's band of 1,000 men in the first descent upon Sicily, which was garrisoned by one of the large Neapolitan armies, until the end, when all those armies are beaten, and the two Sicilys are conquered, we follow with the keenest interest the exciting adventures of the lad in scouting. in battle, and in freeing those in prison for liberty's sake.

JOHN HAWKE'S FORTUNE
A Story of Monmouth's Rebellion

Living in Dorset at the time of the landing of the Duke of Monmouth, the hero is of service to the rebels after the battle of Sedgemoor and becomes a friend and retainer of the Duke of Marlborough.

WON BY THE SWORD
A Tale of the Thirty Years' War

The scene of this story is laid in France, during the time of Richelieu, of Mazarin and Anne of Austria. The hero, Hector Campbell, is the orphaned son of a Scotch officer in the French Army. How he attracted the notice of Marshal Turenne and of the Prince of Conde; how he rose to the rank of Colonel; how he finally had to leave France, pursued by the deadly hatred of the Duc de Beaufort – all these and much more the story tells with the most absorbing interest.

ON THE IRRAWADDY
A Story of the First Burmese War

The hero having an uncle, a trader on the Indian and Burmese rivers, goes out to join him. Soon after war is declared by Burmah against England and he is drawn into it. His familiarity with the Burmese customs and language make him of such use that he is put upon Sir Archibald Campbell's staff. He has many experiences and narrow escapes in battles and in scouting. With half-a-dozen men he rescues his cousin who had been taken prisoner, and in the flight they are besieged in an old ruined temple. His escape and ultimate successful return to England show what a clear head with pluck can do.

BOTH SIDES THE BORDER
A Tale of Hotspur and Glendower

This is a brilliant story of the stirring times of the beginning of the Wars of the Roses, when the Scotch, under Douglas, and the Welsh, under Owen Glendower, were attacking the English. The hero of the book lived near the Scotch border, and saw many a hard fight there. Entering the service of Lord Percy, he was sent to Wales, where he was knighted, and where he was captured. Being released, he returned home, and shared in the fatal battle of Shrewsbury.

A SEARCH FOR A SECRET
An Heiress Searches for a Hidden Will

Agnes Ashleigh inherits the estate of Gerald Harmer, but his two sisters conceal the secret of his lost will and determine to give the estate to the Catholic Church. Ultimately, after much intrigue and action, the will is found and the efforts of the sisters thwarted.

DOROTHY'S DOUBLE
The Story of a Great Deception

Dorothy Hawtrey's life is turned topsy turvy by a rogue enemy who cultivates a poor girl who resembles Dorothy and uses her to impersonate Dorothy. The tale expands to the California gold fields where the double and her captor are eventually discovered. The double turns out to be a long lost sister, the rogue is killed, and all ends well.

WITH BULLER IN NATAL
Or, A Born Leader

The breaking out of the Boer War compelled Chris King, the hero of the story, to flee with his mother from Johannesburg to the sea coast. They were with many other Uitlanders, and all suffered much from the Boers. Reaching a place of safety for their families, Chris and twenty of his friends formed an independent company of scouts. In this service they were with Gen. Yule at Glencoe, then in Ladysmith, then with Buller. In each place they had many thrilling adventures. They were in the great battles and in the lonely fights on the Veldt; were taken prisoners and escaped; and they rendered most valuable service to the English forces. The story is a most interesting picture of the War in South Africa.

THE LOST HEIR
A Tale of Intrigue in India and England

A child, the heir to the fortune of a wealthy Indian Army officer, disappears. The general has died leaving a will in favor of the child, but, in the case of the child's death, of the rogue, Sanderson who poses as John Simcoe. At length, after many intrigues and adventures, Sanderson is exposed as the murderer of the General and forger of his Will, and the child is found.

THE CURSE OF CARNE'S HOLD
A Tale of Mystery in England and a Kaffir War

Falsely accused of the murder of a relation in Devonshire. Ronald Mervyn emigrates to South Africa and participates in a Kaffir war. He rescues a family from death in Africa, who subsequently return to England and work to establish his innocence. All ends well, as another relative confesses to the crime.

ALL BUT LOST – VOLUMES I, II, & III
A Novel of Cambridge and British Life

True to its title, only three copies of this three-volume work are known to exist. In recent years, reproductions were permitted of one of these copies, which makes this printing possible. Frank Maynard and Alice go through many adventures in this absorbing tale of British society.

COLONEL THORNDYKE'S SECRET
The Brahmin's Treasure

Our hero, Mark Thorndyke, pursues his father's killer through England and English society. The apparent curse placed upon the possessor of a lost bracelet, first upon John Thorndyke and then upon his son, is finally unraveled, the "curse" is lifted, and Mark marries his intended cousin Millicent.

FRIENDS THOUGH DIVIDED
A Tale of the Civil War

England is torn by a great conflict between the Cavaliers and the Roundheads. The two heroes, Harry Furness and Herbert Rippinghall, are on opposite sides of the struggle, with adventures that spread to Ireland and Bermuda and the efforts of Charles II. to regain the throne.

GABRIEL ALLEN M.P.
Frank Allen's Search for His Identity

Gabriel Allen, a member of Parliament, turns out to be a clerk who escaped from a shipwreck and established himself as a wealthy industrialist. His son, Frank Allen, is found, after many adventures, to be the son of his dead former employer. The villain Ruskoff is lost and all ends well for our hero.

IN THE HANDS OF THE CAVE DWELLERS
A Tale of the American West

The hero is an American sailor who saves a young Mexican from thugs. The story spreads to an Indian attack, the loss of the heroine to cave dwellers, her rescue, and the eventual happiness of hero and heroine who have overcome adversity.

JACK ARCHER
A Tale of the Crimea

Our hero survives adventures at Gibraltar and the battles of Alma, Bacalava, and Inkerman, but is captured and is involved in the death of a Russian official. He escapes, goes through the fall of Sebastapol, and ultimately marries a wealthy Russian girl.

THE SOVEREIGN READER
Scenes from the Life and Reign of Queen Victoria

This is Mr. Henty's original chronicle of the life of Queen Victoria published as a reader for school children at the time of the Golden Jubilee. It was later updated to the time of the Queen's death and published under the title, *Queen Victoria.*

QUEEN VICTORIA
Scenes From Her Life and Reign

First produced in 1887 as "The Sovereign Reader" to celebrate the Golden Jubilee of Queen Victoria, this book was updated at the time of the Queen's death. It chronicles the Queen and the events during her reign, both military and domestic.

RUJUB THE JUGGLER
A Tale of India During the Mutiny

Ralph Bathurst overcomes his fears and, with the help of Rujub, rescues the girl with whom he has fallen in love from a wicked Rajah. The setting is an English community struggling to escape death during the Indian Mutiny.

THE CORNET OF HORSE
A Tale of Marlborough's Wars

Rupert Holiday flees England as a result of a fight with his stepbrother and joins Marlborough during his campaign in the Netherlands. Set during the battles of Blenheim, Ramillies, Oudenarde, and Malplaquet, Rupert has many successful adventures before marrying a French girl and settling down in England.

THE QUEEN'S CUP
A Novel

A yachting adventure and romance involving a former British soldier turns into scenes of high adventure and peril with the heroine kidnapped and the action ranging from England to the West Indies. Ultimately, she is rescued by the hero, Frank Mallett.

A WOMAN OF THE COMMUNE
The Two Sieges of Paris

The adventures of Mary Brander and Cuthbert Hartington in recovering a lost estate are set against the episode of the Commune in Paris. After many adventures, all ends well with the hero and heroine married and living in London.

THOSE OTHER ANIMALS
A Humorous Tour of the Animal Kingdom

This is a series of short essays about various animals with tongue-in-cheek derisions of human interactions with them, their own personalities, and some of the extant myths about their origins including Darwinianism. These are not historical novels, and they display some of the author's prejudices about people and their behavior.

THE YOUNG BUGLERS
A Tale of the Peninsular War

Two brothers enlist and serve in Portugal under Wellington's command. The story revolves around the family's loss of its fortune to intrigue, while its setting is an in depth history lesson of Wellington's famous campaign.

THE MARCH TO MAGDALA
A Chronicle of the Abyssinian Campaign

As Special Correspondent for the *Standard* newspaper, Mr. Henty chronicles the March from Annesley Bay to Magdala. This 400 mile ordeal was a logistical nightmare during which the British emerged victorious over the terrain, the human enemy being a minor difficulty. With rich description of the country through which this March was made, this account is a brilliant, in depth description of the determination and endurance of the British Army and also of some of its foibles and weaknesses.

THE MARCH TO COOMASSIE
A Chronicle of the Ashanti Campaign

This is a compilation of Mr. Henty's reports to the *Standard* newspaper while he was serving as a Special Correspondent during the Ahanti Campaign. It reports the march from the coast to Coomassie and the return. The chronicle gives great detail about the hazards of the March, and the native country, as well as the struggle with the Ashanti.

IN TIMES OF PERIL
A Tale of India

Dick and Ned Warrender are the sons of an officer in the Indian Army at the time of the Indian Mutiny during the reign of Queen Victoria. The action includes the massacre of Cawnpore, the siege of Lucknow, and many adventures. The mutineers are beaten, and the heroes prevail and return with honor to England.

OUT ON THE PAMPAS
Or, The Young Settlers

This is a tale of young Englishmen who go out to the Argentine with their family. They have many adventures at the time of the Mexican-American War including a raid by the Pampas Indians in which their sister is abducted. They rescue the girl, make peace with the Indians, and return prosperously to England.

WINNING HIS SPURS
A Tale of the Crusades

The hero, Cuthbert, joins Richard the Lionheart and participates, at his side, during stirring battles and great adventures. This novel is an excellent example of Mr. Henty's talent in spinning an adventure that so captures the mind of the reader that the history and customs of the times and events become fixed in memory along with the hero's deeds.

THE YOUNG COLONISTS
A Tale of the Zulu and Boer Wars

An adventure of Dick Humphries whose family lives in Natal. He participates in British defeats and victories during the Zulu war and then becomes involved in the First Boer War.

THE YOUNG FRANC-TIREURS
A Tale of the Franco-Prussian War

The two heroes join the French forces during the Franco-Prussian War and have many escapades and adventures including especially their entry into Paris in disguise by swimming the Seine and their escape from Paris in a balloon.